WOLVES
AND
WAR

CANDY RAE

WOLVES AND WAR
Copyright © 2016 by Candy Rae.

No part of this book may be used or reproduced in any manner whatsoever without written permission except in the case of brief quotations embodied in critical articles or reviews.
This book is a work of fiction. All characters in this publication are fictitious and any resemblance to real persons, living or dead, is purely coincidental.

Cover Artwork by Jennifer Johnson
Book interior by Candy Rae with help from Creativindie Design.

First Edition: December 2016

All rights reserved.
ISBN-13: 978-1522844051
ISBN-10: 1522844058

Wolves and War is dedicated to my husband Jim. Without his support I would never have begun to write and Planet Wolf would never have been anything more than a dream.

BOOKS BY CANDY RAE

PLANET WOLF SERIES
(1) WOLVES AND WAR
(2) CONFLICT AND COURAGE
(3) HOMAGE AND HONOUR
(4) DRAGONS AND DESTINY
(5) VALOUR AND VICTORY
(6) AMBITION AND ALAVIDHA
(THE PREQUELS) PAWS AND PLANETS
(SHORT STORIES) TALES AND TAILS

DRAGON WULF SERIES
(1) JOURNEY AND JEOPARDY
(2) GOSSAMER AND GRASS
(3) FLAMES AND FREEDOM

T'QUEL MAGIC TRILOGY
(1) EPHEMERAL BOUNDARY
(2) ENDURING BARRIER
(3) ETERNAL BULWARK

KILL BY CURE

CHAPTER 1

NORTHERN CONTINENT

In the twenty-fourth century, a convoy of seven spherical deep-space vessels set out from the main space facility that sat in permanent orbit over a dying Earth. Six were bound for a colony world light-years away.

The seventh ship was different. Although the World Coalition Prison Ship *Electra* would eventually head for Riga to drop off the much needed heavy machinery, tools and transport vehicles, it would first make a detour to another, less hospitable planet, where it would unload its animate cargo before rejoining its sister ships. The *Electra's* animate 'cargo' was made up of some of the vilest criminal classes on the planet.

The journey of the seven ships was planned to take twenty years. The on-board living quarters were extensive. The colonists spent the time training for their new lives in the ship sections designed for that purpose and were looking to the future with a great deal of optimism.

Twelve years out from Earth, disaster struck.

The seven ships plunged one by one into a huge cosmic storm and only two survived. One was the World Coalition Colony Ship *Argyll* with some eight thousand colonists and crew on board, the other the WCPS *Electra*, carrying twenty thousand male convicts.

Independently of each other and against all odds, both ships endeavoured to find and safely land on a planet that could sustain human life.

Unknown to the humans, they were not the only sentient life forms inhabiting this strange new world.

The WCCS *Argyll* entered the atmosphere, heading towards the soft flat area designated as the landing site.

"Prepare for landing."

The klaxon gave two sharp toots.

Commander Stuart MacIntosh flicked the toggle on his console that turned the thrusters over to manual control. His fingers moved over the keypad. The ship descended, heading towards the soft marshy ground. Tension mounted.

The reversing thrusters fired. The manoeuvre was not as effective as it would have been in deep space; the thruster-units were not designed to operate in above zero atmospheres but they did slow the *Argyll* down. Before the engines had a chance to stall, Stuart pressed the yellow button warning the engine room that he needed that bit of extra power for the landing manoeuvre itself. Petty Officer Jim Cranston reacted at once.

Both men's index fingers had been hovering over the improvised landing buttons. The Commander nodded. Two fingers pressed down. They heard the engines responding, labouring mightily to keep the ship in the air long enough to achieve her landing trajectory.

The mesmerised bridge crew gazed at the scene unfolding on the screens. The land was approaching so very fast, the ground rushing up to meet them.

At a nod from Stuart MacIntosh the young engineering lieutenant cut off the engines. The WCCS *Argyll* plunged the remaining few metres to the ground, still maintaining some forward momentum, hull protesting. Metal screeched, and anything not securely bolted down bounced around, as she landed on their new world, ploughing through anything that got in her way. Bushes and trees were swept aside and she left a swathe of destruction behind her. She began to slow down as the bottom of the sphere met the resistance that was boggy marshland before swaying to a stop.

There was silence, broken only by loud bangs and thumps as items dislodged in the descent settled themselves.

Against all the odds, they had made it; they were safe, for the moment.

Jim Cranston and Stuart MacIntosh's eyes met, each mirroring the other's relief at a job well done.

The challenge of getting the colonists to Planet Rybak had been accomplished. Now they must meet the challenge of survival.

The colonists stripped the WCCS *Argyll* of anything remotely salvageable, blissfully unaware that they were being watched.

The natives of the planet were more than a little interested in what was going on.

Their wide patrol had come across the frantic activity beside the marshlands when investigating the reason why the large herd of silly kura who usually inhabited this part of the coast had suddenly decided to stampede towards the forest as fast as their short legs could carry them.

Now they knew the reason why.

It was not an incursion of Larg as they had first thought. The peculiar creatures hammering away below did not remotely resemble their eons-old enemies, the Larg. They walked on their two hind legs for a start, and did things with their forepaws and chelas that the Lind could not have imagined in their wildest dreams.

The rest of their patrol went back to report to the Commander of their Lindar. Kolyei and Tarmsei dug themselves deep enough down into the dry mud of the high ground at the edge of a small copse of trees so that not even the blue-pointed tips of their furry ears could be seen, and settled down to wait. From time to time, and with understandable caution, they lifted their heads and gazed at the activity down on the plain, wonder in their eyes.

The strangers did not appear to be coming their way, so the two Lind began to converse. The language of the Lind was rich and diverse and spoke of a culture deep in knowledge and tradition. The two discussed the situation at length; their conversation ceasing only when one or both raised his head to survey the amazing scene below.

The Lind's vocal speech pattern was augmented by colourful and diverse images and feelings, which they placed into each other's minds when words were not enough to fully describe what they were trying to say aloud. The Lind could converse telepathically in words, but it took a great deal of energy and effort. So the ability was usually reserved for emergencies and for when one wished to have a private conversation, perhaps with one's mate.

"Think you Tarmsei, that these creatures are dangerous?" asked Kolyei.

"They have entered our rtathlians," Tarmsei answered.

"But not, think I, to make war upon us. Look, they have ltsctas with them." Ltscta was the Lindish word for 'young one'. A Lind did not reach adulthood until he or she reached the age of fourteen summer seasons and until then was known as a ltscta.

"They are not Larg."

"Many things are not Larg."

"Think you that these strange two-legged creatures come from the skies above?" asked Tarmsei after some thought. "Myself, I cannot think of another explanation. Indeed, look you at that huge shiny round thing that sinks into the wetlands. They must come from the skies as with our oldest legends that are sung about the Lai."

There was silence as both thought about what the arrival of these strangers portended. For almost the first time in his life, the normally insouciant Kolyei found himself lost for words.

The colonists had no idea about the interest they were generating and on the solid ground some half a mile from where the WCCS *Argyll* lay; they were working hard to build temporary shelters before nightfall. Everybody had disembarked, it being the considered opinion of the officers and the other specialists that the ship was in far too precarious a position for anyone to remain on board. Her tonnage was forcing her down into the boggy ground that had been their saviour on landing, but which was now inexorably swallowing her up. The one geologist on board was of the opinion that even the ship's upper entranceways would be submerged within a few days.

The evacuation and landing plan was working well, with only one potentially fatal mishap.

In a rash moment, a group of pre-teens decided to explore the immediate vicinity on their own, while the adults were too busy to be aware of any mischief they were up to. They evaded those who were supposed to be looking after them and ventured some distance north of the ship. Poking around with sticks of wood they found lying on top of the marshy ground, two of them managed to fall into a deep and muddy pool of stagnant water. They were only saved from drowning by the prompt action of their fellow miscreants and with a great deal of effort on the part of the adults frantically summoned to their rescue.

All participants in the escapade got a severe fright and the perpetrators received a sound telling-off by no less a personage than the Commander himself. Stuart MacIntosh did not mince his words. It was five very chastened boys who later joined their compatriots for their evening chores. The marshy ground and everywhere else outside the marked perimeter was placed out of bounds for all those aged under fourteen and the five became very unpopular.

Guards were detailed to protect the perimeter. Adults were erecting shelters; others were preparing meals from the pre-packed foods. Temporary nurseries had been set up, staffed in the main by youngsters and older adults deemed too frail for heavy labour.

The land was strange to their eyes, ears and noses. There were alien smells and even stranger noises. The air had a spicy tang to it, resonant of lemons and nutmeg and it smelled wonderful to those accustomed to the recycled air of the ship. Scouting parties investigated the immediate vicinity and did not find anything of a threatening nature, but it was still an unknown land, fraught with unknown perils.

When dusk fell, the colonists from the WCCS *Argyll* settled into an exhausted and uneasy sleep as the Lind continued their vigil.

"Can you sense thoughts from them?" murmured Tarmsei after a while.

"Too many," answered Kolyei, "some strong, others not."

They stored up this piece of information to add to their report.

When night came again, the two Lind flitted away quietly from the noise and disruption that was the colonists and sped off to report their findings to the rest of their Lindar, the warrior section of their rtath, their pack.

At pack Zanatei Lindar's dom, a half-sun's hard running away, all was in turmoil.

Heated discussions were in progress when the two scouts arrived. The atmosphere was tense.

At the edge of the circle Tarmsei and Kolyei waited to be asked by the Susa to speak, listening hard, both with their ears and minds, to what their fellow Lind were saying. They sensed acute agitation and in some cases intense anger that the rtathlians were being disturbed in this way. A bloodthirsty minority was in favour of rushing down on the encampment and slaughtering all they found there.

The two looked at each other in consternation.

: *This will be very tricky* : said Tarmsei to Kolyei in a tight beam of telepathic speech.

: *Yes* : answered his friend. Kolyei was a master of the understatement, even for a Lind. : *We must be most careful of our thoughts and words* :

The large white Lind in the middle of the circle motioned for them to approach. His name was Afanasei and he was the Leader, or Susa of the Lindar. Kolyei and Tarmsei bowed their heads in respect before taking their places.

"Tell us of your findings," ordered Lindar Susa Afanasei. "Permit that Tarmsei and Kolyei speak. Be silent." The last two words were barked out as a command and with an accompanying growl.

It was obeyed at once. Afanasei did not raise his voice often but when, on rare occasions he did, every Lind paid heed.

Kolyei and Tarmsei had planned in detail what they would say during their journey back to the dom but they were not sure of how their rtathen, or pack-mates, would react. Theirs was a warrior rtath. They were defenders of the rtathlians, the lands of their fellow Lind. This Lindar would be difficult to convince, used as they were to meeting all incursions with chela and tooth.

"The strange creatures are not Larg," Kolyei began. "There is no cause to kill."

There were low growls of disapproval of such a sentiment from some of those sitting in the circle.

Kolyei continued, in no way intimidated. "We of the Lind battle only our enemy the Larg who destroy and kill."

Tarmsei butted in, his snout raised belligerently. "I have watched them for two sun-downs. This is not an army sent to kill in our rtathlians. There are ltsctas with them."

There were some mutterings from the back of the circle where the unmated females sat. The Lind were very protective of their own youngsters. The females would find an affinity with a species that loved and cared for their young. They would oppose an attack for that very reason.

Tarmsei continued. "It is not our way to kill for killing's sake. You must need good reason for attack. They give us none as yet. Different than us, yes, the two-legs are, but in some ways the same. We must watch, then decide."

There were more growls of dissent. Both Kolyei and Tarmsei could 'feel' the heaviness in the air.

"We must watch and wait," advised Kolyei.

Afanasei was listening. Kolyei and Tarmsei received a sense of approbation from his direction. He spoke up now, quelling incipient barkings, shoutings and bayings with a severe look and a stare. One or two of the assembled hung their heads.

"Shame. Judgement without knowledge is a bad thing," Afanasei pronounced. "Do you not remember the teachings? We will send a message to Elda Zanatei. The two-legs do things we cannot. We know the Larg come in the next hot season and our spies tell us in great numbers."

"I should like to know more." This came from the slight young female nearest to Kolyei. "Their young they care for?" Kolyei noticed that the blue stripe pattern on her face and around her withers was most attractive. He nodded.

"Then to attack, volat it would be. The young of any *must* be protected."

There was more growling and whining. Volat was the Lind term for the wanton and needless slaying of any creature. Their enemies, the Larg of the southern continent, committed volat. The Lind did not, being taught from their earliest years that to perform an act of volat was the worst crime any Lind could commit. The Lind killed to eat, not for fun.

"We shall not attack." It was her final comment and she sat back down on her haunches and looked placidly around the circle. The females behind her whined in agreement.

Kolyei eyed her with much interest.

The Elda caught the eyes of two young Lind at the edge of the circle. They approached, tails swishing and eyes alight with anticipation.

"We are to watch two-legs?" they asked eagerly of white Afanasei.

"No you shall report. Tell Zanatei all we have seen and said. Run fast."

Afanasei did have the mental telepathic strength to send his own report to his pack leader but such an undertaking would sap him of much of his energy. He had enough on his paws to keep control of the Lindar and, he reasoned, the two-legs were not an immediate threat to the packs. Also, he trusted Tarmsei and Kolyei.

The two looked and felt disappointed but ingrained obedience to the Susa won and they turned and sped away.

As for Kolyei and Tarmsei, Afanasei sent them back to watch the colonists after they had eaten their fill from a plump young kura caught by the hunters earlier in the day.

Many suns passed before word came back from the leaders, or Elda of the Lind. Kolyei, Tarmsei and others shared the watches and learned much.

These two legs could control fire! This was an amazing thing to the Lind, accustomed as they were to the fear of fire. In the forest glades of the Lind large firestorms often broke out in the hot season and many lives could be lost. They were also thunderstruck when they looked at what else the creatures could do. They held and used the 'things' they held in their forepaws and these 'things' were completely unknown to the Lind. The possibilities were enormous if they could but learn to communicate and then to work with, and perhaps share wood-space with these newcomers.

From their well-concealed dugout (it had to be well concealed – when the strangers had started exploring the countryside the watchers had had to move their hide further away – deep inside a large prickly dugo bush on a nearby hillock) they saw that the two-legs were taking insufficient precautions against hostile attack. The perimeter fence of their domta was only half the height of an adult Lind and wouldn't hold back the hordes of Larg for long, however valiantly it was defended.

"We must warn them," growled Kolyei.

Tarmsei urged caution.

"Can we not go closer?"

"You are incorrigible, Kolyei my friend."

Kolyei cocked a pointed ear in inquiry.

"You are the most incorrigible Lind I have ever known."

Kolyei's plea had been full of wistful longing. He was renowned amongst the members of his pack for his eagerness to explore the unknown and the new, which was why, if Tarmsei thought about it, Kolyei was one of their Lindar's best scouts.

"Have you forgotten all training?" Tarmsei asked with a lopsided grin.

Kolyei looked shamefaced as Tarmsei continued. "You shall not move one single paw closer to these strangers than where you are now. I have lost too many of my friends and family in battle to lose any more."

Kolyei sighed in frustration but did follow his friend's advice.

The watches continued. Regular updates were relayed west to the Elda of Lind.

During this time of watching and waiting the young female that had spoken that first night in the circle approached Kolyei. "I wish to see the ltsctas of the two-legs," she requested.

Kolyei was happy to comply, taking her with him on his next watch. Tarmsei was only too glad of the respite from the often boring watches. He was not as interested in the situation as Kolyei who felt a strong compulsion to get closer to the newcomers. Once at the dugo bush she hunkered down beside him and with great daring, lifted her head up to survey the scene below. She gasped in surprise and her head came back down at once.

"Radya," said Kolyei with concern. "Are you alright?"

"Yes," she replied and raised her head for a longer look. They spent the rest of their watch in silence and after this Radya often accompanied Kolyei on his watch-shifts.

At long last the Gtratha, or High Council of Eldas came to a decision. Orders went forth to all the packs.

The newcomers were not to be attacked. They were to be watched and as much learnt about them as possible. More watchers were detailed to keep a close eye on the settlement, now sitting proud on a substantial area of dry ground and surrounded by a low palisade.

Other Lind were detailed to keep an eye on the hunting and exploration parties and to report back on how these creatures dealt with the land and wildlife. It came as a great surprise to the Lind when they heard of the rounding up of numbers of kura and other animals. After much discussion it was decided that this was not a dangerous thing. After all, the two-legs were slow, very slow compared with the Lind. They could not hunt the Lind way. It was sensible of the slow running two-legs to keep their meat nearby.

The reports continued to be favourable. The newcomers did not kill for killing's sake. They cared about their surroundings and for their younglings. It was decreed that closer ties were to be formed. The Larg would come in the summer bringing with them the killings and the maimings. The Lind would warn the newcomers of the Larg. In return the two-legs would join with the Lind to defend the land. Both species would benefit. Both species would survive.

Kolyei's report that he could sense some of the two-legs' thoughts was heeded. Some watching Lind were also being drawn to others among the newcomers in much the same way as when a Lind was drawn to one of their own as a potential mate. It was all very strange.

Kolyei himself found his thoughts straying in one particular direction. He sensed strong emotions emanating from a young female. Using these emotions as a focus he had little trouble singling her out from the other youngsters gathering fruit at the edge of the lian. Radya, who accompanied him often now, was just as attracted to a young male youngling slightly smaller than the female.

From his hiding place in the dugo thicket, Kolyei tried insinuating some simple thoughts into the young female's mind and to his surprise, found it to be extremely receptive, much like the mind of a young Lind. One day he became aware that a rainstorm was in the offing, common enough in this season. He sent a tentative warning straight to the youngster and, to his great satisfaction saw her look at the sky then dash back to the settlement as fast as she could go. He didn't think she even got slightly damp.

One further ruling from the Gtratha pleased the adventurous Kolyei greatly. It had been decided that contact must be made. Wary of a negative and potentially lethal reaction if a large Lind appeared outside their domta (the Lind had by now seen bow and arrow in action) it was decided that a group of twelve should be detailed to send thoughts to those two-legs receptive to them, preferably the young who would be able to adapt, it was hoped, more easily to contact with an alien species.

The plan was that the twelve should 'persuade' their chosen two-legs to come with them deep into the rtathlians of Lind. There were to be no confrontations. The younglings were to be spirited away secretly. It was a tall order, but the twelve chosen, chosen because they had already established some form of mental contact with one of the young two-legs, started work on their more detailed plan at once.

When the time was right, they would put this plan into action.

For the newly-orphaned Tara Sullivan, the girl to whom Kolyei was attracted, these first weeks were uneasy ones.

Although the nights were warm with a soft breeze she wasn't sleeping well. She was sharing tent-space with other girls her age or a little older. Their chatter unsettled her; they talked of the future and of their own families. At this point in Tara's life, she didn't have any plans and had no family left to chatter about. The girls largely steered away from talking about her recent loss so Tara found herself, on the whole, ignored.

She was part of a team whose responsibility it was to gather seaweed from the shore and to go wood gathering in the area next to the trees.

The team was under the command of a bright-faced lad of sixteen, therefore almost grown-up to Tara's twelve-year-old eyes, whose mission in life seemed to be to lead the most successful work-group in the colony. Bill, for that was his name, knew what had happened during the space storm when Tara's parents and little brother had died and was kind to her in his own way, keeping her beside him as they toiled on the beach and at the fringes of the woods. The two talked about generalities and Bill did not mention his own family.

As more cabins were built and the temporary campsite began to empty, Tara remained.

Stuart McIntosh ordered that not all the cabins should be built in the immediate settlement area. Streams and rivers were plentiful and as the majority of the colonists were from farming stock they were naturally keen to branch out and to stake their claims in the surrounding countryside.

Once the botanists and other scientists had found out which native plants were poisonous and which were not, there was little to stop them. Indeed, the remaining food supplies taken from the *Argyll* were pretty well finished by now and there was little choice but to sample the native edibles.

Test fields were springing up. One ground-root in particular became very popular. It grew in profusion everywhere you looked and was packed full of nutrients and vitamins. Uncooked it was harsh on the taste buds but when heated had a pleasant, if unfamiliar, taste.

All cultivation was done by hand; even children as young as ten were expected to work part of the day. Willing teams of colonists tended the embryo crops. The wild cereals were being studied with a view to finding suitable edible varieties that could be grown to mill down for flour.

Small fruit trees and bushes were transplanted from the woods nearby to form baby orchards. Tara's work-group moved from the beach and spent many hours gathering the young plants.

Apart from the loneliness, Tara was far more content than she should have been.

Perhaps the dreams had something to do with it. The haunted nightmares about that last day together with her family began to disappear and she was sleeping soundly each night. Colour came back to her cheeks. The medics put the improvement down to fresh air, hard work and time.

Tara knew better.

At the end of the second month, Tara moved from the camp to a small cabin with a group of six other children who had neither parents nor close family. In the tiny hamlet were two other cabins.

A river rippled at the hamlet's edge that provided water and also fish that the children learned to tickle out and which provided a tasty alternative to their, as yet, limited diets.

The two other families kept an eye on the children in the third cabin, which had two adults in nominal charge, an elderly lady who had lost her family during the space storm and another younger woman who was not best pleased with her appointment as assistant foster mother to seven children.

Tara did not like her and grew increasingly unhappy with the situation. When the woman decided that enough was enough and left one night, she shrugged her shoulders and got on with it. She was doing the majority of the chores anyway she reasoned and said as much to the other adults in the hamlet. The desertion was not reported to the authorities.

The eight of them managed well enough. If Tara wasn't exactly happy, she wasn't massively unhappy either.

The weeks passed. The Lind continued to watch and to listen.

The main settlement was, by now, built although it was still rough and ready. A narrow river ran through the centre and provided the settlers with fresh water. There were plans to build water and sewerage pipes. Both outer palisade and buildings were built of the hardwood trees found in the nearby forest. The trees on this planet were of two types; hard and soft. The latter was dry and fibrous and was primarily used for burning, although experiments were exploring its use as matting for roofing and floor coverings.

The hardwood was used for projects that needed strength. One type proved to have much the same attributes as steel and was being used as such. The single metal-smith amongst the colonists was on a rapid learning curve in this area, making ploughs, shovels and knives out of this strange new substance.

Dogs and cats from the ship roamed the settlement, providing both an early warning system for any predators, although none so far had shown themselves, and as a means of keeping down the small native pests. A particularly annoying creature was a small burrowing animal that resembled the Earth rat but without a tail. It could eat its way into any storeroom and devour twice its own weight in food within a few hours. Unfortunately, there were a lot of them about.

More farms, villages and hamlets sprang up in the fertile plains to the north of the landing site and west of the marshlands. To the west, a few miles from the main settlement, was a long forested hill. This forest was very extensive and only the fringes had been explored. A few outlying farms were being built at the edges.

Small groups of intrepid settlers built their cabins on the shoreline, both east and south of the settlement, intending to satisfy the colony's need for protein by farming the seas.

A number of rabbits had managed to escape from their pens during the early weeks and were thriving in the wild. Although the biologists were worried about the impact this would have on native species, the majority of colonists were far too busy to worry about it. The remaining rabbits were being bred as a means of providing extra protein. Children were encouraged to think of them as a resource to be eaten and not as pets. Guinea pigs were acceptable as pets; there was not enough meat on their bones to make resource breeding a viable option. The children were more than delighted with this decision and the animal lovers amongst the adults felt much the same way.

They had been lucky, arriving at the beginning of the summer season when game, fruit and vegetables were plentiful. There was time to prepare for winter. A start was made to replace the larger livestock lost in space with native species.

The ruminant herds which had been recorded by the probe were numerous, and more importantly, edible, although the meat tasted oily. The livestock breeders were working on the problem but without much success. The seaweed the animals preferred was on the oily side and proved, when attempts were made to cook it, to be inedible by humans.

Three types of native animals inhabited the paddocks. One herd consisted of some eighty beasts that resembled the mountain goats of Earth, but with much shorter legs. They had woolly coats of a dull brown and as well as being edible, provided wool for clothing and milk that could be made into a crumbly cheese with a tangy taste. Gentle in temperament, they were easy to catch and had adapted to captivity well.

The animals that inhabited the second paddock were not so gentle. Milling about restlessly was a small herd of long necked creatures that were being bred to satisfy the colony's need for meat.

Eighteen creatures that resembled Earth's New Forest ponies inhabited the third. They were proving even more difficult to tame but there were high hopes that eventually these eighteen might become the nucleus of the colony's transport system. There was no other way to get around except on foot with the consequence that exploration of all but the nearby area was patchy at best.

The planet had a ten-month yearly cycle and just two seasons. The colonists were working every daylight hour to reap and store enough edibles to see them through the first all-important winter. Thankfully, there were plenty of wild nutritious edibles that could be gathered and before long storerooms were piled high with the drying fruit and roots that had been gathered in from the plains and edges of the wooded areas.

It was beginning to feel like home for many but for twelve

youngsters, it was an unsettling time.

The dreams had begun not long after landing. The twelve felt compelled, in a way they did not understand, to keep silent about these dreams but some adults, especially the mothers, were beginning to suspect that something was seriously wrong. As it was a tenuous suspicion, they did not report it.

Candy Rae

CHAPTER 2

NORTHERN CONTINENT

The hardwood door slammed shut behind Tara. It was raining hard.

I'll be soaked through within minutes, she thought with a jaundiced look up at the sky. Like last night when I was dreaming.

They were the strangest dreams she had ever had. There was a peculiar compulsion about them, a compulsion to find out more about where they were coming from. Over the last few nights the compulsion had grown stronger, to that of a most foolhardy one – to leave the safety of the settled area and venture out into this exciting new world, to explore, to find out why she was dreaming in this way. She also felt a tenuous sense of belonging, to whom or what she did not know, but she wanted to find out.

Pulling the hood of her grey cloak over her head, she shivered.

A crotchety voice called out. "Don't forget to bring back enough firewood to last us until tomorrow."

Tara sighed again. Still, it was good to be out.

The cabin at the edge of the small hamlet that housed the orphaned youngsters was cold and dismal this early in the morning. The nights were getting colder. Snow had already appeared on the tips of the mountains in the north.

The voice continued. "You can fill the water cask when you get back."

Like Tara, Mrs Mackie had been the only member of her own family to survive the cosmic storm. She was somewhat rambling and incoherent on occasion, but this was not surprising. The old lady was over eighty years old.

Marion Mackie liked Tara, associating her with happier times when both their families were alive and she had, unknown to Tara, stopped more than one family from taking the girl in. The main drawback for Tara was that because Mrs Mackie was old and not able to move around easily, the majority of the heavy tasks fell to her. Firewood gathering was one of them. It was becoming hard to find manageable branches of burnable softwood close to the inhabited areas. Tara had to go further away each day and that was hard on the legs, especially when she was pulling a heavy sled full of wood, was only twelve years old and slightly built at that.

Dragging the sled behind her, Tara started her trudge towards the copse of trees that was the hamlet's designated wood gathering area. She kept her eyes on the ground, the better able to see any of the many potholes that could trip up the unwary.

It was still strange to see grass that wasn't green.

Her mind wandered as she progressed up the incline towards the edge of the wood. It could have been worse, but not by much, she was thinking as she pulled the sled behind her. Old Marion Mackie did her best, but Tara was used to the love and companionship that came with being part of a loving family. She missed her parents and little brother who had died during the space storm with a terrible anguish and it seemed that nobody cared overmuch about how she was coping with it all. It was all very worrying.

As she walked she thought again about the dreams. Over the last few days it had become difficult not to think of them, often at the most inconvenient times and places. Last night's dream had been different, more intense than the ones before. For the first time an image of a large wolf-like creature had appeared. In the dream Tara had not been afraid, had been convinced that the wolf was friendly and was welcoming her in some strange way.

When she reached the wood's edge she stopped for a moment to catch her breath, turned round in her tracks and surveyed the scene that met her eyes. She almost smiled. How her Mama and Papa would have loved it here. Shrugging her shoulders, it did no good to dwell on what might have been, she turned and dragged the sled under the branches and into the clearing.

Good, plenty of softwood here. This shouldn't take too long and then she could explore a bit, perhaps find some of the greenfruit to take back. The little ones would enjoy them, with their peculiar sweet-tart taste.

She bent down and hefted the nearest fallen branch on to the sled. This action she repeated for some time, packing in the larger pieces first then fitting in the smaller bits and kindling, but as she toiled she grew more and more uneasy and this feeling grew apace when she heard a number of crackles from the undergrowth. She straightened up and looked around, feeling for the steelwood knife she kept in her belt.

Another sharp crackle and Tara shivered. Gone was her idea of gathering the greenfruit. All she wanted was to finish her task and get home as fast as her legs could carry her. Placing the last of the wood on the top of the load she turned to fit the pull straps up and on to her shoulders.

She looked round and caught a flicker of movement. There was something out there, an unknown something, a scary something, a *very* scary something.

There, no, yes, there it was. There it was in the thick undergrowth to her right. She would go left. She began to haul the sled in that direction. The sense of being watched ceased for a moment and Tara breathed a deep sigh of relief.

This relief was short-lived. Now to her horror she sensed rather than saw movement right in front of her. She was getting really scared now. This area had been declared safe. There were no large predators in this part of the continent. An unknown something was stalking her. She stood frozen to the spot. She wanted to scream but found that her lips wouldn't open so she stood there waiting, her heart hammering.

A shadow was forming.

Tara regarded it in stupefied horror.

It was too big to be a man and it was the wrong shape. It was larger for one thing and had four legs rather than two.

The shadow began to solidify and a large creature loomed out of the undergrowth. She gasped in surprise, half enthralled, half terrified. Strangely, she was becoming less afraid.

The events of the previous night's dream came to her. This was nothing to be scared of. She was perfectly safe. This was what she was waiting for. This was the culmination of these dream-filled nights. They had been the preparation; this was the reality.

The creature that emerged was large, taller than Tara at the shoulder. Even though the dreams had prepared her, she was still nervous. The creature was big, three or four times the size of the pictures of Earth wolves shown in the wildlife datdiscs. This was a coloured animal whose pelt was a mixture of variegated light brown and blue hues. There was intelligence in its eyes; intelligence and a certain questioning look as if it was trying to communicate with Tara in some way the girl could not understand. Tara recognised the creature; it was the same as in the dreams. In her mind the creature was telling her not to be afraid, that he, how did she know that it was a he, was not going to hurt her. She believed him. He hunkered down, looking at her out of his deep blue eyes, eyes that matched the blue stripes on his coat.

She started to relax, just a little bit, and took an involuntary step towards him.

He looked at her encouragingly as if daring her to step nearer.

Tara couldn't help it; she took two more steps.

The creature raised himself up to his full height and padded towards her, one careful step after another. Once he had placed himself directly in front of her, he stopped and gazed down at her again.

Her mind was a mixture of emotions, confusion being predominant.

Kolyei, for that was who he was, gazed even more deeply into Tara's eyes. His mind was filled with regret about what he was about to do. He had to do this, take her away. The Eldas had decreed that he must. It was his duty to do so. He uttered three distinct sounds.

"Come with me."

Tara jumped. Why, that sounded almost like the wolf was talking to her.

A picture formed unbidden in Tara's mind, a moving picture showing her leaving with him, leaving her sled and its contents behind.

Kolyei's 'words' became more insistent.

"Come with me."

In a daze, Tara found herself doing just that, following him out of the clearing and into the deep undergrowth. The sled remained, mute testimony of her presence in the clearing. No other clues were left for the search parties to follow when they arrived some hours later.

When darkness fell the search parties returned to the settlement. They had found none of the missing children.

The Council met in emergency session.

"Twelve of them," said Stuart MacIntosh, Leader of the Colonial Council in a perplexed voice. "All vanished without trace."

"There were no tracks," volunteered Jim Cranston, another member of the Council. Like Stuart MacIntosh he had been a crewmember aboard the WCCS *Argyll.*

"No sign of any struggles either," said another man.

"We have to keep looking," declared Jim. "I vote that all of us hunters go out again first thing in the morning."

"I agree," Stuart said, "and any trail will be easier to find in the sunlight."

The ex-crew of the WCCS *Argyll* had, on the whole, kept together, performing tasks that the farming colonists did not have the time or inclination to do. Jim Cranston had become the colony's expert with spear and bow. The other more advanced weapons had not survived the storm having been locked away on the officers' deck in the section of the ship that had sustained a lot of damage when the space debris had hit.

"All the hunters?" spluttered Robert Lutterell, one-time Chief Petty Officer on the spaceship.

"Of course."

"No. We can't spare that many personnel to make up search parties to hunt for youngsters who may merely have run away. We need all of them here to bring in enough food to last us through winter. We must concentrate on that. Food stocks have not yet reached the required level and there aren't enough live animals in the corrals."

Jim glared at him. "Run away? All twelve?" he said, disbelievingly. "I think not. There is something strange about all of this. Why these twelve? Why was there no warning? There must be a reason. We must keep looking. One of the missing is Kath Andrews. She is almost adult, seventeen, rising eighteen and a member of the crew. I do not think she ran away. We will go out again in the morning."

The Council members looked worried as Jim continued. "Then there are Will Armstrong's twins, Bill and Geoff. Their sixteenth birthday was only days after landing. Will wants something done about finding them and pretty pronto too. His wife's in a state; she doted on these two boys."

"Who else exactly has gone?" asked Jean Farquharson. "I came in late to the meeting, remember?"

"Moira Craig, Brenda Urquhart and Yvonne Benoit. They're a year younger than the twins," answered Jim Cranston with a glance at the list he was holding.

"I know these three," declared Jean, "always skiving off when there's work to be done. The only thing that concerns them is their looks and how to attract the opposite sex."

"That's true," said Jim with a smile. "Thomas Wylie is next in age, he's fourteen. He's the mechanical one amongst them, a clever boy, and excellent grades in all his learning outcomes, especially science and mathematics. Good with his hands too. Then there are three thirteen-year-olds, Emily Stanton, Mark Ampte and Alan de Groot. Alan's one of the survivors of colony section six; he's being raised by his uncle. Mark's from farming stock same as Bill and Geoff."

"Emily?" questioned Jean.

"Bit of a dreamer with a passionate interest in language and history, at least that's what the personnel datdisc has recorded about her. Peter Crawford is the youngest. He's only ten, small for his age but a normal wee boy, leastways he was until a week or so ago."

"That makes eleven," said Jean, totting up the names she had jotted down. "Who's the twelfth?"

"Tara Sullivan, aged twelve, another section six survivor."

Winston Randall raised his head.

"I remember that one. She lost both parents and a little brother when their cabin decompressed. I intended to keep an eye on her after we landed but you know how it is – never enough hours in the day."

"She was billeted at Lower Hamlet with the rest of the orphans," said Jim. "Her disappearance was the last to be reported. Old Marion Mackie is getting on a bit and lost track of the time. I think though that she was probably the first of them to vanish. Nobody's seen her since early morning. The last one for which we have a positive ID sighting is Mark Ampte. He was last seen walking in the general direction of the woods by his father who told him to be back by suppertime. By then of course the first missing person's report was coming in but we hadn't got round to warning everyone."

"So," said Stuart, "a farmer's three children, one ex-crewmember, three work-shy girls, one embryo mathematician, one dreamer, two orphans and a young boy still in junior school; quite a varied bunch. Why them and how, for heavens sake?"

"All of them bar Thomas Wylie were living outside the settlement area proper," ventured Jim, "and we know Mark, Kath and Tara were in the woods."

"It's a conundrum," said Robert Lutterell.

"A conundrum?" exploded Jim. "It's a disaster for the families. Agnes Crawford is hysterical and the rest of the parents not in much better shape. There's something going on here we don't understand, but we will, I promise you. We've got to find them, get some answers."

"Now wait a minute," said Robert in his loud, forceful voice. "We can't all go out looking for them. We don't even know in what direction they went. It's all supposition. You said there were no tracks, no sign of any struggles. Get this into your head; we simply don't have the manpower."

The discussion rumbled on.

Robert let them talk for a while then interrupted again, with more bluntness this time and uttering the words that most of those seated round the table were thinking.

"They might have been taken by predators. We know so little about the planet outside the immediate area. We must warn all personnel. Youngsters may no longer wander around unattended. I advise one hunting party to search for traces. I wish we could spare more." He looked at Stuart MacIntosh. "Surely you must agree sir?"

There were reluctant nods from the rest of the Councillors and Stuart MacIntosh.

"I will lead the search party," Jim announced in a very loud voice, "and I will find them! I leave first thing in the morning and no one is going to stop me!"

He rose from the table.

"Who are you taking with you?" asked Stuart. "Better make it four or so. A small party will make better speed than a larger one."

Jim thought for a moment. "Young James Rybak. He was out searching with me earlier and is most distressed about young Kath. McAllister too I think. We may need his strength before this is over. Laura Merriman would also be a good choice. She is adapting better than most to the alien environment and is developing into a rather good tracker."

"I don't think you'll find them," muttered Robert Lutterell, "and I say again how sorry I am that we can't spare more to look, but go. If you can't find them then no one will."

"I concur," said Stuart MacIntosh looking round the table. "Is everyone in agreement that Jim here should take an away team and go and look for them?"

There were murmurs of agreement, tinged with regret from those who felt bad that they could do little more, but most felt that Robert Lutterell had the right of it. The winter season was almost upon them and the eight thousand colonists needed all the food they could catch and gather if they were to survive.

Jim vowed to himself that he would do all in his power to find the missing children and if it should take months, then that was just too bad. He, unlike Robert and some of the others, did not believe that the children were dead.

He left the Council meeting and went straight to find James Rybak. It was not hard. The young man was pacing up and down outside the medical facility, face set with worry.

"Well?" James asked. "When do we leave? I'm going no matter what they say. I know the Chief is against it. Give him his due, he *is* trying to see the bigger picture but we can't just let twelve youngsters disappear into the blue mist like this."

"He was in the majority," growled Jim.

"We leave tonight?"

"No, in the morning, early," was Jim's terse reply, "and had they said no I would have joined you anyway."

"How many of us?"

"You, me, Laura and Francis McAllister."

"You think that is a good idea Jim? He's a bit of a troublemaker."

"He is as upset about the children going missing as you and I."

"What do you want me to do?"

"You go and tell Laura and Francis. I'm going to speak to some of the families. The children may have said something. As I said before, I think there is far more to all this than meets the eye. We'll meet back here in two hours. Tell them to prepare for a *long* trip."

James chuckled as he nodded. He understood perfectly. They would not be returning without the children, no matter how long it took.

In the hardwood cabin that housed the Crawford family, young Peter Crawford's mother was in tears. The face that faced Jim when he arrived was one of anguish, the anguish of a mother who has lost her only son.

"He is only ten years old," she cried, "he's just a little boy."

"I know," said Jim sitting down beside her, "and I am going to bring him home."

Her tears stopped for a moment and her face changed to one of entreaty.

"You will find him, won't you? He's not dead?"

"I will not return without him, and no, I do not think any of the children are dead," he vowed, devoutly hoping that he could make good the promise, but he couldn't leave her like this. She had to have some hope. "Now, you can help me if you will?"

Her face was raised to his.

"Anything, just ask."

"Did Peter say anything to you that sounded odd over the last few weeks? Was he acting strangely at all?"

Agnes Crawford considered for a moment and then shook her head. "No, he was much the same as usual, perhaps a little quieter, that's all."

Jim sighed. This was much the same reply as he had been getting in all the cabins that he had visited so far. He was none the wiser than when he had set out on his round of visits over an hour before. One or two parents had said their children seemed preoccupied about something but they had no idea what.

A very matter of fact young voice piped up from the huddle of bedclothes in the corner.

"Was it the wolves that took Peter?"

Jim pivoted round at once. "Wolves?" This was the first he'd heard of any wolves.

A small tousled-haired girl was sitting up in bed staring at him, her eyes puffy with sleep.

Agnes Crawford looked at her daughter. "Wolves? What wolves? Has Peter been scaring you with his tales again?"

The girl shook her head.

"Not *bad* wolves, good *big* wolves. They have been talking to Peter, in his head. He said it was a ginormous secret and I wasn't to tell anyone but now he's gone."

Her face crumpled and the tears began to flow.

Agnes rushed to her daughter's side and gathering her up in her arms, carried her over to her seat beside the fire.

"Ask her if she remembers anything else," Jim prompted, but the little girl did not.

As he left the cabin, Agnes rocking the girl back to sleep, Jim was thinking deeply. *Good big wolves? What the Dickens does she mean?*

When he discussed it with the other three they were inclined to dismiss the girl's words.

"An over-vivid imagination," was Lesley's comment.

Francis McAllister was more blunt, "Balderdash."

Jim was not so sure.

"Let's not discount it without investigation," he said. "It's the only clue we have so far."

"Clue or fairy story?" was Laura's rhetorical question.

"I'd better take a large spear with me," Francis said sarcastically, "in case we meet up with these imaginary wolves."

"I thought you'd be taking it anyway," was Jim's laconic answer, half serious, half in jest.

Soberly, the other two smiled. Although they said they did not believe the Crawford girl's story, they would take no chances and none relished the thought of meeting up with large wolf-like creatures, however friendly they might turn out to be.

Kolyei and Tara travelled all morning and well into the afternoon.

She walked beside him not really thinking at all, merely placing one foot in front of the other. She did not need to think. She was not sure she wanted to think. Then her stomach started to rumble. She had had but little breakfast, Marion Mackie being accustomed to feed the littlest ones first, herself and Tara later.

Kolyei matched his pace with hers, slow that it was. It was not his plan to exhaust the youngster. He had been lucky; she whom he had chosen had been easy to take away. She had come with him without any demur. The others might have to wait until their youngsters were alone, they might even have to wait until nightfall when the two-legged creatures were relaxed and sitting round their fires before they could plant the compulsion to seek them out into the young minds but he was confident that he would see the rest by first light.

Tara stumbled once and again a few paces later. Her companion sighed mightily. He would have to let her ride else they would not arrive at the dom before nightfall. Two paws were not as good as four.

He stopped and sat down. Tara looked at him.

"I am hungry," she said.

Kolyei cocked his ear at her, trying to understand, but he thought he did realise what the problem was.

An image of a large hunk of raw meat appeared in Tara's mind. She recoiled with a shudder.

If Kolyei could have frowned he would have. Instead his eyes crinkled up as he tried to make sense of her reaction. Was the youngster not hungry? Did she not like kura? Something else then?

The next image was better from Tara's point of view, that of a bush of greenfruits.

She nodded, smiling just a little.

Kolyei nodded his head in reply. This must be the sign for yes. He was making progress. He led her to the greenfruit bushes. He himself would not need to eat until the sun rose again having dined with his rtathen on a large zarova buck early that morning. These two-legged ones must have to eat more frequently. He stored up this extra piece of information for future use.

When they reached the bush, he watched the youngster's eyes light up then she picked a fruit and began to eat. He moved closer and sat down to wait.

Tara looked at him, faintly alarmed.

"Kolyei," he said, enunciating both syllables. He nodded his head.

His voice was low yet resonant, not like a human at all.

Why should I expect him to sound like us? thought Tara, munching steadily through her fruit. *He is an alien, or is it us who are the aliens? I don't know. He seems friendly. I only wish I knew exactly why I followed him and how does he plant these pictures into my mind?*

Truth be known, Tara wasn't too bothered. He seemed to be friendly; in fact he was being more that just friendly. He really appeared to care about her. The sense of belonging that had come across her in the clearing so many hours ago and in her dreams over the last weeks came back tenfold.

Kolyei nodded again and his long bushy tail started to wag, just a little bit. He spoke again.

"Kolyei."

Does he know what I am thinking? Is Kolyei his name? She stood up and placing her two index fingers on her chest said aloud, "Tara."

"Tara?" His inflection emphasised his enquiry.

She nodded, bent down and picked her fifth greenfruit from the bush.

"Tara," he said again, enunciating the two syllables and pointing one forepaw towards her.

"Yes," she replied and nodded. She realised that if she was going to spend a lot of time with this Kolyei, she had better start communicating. She sat down beside him, still munching.

"Yes," she said again. She then repeated both sound and action. Kolyei nodded to indicate that he understood.

"Yes Tara," was his reply.

He was rewarded by a tentative smile.

"Ceja Tara," he said.

Zowie! He is teaching me his language. Does Ceja mean yes? I wonder what no is?

"No," she said and shook her head. She made a face as if to indicate displeasure.

He looked at her blankly. It was clear to Tara that he did not understand. Tara racked her brains for inspiration.

It came to her.

I wonder if this will work? He thinks thoughts at me so why shouldn't I be able to do the same? She thought hard as she formed a picture of a large piece of uncooked meat in her mind, together with a strong feeling of her dislike of it.

"No," she repeated and tried to fling the thought through the air towards her companion.

Kolyei's eyes opened wider as he realised what he was 'seeing'. She could implant pictures in his mind. What an unexpected and wondrous thing! It would make this whole assimilation process so much easier. It would not take many long moons to learn each other's language. Why, they could do it in one.

"No," he said in Standard and shook his head.

Tara laughed and clapped her hands together. Kolyei did not try to imitate this. It was virtually impossible for him, after all, preferring instead to show his pleasure by wagging his tail. He proceeded to do so, very fast. Emboldened, Tara gave Kolyei a quick pat. He grinned at her. His eyes twinkled. Tara laughed again, louder this time.

They did not know it then, but it was at this moment that their lifelong mind-linkage was cemented. They would never again be separated, except by death, and as if this was an omen, the sun chose this moment to shine through the clouds and the rain ceased. They were the first paired human and Lind. She was the first of those who would go down in history as the 'Children of the Wolves'. Tara and Kolyei were the first of what would become known as a vadeln-pair.

After Tara had eaten no less than ten greenfruits they set out again. Periodically they stopped for a rest and Kolyei would point with his paw at a flower or a plant and say its name. Tara repeated the words and taught him some of her own. Both the Lind male and the girl were enjoying themselves. As the afternoon drew in and Tara started to stumble again, Kolyei drew closer to her.

How was he to tell her to climb on his back? The Eldas had given approval, realising from the sorties near the settlement that there was no way that the newcomers could match the Lind for speed and stamina. Traditionally the only other time when this was done was when mothers were forced to carry their young out of danger. Certainly within living memory no male had ever done so except in dire circumstances. Once she was on his back they would be able to go so much faster. There was still a long way to go to reach the dom.

He stopped.

Tara looked at him.

"Ptatch," he said aloud.

"Ptatch? What does that mean?" asked Tara.

He nudged Tara with his shoulder then lowered himself. Crouching beside her he sent an image of her riding him directly into her mind.

Tara smiled and nodded. She lifted her right leg over his haunches then, after a struggle, settled herself on his back. Kolyei stood up. He was large; her weight was nothing to him, slightly built as she was.

He began to walk then to trot. Tara grabbed hold of the longer hairs at his withers, surprised at its length and softness. Feeling that much more secure she gained confidence, tightening her legs round the barrel of his body. Kolyei moved into a canter then into a ground-devouring lope that was much faster and, as Tara was to learn, far more sustainable than what she'd been taught concerning a horse's gallop.

Laughing, she shouted out in delight. "Oh this is wonderful!" Indeed it was.

They reached the temporary shelter at dusk.

"Dom," said Kolyei as he slowed down.

CHAPTER 3

NORTHERN CONTINENT

Tara looked around at the campsite, or dom as Kolyei had called it. There were, what could only be described as small lairs, dotted around the clearing. A stream bubbled to one side. Bundles of what might be food lay heaped by type in one corner, and beside them sat another Lind. This one was white, white as snow, and he stood up with grave courtesy as they approached.

The two Lind stared into each other's eyes. Tara was sure that they were conversing mentally with each other.

Telling each other all the news I'll be bound, she thought, slipping down from Kolyei's back with relief. Her tired muscles ached in protest at the unaccustomed exercise. All she wanted to do was to lie down.

The white Lind approached Tara.

"Dedta Tara." He greeted her.

I was right. They talk aloud and send pictures to each other's minds just like Kolyei does with me.

She looked longingly at the bundle of food. It was a mixture of fruit and roots.

"Jeza Tara," invited the white Lind, pointing to the nearest pile with his forepaw.

"Eat," translated Kolyei.

Tara did just that.

The two Lind looked at her, then at each other, as she ate. Their tails swished in a tranquil fashion. The plans were progressing well.

Kolyei introduced Tara to the white Lind.

"This be Afanasei," he said, pointing his snout at him.

Tara bowed slightly. It seemed appropriate.

Afanasei looked pleased at this show of courtesy and dipped his head once in reply.

The two Lind started to talk to each other. They talked so fast that the only word Tara could distinguish was her own name.

Then Kolyei brought twelve white pebbles in his mouth and spat them out in front of her. She counted them carefully.

"Twelve," she said aloud.

"Duntanvad," he agreed.

Then twelve black stones were placed beside each of the white ones. A larger white stone was placed to one side. Tara watched, wondering what they were trying to tell her.

Kolyei moved one black stone with his paw and placed it at her feet.

"Tara," he said. He then nudged the white one from the other bundle to a position in front of his other paw.

"This be Kolyei," he said.

Afanasei pawed the larger white one over towards himself.

She looked at them wonderingly. The black stone must represent her. If she had got that right then the three stones apart from the rest represented the three of them here. What was the significance of the other eleven pairs of stones? In a rush, understanding came to her.

There were more on their way to the dom. She had not been the only one kidnapped by the Lind. They were waiting for another eleven Lind and eleven people.

She looked at Kolyei and nodded to show that she knew what he was trying to say.

She formed a picture of eleven other pairs of Lind and humans arriving in her mind and, concentrating hard, pushed it out towards him, smiling and nodding as she did so. She wouldn't be the only person here with the Lind. He wagged his tail rapidly, delighted with her reaction and her ability to transmit the image.

Tara went to sleep that night with a light heart. She felt safe, secure and for some reason, loved. Nestled into the warmth that was

Kolyei she did not stir, even when the second pair that was Kath Andrews and Matvei loped into the clearing in the middle of the night.

Kath Andrews was sitting beside Tara when the younger girl woke. With a sharp cry of gladness, Tara opened her arms and fell into the older girl's embrace.

"Well kitten," Kath said with a smile. "You too?"

Kitten was Kath's pet name for Tara.

Tara grinned at her. "Fraid so. I am so glad you're here Kath. It felt so strange on my own."

"Not really on your own, your Kolyei was here."

"Yes," Tara pondered, "but that's different."

Kath understood perfectly.

"Want some breakfast?"

"More raw roots and fruit?"

Kath laughed. "No, I came better prepared than you! I was out hunting when Matvei came across me. I had my pack with provisions and other things. The provisions are all gone, but I do have my fire-starter with me so we can at least make something hot. Far nicer that way."

Tara stood up with alacrity. She was hungry again.

"Where?" she demanded, looking around the clearing. Then she saw the small fire some six or seven feet away. A small pot was bubbling in its midst. Her mouth started to water in anticipation.

Over breakfast the two of them talked. The Lind were resting not far away. Kolyei lifted one forepaw in greeting but did not interrupt. He did send into her mind however, a feeling of utter contentment combined with a picture of her sleeping quietly by his side.

"Do you know why they brought us here?" asked Tara munching her way through a mixed plate of whiteroot and salad. The whiteroot was cooked to a tee and Tara was enjoying it immensely.

"A wee bit," answered Kath. "I don't think they'll tell us the full story until we reach our destination. Matvei says we are going to a place called domta. I presume that is where the rest of their pack lives."

"You understood that much?" asked Tara in amazement.

"Most of it is just a guess," Kath admitted. "The words I know relate to actual things. Verbs, adjectives and pronouns are more difficult."

Tara nodded her agreement, her mouth being too full of good food to answer.

Kath continued, "I think the white one is some sort of teacher of the young. I got the weirdest images from Matvei of a large white Lind sitting in front of a crowd of young ones. It looked like a school!"

"Will we have to join in?" asked Tara apprehensively.

"I think they might have special classes for us," was the less than reassuring answer but Tara accepted this pronouncement in her usual matter of fact way. "Will we rest here today do you think Kath? I am really tired. I'd like to sleep some more."

It was with sympathy that Kath looked at the white-faced youngster. "Yes," she answered, considering the matter. "We're waiting for the others to arrive. I would go and have that lie down now if that's what you want, while you have the chance."

"Good." Standing up slowly, how her muscles protested, she looked down at Kath. "I think I will." She yawned, showing two rows of perfect white teeth. "Will you wake me up when the rest get here?"

Kath nodded and watched as Tara went back to her sleeping niche. A few moments later the girl was sound asleep so Kath covered her with her hunting cloak to help keep out the chilly morning air and went over to join the three Lind.

Kath, being almost adult, felt responsible for all their safety. She had realised early on that the children would look to her as the eldest. She sat down beside Matvei. "The others when they get here will be confused," she began, "and I have to confess to being a bit on edge myself."

Afanasei, Kolyei and Matvei turned their heads towards her.

Grasping at her courage, Kath added. "And I'd like to know what you are going to do with us."

The three Lind did not comprehend the actual words Kath spoke, but they understood well enough the meaning behind what she was saying. Matvei's mind was attuned to hers and he managed to make sense of her question.

"Kath wishes to know why she is here," he explained to Afanasei. *: Kath has nervousness to our intent :* he added telepathically. *: Kath* *feels responsible for those younger than herself but has no fear about herself :*

: We wish no harm, you must tell her : replied Afanasei. *: Can she not feel the love you have for her? :*

: I would die to protect Tara : affirmed Kolyei.

: Tara is not scared : added Afanasei. He turned towards Matvei and added *: You must explain to Kath :*

Matvei began to speak, attempting to make clear why they needed to make contact with their people. He glossed over the dangers foretold for the summer. Kath understood perhaps a half of it, but she did emerge from their conversation with some answers to her questions.

The Lind had a serious reason for 'persuading' her and the rest of the children, even now approaching the dom, to run away with them. That it was something that was a threat to them all she also understood. It was enough to be going on with and she walked away rehearsing what she would say to the others when they arrived but content that they were among friends and in no immediate danger.

Many miles to the east, Jim Cranston and his three colleagues were making themselves ready. They were equipped for a trip that, he was sure, would be a long and arduous one and fraught with many dangers. Along with their food packs and spare clothing they all carried weapons, including bows and arrows for Jim and Laura Merriman. Francis McAllister held a large spear with a steelwood shaft in his large hand and a wicked-looking dagger tucked in his leather belt. Jim knew how far Francis could throw this spear and just how accurate he could be. He hoped his skills would not be needed. James Rybak carried nothing but the knife carried as standard by all colonists venturing outside the settlement. He was impatient to be off and moved around in a restless fashion.

As they intended to live off the land for the most part, their packs were light.

Agnes Crawford, her young daughter in her arms, stood with the other families whose children had vanished.

Stuart MacIntosh appeared, his eyes straying to the palisades where, for the first time since the second week after landing, a guard detail patrolled the perimeter on a day and nightlong vigil. Although

Robert Lutterell and others were of the opinion that the twelve had either run away or been taken by predators, the majority of the settlers agreed with Jim that there was far more to it than that. Other snippets of information had emerged as Jim progressed with his enquiries after he had left the Crawford cabin.

One mother had confided that her daughter had complained that she had not been sleeping well and was plagued by dreams of friendly wolves wanting to talk. Another said the same. When asked why they had not reported this to the authorities they had answered that they had not believed their children were talking about something that was actually happening, thinking, like Lesley Merriman, that these dreams were just that – young imaginations running riot due to the excitements they were experiencing on their new planet. They deeply regretted not reporting it now, but that was after the fact.

Stuart MacIntosh said two simple words to the party as they picked up their packs.

"Good luck."

Jim looked at his captain, his blue eyes serious.

"Thanks Stuart. I think we may need a surfeit of luck before this is all over. I don't think we'll find these kids easily. We have to assume that they have been kidnapped for a reason and the fact that they have disappeared so very completely may well mean that they don't want them to be found."

"Kidnapped?"

"Well, what else would you call it? I'd be the first to admit that we don't have the full story, just some rumours and reports from tearful mothers and siblings, but I think the mass disappearance has been planned and planned carefully by some sentient species on this planet that we haven't come across yet."

"You're not serious?"

"Yes I am. Deadly serious. You know how little of the surrounding area has been explored. For goodness sake man, how many planets do you know of that don't have carnivores preying on the herbivores? We see plenty of grass eaters but predators?" He looked at Stuart, square chin thrust out as if daring him to contradict. Stuart said nothing. In his heart he knew that the ex-petty officer was talking a lot of sense and was probably correct in his assumptions.

Laura walked over to stand beside Jim and added her bit.

"Because we have not seen them does not mean that they have not been present all along, watching and evaluating us."

As Jim continued with his theory, Stuart listened, a stunned expression on his face.

"That they have managed to persuade twelve normally well adjusted youngsters to go away with them and not say anything to anyone, speaks of their intelligence and also, I think, their intentions. They have not taken the kids off to make them the main course of their next meal. I think that this species, large wolves or whatever they are, have made contact in their own way and have taken the kids to try and find out more about us. They would realise that if they approached us directly that some trigger-happy bowman would start taking pot shots at them. If they have been watching and I think we can take that as a definite, they would have been very wary indeed."

James and Francis were listening. James spoke up. "I also think that these creatures must have some form of telepathic powers."

"What? Telepathic powers?" was Stuart's incredulous stutter.

"How else would you explain it? The kids have been dreaming, not sleeping well. They tell a few close siblings or mothers about their dreams. Not a lot of information and it is as if they were being compelled somehow to stay silent. Remember, the Crawford girl said that Peter was not supposed to tell anyone. Then, before anyone has the chance to start getting suspicious, the twelve disappear, all on the same day, leaving very few traces of their passing. How else would you explain it? Even Kath closed up on me a few weeks ago. She told me that she was having some unsettling dreams but even when pressed would not tell me what these dreams were."

"Well, I don't know if I want to believe what you have just said. Telepathic wolves? It's like something out of a child's fairy story. Still, better that than the children all being dead. I'll do what I can with the Council. The colonists are worried and unsettled about all this. Some have taken to confining their children to their cabins. Now get on, leave now, before Robert Lutterell thinks of a reason to keep you here."

He stepped back. The four hunters picked up their packs, turned and headed towards the gate. They did not look back.

The guard detail watched silently as the small party headed up the hill towards the tree line. In the lead went Jim, his not inconsiderable frame dwarfed by the bulk that was Francis treading close at his heels. The tall lanky figure of James bounded up the incline after them, then Laura, her slight wiry figure being the last to disappear into the dense foliage. The guards looked at each other; they did not think they would see the four again.

When Tara woke up from her nap the clearing was buzzing with activity. She pulled Kath's rain-cloak from her shoulders and stood up, eyes wide as she took in the scene.

Children and Lind were scattered around. Some were resting; others were talking. There was much laughter from the humans and merry whining from the Lind as they demonstrated their enjoyment the Lind way.

Kolyei, talking to Matvei not far away, saw that Tara was awake and padded over to her, tail swishing. The girl's mind filled with a warm feeling and the accustomed sense of belonging. It was a very pleasant feeling for one who had lost her entire family such a short time before. He sat down in front of her and she lifted her head so that she could look into his liquid blue eyes.

"Good morning," she said in Standard.

"Good morning," he translated into Lind. "You wish to eat? You will be hungry. You must be strong. We walk a long way this day."

Tara only understood a word here and there; certainly not enough to make sense of what Kolyei was trying to say. Her face showed her confusion.

He lifted his forepaw towards his head and then pointed it at hers. Tara understood. He was going to 'send' her some telepathic images that would help her to understand what he was saying. Three pictures formed in her mind. The first was of her eating.

Tara nodded to show that she understood that part.

The second picture was of them leaving the clearing and starting to walk. The sun was bright in the sky. The third picture showed them still walking but it was twilight.

"Long way," Kolyei repeated.

Enlightenment came to Tara. *It's as Kath told me. We are going on a long journey to their home.*

Looking at Kolyei, she said clearly, enunciating each word with care. "Yes, I will eat. Long journey ahead." She nodded and walked towards the campfire, over which Kath and a boy somewhat older than Tara presided, doling out food.

Kolyei watched her go with intense satisfaction. Communication with these strange two-legs was progressing famously. Attuned to Tara's mind, he understood a surprising amount of what she was saying. It would not take them both long to learn the other's tongue. He wondered how the other Lind would manage.

Radya and young Peter Crawford were lying resting not far from the campfire. Peter was sleeping; the female Lind curled up protectively around him. Her eyes were open and she was eying Kolyei speculatively. He pretended not to notice and walked away, head in the air.

This nonchalant effect was spoilt somewhat when his front paw tripped over a fallen tree trunk and falling, he banged his snout on the ground. Kolyei shook himself as he picked himself up and walked over to Afanasei, all the time wondering why Radya affected him this way. Why, he was as clumsy as a ltscta not three moons old when she was around!

Candy Rae

CHAPTER 4

NORTHERN CONTINENT

Unbeknownst to the thirteen Lind and their twelve human friends in the clearing to the west, Jim Cranston and his fellow hunters had found traces of their passing. It was Laura who found the first clue, a twig broken off a bush beside where Kath Andrews had last been seen. Nearby, the hunters found faint tracks, almost undecipherable due to the heavy rain that continued to fall but Laura's sharp eyes managed to make out two sets of tracks, one made by a human (the imprint of the leather boots all hunters wore was clearly marked in the mud), the other made by a large four-footed animal. She could see that the animal did not have hooves. The shape imprinted on the wet soil was akin to that of a dog, but if a canine, it was a very large one, very large indeed.

She straightened up from where she had been examining them and looked at the other three.

"I've found them!"

Jim, Francis and James looked over.

She pointed at two-footed tracks. "These are Kath's, of that I am sure." She moved her head down for a closer look. "The other is a large animal. Just look at the distance between the strides. At least the size of a horse I would guess. There is no sign of a struggle. I think Kath went with the creature willingly."

"That would bear with what we learned back at the settlement," said Jim.

James nodded his head in agreement.

"We follow?"

"What do you think?" Jim said witheringly. "Of course we follow."

Francis added his bit, "Are they wolf prints?"

"I don't know for sure," answered Laura, running a hand distractedly through the dark brown curls of her hair, "I've never tracked a wolf. I have seen dog prints though and these are similar. They will not be easy to follow. For a large beast, it is very light on its feet, as if it is being very careful about where it is treading. The tracks are all on the lighter soil where an imprint is not so obvious. A clear sign of intelligence, wouldn't you say?"

Francis nodded. He noticed that Laura's curls were rather appealing and matched her elfin looks perfectly. They were certainly an improvement on the severe bob that had been the norm for female crew on the ship.

The four lifted their packs on to their shoulders and followed Laura out of the clearing and back into the undergrowth.

The hunt had begun.

The thirteen Lind and their human companions had already set out for their trek to the Lind pack-home. They walked for the most part and were led by Matvei and Kath. Afanasei walked beside Tara and Kolyei, learning all he could of this alien language. Tara began to think there would be no end to his questions. It was a slow process; what each knew of the other's language was still limited but both species found that being able to illustrate words and ideas with mental images was a great help. As the day wore on, every pair began to speak to each other more vocally, their thoughts being more and more reserved for emotions rather than explanations. Afanasei wondered at the phenomenon. What unbelievable luck that some members of this off-world species were able to communicate the Lind way.

"How long will the journey take?" Tara asked Kolyei with a long-suffering sigh after Afanasei had moved ahead to inflict his endless questions and tuition on another unfortunate pair.

He considered her question. The journey would normally take a

Lindar all of nine sundowns; a smaller party could do it, perhaps, in a little less. Encumbered as they were with these slow two-legged creatures he was not sure.

"Eleven sundowns," he answered at last, but Tara got the impression that it might be a lot more.

They set off.

It had been planned that for the first part of the journey through the forest both species would walk. It was realised by the Lind that their two-legged partners had not the stamina nor the speed to keep up with a Lind running and, when they reached the grass-lands the two-legged younglings would again be permitted to ride. If the Eldas had not given this concession the journey would take too long and it would also give any search parties the opportunity to catch up with them. That was not in the plan.

Matvei had discussed the situation with both Kolyei and Afanasei on arrival at the dom the previous evening and they concluded that riding would be the norm when vadeln-pairs needed to traverse large distances in the future. Matvei had laughed as he mentioned that it was his considered opinion that ltscta not five moons old could traverse the ground faster than his Kath. The Lind were in high spirits. It was a great honour for pack Zanatei to be the one chosen by the Eldas to pioneer the twelve first inter-species bondings. Why, they would be sung about for many moons and seasons to come.

When Tara was informed that riding would again be necessary she was eager to ride at once. Her legs were tired from the previous day as the walking pace set by the Lind was much faster than she was used to and often she had to run to keep up. To be carried on Kolyei's back would be unadulterated pleasure. It would also remove Afanasei from their side. He could not run at speed and ask questions at the same time, at least she hoped he couldn't.

During a short break, the twelve human youngsters ate some of what they had brought with them from the first campsite. The Lind had eaten their own meal earlier and would not need to eat again until the following day. They set off again, mounted this time. It was amazing the speed at which the Lind could traverse the ground. Tara, her knees clamped tight to Kolyei's side and her hands once more entwined in his thick neck fur, became almost mesmerised by the sight of the trees and undergrowth flashing by. Before nightfall, they had left the woods and were going even faster, the land being prairie-like, the grasses almost uniformly mauve and the ground undulating only slightly. In the distance Tara could see a faint smudge of what might be hills on the horizon and wondered if they were their destination.

They slept that night at the bottom of a slightly larger undulation. The rain stopped and with relays of Lind keeping watch through the dark hours, the children slept the sleep of the exhausted nestled into those Lind not on watch.

When morning came they were surprised to see a bundle of edibles waiting for them. The Lind said nothing but Kath, Tara and a few of the others correctly surmised that other Lind were in the vicinity and had brought it for them.

When questioned, the Lind only looked wise.

"They are our friends and rtathen and they guard us," intoned Kolyei.

It took quite some time to explain just exactly what the Lind meant, but the humans understood that there were dangers on these plains, dangers that only the Lind knew existed and that they were taking steps to protect the party. Kath, older than the rest realised that these protective parties could also be used to stop searchers looking for them but she kept such thoughts to herself.

They set off after they had eaten. That night they rested beside a small copse of dugo bushes, about the only vegetation larger than a stalk of grass that grew on the plains. The smudge of hills on the horizon was closer now and as the days passed, became ever bigger and more distinct.

These hills were their destination.

The hunters found the site where the children had spent their first night.

Laura strode into the clearing, bow at the ready, her eyes raking its length and breadth for any danger. "All clear," she shouted back to the three men as she stopped in the middle of the deserted campsite, waving them forward.

They stepped forward warily, hands poised to grab their weapons if danger threatened.

"Long gone," stated Jim with a sigh of resignation. Looking

round, he added, "They *were* here though. There are traces of their footsteps passing back and fro and indentations where they rested."

"I agree," said James, bending down and picking up a half-buried food wrapper. "A lot more of these overlarge paw prints as well."

"Fire too," stated Francis, kicking the ashes with one large booted foot. "Been at least a couple of days since they were here I reckon, perhaps more."

"It's taken us time to track them through the woods," stated Jim, sitting down on a fallen tree stump after looking over it thoroughly for any infestations of the nasty little yellow ant-like creatures that bit like fury if they were disturbed. "We kept losing the tracks, especially when the footprints disappeared."

"I believe they're riding the beasts," was Laura's contribution.

"You may well be right," said Jim. "It'll make them that much harder to track though." He sighed gustily, "I'm tired to the bone. I vote we stay here tonight. We need a decent rest and we may pick up some clues before nightfall." He was still breathing hard from the climb up to the campsite. Older than the other three by more than a decade, he was finding the going tough. He was absolutely certain that before this hunt was ended he would be much fitter and have shed more than a few pounds in weight. He had already tightened his belt a notch.

It was during an exploration foray just outside the clearing that they came across the note. It was from Kath who, realising that someone would be detailed to follow them, had decided to put that someone in the picture. Francis found the note when he was poking around in the undergrowth where, had he known it, Kath and Matvei had rested together before setting out again.

He ran back into the clearing waving the small piece of folded durapaper excitedly.

The other three clustered around as with trembling hands he carefully opened the folds.

"It's from Kath Andrews," he said. "It says, 'Don't worry. We are twelve. Will return three months. No point following. Tell parents well and happy. The Lind are friendly. Kath.' Well, what d'you think of that?"

"The Lind? Who or what are they?"

"Don't worry! That's a bit rich!"

"Doesn't tell us much does she?"

Jim interrupted what was turning out to be a tirade of exasperated comments.

"It does tell us that they are safe and well. What we have to decide is whether to accept this note and return to the settlement with the news or to go on regardless."

"I think we should go on," said James. "Perhaps Kath was coerced into writing the note. The parents would expect us to go on until we find them and I must find Kath."

"I agree with James," said Laura decisively. "We cannot return without them. Anyway, James would continue on his own if need be."

She looked at James mischievously, her brown eyes twinkling. "I think the lad's smitten."

Jim chuckled.

James looked embarrassed, blushed a deep red and Francis broke out into an ear-splitting guffaw. This type of banter appealed to his sense of humour.

"She got you there mate," he said and laughed some more.

Jim looked at Francis.

"Well?" he asked. "What do you think? Do we go on?"

Unaccustomed to his opinion being sought, Francis looked surprised. "We go on," he said, "and now that's decided, I'm going hunting. We need decent food. Nuts, roots and fruit are okay for a short trip, but more protein is a necessity. We can cook the meat from one of these sheepy animals; it should keep for quite a few days if wrapped."

On the word, he was gone, Laura following in his wake. Hunting was easier with two.

The two remaining hunkered down, backs against a large tree.

"Let me have a look at the map," said Jim.

"It's a bit vague," said James as he took it out of his back pocket.

Both men examined it. Jim's forefinger pointed to a grid-point within the forest. "We are about a one-day walk from the edge of the plains," he declared with confidence. His finger moved across the expanse of plain on the map. "Jumping cockroaches, it must go on for miles!"

James agreed with him. He was by far the best map-reader in the party. After the intricacies of three-dimensional star maps, the two-dimensional durapaper map in front of him was child's play.

"We are about a day's walk from its edge, maybe two," he agreed. "After that it is miles and miles of open grassland. Virtually no cover either. We should be able to track them easily. Only problem I can see is that anyone watching us will also have no trouble seeing us, with few if any places to hide there. If they are riding then they will be able to go much faster than we can. Remember the length of those strides?"

"Yes," his companion admitted ruefully, "we are in for a long trip."

"Aye, but what is at the end of it, I ask you that?"

Silence. There was no answer Jim could offer.

By now verbal conversations between the children and their Lind were improving. All twenty-four and Afanasei talked in a polyglot mixture of Standard and Lindish and could make themselves understood in all but the more abstract ideas.

The quickest at this were Tara and Kolyei and it became usual for them to interpret. It was Tara who Kath approached when they were about halfway across the plains to discuss a specific problem.

"Tara," said the elder girl, "is Alan happy? He seems so quiet and withdrawn. Even Peter, homesick as he is, talks more about his home and family. I wondered if you could talk to his Kiltya?"

"He's not missing his home if that's what you think," answered Tara, who was an astute young person.

"I've noticed he never mentions his family. Last night when we were all talking even you were laughing about what our people will say when we return."

Their Lind had taken great pains to explain to their children that the separation was to be a temporary one only and that they would be going back east one day.

"Alan never said a word," added Kath.

Tara pondered the problem.

"Kolyei says that Kiltya told him that Alan doesn't want to go back. It's only him and an uncle and Alan doesn't like him very much."

"Has he no other family?"

"They died in the storm, like mine."

"Sorry kitten, I didn't want to open old wounds."

"It's okay, I've accepted it now, more or less. I still miss them horribly but Papa wouldn't have wanted me to fret. He always said that if anything happened to separate us that I must go on and be happy. I'm trying very hard. Kolyei helps a lot. Kiltya would too, if Alan would let her, but he won't."

"Would it help do you think if I tried to talk to him?"

"Don't think it'd do much good," said Tara. "You were a member of the ship's crew. I think he blames the crew for not getting to his family in time. You talking might make him worse."

"I've seen him talking to you."

"A bit, nothing more than being polite, but he's not rude to me. The rest shy away from him."

"I'd noticed that too."

Kath thought for a bit.

"Could you try to get closer to him? You lost your parents too and he might open up to you, tell you what's wrong. I hate to ask, but Matvei says his behaviour is upsetting Kiltya."

As if things weren't difficult enough already, thought the younger girl, but being Tara, she hated to see someone unhappy.

"I'll try," she said at last.

The next morning they breakfasted early and prepared to take the trail. Tara, with an apologetic look at Peter who liked to travel with Tara and Kolyei, stepped up to Alan.

"Would you care to ride beside Kolyei and me?" she offered in a bright voice.

"No."

Tara tried again.

"Please Alan, I would like to get to know your Kiltya."

Alan shrugged and replied indifferently. "If you like."

Kath watched with approval and turned to a stricken-faced Peter, who was already mounted on Radya.

"And I will ask Peter if he and Radya will be Matvei and my partners," she looked up at the boy with a smile.

Peter perked up at once. Kath and Matvei usually led the way and he was young enough to think that it was a great honour to be in the lead although he would miss Tara's stories.

Kath, primed by Tara, was ready for this.

"I'll tell you about the time on the ship when I started crew training," she said persuasively. "Would you like that?"

"True stories or make-believe?"

"True stories," she said firmly as she swung her leg over Matvei's back and made herself comfortable. Kath's story-telling abilities were on a far lesser scale than Tara's, who could keep her friends entertained for hours at a time, but she was sure she would be able to keep one ten-year old boy amused for one morning.

Meanwhile, Tara was finding the going tough with Alan. He responded in monosyllables if he deigned to say anything at all. After a few hours Tara wished Kath had given the task to someone else. At lunch break he moved away, ignoring her invitation to come and sit beside her.

She caught Kath's eye and grimaced, but Kath knew her Tara, she wouldn't give up easily.

Despite Alan's pointed disinterest, she moved over to sit beside him and began again, chattering away about nothing and everything.

When they set out again she placed herself and Kolyei beside him and Kiltya and began to talk about the space storm and what had happened to her own family.

Alan tensed up as she began, his back ramrod straight and his visage one of affronted disapproval.

"How can you talk about it?" he burst out.

"Why not?" was her reasonable answer. "It happened, nothing can change it."

She caught a quick encouraging look from Kiltya and 'felt' Kolyei's support.

"Why shouldn't I?" she asked again.

"Because it's wrong."

"What? Wrong to remember them? Wrong to talk about it?"

"I lost my family too," he whispered, "and it's all my fault."

"Why?"

He raised a stricken face towards her.

"I should have helped get my brothers and sisters into their cabinets but I didn't. I just ran into the nearest one and shut the door."

Tara prayed for guidance. She certainly hadn't expected this.

"It wouldn't have made any difference," she said. "It all happened so quickly, I know. All that would've happened if you'd stayed to help would be that you died too."

"Better that than this."

"You mustn't say that. Life is precious. I may be younger than you but I realise that. Your family would be glad you've survived. It's up to you now to make the most of your life. Don't live in bitterness or thinking of what might have been. I think of my parents and Mark every day, but not sad thoughts."

She fumbled for the next words.

"I share my memories with Kolyei. It helps. You should do the same with Kiltya. She's lost family too."

Kolyei had told Tara something about Kiltya's history so she felt pretty sure this advice was right. "At least promise me you'll think about it."

Alan's reply was a bad-tempered grunt.

Tara had shot her bolt and they rode on in silence.

That evening, however, and for the first time, she noticed Alan taking his time settling Kiltya for the night and although he remained separate from the jolly banter round the fire, he cuddled down beside her to sleep.

As, in his turn, Kolyei settled down, wrapping his bushy tail round her legs, she noticed Kiltya doing the same.

: *Kiltya says a big thank you* : 'sent' Kolyei.

: *I did okay then?* : she asked sleepily.

: *More than 'okay'* : *Kolyei replied* : *I think…* :

But Tara never heard what he was thinking. Tired out, she had dropped off to sleep.

"Were you part of a large family?" asked Alan of Tara the next day.

"No, just Mama, Papa, me and my little brother Mark."

"There were seven of us."

"Tell me about them."

"No."

Tara ignored that.

"I miss them," she contented herself with saying, "and I think of them every day, as I think I told you already."

"I don't think of mine at all," he admitted.

"But you should you know, don't lose the memories."

"I'm not."

"You are," she flashed back. "Now think about what I've said and don't come back to me until you have."

"You've no right to talk to me like that," Alan flared, his face scarlet with rage.

"So you *do* have feelings?" she retorted back. "And as to rights, I have every right and if you weren't so sunk in self-loathing and self-pity you'd see it. Think of Kiltya, you're upsetting her more than the rest of us put together. Do you want her to decide it would be better if she left you and not come back? Keep going like this and she just might."

Tara was in full flight.

"Don't care about yourself if that's what you want, but what you're doing to her is unforgivable."

"I didn't realise," he mumbled.

"I think you did. She wouldn't have chosen you if she didn't want you, if she didn't love you."

"I'm afraid."

"Of what?"

"That she'll leave me like my family did."

"Now that's just plain silly and you know it. Kolyei loves me. Kiltya loves you. She's not going anywhere without you. Now, open your mind to her, let her in. If you don't I'll be very cross."

She 'felt' Kolyei's mental chuckle at her words.

They trotted on in silence for a while and Tara began to calm down. She began to worry that she had gone too far. Alan was deep in thought. She could hear the others chatting but she kept by Alan and Kiltya's side. She sensed she might be close to a breakthrough.

That night, as Tara tried to comb through her tangled hair, she felt Alan approach. The boy looked embarrassed as his eyes met hers.

"I wanted to say thanks," he said awkwardly, "you were right."

Tara's eyes softened.

"She's there for you always, you understand that now?"

He nodded shamefacedly. "Sorry I was such an idiot."

Tara giggled.

"We've all been idiots some time or other. You just took it to extremes, that's all."

It is strange, that one of the youngest should be one of the wisest, thought Kath at intervals as she watched Alan reply to a tease from one of the twins with a grin, a retort and a playful shove. At twelve, Tara had become the repository for most of their secrets and fears. Even Bill and Geoff hunted her out at irregular intervals for a chat.

Peter adored her and Alan wasn't far behind. The others treated her with affection. Kath herself thought of Tara as the younger sister she's never had. The threesome of Moira, Brenda and Yvonne opened their ranks and treated her as almost their equal and Mark, despite his misgivings and at Tara's urging, took Alan under his wing and found that Tara was right. Alan wasn't nearly as bad a friend and companion as he had feared he would be.

Kath's heart lightened as the hills got closer. Their adventures were only now really beginning she suspected. At least the twelve children were as one with their Lind now and that was thanks to Tara.

"We are being followed," said Afanasei some sundowns later. "Four two-legs." He corrected himself with a whine of a laugh, "I mean humans."

"In two sundowns we shall reach domta Zanatei," stated Kolyei.

"They will not catch us," was Matvei's confident comment, "and I shall see Rozya and young ones." He wagged his tail with pleasurable anticipation. It had been two long moons since he had seen his mate.

Kolyei sighed, his ears drooping just that little bit. He had not yet found a mate to his liking.

"Radya likes you," Matvei said suggestively.

If Kolyei could have blushed he would have. As he couldn't, he tried to ignore Matvei's comment.

When at last the weary travellers arrived at the Lind domta, it seemed as if the entire pack had turned out to greet them. Walking beside their partners, the human children were quite overawed by it all although the Lind explained that there was nothing to fear. The inhabitants of the pack were curious, nothing more. The Lindar was still on patrol but were expecting to be relieved by a Lindar from another pack within the moon. Then the whole pack would be in the rtathlian, the pack-home wood-range.

Amongst their audience Tara could see many young Lind, the

older ones standing quietly beside their dam but also ltsctas playing together in rough and tumble games, growling squeakily and batting each other with their paws.

"We will go to my daga," Kolyei informed her. "It will be quiet there."

"Good," she answered with relief. "I would like to rest."

"Teachings start with the sunrise."

Tara groaned; she could not help it. Kolyei looked at her out of one twinkling blue eye.

"You have much to learn," he stated, laughing at her. He was looking forward to the morrow.

Kath followed Matvei to his daga, home for him, his mate Rozya and their five ltsctas. He assured her that she would be a welcome addition to their family, albeit an unusual one. Orphaned Lind pups were taken in by families, but this would be the first time someone from another species and an inter-planetary one at that, would be adopted.

Rozya sat waiting, her brood beside her, their eyes alight with curiosity.

As they entered the dim interior, she wagged her tail in welcome.

Kath smiled at them all uncertainly. Matvei had not seen fit to inform her of how a visitor behaved when in a daga. The normally confident Kath was very nervous and unsure of herself. *Do I offer to shake her paw or what?*

The daga was round in shape and the frame made up of naturally growing trees. Their branches made the roof. The twigs were roughly layered in between the sides to make the walls. On the whole Kath concluded it a most unfinished creation. Part of the roof was open to the sky and would let in vast amounts of water when it rained. The walls looked draughty as well. *I can do something about that,* she thought, *if I don't I will get soaked. It may not bother them but I don't have a fur coat to keep me warm and dry. I suppose their paws are not really suited for the more delicate work.*

"Welcome," said Rozya in Standard, enunciating both syllables with care.

Kath gave a start. She had not expected to be greeted in her own language. She decided they must have some sort of bush telegraph system. Perhaps they could 'send' thoughts greater distances than she had realised. She wondered if all the Lind had been learning Standard or just a few. Thinking of the forthcoming lessons she became uneasy about her own abilities to learn Lindish. She did not think it even remotely possible that she would be one of the star pupils. That would be Tara; she was picking up their language as if she was born to it.

Matvei was watching her, waiting for Kath to speak.

"It is very nice," she said at last, not knowing what else to say. She smiled admiringly. Her thoughts betrayed her, not fortunately to Rozya but to Matvei, attuned as he was to her. It was almost the first time he had picked up her actual words and the meaning behind them.

: *But it is very, well rustic and that bed thing looks very uncomfortable* :

She decided there and then that she would take steps before she was very much older to ensure she made herself both a decent bed and repaired the leaky roof and sides.

Matvei blocked her thoughts and conversation so that any Lind nearby would not overhear, resolving to teach her how to blanket private emotions before she got herself into trouble. Some Lind might not be that understanding of alien thought patterns and cultures and treat an unguarded thought as an insult. That would not be good for the inter-species relationship that was developing.

He was not surprised that he could actually hear Kath's words as well as sense her emotions. Kolyei and Tara had been managing it for days now and for a Lind it was but a small step from sharing images and emotions to being able to talk telepathically. After all, did not mothers listen to their ltsctas' babblings from an early age? He and Kolyei had known it would only be a matter of time for the rest of the vadeln-paired to do the same.

: *Quietly* : he advised.

Kath's' eyes opened in surprise and she looked at Matvei with consternation.

: *Did Rozya hear me?* :

Matvei shook his head and wagged his tail.

Kath breathed a sigh of relief.

The four hunters had reached the edge of the forest. They had arrived at the western edge of the plains in the most roundabout way imaginable, following tracks that went nowhere, others that went round and round in circles and it had taken six days instead of the one foretold by James. Laura was convinced that what they had by now realised were false trails had been put there to put them off the scent. Only the day before these false trails had petered out and the real trail showed up loud and clear again.

"There must be a reason for this," she muttered as she followed Jim (it was his turn to take lead-point). "These wolves want us to follow the trail now. I wonder why?"

Jim mounted a small rise to their right. Raising his hand over his eyes he squinted into the distance.

"I can see their tracks through the long grasses," he shouted and pointed excitedly toward it, "they're as clear as day."

"And what do we do in the dark?" asked Laura in a disgruntled voice. She was not looking forward to a long wet tramp through the never-ending grasslands.

"Sleep." The disembodied word came out of the undergrowth behind her. James and Laura turned in that direction.

"Francis, is that a joke?" teased Laura.

Laura was finding that the Francis here on the planet was a far nicer person than the argumentative troublemaker on the ship. She respected and liked this new Francis. His droll sense of humour was certainly refreshing.

He shrugged. A loner all his life, he found it difficult to return the banter his shipmates considered the norm. He was, however, becoming closer to these three people than he had ever been to anyone before. He was actually finding that he liked them and wanted to be liked by them.

They set out across the plains after a meal and a short rest. It was raining hard and it continued to do so over the gruelling days, then weeks, that ensued as they followed numerous tracks and trails which also turned out to be false.

"Doesn't this planet ever let up?" grumbled Francis as he followed the rest. "Rain, rain and yet more rain. What about a bit of sun?"

"Don't think it's the season for it," was the laconic answer, he did not know from whom.

Candy Rae

CHAPTER 5

NORTHERN CONTINENT

The children had been at the domta for a moon. It had been waxing when they arrived, now it was waxing again. At the instigation of Kath they had 'improved' their pairs' dagas and now slept snug, warm and, more importantly, dry. They did such a good job that they were much in demand by Lind families who did not have the good fortune to have a member paired with a human. The twelve were therefore kept more than a little busy after language class was over for the day weaving twig and branch into holes in walls and ceilings. It was widely considered by the Lind that human forepaws were very useful and the children a welcome asset to their community.

The children settled into the life of the domta. There were daily language lessons for both species. As predicted by Kath, Tara became their star pupil in Lindish and Kolyei was making quite incredible strides in learning Standard. As the days passed, the lessons were expanded to include other, non vadeln-paired Lind. The bond between the pairs increased. The children learned how to control the 'sendings' of emotions and then pictures to their Lind partners. From there they began to share mental conversations (they learned each other's language much faster this way), although it took a great deal of effort. It did however, become marginally easier with practice.

One Lind who found the tightening of these bondings hard to cope with was Matvei's mate Rozya. She had been mated with Matvei for over eleven seasons and began to resent the bond he had with the young human. She was not exactly jealous; their lovemaking was as good as ever it was when they did manage to be alone together. When one had a boisterous family like they had one could and did find time alone to be at a premium. It was just the fact that Kath was there so much of the time. Rozya began to long for a bit of privacy, even if it were merely to converse with her mate.

One day after Matvei had gone hunting she spoke to Kath who was sitting contentedly combing one of Rozya and Matvei's ltsctas. The Lind loved to be combed, finding it pleasantly soothing as well as getting rid of the nasty burrs in their coats that were otherwise difficult to eradicate. It also helped deter the black bloodsuckers that attached themselves and itched unbearably.

"You have a mate?" Rozya asked Kath.

"No one has asked me," replied Kath, continuing with her self-appointed combing duties.

"The male ask this of the female?" said the Lind in incredulous tones. "That is most strange. Here female ask. That is very better way."

Kath laughed.

"Well, there is someone," she admitted. "His name is James but he is at the settlement. He's probably forgotten me by now."

She moved one ltscta over so that she could sit the next one to be combed in the vacated space.

"Rozya," she said as she settled the young one, "do you mind me being here?"

"No," she replied, "but if I wish to be alone with Matvei, you tend ltsctas?"

Kath agreed with a smile. "Of course I will. You only have to ask. Babysitting is my speciality."

"Babysitting?"

"Wrong word," admitted Kath, "ltscta-sitting sounds rather peculiar, that's all. When you and Matvei want some time to yourselves, just ask."

Rozya felt a lot better.

Each evening the children usually congregated round their

campfire. They all felt the need to be together at this time, especially Peter, whose homesickness hit him in waves at periodic intervals.

It was Kath who thought of something to keep his mind occupied with a game she and her fellow crewmembers of the *Argyll* had played during the long watches on the ship.

One dull evening when the twelve were sitting silently, most simply gazing into the flickering flames and Peter's face looked sad as to breaking, she suggested it.

"I know," she said in a bright voice, "let's play *Quickrhyme*."

"*Quickrhyme*?" Peter asked, "What's that? Is it fun?"

"It's easy," promised Kath, "and it can be funny too. When it's your turn someone gives you a word and a subject and you have to make up a poem, on the spot mind you, on the subject and using the rhyming word."

"It's a baby game," protested Bill.

"Nonsense," replied a bracing Kath, "and you don't have to join in if you don't want to. Peter will, and Tara. Anyone else want to beg out?"

"We'll play," said the more tolerant Geoff, "there's nothing better to do. Who's going to start it off?"

"I will. You give me the subject and word."

"Okay then," Geoff thought for a moment, grinned and said, "the rhyming word is 'smell' and the subject is 'noise'."

Kath gave him a withering look as she protested. "That's virtually impossible and you know it."

"The game was your idea," he said with a laugh.

"All right, I'll give it a go." She thought for a moment then began.
"The smell,
from the dell
was well.
The sounding bell,
Fell,
I will tell- ..."

Her voice petered out and she shrugged off her inability to go on any further with a laugh, "I can't think of any more."

"That was rubbish," declared Geoff, "but you've scored six, and you only get one bonus point because you only kept to the subject once. Now it's your turn to nominate and give out the words."

Kath looked at the others. "You see how it is played?"

The children nodded. This sounded as if it might be rather good fun.

"I choose Moira, the word is 'reap' and the topic is 'fire'," said Kath.

Moira giggled. She also thought of the game as rather on the babyish side but was prepared to give it a go.

"The farmers reap.

The children weep.

The mothers keep.

The spacers leap.

I don't come cheap.

Do you want a peep?"

"Watch it," warned Bill, "there are children present. You get six points but no bonus points because you didn't mention Kath's topic once. Now it's Tara's turn. What word? I know, 'mine'. That should be pretty easy."

"The topic, the topic?" chanted Peter. He had forgotten all about feeling homesick.

"The Lind," replied Bill in a bland voice, with a teasing glance at Tara who looked horror-struck at this. She thought for a moment, grinned benignly at them all then stood up.

"You are mine,

And I am thine,

Our thoughts entwine,

You are mine.

You are mine,

Your coat does shine,

From paw to spine,

You are mine."

"Hold on," protested Yvonne. "You used 'mine' more than once. Points taken off."

"Nobody said I couldn't."

"Oh, carry on Tara," interjected Kath, "at least you're *on* the subject."

Tara continued as if the interruption hadn't happened.

"It's a fine line,

The air's like wine,

So do not whine,
We're about to dine.
From the grapes of the vine,
It's a grand design,
Would you rather I drank wine,
Shame, you swine."

"Get back on to the subject," ordered Moira, and Tara nodded.

"Our lives combine,
We're doing just fine,
More than ten times nine.
Tied together with more than just twine.
To thee my Kolyei I do my life assign,
A partnership from which I will never resign,
You are mine,
And I am thine."

"I can't think of any more," said Tara with a grin and sat down.

Everybody laughed and clapped with appreciation, all but one of the listeners.

"Too many repeats," said Yvonne.

"Don't tease," ordered Kath, "it's really good for someone not yet thirteen."

"A mix of Lindish and Standard," complained Yvonne.

"It sounded okay to me," Bill disagreed, "and I think Tara is most definitely in the lead. Think you could do better?"

Kath was thinking hard. They all knew that Tara was a good storyteller; it now looked as if she had leanings towards the poetical as well. She wondered what the future would bring for Tara.

They played the game for a little while longer then started talking again..

To the humans' chagrin the Lind had been much faster at learning Standard than they were at learning Lindish.

"It's all these consonants all jumbled together," complained Thomas who was vadeln-paired with a young female Lind called Stasya. "I just can't do it."

"I know what you mean," agreed Tara. "It's also hard to get the pitch right. Yesterday I said the word vuz, meaning that small red and white striped animal that they were hunting by the river the other day and Kolyei shook his head and growled as if I was insulting him!"

"And were you?" teased Kath.

"Zowie! Of course I wasn't! What I didn't know at the time was that vuz spoken softly means the animal but when spoken growlingly hard it means idiot. You know how the vuz are not very clever. Kolyei thought I was calling him an idiot."

They all laughed. Mispronunciations like that were ten a penny here at the domta. No one had escaped Lind teases about misspoken words.

"Does anybody know what is going to happen now?" asked the girl sitting beside Tara. "We can all understand each other, more or less."

"I don't know, Emily. The Eldas have been teaching their adults and young. Even the pups can hold quite a sensible conversation with us now," answered Kath. Then she added judiciously, "at least sensible conversations for their age group, that is."

They all laughed again. Lind young were very similar to their human counterparts in this respect.

"Seriously though, I get the impression that we are waiting for something, but what it is I haven't a clue."

They left it at that.

It was some days later when Tara, Peter, Emily and with Thomas in tow, hunted out Kath.

"Do you think it true?" asked Tara.

"What's that kitten?"

"That there's going to be a war."

"It doesn't seem real somehow," said Emily. "It's so peaceful here, but Ilyei has been painting pictures in my mind. They are horrible," gentle Emily shuddered.

"Kolyei and Radya haven't imagined any battles at me or Peter," said Tara, "but he's shown me pictures of afterwards and that's terrible enough."

Kath turned surprised eyes towards their two youngest, but this wasn't the first group who had spoken to her about nebulous threats of a war.

She wondered why neither Tara nor Peter were included in these mental interchanges. Even Mark's Aya had unsettled him with life-like scenes of fighting.

A quick mental call to Matvei and she had the answer. Both Tara and Peter were under fourteen summers in age. They weren't adults the way the Lind saw it.

"Well," began Kath, "you've all seen the scars many of the Lind have. Now we know why. Now, don't panic. Matvei tells me if it does happen it won't be tomorrow or even the next day. Anyway Peter, you and Tara are too young."

"That's true," said Thomas brightly, "I get the same from Stasya."

Peter relaxed.

Kath glanced at Tara; it was obvious that the girl was upset. She was as white as a sheet and was shaking.

Kath gave Thomas a barely imperceptible wink.

Thomas did not see it, but Emily did.

"Thomas, Peter," she said, "let's all go and explore the pond. We can take rods and try to catch some fish for supper."

"Good idea Em," Thomas replied and placed a comradely hand on Peter's shoulder.

The three walked away in search of their Lind. Ilyei and Radya loved watching their humans fish for tranet, a flat fish that inhabited the pools and rivers. Stasya did not care for fish but she liked to go with them anyway. She never strayed far from Thomas's side, except to hunt.

That left Tara with Kath.

"I don't want to see any fighting, people die fighting," Tara whimpered. "You and the others are all the family I've got now."

Kath wrapped the child in her arms, feeling the tension in her slight frame, the terrified shaking. Tara acted and spoke so responsibly and grown-up they often forgot how young she really was.

"I'll be here for as long as you need me to be here," Kath offered quietly, hoping she could make good the promise.

The days passed, summer disappeared almost overnight and winter arrived with a vengeance.

Not that the children were cold and miserable, far from it.

Their dagas were warm and dry. They had plenty of furs, from the zarova the Lind caught, to keep them warm. They had learned how to cure them so they didn't smell. Shoes were made from the same furs.

The kura had thick woolly coats. The children learned how to first pluck them then how to make wool. Emily taught them all how to knit, even the boys (to their secret disgust). From animal bone they made implements such as scrapers, eating utensils and combs.

As Emily laughingly said, it was like living in the Stone Age when hunter-gatherer man must have done much the same thing. And of course, there was an abundance of wood of all types, from the steelwood from which Thomas made (with Bill and Geoff's help) rudimentary knives and shovels, to the softwoods whose strands went to provide floor coverings and wet capes.

When Kath thought about it, the twelve, plus their Lind partners, were close, like a large and noisy extended family.

"We are the 'Children of the Wolves'," said Yvonne one evening as they settled down to a supper of fried tranet and whiteroot washed down with mugs of piping hot kala.

Bill glanced at his twin then at Yvonne, "I wouldn't call myself a child exactly. You, however..." his eyes were twinkling.

"You know what I mean," she retorted, her voice rising. Bill always managed to say things that riled Yvonne.

"Yvonne is half right," interposed Emily, trying to put a brake on what was likely to turn into yet another quarrel between the two.

"I'm young enough to be called a 'Child of the Wolf'," said Tara who hated quarrels and always tried to find a way to stop them, "Peter too." She smiled at Yvonne who grinned back, understanding what the younger girl was trying to achieve. "But I have to agree that Kath, Geoff and Bill cannot be called children, any more than you can. You're almost grown-up too."

Yvonne sat back, a pleased smile on her face and shot a triumphant look at Bill who studiously avoided looking at her.

Kath bit back a laugh. Everyone knew that Yvonne fancied Bill like mad. He, however, thought of her as a silly kid and had said so, aloud and often.

Yvonne appreciated this very public declaration of her almost adult status and said nothing more.

They liked to gather together in the evenings round the fire and relax, even Kath and Matvei, though they didn't come as often as the others, spending the majority of their evenings with Rozya and the family.

Kath still felt responsible for them all and tried her best to be a surrogate mother, especially for Peter, and to a lesser extent Tara.

Although the youngest but one in age, Kath always thought of Tara as much older; she was certainly the deepest thinking of them all, except for Emily.

The first moon of the winter season was waning when Tara approached Kath, a seriously worried look on her face, one that Kath had learned to recognise. With Tara looking like this, it was wise to put aside one's current task and pay attention.

"I've been having an interesting conversation with Kolyei," Tara began in a diffident manner. Tara always expressed herself shyly as if she thought she might be in the wrong or if she considered her news unpleasant.

"What has Kolyei been gossiping about now?"

Kolyei liked to gossip. It was one of his favourite pastimes, that and teasing all and sundry.

"Kolyei says life is for enjoying yourself," said Tara defensively. "He thinks I take life too seriously."

"So what have you picked up this time kitten?"

"He's excited. His friend Tarmsei, you know the one? Well, Kolyei thinks he's let something slip. Tarmsei and others in the Lindar have been sent out on an escort mission. Kolyei and I have been sort of wondering who or what he is escorting."

"Visitors from another pack?" hazarded Kath.

"They don't usually have an escort," Tara reminded her, "they just appear."

"True."

"Kolyei wondered if it might be some humans sent to look for us. Remember when Afanasei told us that the patrols had found tracks when we were coming here?"

Kath snorted.

"It's the middle of winter. If someone was coming after us don't you think they'd be here before now?"

"Maybe more Lind have paired with more of us like we did."

Kath shook her head.

"Matvei says not. It has been forbidden."

"What do you think if it isn't that then? I'm scared it might be something about the war you older ones have been dreaming about."

"You know, I have no idea and I think I'll wait and see. The Lind I have noticed are very good at keeping things close to their chests when they want to."

"You don't think it's anything to worry about?"

"I'm not going to lose any sleep over it," stated Kath, "and neither should you."

Meanwhile, Zanatei and Afanasei were talking.

"Vadeln bond is strong now," said Afanasei. "It can not be broken now."

"Yes," agreed Zanatei, Chief Elda of the pack. "Now is the time. We shall tell Lindar."

"Janya says they enjoy much fun with human four."

"Fun later. It will be hot season in four moons. We start next part of plan."

Afanasei bowed his head in agreement and left to arrange the necessary orders.

It was with great surprise the next morning when the twelve vadeln-pairs were summoned to the Chief Elda's daga. Once there they were kept kicking their heels (or paws) whilst Zanatei and Afanasei stood watching them. Even Kolyei and Matvei were not sure what it was all about.

Eventually a large male Lind approached the assembled.

"They come," he announced in stentorian tones.

"Who?" whispered Tara.

Kolyei looked at her; he was beginning to suspect what was happening. "Wait," he told her.

They heard the noise of an approaching party. The members of the party were talking loudly in Standard and their complaints were sharp and to the point.

"Stop pushing me you thrice-blasted beast. I am going as fast as I can."

"Gerroff." This was Francis. He never minced his words.

"Blooming heck Jim, where are they taking us?"

To Tara's astonishment it was Laura Merriman who led the group into the small clearing, the sailor who had saved her when the spaceship had been damaged. Kath was equally astonished to see Jim Cranston and James Rybak, followed closely by a dishevelled Francis McAllister.

The four looked lean and fit, Jim Cranston especially. He had dispensed with any surplus body fat and looked far younger that his forty-five years.

Jim strode towards them; chin thrust out, eyes sparking with barely suppressed anger and irritation.

When he spied the twelve children his face broke into a fleeting grin of pleasure and accomplishment, then the grin vanished as though it had never been.

"So there you all are," he declared. "Fine dance you've led us."

The children and Kath were somewhat taken aback. This was not the greeting they had been expecting.

Jim was not finished. He was still complaining in a loud voice as he approached them.

"We've been herded around these hills and woods by these damned animals for weeks," he exploded.

Beside her Tara felt Kolyei bristle with indignation and despite Tara's telepathic warning he could not help himself. He took three steps towards the four adults.

"We are not animals but are Lind."

Jim bravely stood his ground, rocking back and forth on his heels. Kolyei stepped closer until he was standing directly in front of the man. He drew himself up so that his eyes were slightly higher than Jim's and looked down into the man's face. Jim met his stare with one of his own.

"Animals are for eating. Would you eat your friends? I think not."

Kolyei pronounced this remarkable statement with a tone of finality and, to Jim's absolute astonishment, in very clear and understandable Standard.

Impasse.

It was James Rybak who broke the tableau. When he spied Kath he shouted with delight, dropped his pack and started to run towards her.

Matvei growled threateningly and the young man stopped. Kath laid one hand on Matvei's snout, a Lind gesture for caution.

"Matvei," she said sternly, "stop that."

His growls reduced in volume but did not go away.

: *He is a friend. His name is James* :

Rozya, who was sitting sedately some distance away watching the proceedings, started when she heard the name. She began to inch her way forward. Each time she stopped she stared hard at James. He was not aware of her scrutiny to begin with; his thoughts and gaze centred on Kath, who it must be said, was also looking at him, pleasure on her face. So engrossed was she with her newfound life-partner Matvei, she had not realised just how much she had missed him.

Gradually, James became aware of Rozya's approach and turned his gaze in her direction. He began to smile.

"He is mine," Rozya said.

The assembled watched as she closed the intervening distance between them. Nobody moved, not even an ear twitched.

Then a look of almost wondrous joy appeared on James's face. He seemed to have forgotten all about Kath.

As Rozya reached her target she looked him straight in the eye and repeated, "Mine." Her tail began to wag.

Matvei gave out a short whine of approval.

Rozya turned and looked at the small bunch of Elda beside Zanatei and Afanasei.

"San is right. Lok is not good."

And that was that.

The four of them left the clearing, Matvei and Rozya leading the way. James followed them in a daze, and did not even notice when Kath slipped an arm round his in order to guide his steps.

"Rozya says that four is the right and proper way," translated Tara for the benefit of the newcomers.

"What is right and proper?" asked Jim. "What is going on? I want answers."

"You will get your answers. Sit," responded Zanatei.

The three remaining adults approached the white Lind.

"We talk," said Afanasei from his position to Zanatei's left. "There is much danger."

"To whom?" asked Jim, standing his ground, then sitting down on the springy moss that covered the clearing. Laura and Francis sat down beside him.

Kolyei nudged Tara forward with his snout. She had been expecting this, being the most proficient in Lindish out of all the children 'borrowed' from the settlement. She and Kolyei would need to translate. Both Alan and young Peter moved closer to her to give her some moral support and to help with the translations if things got difficult. Radya sat beside Kolyei. For some reason her closeness made him feel uncomfortable. She seemed to be sitting rather closer that was absolutely necessary.

The Lind talked briefly together in Lindish then began. Tara, with help from Peter, Alan, Kolyei, Kiltya and Radya, translated when it was needed. Alan stayed silent. He was still rather more withdrawn than the others.

By the end of the conversation the heads of the humans, young and old, were reeling.

Afanasei started the ball rolling with his first pronouncement. His Standard was by far the most fluent amongst the Elda. Jim struggled to understand the polyglot mixture of Lindish and Standard. Interspersed with the Standard words were many Lindish ones and understanding was correspondingly not easy even with Tara's help.

"There is great danger. Larg will come when warm season come again. There will be much killing. You must defend yourself, your rtathen and your rtathlians. You must protect your lairs, your pack and your rtathen."

It was the first they had heard of the Larg.

At the end of the meeting, which lasted until well into what the humans called the afternoon, Kolyei and Tara invited the three adults back to share her and Kolyei's daga for the night. Peter and Radya followed. Young Peter had had a shock and needed company. Now that the adults had arrived at the domta he gravitated towards them, seeing them as his protectors in this dangerous world. They were also a link with home. He missed his mother, father and little sister unbearably. When asked by Peter if she minded going with them, Radya told him that she was more than pleased with the idea. Her tail wagged constantly and continued to do so as they entered the daga.

Tara had tried to make it comfortable and as similar to the cabins back at the settlement as possible. The roof and walls were sound and she had made a soft bed in a corner, lined with kura pelts. There were also some blocks of wood that could be used as seats and a wobbly table.

"Well," said Jim, "That was certainly an eye-opener and no mistake."

"Looks like this planet is not as idyllic as we thought," was

Laura's contribution.

"Will we all have to fight?" asked a very small voice from the corner.

Jim looked at young Peter with compassion. The boy was sitting hunched up, his face strained and white. "I hope not son," he answered. "At least you, I think, are too young. The adults will have to I think; if the Larg are as numerous and as vicious as they tell us they are."

"You must fight if you wish to survive," agreed Kolyei, "and yes, young fight not, adults protect ltsctas."

Radya spoke up, "The Larg will kill all if we do not."

"What exactly are the Elders?" asked Jim. "They keep mentioning them."

Tara laughed. She knew the answer to that one. It had provided a fair bit of amusement. "It's not 'Elders' Jim, it's 'Elda'," she replied, with a twinkle at Kolyei. "The Lind call their white Elders Elda, a very similar word to ours for someone older than the others. They are in charge of the packs. Zanatei is the Chief Elda of this pack and it is called after him."

"So these Larg will invade when the summer starts?" asked Laura, turning the conversation back to her immediate concern. "That doesn't give us much time."

"In warm season they come. Spies say satalrdn," said Kolyei soberly.

"He means more than ever before," said Tara, benefiting from the explanatory pictures Kolyei was planting in her head. The word satalrdn was new to her as well as to Jim. "Do you want me to explain in more detail? I have very clear pictures in my head."

"No need," came a Lind voice from the entranceway. "I will this do."

A large female Lind was sitting there. No one had heard her approach but it was obvious she had been sitting listening to their conversation.

She looked at Peter and said, "You must not fear. My rtath will protect all ltsctas."

Peter seemed to take a little comfort from her words.

The female was large, larger than Kolyei and in her fur, although coloured in the blue and brown hues like the rest of the pack, there were tinges of white showing. Tara knew what that meant. When a Lind reached many seasons and survived that long, the coat would turn white. When white any Lind could become an Elda of the rtath, although not many females chose to take up that option, preferring to stay with their extended families. To be an Elda was a lonely and often dangerous occupation.

The female continued, "My name is Larya. I will join with you."

Predictably, Tara was the first to understand the meaning of what Larya was saying.

"Jim, she wants to pair with you as Kolyei and I did and all the others! She will explain what is going to happen with the Larg."

Jim Cranston stared at her in disbelief. He looked stunned.

"I am too old," he protested. "I'm over forty for stars sake."

"Many seasons have I," was her answer. "Come with me."

Tara jumped. Those were the words Kolyei had used with her and she had dutifully obeyed. Would a grown man be any different?

She need not have worried, Jim stood up. He complained ever afterwards that he just couldn't help himself.

He looked at Larya. "I'll give it a go if you're sure." He grinned wickedly at those in the daga. "You know, this might be fun. I've always wanted to ride fast over the countryside. Never had the chance before, never being dirt side long enough."

Larya looked at him witheringly. She stood up and moved away, expecting Jim to follow. With a rueful grin, Jim went.

"What about us?" asked Laura indignantly. "Walking out like that."

"You will join yourself soon," promised Kolyei. "You will not be alone in domta Zanatei."

Tara explained what he meant.

Laura was silenced.

Jim walked beside Larya. Unlike James a scant few hours earlier, he did not walk in a silent daze. He had a great many questions so he made hay while the sun shone and asked away.

She stopped, looked at him but did not answer his questions.

"Wait," she commanded.

Candy Rae

CHAPTER 6

SOUTHERN CONTINENT

What none of the twelve children, or their families too for that matter, knew was that the WCPS *Electra* had also landed on the planet.

The prison ship had crash-landed in the desert wastes of the southern continent. With the breakout of the twenty thousand or so convicts unstoppable, the crew and their families had fled. Commander Camilla Todd, the *Electra's* second-in-command, was leading them. This group of refugees had travelled north up the course of a wide river until they had reached, in the more hilly country, a high rocky tor, the top of which they had occupied and called Fort.

Camilla knew that the convicts, once free, would hunt them out and she had a good idea what would happen when they found them.

She was in command because the Captain, Peter Howard and three others had taken the *Electra's* power-core, an extremely dangerous object were it to fall into the wrong hands, east and further into the desert where they intended to bury it in the most inaccessible place they could find. The four hadn't been in contact for some time and Camilla hid a private fear that they had come to grief. She did not voice her concerns to Peter Howard's wife Anne.

How am I going to keep them all safe? she asked herself repeatedly but never came up with a satisfactory answer.

The self-proclaimed convict leader Elliot Murdoch and the rest of the ex-prisoners from the WCPS *Electra* rested at their camp for over two months, getting ready for their march north to search for the crew. It was late summer when he decided that they were ready, and some seventeen thousand men set out, loosely organised into groups of some five hundred each and led by their one-time block leaders from the ship. The day was hot; and more than hot, but this was normal had they known it for this time of year in the equatorial south. The men found that the heat sapped their will and their strength in a manner to which they were certainly not accustomed, acclimatised as they were to the cooler atmosphere on board the prison ship. The heat was purgatory to walk in and the least fit were unable to keep up with the pace set by Murdoch. He was forced, therefore, to reduce the planned daily mileage. He was not at all loath to do so. His captivity over the last eighteen years had made marching no easy matter for him either.

The men ambled along the riverbank in an undisciplined and chattering mass, stopping at frequent intervals to drink from the river to sate their overwhelming thirst. All the men, that is except for Murdoch's immediate five hundred, who marched in a semblance of parade ground precision, much like a bunch of recruits, which was how their colonel saw them. Elliot Murdoch's deputy, Smith, had received military training in his youth and he used this knowledge to good effect now. Smith had been an efficient soldier but hard on the men who had the misfortune to be under his command and had been court-martialled and expelled from the army after causing the death of three young recruits.

Even now, after nearly twenty years imprisonment and re-education he still considered that he had been in the right. Army life was supposed to be hard and cruel according to Smith; those who were inefficient, stupid or lazy must be considered worthless and therefore expendable. This five hundred were the nucleus of Murdoch's army and were becoming known as Smith's Regiment. Smith planned to organise the best of Murdoch's other followers in the same way.

Each regiment would consist of some five hundred men led by a colonel and would be divided into five companies, each led by a lieutenant. There would be four fighting companies within each regiment, the fifth company being made up of specialists such as medics and other support personnel. It had been agreed the previous evening that approximately twenty-four regiments of five hundred would be available for the planned attack on the ex-crew and guards when they located them. The remaining five thousand men would be non-combatants and therefore would be kept down the pecking order when it came to dishing out the spoils.

Marching proudly at the head of his column, head held high, Smith felt very pleased with his achievements over the past weeks. He fully intended that his men would be the elite of all the regiments, and closest to Murdoch, who marched some twenty paces to his front, his bodyguard, led by an indomitable ex-convict called Cracov, surrounding him in a protective shield. Murdoch was under no illusions that he was secure in his position of leader. He was taking no chances.

They were in no hurry. The escapees would have to stop and make a stand against them somewhere, encumbered as they were with women and children. Murdoch had plenty of time to train the men, weeding out those incapable or unwilling to fight and welding the remainder into a cohesive force, an army, *his* army. To those who fought well and who obeyed him would fall the spoils of this campaign.

Those that could not follow due to old age or injury; those not prepared to obey; and the men who were of no use to him, he left behind without a second thought. This night he would call the prison block leaders, now his colonels, for a conference and explain his great plan in detail.

His mind was busy as he marched. He, like any good commander, was thinking ahead to the day when the campaign would be over and he would put down roots and begin to live the free life. Once the guards and male crew were disposed of and the women allocated to the most deserving, he would *have* to be strong and ruthless to keep his position. He was a general now. Smith had informed the other leaders in no uncertain terms that that was how he was to be addressed. As Smith had been fingering his lethal looking knife at the time, all took his words very seriously.

Murdoch did not want just to remain a general; that was only the first step. He wanted to be the undisputed ruler of their new society. Murdoch wanted to be a king. Anyone that stood in his way would be eradicated. No challengers to his position could be allowed to survive. It was not an army he was leading; it was a nation, his nation.

To that end, he had insisted that all those who could be of use must be brought along, even those who might otherwise have been left behind due to age or infirmity. They were finding the march almost impossible. There were only so many doctors amongst the ex-prisoners. They would later train others in their craft and so medicine would be available for those who needed and deserved it. Hi-tech specialists were few, Murdoch having realised early on that this new society must function on a low technological level. If these specialists were not able or willing to fight in his army they were left behind. He had cannily brought along all that were good with their hands; mechanics, metal smiths and woodsmen had been specifically selected, also tailors and shoemakers. He would use them all.

Cocteau, a dark swarthy man of southern European extraction, Murdoch put in command of this non-combatant and diverse group. An intellectual man, but also a hard and unforgiving one, he was well suited to the job, being able to talk to his men on their level whilst not giving away an iota of his authority.

All in all, Murdoch was feeling well pleased with himself when he called a halt that first afternoon out from base camp, where the unwanted had been left to fend for themselves.

"We'll stop here for the night," he announced, turning towards Cracov, who was, as usual, not six paces away from him. *The man certainly takes his duties seriously*, thought Murdoch as he walked towards an attractive looking copse of trees some twenty yards from the riverbank. He knew what drove the man; Cracov wanted a fair share of the booty and that included one of the women for his very own. He was certainly not the best looking of his followers; in fact Murdoch could only describe him as a brute, a man whose coarse face almost never broke into a smile.

Murdoch smiled to himself. An exceedingly good-looking man when in his twenties, his good looks had faded but little during the long years in jail. In those younger days on Earth, before the security police caught him, he had led a life of luxury, paid for by the high fees he commanded as a world-class assassin. He had owned a beautiful villa in the Mediterranean and women had chased after him like moths to the flame.

Even in those halcyon days, Murdoch had wanted more, more women, more riches, but above all, more power. He needed people to listen to him, to obey him.

It was because of this yearning that he was caught. In his late twenties, he had accepted a lucrative job from an unpopular head of state who had wished to dispose of one of his popular rivals. Murdoch had tried to double-cross the aforementioned head of state, had approached the minister in question and persuaded him to attempt a coup. If successful, Murdoch had intended to be the power behind the government.

The plotters' security measures were as inadequate as a leaky bucket and before long the head of state knew all about it. He had informed the World Coalition Security Forces and Murdoch had found himself running for his life. After a month on the run (an experience he never wanted to repeat) he had been caught, tried and sentenced to life imprisonment.

During the long years of his incarceration, Murdoch had never forgotten the dreams he had had in his twenties.

When the news came to the prison that the long-term prisoners were to be exiled on a prison planet, he had pondered long and hard about how he could rise to prominence there, but this was far better. If he played his cards right he could make himself the undisputed dictator of this entire world and not merely of a small sector of people on the harsh prison planet.

His plans were panning out well so far. He was the leader of the convicts; now it was time for the next step.

Cracov walked heavily up to his mentor, breathing hard. He suffered from the problem of flat feet, not a comfortable disability when one was walking a set distance each day.

"How many miles to them hills?" he asked, gasping.

Murdoch squinted towards them and thought for a moment before he answered.

"Map is unclear about this area, but about another month's march I should think, maybe more. Distances can be deceptive in this haze. No point exhausting ourselves. Six miles a day is probably as much as any of them can cope with and perhaps not even that."

"Crew there?"

"They can't be anywhere else. The tracks are clear." Murdoch rubbed his hands together in anticipation of what was to come. "I can't wait."

Cracov grinned. He knew what the General was thinking.

They stood for a moment in silence before Cracov spoke again. "I'll get you your dinner."

Turning to the assembled bodyguard, some thirty strong, he issued his orders then sat down some distance away, thinking, correctly as it turned out, that Murdoch would want to be left alone to catch his breath and recover before he did anything else.

Once he finished his meal, Murdoch swept aside the crude dishes for his minions to pick up and turned to Cracov.

The man stood to attention at once. He had seen Smith approaching and wanted to make a good impression.

"Get the rest of the colonels," Murdoch ordered. "Time to talk about plans and organise final training. Get Cocteau in on it as well. He'll have to know what we are about."

When the twenty-four colonels (and Cocteau) were assembled, Murdoch was ready and waiting for them, sitting astride a large tree trunk that Cracov had positioned under a shady branch. Smith and Cracov stood at once behind him, reinforcing his authority. With the bodyguard positioned nearby and Smith's regiment armed and within call, it would be a brave colonel who would argue with Murdoch's orders.

Unaccountably courteous, Murdoch asked them to sit down. This conference would not be a short one. There was much shuffling about as they did so, eyeing each other, their leader and warily wondering what this was all about.

Murdoch cleared his throat and began to talk. "No interruptions," he said. "Hear me out and then if you want to ask anything stand up. Smith will tell you when it's your turn."

There were some mutterings at his didactic and peremptory tone but no one said anything. One look at Cracov's threatening face was enough.

"We march each morning; six to eight miles a day. In the afternoons we train. It'll take us at least three weeks to get to the hills, a bit longer to locate the crew. They will have tried to hide but we'll find them. When we do, we'll overrun their hideout and take the women and whatever they have with them – livestock, tools, clothes – everything; it's as simple as that."

He sat back, waiting for their reactions, eyes half-lidded against the sun and was, on the whole, pleased with what he saw. He noted two called Weiss and Gunnarsson who were looking doubtful. These were the men whom he would instruct Smith and Cracov to keep a closer eye on. These two could be a real threat to him.

"You may speak now," said Murdoch graciously, opening his hands as a king would grant audience.

There was a moment of silence. Nobody wanted to be the first to speak.

It was the fox-faced Baker who took the bull by the horns and asked the first question. A tall, dark and angular man with three deep parallel scars on his left cheek, he was already getting the reputation of being a strict and forceful leader of his men.

"Do we all attack or just some of us?" he asked.

"The best only," answered Murdoch with a smile. "I will only select the most efficient and well-drilled to take the crew out. To these regiments will go the spoils of the battle, and mark my words, I, and only I, will divvy out the women and the goods. No one else."

"There's still not enough women to go round," said Colonel Duchesne. "Even if only the eight best regiments attack their hideout, there can't be more than three hundred women there, if that."

Murdoch nodded. He had been expecting this and he had the answer ready. "The women will be shared out – a woman of your choice. That is a promise. I get first choice of them all, Smith second, Cracov third. After them, the colonels of the regiments who did the fighting, then the other colonels. Some men who fight well may get one as a reward. Tell that to them. It will make them keen."

He paused.

"What then?" came a voice from the back.

"The rest of the women? I think all the fighters should be rewarded, don't you?"

They all laughed and on that high note Murdoch led them on to the more mundane topic of battle training.

Upwind, the Larg scouts were watching. They were for the

moment content to watch, but plans were being laid, plans that would include Murdoch and his men.

Miles to the north, the crew and families from the *Electra* were preparing their defences, unaware of Elliot Murdoch's plans for the womenfolk. The high ground where Gerry had led them had certainly fulfilled their expectations. It could be described as a natural hill fort, surrounded as it was by three sheer cliff faces to the north, east and west. These cliffs were, decided Camilla, almost unassailable, almost but not quite. A determined force could, with much effort, climb them, although they would lose many men in the process. Unfortunately, the prisoners could well afford to throw away lives to keep the defenders busy on these three sides, whilst their main attacking force rushed the easier southern approach.

Camilla was under no illusions. The place would be pretty nigh impossible to defend long term with the numbers and weaponry available to her. Not that she had any choice. Negotiation would not be a viable option with these men, of that she was certain.

From the highest rocky crag in the middle of their bolthole she could see with binoculars the southern continent's northern coastline in the distance, a faint smudge on the horizon. She knew that there was another landmass in the north, over the water. There was no point in trying to reach it, much as she wanted to put the vast expanse between them and the convicts. If they did reach the coast, just how could they get there? How could they cross over to the northern continent? Boats of course, but boats took time to build. The ex-prisoners would catch them in the open and any defence would be as a laughable charade. They had a chance here in the hills, albeit a slim one. Perhaps they could at least get a few of the most vulnerable away? She made a mental note to examine the possibility.

She appeared to be everywhere at once, checking that the barriers were being placed correctly on the southern slopes. Large tree trunks formed the mainstay of the defences, wedged in place between the rocky buttes that formed an intermittent semicircle at the edge of the southern slope. If she had had more men and modern weapons she would have been happy. They could have held back a storm of attackers. As it was, they could only do their best and hope that they could hold out.

Gerry Russell, who had been the head livestock handler back on the ship, mounted on his gallant grey mare, was waiting for her some paces downhill from where the workers were toiling. He had been riding this mare ever since they had landed and Camilla doubted very much if he could be prised away from her now. The approach path leading south from Fort had a gentle incline, only growing steep right in front of where the barriers were being built. The natural corral where the livestock was situated was at the bottom of the slope. It was guarded day and night, protecting the animals from any predators that might be in the vicinity.

Camilla walked down the hill to join him.

He smiled down at her.

"You wanted to see me?" he asked. "All is quiet with the animals. No problems."

Camilla ran her hands through her sticky hair whilst she marshalled her thoughts. Gerry would not like what she was about to say. She took a deep breath.

"It's about the animals I need to speak to you Gerry," she began, "I don't know how we can defend them when we are attacked. We'll need every adult we can muster up there." She pointed back uphill.

Gerry stared at her as if he couldn't believe his ears. A man passionately devoted to all animals, he could not understand how and why the Commander was suggesting such a thing. Humans, he felt, were more than able to look after themselves. Animals could not.

He shook his head decisively. "No," he said, "I cannot abandon them."

Camilla looked at him. "You must."

He continued to shake his head.

"Well, what do you suggest then?" she asked.

"Take them inside Fort with us. There's enough water from the spring up top. You can't leave them down here. Anything could happen to them."

It was Camilla's turn to shake her head.

"There's just not enough room. Quite a manner of things could happen to them if they are squashed up with us as well. There will be, in all probability, a lot of fighting up there. You can't want them amongst it all. They will get hurt." Camilla continued. "When we see the convicts approaching I think we should bring in the goats, but only the goats."

"And the horses," finished Gerry, "you must give me that at least." He patted his mare; her ears flickered as she responded to the caress.

Camilla nodded. He could have his horses with him inside the barricade. At least the man seemed to realise that it would be impossible for them to protect all the livestock from the prisoners. The horses might also prove useful. She wished she had more of them. A germ of an idea began to take form in her mind.

"You do understand, Gerry, don't you?"

He nodded. "Yes. I suppose you're right. If the worst happens, these men, they can't all be bad. Some must love animals surely? They will look after them," he paused, "but not as well as I."

"Indubitably," agreed Camilla. "You make the arrangements about your beloved horses and the goats. We'll need the milk they provide if we end up in a siege situation. I am quite sure you're right, they will be looked after."

"Maybe the convicts will give up and leave us alone."

And cows might fly. "Perhaps," Camilla answered but by her tone of voice Gerry knew that she didn't think so.

Up behind the barricades, the other inhabitants were coming to terms with what was ahead of them.

The Howard family, still minus Peter Howard who was still in the desert with the away-team, burying the dangerous power-core from the *Electra*, was in the middle of a family confab.

"Do you think Dad is all right?" fretted Jessica. She was close to her father and missed him.

"They've activated the locator unit," said young Joseph, aged seven-and-a-half. "He'll find us Jessica, never fear."

He put his arm awkwardly round his big sister. It was strange, he reflected as he did so, to be comforting her. It was usually the other way round.

Anne Howard, worry for her missing husband and for what lay ahead of them etched on her face, her arm round her younger daughter Cherry, spoke up, "I am sure he will be with us very soon," she comforted.

Under her breath, Anne was never sure if she actually heard her or if it was her imagination running away with her when Jessica muttered, "But perhaps not soon enough."

At that point Jenny, Jessica's best friend popped her head round the tent flap that served as the door to their little domain. A stocky, sturdy girl three months younger than Jessica, the two were almost inseparable; even on the ship they had rarely been seen apart.

"Coming Jess? We've got cook duty."

As Jessica bent down to put on her boots Anne Howard sighed, thinking about their situation where children were being forced to work, and hard. The adults did the heavy backbreaking labour building the barricades. To the younger teenagers fell the day-to-day tasks ordinarily performed by these adults. Jessica and Jenny, the two Jays as they were known, were working at least ten hours a day on various necessary jobs, thus freeing their elders to work on the defences and to learn how to fight.

In fact, although Camilla deplored the necessity, all personnel, male or female over the age of fifteen would be manning the barricades when the time came. Anne herself had been given a duty station on the north face. When she was ordered to take up her position she would place Cherry and Joseph in the hands of their big sister. They and the rest of those under sixteen would enter the comparative safety of a large cave situated not far from their tent. It was hoped that the youngsters would be safe there until it was all over, one way or another.

The days and nights passed as the ex-crew and their families tried to keep some semblance of normality in their lives whilst working hard to prepare for the inevitable day when the ex-prisoners found them.

Candy Rae

CHAPTER 7

SOUTHERN CONTINENT

Elliot Murdoch, self-appointed general, was facing problems of his own. The first was short and bloody and was one that he dealt with in his normal ruthless manner. The second was far more serious.

The convicts had been travelling north for some time before the first manifested itself early one evening.

The only warning Elliot Murdoch had of trouble was a yell from Cracov as he lifted his heavy sword high in the air and brought it down on Colonel Weiss's head. The head split open with a gush of bright red blood and the body spun slowly as it slumped to the ground. Mesmerised, Murdoch stared as his assailant's brains spilled out on the grass.

The other bodyguards arrived at the run and formed a protective circle.

Murdoch knew what was happening. He had been warned by Cracov of a planned revolt by Weiss and Gunnarsson; all the indications had been there. He wondered why the man had waited so long. If he had made his move even a few days before he might have stood a chance but not now. Murdoch had been talking to and working with some of the colonels. Baker, Duchesne and Mahler were now his sworn men and, with Smith, would viciously counteract any perceived threat.

The revolt was short-lived and the survivors, some four dozen, were kicked and pushed into a small wallow beside the riverbank and guards set over them.

Murdoch's face showed clearly the satisfaction he was feeling. His position was secure. He would make such an exhibition of the rebels' deaths that it would be a brave man who ever tried to topple him again. In front of him and slightly to the left stood Cracov, eyes alert for any further trouble. Beside the huge man another smaller man was on his knees, blood streaming from a wound on his scalp but otherwise unhurt. It was Weiss's accomplice Gunnarsson and he was moaning loudly and piteously.

The man knew that he could expect no mercy from Murdoch. He had failed to usurp the General and the consequences of this failure would be slow and painful. At this point he was not to know just how agonising Murdoch's punishment would be. He would have to wait a long three days to find out.

"Tie the ex-colonel up," ordered Murdoch. "I will decide what to do with him later." His eyes bored into Gunnarsson, full of promise of torture and pain. Murdoch would enjoy watching him writhe as he died. Gunnarsson remembered all too well how the man had dealt with the paedophiles back at the ship. His own experience would be much worse. He shuddered in terrified apprehension.

Cracov tied him up, a sardonic grin on his face. The bonds were tight and his victim grimaced as they dug deeply into his wrists and ankles. He was then kicked and prodded as he was forced to crawl towards the surviving members of the rebel force who sat waiting in the wallow. As he crashed to the ground in their midst, not one attempted to help him. They had hopes of a merciful death and none wanted to be seen aiding their ex-colonel.

Closely guarded, the worried men were left alone.

Murdoch's second problem manifested itself as sunset passed into night.

Preparing for sleep, well pleased with the way the abortive revolt had been countered, he wrapped himself in the quilted coverlet and lay down on the groundsheet. He shivered; nights could be chilly, although during daytime the heat was insufferable. Snuggling into his covers, his thoughts began to drift. He was very tired.

He woke with a start and sat up trying to make sense of strange noises emanating from the very edge of the encampment. There was the sound of excited shouting from the men and the sound of an engine spluttering in the distance. The only truck Murdoch was aware of (except for those disabled back at the ship and the ones with the crew and their families) was the one left behind at base camp. Whatever was it doing here? The engine noise got louder as it laboured hard up the incline to reach them. Murdoch extracted himself from his covers and stood up. Smith, or perhaps Baker (he was not sure who had guard duty) would report, there was no need for him to investigate personally.

"Mug of caffee while you're waiting General?" asked Cracov, appearing at his side. Murdoch hadn't even been aware of the big man's approach. Murdoch grunted and took a long swallow, savouring the flavour. Caffee stocks were low now; he hoped someone would find a replacement beverage from the native edibles before the stocks ran out completely. The last experiment, he recalled, had been less than successful. He had not been amused and had spat the offending drink straight in the hapless cook's face.

So Murdoch stood waiting, sipping the hot drink and wondering what was happening, then saw Smith approaching at the run, three of his men following close at his heels and escorting another older, grey-haired man who was gasping and gulping for air as they forced him to keep up.

When they reached him, Smith came to attention and gave Murdoch a smart salute. The older man's eyes widened with surprise. He tried to hold himself erect, unsuccessfully; his breath was laboured and sounded very loud in the silence of the clearing. Everyone who wanted to hear what had happened drew closer.

"Truck arrived General," began Smith, "with this man driving and about twenty or so wounded in the back. Some quite badly."

Murdoch turned an inquiring glance at the newcomer, who, to give him credit considering the state he was in, was fast to respond to the unspoken request for information.

"It started last night," he started to babble, his words running into each other as he tried to explain. He swayed on his feet, at the very end of his energy resources.

"Sit down man," commanded Murdoch. The man did so with an alacrity born of exhaustion, his legs folding beneath him. Baker moved forward and helped him into a sitting position, then hunkered closer to better hear what he was saying.

"Tell us slowly and calmly," he said. "Don't leave anything out. It might be important."

The man nodded, his chest still heaved spasmodically but his breathing was certainly getting easier.

"Name's White," he said.

"And?" prompted Baker.

"Me and my mates were bunking down near the truck. Most of those you left had split into small groups, some quite far up or down the river."

This was better, his words were clear. This White was an educated man.

"I was asleep when I was woken up by screaming and shouting. The loudest screams were coming from downriver where a group had built a campsite in the woods near the water. The woods scared some but not them."

He licked his dry lips.

Murdoch passed him his half empty mug of caffee. White's hands grasped it with shaky relief and he lifted the mug to his mouth, gulping down the contents with evident pleasure. Caffee had not been on the menu on the prison decks.

"And then?" prompted Murdoch. "What happened then?"

White looked directly at him, haunted horror in his eyes.

"The beasts were bigger than huge. Great big tawny wolves as big as a landcar back on Earth."

Words failed him at this point. He gazed round at those assembled, begging them to believe him.

"A landcar?" derided Smith. "You can't be serious? No animal is as large as that!"

"They were," answered White. "I'm not lying, honest. They were gigantic, with sharp claws and big snarling mouths full of teeth. Hundreds of them. They just fell on us, we didn't stand a chance."

Murdoch looked at his colonels.

"Double the perimeter guards," he barked and Baker moved away to issue the order.

"How did you manage to get away?" asked Duchesne.

"Just jumped into the truck, pressed the start button and drove," said White. "I was driving slowly at first and some managed to climb in the back. No point trying to fight. When I got out of the trees, I drove faster. They chased us for a while then gave up. Better pickings back at the camp no doubt."

"Do you think any survived?" asked Murdoch.

"Don't know. Don't suppose so."

"Why did they attack?" asked Cracov.

"For food," White said. "Could see them starting to eat as I drove off. It didn't seem to matter whether the men were dead or alive."

The words chilled the listeners.

"Will they attack us?" Cracov asked, bile rising in his throat.

White shrugged his shoulders. "There were not as many of us at the base camp. As I said, we had split up into small groups so we were easy to pick off. Some men tried to fight the beasts off but it was useless. They were very large and very fierce. They attacked in twos, one pinning a man down whilst the other went for the kill."

"We are well armed and organised," announced Murdoch. "They won't find us easy prey. There are thousands of us."

He turned to White. "Are they heading this way?"

White didn't know, and at that moment didn't care. He was safe now. His eyes started to close and his head drooped as he slumped over to one side. Within seconds he was fast asleep.

"Our plans don't change," Murdoch ordered. "We continue the march in the morning. Keep our eyes and ears open for any threat."

Nobody argued with him. It was strange, Murdoch thought as he settled down for the third time that night, that, instead of being the hunters, they appeared to have become the hunted, but there must be a way to get out of the predicament. He wondered if he should pick up the pace of the march but discounted the notion. It would be a sign of weakness to be seen running away. No, he would stick to his original plan and take the appropriate precautions. He might however, let someone else take the lead on the march. If the beasts attacked, he did not want to be the one wielding his sword in earnest.

When Murdoch and his army left their campsite the following morning, a partially recovered White went with them, determined to keep up. There was no way he was going to be left behind. At almost seventy years old, he would find the going tough, but Cocteau had very precise instructions. He was to be brought along, carried if necessary. Three of the twenty injured whom White had brought with them in the back of the truck went too, the others were too badly hurt and as was becoming the norm, were left behind.

To their surprise, the captured rebels went too, hands tied with casual ruthlessness behind their backs but suffering (for the moment at least) nothing more from their guards than a shove and a curse if they lagged behind. Some began to hope that they might survive after all, that Murdoch would forgive and forget.

Elliot Murdoch's master plan had not changed. The only concession he had made to danger was to increase the guard and to put everyone on high alert. As he marched away that morning, now ensconced within, rather than in front of, the lead regiment, he remained in fine fettle.

The Larg kohorts at base camp had not enjoyed themselves so much for many moons. Although some of the two-legs had fought back, the vast majority had tried to run. These attempts to flee had been to no avail. The Larg could run faster. A kohort had been detailed to surround the camp and the terrified runners had run straight into their waiting mouths, teeth and claws.

Within the camp, after the initial killing spree, the kohorts played with the men still alive, taking a nip here and a bite there, and then moving on to play their favourite 'game'.

The favourite killing method amongst the Larg was particularly messy and painful but in the Larg lexicon it came under the heading 'Sport'. One Larg held the victim at the head; the other at the tail and whilst their victim lay there, quivering with fear, a third Larg would appear. Using his sharp claws, this Larg would quite deliberately and slowly rip open the victim's torso. As the rent grew and as the intestines and other organs spilled out, the three would began to eat, even as the victim's heart pumped out its few last breaths.

All but forty of the men were dead. The Larg had done their work well. True to form, they had enjoyed both their sport and their meal.

Herded into a circle, the forty survivors huddled together in the darkness, too shocked to speak. The Larg prowled around, growling threateningly as they gazed at the men out of baleful yellow eyes, as if daring them to try and make a break for freedom. Nobody did. When dawn broke, these Larg stepped back three paces and sat down, tongues lolling with excitement. This made the men even more nervous.

Aoalvaldr, the Warrior Chief of the most senior kohort, had promised them some fun with any two-legs that proved unsuitable for his purpose. They eyed the restless milling men with greed, wondering which ones would be given to them as a reward for their long night's guard vigil. Aoalvaldr appeared, his more junior leaders in tow. A huge beast, even by Larg standards, Aoalvaldr towered over the waiting men.

Andrew Snodgrass, sometime thief and spy, viewed Aoalvaldr's approach with a great deal of terrified trepidation. Outside their guarded circle, he could see other beasts sating their appetites on the bodies lying nearby. He shivered. Whatever they intended to do with him, he hoped that the end would be quick.

Andrew's death however was not what was uppermost in Aoalvaldr's mind. He was no longer hungry. An intelligent beast, he had plans for one of these two-legged creatures. He singled out Andrew.

The Larg were telepathically similar to the Lind in the north, similar but not the same. The Larg could hear thoughts and even send images to each other, although not with the same proficiency. They were descended from the same genetic gene pool many eons in the planet's past. The Larg were larger and predominantly tawny in colour, the better to blend in with the desert sand. The Lind were, in general, smaller, with variegated and colourful stripes and patches, the better to blend in with the dense forests in which they made their homes. There the similarities ceased. The Lind were a peaceful species and lived in harmony with their surroundings, whilst the Larg were warlike and frequently at war with each other.

The Larg despised the Lind of the north with an undying hatred.

The Larg warriors had watched and taken careful note of the recent happenings in their land. They had seen the *Electra* arrive and had watched as the crew and their families departed at speed to the northern hills. They had watched and done nothing. The trucks they had been travelling in were beyond any of their experiences and anyway, there were not many in that strange-looking herd; they could be dealt with later. The mass of men that spilled out of the ship after they had gone was an entirely different matter. They had watched as Murdoch executed the men accused of paedophilia with approval and excitement. The Larg also disposed of their unwanted pack-mates and enemies. When the old and sick were left behind by Murdoch at base camp they lifted their heads in agreement with what the two-legged Chief Warrior had done. The Larg also did not encumber themselves on the march with those that could not keep up.

They had waited until the fit were far enough away and then pounced. They were hungry; there was not enough game that could be hunted in the harsh southern plains. The last few summers had been dry and the herds had not bred sufficiently well to provide enough food for all. So the adult males had gone northwards and had been heading towards the hills and the herds that lived there when they had come across the humans.

Plans were being laid to invade the northern continent come summer.

Aoalvaldr walked towards Andrew, placing one paw slowly one after the other in deliberate fashion and calculated to frighten. What a puny creature! The men standing next to Andrew melted away. Andrew stood motionless as the beast closed in on him, the vast menacing shape like something out of his worst nightmares.

What happened next made him soil himself in fright. Not only did Aoalvaldr open his mouth, displaying a mass of white and very sharp teeth (Andrew cringed at the sight) but also a strange harsh growling sound came out. At the same time Andrew felt his mind being invaded by an alien presence as his consciousness filled with inexplicable images. His knees began to shake.

These images were clear, and he realised at once what the Larg had been doing since the *Electra* landed. They had been watching and waiting. As clear as if it was a replay from a datdisc, he saw the crew and their families disembarking and then preparing the vehicles. He watched the convoy leave and wondered at the sight of a single vehicle departing in the opposite direction, into the desert. The images flew past, moving on to the convicts' experiences.

Then the images changed, away from the overview of the convicts as a whole to ones in which he alone featured. Aoalvaldr wished to get to know Andrew for some reason; needed to learn about these creatures that had appeared out of the sky.

It was a split second decision. Andrew wanted to live. He was not a brave man, he abhorred violence and not having the skill-set that

Murdoch needed had been permitted to remain behind with the old, the infirm and the unwanted.

Greatly daring, he took a single step towards Aoalvaldr and signalled his assent with a nervous nod. The great beast appeared satisfied with this gesture and began nosing Andrew away from his apprehensive peer group.

Andrew let himself be prodded towards the river, trying all the time to avoid the blood, the shreds of bodies, and the bits of bone that lay scattered around. He retched as his foot slipped then crunched on some of the detritus.

Aoalvaldr watched with amusement. This creature must learn to control himself and Aoalvaldr would make it his business to make sure he did.

The Larg encircling the remaining thirty-nine moved in for the kill. Andrew heard the anguished screams as the Larg pounced and began to play. He put his hands to his ears in a vain attempt to block out the noise, but he was unfortunately as unsuccessful at this as he was at avoiding the horrendous sights that met his eyes and crunched under his feet. Both recollections haunted his dreams for years to come.

By then Captain Peter Howard and his three-man away-team, having buried the power-core, had reached the scrubby foliage that marked the western fringe of the hills. They had not even attempted to make for the rendezvous site, knowing well that Camilla would not wait for them. Instead, they made for the hills at an oblique angle from where their vehicle had broken down, realising that this would cut out at least two weeks' journey time.

Johannes Pederson turned on the handheld locator. To his relief it gave out the expected start up chime and began to scroll through data as it hunted for a fix on the mother locator unit with the convoy. It would bleep if they were moving off course and the small screen would display an arrow indicating the direction they must take.

"They're still there," he announced, "but a long way off. I'd hoped to reach them soon but they're further north than we thought they would be."

"Can't be helped," stated Peter Howard. "We have enough food and water for three to four days and there will be fresh water when we reach the woods proper."

He turned to Angus and Tom.

"Let's go," he said encouragingly. "We're on the home straight."

The four began to walk.

CHAPTER 8

NORTHERN CONTINENT

When Jim, until recently World Coalition Petty Officer Cranston of the colony ship *Argyll*, followed the Lind known as Larya across pack Zanatei's domta and into her daga he was of the jaundiced opinion that he had stumbled into some sort of surreal dream.

First the children's disappearance, then the long, wet and exhausting hunt for them. To cap it all, the creatures that had spirited the youngsters away had then merrily proceeded to lead him and his companions a long and arduous dance among the foothills below. They had laid one false trail after another in order to prolong his search for some nefarious purpose of their own. He had not yet forgiven them for that. He was footsore and weary and in no mood to play games.

"It was necessary," said Larya, surprising him with her insight, he not being aware as yet just how the Lind could pick up thoughts and emotions from their human partners.

He frowned at her.

"Maybe, but I want to hear some answers pretty sharpish."

Larya cocked her head to one side. She didn't understand the words or perhaps chose to ignore them. "You learn our language first," she answered and padded away. Jim made haste to follow her. He most definitely did not want to be left floundering in the dark in the midst of the domta. The Lind had far better night vision than humans.

Of the six who remained behind in Tara and Kolyei's daga it was Laura who broke the silence.

"What did she mean when she said that she would be white soon?" she asked. "I don't understand. In fact, I don't understand a lot of what's been happening, but this question will do to be getting on with."

Tara marshalled her thoughts and got the answer clear in her mind before she spoke.

"The Lind age in a different way from us," she began, feeling her way. "If a Lind survives for a certain number of seasons, he or she turns white within a year or so. Then they can become an Elda of the pack. Not all do."

She looked at Kolyei for confirmation.

"Did I get it right?"

"Yes," he answered her. "We become white in perhaps fifty cold seasons, some more, some less."

"I didn't see many white ones," Laura said.

"No," agreed Kolyei, "Rtath Zanatei is a warrior rtath."

"Do many die young?" persisted Laura, not fully understanding what Kolyei was trying to say. He was still talking in a mixture of Standard and Lindish. Tara and the other eleven children could understand him perfectly well but it would be some time before Laura and Francis could, as they did not have the advantage of the telepathic link of being vadeln-paired.

"Larg come. Many will die," stated Kolyei.

"Do they come every year?" asked Francis.

Kolyei considered the question carefully. He was unsure of what the term year meant, guessed and nodded (the Lind had taken to this human expression of agreement with alacrity).

"Most. Satalrdn, many, this warm season. They will attack us within four moons."

You mean in the summer?

"Summer?"

The explanation followed. At the end of it Kolyei and Radya concluded that it was easier to use the word 'summer' than 'warm season'. Tara wondered how long it would be before all the pack members were using the term. Not long she was thinking, knowing how fast information could permeate throughout the pack. The conversation moved away from the subject of the impending war. Tara, for one, was very glad that it had and hoped that they could talk of lighter things until bedtime. She went over to the shelves fixed to the sturdy and comparatively draught-free wall and took down some ripe pinkfruit and a cup. Kolyei's daga was one of the few this side of the domta that sat beside a little stream.

"Help yourself to water everyone," she said placing the cup down beside the fruit. "I'm hoping to get some more cups soon but at the moment we'll have to share."

Laura took one of the fruit and bit into it rather doubtfully, it didn't look very appetising from the outside, resembling as it did dusky pink boot leather; but as she chewed her face broke into a delighted smile.

"This is delicious. Tastes of ripe cherries." she said. "Try one, Francis."

But Francis had other things on his mind. He turned to Kolyei. "Can we get back to the subject now?" he asked.

Kolyei stopped chewing his fruit. The Lind were well aware of a balanced diet and ate copious amounts of vegetables and fruit as well as meat.

"What subject is that?" asked Kolyei humorously. He did so enjoy teasing the humans.

Francis frowned. Although he had become far more open-minded and relaxed of late, he was still getting used to the feeling of being a part of, rather than apart from, his fellows. He accepted the gentle teasing of Jim, James and Laura (especially the latter) and could give them as good as he got. Now it appeared that these alien beings also delighted in the play of words and the tease. He was not to know that Kolyei had quite a reputation as a practical joker amongst the pack. He was a master of wit in his own language. Now he was developing this skill in Standard as well.

"The war of course," he said, half-annoyed, half-amused.

Tara sighed. She just couldn't help it. They were going to start talking about the Larg again. She looked over at Radya and Peter. The boy was fast asleep.

Laura stopped the conversation right there and then. "It is late," she said in a no-nonsense tone. "We can discuss the war in the morning."

Francis demurred, but seeing the determined look on her face agreed, albeit with a great deal of reluctance.

As Laura prepared her bedding she became aware of two mature Lind standing not far from the entrance to the daga. One was slightly larger than the other and its gaze was focused on her, with a look in its eyes that was rather unsettling.

The six spent a restless night, the humans at least beset by dreams or ravaging Larg and battles. Radya and Peter did not return to their daga. No one had liked to wake him. The boy had looked so tired before he dropped off. Radya made no objections, merely wrapping herself round his small body to give him warmth and comfort. Tara cuddled in against Kolyei, sighed with contentment as he likewise pressed against her. She was lulled to sleep by his gentle and loving thoughts.

In the cool of the morning and over breakfast, Francis saw fit to bring up the previous evening's topic once more. He was nothing if not persistent.

Radya and Peter went back to the daga he shared with Alan and Kiltya. The boy was experimenting with making a coat from a kura pelt and wanted to get on with it. He was, after all, only ten years old. He wished to hear no more of war and death. Tara busied herself tidying up the daga and did her utmost not to listen.

"Do many die in battle?" Francis asked.

"Yes and more later," Kolyei answered, looking at the man.

Francis persisted in his questioning. "From injuries sustained?"

"I do not understand. Sustained? You mean hurts? Larg are big and strong."

"Bigger than you?"

"Yes, and many more Larg than Lind."

"Bigger?" Laura squeaked. Why they must be enormous!

"Yes. Each time ltsctas, perhaps breed ten, twelve, maybe more."

"How many in your families?" asked Laura.

Kolyei considered. "Four is usual. Not all survive."

Deciding that the humans were doing too much of the asking, Kolyei decided to ask a question himself.

"How many ltsctas do you Lind have?" he asked.

"One, perhaps two but that's unusual," answered Laura, correctly interpreting the question.

Kolyei looked surprised at that.

"One? That is not efficient," he observed. "How many total?"

"We have two or three in a lifetime perhaps. Probably more now that we are dirtside and there are no restrictions."

"Strange," was his only reaction.

Laura did not try to explain. It would have been far too complicated to make the Lind understand the reasons why it had been necessary to restrict human family sizes on Earth. She would leave it until both species had a deeper understanding of each other.

Francis again brought them back to the subject of the war. He was intensely worried about what they had been told the pervious afternoon and wanted to know more.

"How many Larg will come?" he asked.

"Many. Chief Eldas from the Gtratha will send message soon and we will know more," answered Kolyei.

"Where are these Chief Elders? They are a sort of grand Council taken from all the packs, aren't they?" asked Laura.

"Many suns run and yes."

But Francis was not interested in a discussion about the Gtratha.

"Afanasei said something about you sending spies to the south?"

"Yes. Dangerous it is to be a spy. Many return not."

Tara looked up from her self-imposed task of sweeping the floor, a serious expression on her face. She knew that Kolyei had spied in the south once in the past.

"Know you will when Larg cross over the small lands."

"Small lands?" questioned Francis.

"With water circle outside."

Francis frowned; trying to understand what Kolyei was trying to say. Water circles? He racked his brain, trying to think and ran his hands through his short hair. He had a flash of inspiration. "You mean the islands? That chain of small islands that runs from the northern continent to the southern where the narrow channel is?"

"When summer come then low waters. Larg swim to us over the waters between them."

Francis turned to Laura.

"These islands are not far from the settlement. These Larg will hit there first." Turning to Kolyei, he added, "Is that the only place the

Larg can cross?"

Kolyei nodded. "You must warn your rtath."

Tara finished her housekeeping, (the daga was small, after all and it never took very long) and sat down beside Kolyei.

"Back at the settlement the teachers did say that the planetary year consisted of ten months, five summer and five winter," she interposed.

"That is meant to be reassuring?" flushed Francis angrily.

Tara went red with embarrassment and Laura put a hand on the man's arm, effectively stopping him from saying anything he might regret later.

"Francis did not mean to be unkind Tara," she reassured the girl. "He's just a bit uptight about all that is happening."

Tara nodded. She blinked back the tears that threatened to flow.

Francis looked at her. "I'm sorry Tara," he said, "I did not mean to flare up at you."

Laura's eyebrows rose. It was the first time she had ever heard Francis apologise to anybody.

"Is the only place," Kolyei confirmed, repeating, "you must warn your rtath."

"How do the Larg fight?" pressed Francis.

Kolyei was thinking detachedly that the man would make a good Susa of a Lindar as he formulated his answer. This human asked the right questions.

"They will attack."

"Explain yourself."

"Lindars practise to defeat the Larg. We will defend, retreat, regroup. We will defend rtathen. We will defend rtathlians."

Laura wondered how Kolyei knew these Standard military terms. She assumed, correctly, that Tara had been coaching him.

"Why do the Larg come?" she asked.

"Herds. Meat," answered Kolyei succinctly. "Kura, zarova, jezdic. A Larg will eat much. Females and younglings are left in south and Larg enjoy killing."

Laura struggled valiantly to follow all this.

"What are zarova?" she asked, "and jezdic?"

"Zarova have a long neck and jezdic run fast," was the explanation.

"Now we have the real names for them," she said, satisfaction in her voice. "I was never very happy calling them goats, giraffes and zebras."

"Do the Larg eat the herds?" asked Francis.

Kolyei's reply was chilling. "Ceja. They will eat Lind too."

"Would they eat humans?"

"Yes."

The three humans looked at each other in consternation. "We must speak to Jim," Laura decided, "and the sooner the better."

Jim was getting much the same information from Larya. He was dismayed and appalled at what he heard. With Afanasei acting as interpreter where necessary he quizzed the two Lind unmercifully, eventually getting round to questions about tactics and numbers. He was surprised but relieved when told of the number of Lindars that would be available to fend off the invaders.

"Elda have informed all packs of danger," said Afanasei. "I am Susa of Lindar Zanatei. I lead Lindar to war."

"I with Afanasei go," added Larya.

"And I with you," said Jim instantly. Larya rubbed her snout into Jim's hand in appreciation.

At Jim's request, Afanasei and Larya told him a little about the geography of the Lind lands. "Tell me about the other packs," he asked. "Are there many of them? Do they live far away?"

"Yes," said Afanasei. "Where there lian, woods you call them, the Lind are. Many packs. We of Lind live in high lands north and beside big water far west. Many days it will take you to run there."

"What about the other northern continent?"

"No Lind there. No Larg there."

"Most of your land is forested?"

"Yes. Is forest, woods, lian, flat lands, you call plains, many rivers, hills, mountains where snow big in cold season."

"We must all work together," Jim said at last. "Fight together as well. The humans at the settlement are mostly farmers, not soldiers, but they can learn, they must learn how to fight. The Larg have to be stopped before they are able to gain a foothold. We can set up traps, slow them down. Hit and run tactics. Retreat behind the perimeter fences and hold out."

"This is not the Lind way," observed Afanasei.

Jim ignored that and pressed on regardless. "Have the Larg ever reached here?"

"One time in my memory." The words came out reluctantly, as if Afanasei did not want to remember.

Larya spoke up, "Many died that warm season."

"We shall plan our joint defences and drive the Larg back into the sea," stated Jim, slamming his hand on his thigh in emphasis. He stood up. "However, before we go any further, I am going to do something about the cracks in the walls and roof of this daga. I don't want to spend another night freezing my pants off when I can do something about it."

Some hours later Jim emerged from the daga and Larya led him to the lesson grove. Lessons were in progress. In one corner, youngsters of both species were sitting facing a venerable white Lind listening to a story. Jim couldn't understand more than a few words here and there although the story was being narrated extremely slowly in Lindish. When he looked at the faces of the children he realised that they did understand and were enjoying the tale.

"Hero story," said Larya. "It is about the sire of me, Larya."

"They're telling a tale about your father?" asked Jim in amazement. "Is that white Lind talking about his battles with the Larg?"

Larya nodded proudly.

"Is the white Lind sending pictures into their minds?"

"Yes. Practice is good. He sends pictures to ltsctas."

"Are the human younglings receiving these pictures as well?"

"No. Only from their vadeln."

Clever, thought Jim. Making a lesson entertaining was a well-proven method of good teaching and they got language and thought practice as well. He smiled his approval as another thought struck him.

Larya looked at him encouragingly.

Jim looked at her. "We can send pictures and emotions to and from each other. You can do the same with other Lind. You cannot send pictures or sense emotions with unpaired humans or humans paired with other Lind. Is that correct?"

"I can sense little there."

Jim thought for a moment. Really, it was difficult to follow Lind thought patterns. Then with Larya 'sending' clarification, he nodded as he realised that the Lind could sense a limited amount of human emotion and thought from the unpaired and from those paired with others. It was limited by degrees and Jim realised with a start, Larya had chosen him because she could sense strong emotive thoughts from him. Other Lind who had looked him over had sensed little or nothing at all. He filed this piece of information to think about later. All in all he thought, it was amazing how much of Larya's thoughts he was picking up without even trying. Like the children before him, he was finding that their bonding was growing stronger. They were beginning to share words. It certainly made talking easier.

: *Listen* : she ordered : *Good story* :

Larya wagged her tail, grinned at him and winked. Jim solemnly winked back. He settled himself to listen to the tale with Larya translating and managed to make quite a bit of sense of it. Towards its end, Jim noticed that James and Kath were sitting amongst the pupils. The young man had not lost the half-bemused look of the previous afternoon. Jim wondered if his own face looked the same. James seemed more that content with what this new life was offering. Rozya looked radiant.

Neither the Lind nor their human compatriots knew it as yet, but Rozya's action the previous evening of choosing James Rybak as her paired human thus making a foursome of herself, Matvei, Kath and James, was to become the norm.

Laura and Francis sat to one side, a part of, yet distanced from the others. Another Lind sat with them. They were concentrating hard on what was being told to them because they had to learn Lindish the hard way without the help of telepathic transference. For once, the two Lind who usually followed them were not to be seen.

: *Where are the two watchers?* : asked Jim of Larya.

: *Faddei and Asya wait* :

: *Wait for what?* :

Perversely, she chose not to answer. Her arch look did however speak volumes and Jim began to get an inkling of what was afoot. He smiled. If he was correct and he rather thought he was, Laura and Francis were in for a very interesting time.

Larya pointed to the Lind sitting with Laura and Francis with her forepaw. "Talya is a healer, a Holad," she informed him. "She teaches Laura and Francis our language but also something of how we care for our sick and wounded."

Over their midday meal, which the human inhabitants of the domta spent by themselves, they talked together about various subjects. By common consent, the impending war was not mentioned. Thomas and Emily presided over the cook-fire, frying zarova steaks atop a steelwood frying pan that Thomas had made out of a fallen tree. He was extremely good with his hands.

Hunger satisfied, Jim coughed to get everybody's attention and demanded an impromptu meeting.

"Right everyone," he stated. "We have to decide what is to be done. We adults haven't been here as long as you youngsters – we are still experiencing language difficulties with the Lind. It will take time before we are fluent in Lindish and able to understand all that they are trying to tell us, although their grasp of our language is quite astonishing. James and myself have Rozya and Larya. We can understand a fair bit aided by that useful telepathic thought process of theirs but Laura and Francis aren't paired yet so don't have that advantage." He couldn't resist shooting a teasing glance at the two.

Both Laura and Francis looked mystified.

"I don't want to talk about the Larg," said Peter in a very small voice.

Jim looked at him with real sympathy. "But we must Peter, I am sorry."

Peter sighed. There was no getting away from it. He decided that he would try and shut out the conversation and, if all else failed, escape to Radya. He was becoming more and more homesick as the weeks passed and missed his mother desperately. Radya tried to fill the void and she had spoken to Afanasei privately a few days previously about her worries about him. Afanasei sympathised with her predicament but could offer no help; he was after all not paired with a human and found it hard to relate to specific inter-species problems.

Jim looked around. There was no Lind present, excepting that is, Francis and Laura's two shadows who had reappeared just as they finished their meal.

Kath started the ball rolling.

"Some of us must go to warn the settlement. Others must stay here and learn how these Lindars fight and also introduce the Lind to fighting with two-footed allies who can and will wield weapons to defend their loved ones. We also need to understand how these Lindar regiments are trained."

There were murmurs of agreement.

"Yes," agreed Thomas, the blond fourteen year old. "I have already experimented with making knives and spears. It would be easier back at the settlement. Arthur Knott has a working smithy and could turn them out much faster."

Francis sat up straighter. "A spear is efficient but not I think efficient enough in the close combat fighting that we will encounter. Swords would be better. We must speak to the Lindar Commanders and ask them to give us a demonstration of how they have fought in the past and decide how those with a Lind partner can fight with them."

"Bows and arrows," suggested Yvonne from the back.

Emily raised her hand. "May I say something?" she asked in her soft voice.

At Jim's nod, she continued, "Could the Lind and humans not form a sort of cavalry unit?" she asked tentatively, "like in the Napoleonic Wars on Europe in the nineteenth century?" Emily had a deep interest in historical subjects.

"Not enough time," interposed James, entering the conversation for the first time. "Cavalry need a lot of training." Smiling encouragingly at her he added, "Good idea for the future though. Any more ideas young lady?"

"Agincourt," was her prompt reply. "In 1415 a few English bowmen defeated a huge French force many times their number with arrow storms."

"But the French were crammed into a small space," argued Tara, who had learnt about the battle in history lessons.

"But if we chose the right battlefield, why not? Drive the Larg into a confined space and then annihilate them?"

"Yes," exclaimed Francis. "That might work. I'm sure Arthur Knott could invent something that could do the job."

"We would kill many Larg," said Laura.

"Isn't that the idea?" asked James. "It would certainly please the Lind."

"No," interposed Tara. She looked at Kath. She knew what she wanted to say but didn't have the right words to say it.

Kath responded. "I don't think that is the case. They have emphasised time and time again that they do not kill for fun but only to defend their land and their pack-mates. They deplore wanton killing. What do they call it? Volat or something I think. It's their most heinous crime. They understand the necessity and I don't think they like it, but it's the only way we can drive the Larg off if the numbers they are reporting are correct. Matvei is very worried and says that many Lindars are being brought in from the west to help. This has not happened for many generations."

"Will they definitely attack the settlement?"

"I think they will," Jim admitted. He shrugged his shoulders helplessly. "Remember there are only about five thousand adults at the settlement. They would have to remain there to defend the perimeter."

"How long do we have?" asked James.

"About four months Larya says."

"Better set about it then."

"I can stay here and learn how the Lind fight and then work out how we can integrate with them. Kath, James and Laura must remain too, also Bill and Geoff," Francis announced. He turned to Jim. "You must go back, warn the settlement and introduce the Lind."

Jim demurred. He felt that he should stay where he was. He still had much to learn about their four-pawed allies.

Kath agreed with Francis. "Only you have the authority and the standing, Jim. The Council will listen to you where they would disregard anything we might say."

Jim nodded reluctant acceptance realising that what they were advising made sense. "I will speak to Larya and the Eldas. I think four of us should return and Afanasei should accompany us as well."

"Who?" demanded Francis.

"Myself and Larya of course, then Tara and Kolyei because of their interpretation skills. Thomas and Stasya must go back too so that he can speak to Arthur Knott about weaponry. I'm not sure about the fourth pair."

He looked around the circle of youngsters. His gaze passed over Emily and Mark then rested on Peter who was sitting with a disconsolate face beside Moira and Yvonne.

"I think Peter as well," he announced, smiling at the boy. "He has been very brave but I think he has been away from his mother long enough. He deserves at least to visit her." Peter perked up at once. "It will be no sinecure," he added for the youngster's benefit, "you will need to help us all you can."

Peter nodded, his face one big beam.

Thinking that the conversation had been too serious for too long, Jim changed the subject. "Now, is there any more of that wonderful baked fruit? I could certainly go another plateful."

Talk moved on to other, more light-hearted topics. Tara was even persuaded to recite one of the jolly rhymes for which she was becoming noted. She was given the word 'where' and the topic 'planet' by Yvonne. As Kath had realised early on, the girl certainly had a gift with words.

"Into the vastness of space we humans didst dare,

But it was pure bad luck that we were there,

When the storm didst chuck us who knows where,

Bad luck, good luck, I'm not being fair,

The planet we landed on is more that just bare."

Jim laughed; this was the first chance he had got to hear Tara in full flight.

"But I did get a scare,

When Kolyei came to me, unaware,

And we became the first vadeln-pair,

What a wonderful, and rare,

Life this is, I swear."

"This is good," Jim said in an aside to Laura, "funny too."

But Tara had not finished.

"But alas, there are Larg about who want to tear,

Apart what we have and it's not FAIR."

She stopped.

"I don't want to go on," she confessed to the suddenly silent audience. "The Larg are too close."

They all clapped but nobody laughed, not this time. Tara was right. War with the Larg was too close.

"Well done though," Jim cried. "Kath is right, you do have the gift," and then he made haste to change the mood of the gathering.

The young chatter was pleasant, Jim reflected as he sat back, spooning the delicious fruity mixture into his mouth. He was glad to see young Peter devouring a second helping as well. The lad certainly seemed to have got his appetite back. They began to discuss this morning's lessons and the adults were more than pleased to put their war-worries on the back burner for a while.

The youngsters were exceedingly well organised, Jim realised, with only a little surprise, watching a small group begin to clear up dishes and cutlery. Chore sections had been set up and all seemed to do their part willingly if not very expertly in some cases.

Emily and Thomas excused themselves. They were due for a lesson with the Lind medics to find out more about the diseases that affected their newfound allies and more importantly what natural medicinal resources the planet could provide. Laura and Francis elected to go with them although Jim was surprised at Francis's choice of occupation. He had never appeared to be the caring sort. He surmised that Laura's interest in the subject had something to do with it. When these two left, their ubiquitous shadows rose from their haunches and padded sedately after them.

CHAPTER 9

NORTHERN CONTINENT

James and Kath also sneaked away. One moment they were there, but when Jim looked again they had vanished and he decided they had gone to spend some time alone. Presumably Rozya and Matvei were doing much the same thing. He laid his head against a convenient tree. Despite its hardness, he felt his thoughts wandering and his eyes closing. Tired out with all his experiences his head lolled forward. He was sound asleep within minutes.

Larya found him there some time later. Sitting down at his side, she poked him with her left forepaw, hard. Jim woke with a start and looked up at her out of bleary eyes.

Her emotions, he sensed, were full to the brim of agitation. Something was seriously wrong, of that he was sure. A knot of apprehension started in his stomach. He sat up a little straighter, better to hear what she said.

"Jim. Get up. A message has arrived. You must come to the daga of Zanatei."

When they arrived Jim noticed that this daga was larger than the others. Inside he was pleased to find some tree stumps arranged as seating stools to one side. Good! He wouldn't need to stand. Zanatei, Afanasei and a strangely marked Lind were seated in front of them. They were waiting for Jim.

"Sit," requested Zanatei courteously. It was, after all, his daga.

When he was seated comfortably there was an uneasy silence, as if his hosts were trying to work out what to say. Perhaps they were, Jim had no way of telling. Larya sat beside her partner and prepared herself to listen to what Afanasei said. She was becoming even more agitated as the seconds ticked by and this increasing tenseness communicated itself to Jim. The knot in his stomach grew.

"Spies return," said Afanasei at last, "with news."

He paused.

"Larg come summer."

Jim took a deep breath and nodded. He had been expecting this. What he was not expecting was what Afanasei said next. It was only five words, but they were the last five words Jim was expecting to hear.

"There are other men south."

"Men? How did they get there?" he asked in surprise, rocking back on the stool.

"Same way as you did."

"Another ship?"

The Lind did not answer. They looked very worried. It was obvious that there was more to come.

"Jsei will tell," said Zanatei indicating the strange purple-marked Lind who stepped forward. Jim returned the look he gave him eye to eye. *From another pack, different colour pattern, wonder if all the packs are differentiated in this way?*

This was neither the time nor the place to investigate. He had far more important matters to worry about, like who exactly were these men?

Jsei started to talk rapidly in Lindish and Jim could only understand a word here and there. He shook his head sorrowfully at Afanasei.

"I don't understand him," he admitted. "You will have to translate."

"I know the tale," said Afanasei and began to talk in slow Standard. "They are bad men, they fight and kill."

"Fight and kill?" interrupted Jim, wondering why the complement of a colony ship would start killing and fighting each other. Then, with a sinking feeling in the pit of his stomach he began to realise what the Lind were trying to tell him. He grew hot and cold, all at once.

"The *Electra*! The prison ship!" he exclaimed. "Great stars above, she must have been thrown here by the storm as well. What abominable luck."

"Many men. No females," stated Afanasei.

That bore out Jim's assumption that it was the WCPS *Electra*. He racked his brains trying to remember what he knew about her. She had been a bigger ship than the *Argyll*. Why, she must have been carrying over twenty thousand convicts. He had never seen the manifests but with growing dismay he recollected a conversation in the petty officers' mess one evening a couple of years ago. There had been no female convicts on the transport. Apart from a few specialists and the families of the crew the entire complement on the ship had been male. No wonder the convicts were fighting amongst themselves. He wondered how the female survivors were coping. He concluded that they were probably having a very bad time.

He continued to sit, stunned, his thoughts racing, on the wooden seat, stunned and broodingly silent. Larya tried to comfort him but to no avail. He was too shocked to speak.

"Larg plan alliance with these men."

This was chilling news. It sounded as if they would not just have to contend with the Larg this coming summer but with an army of criminals as well. Jim was glad that the Lind had not called a general meeting. The human youngsters were scared to bits at the thought of the impending campaign against the Larg as it was. This news would seep into their courage with devastating results. This news would have to be broken gently. Let them get accustomed to the thought of war first. It did make warning the settlement that much more imperative. He would have to go soon.

"Do the Larg send spies to the north the same way as you do to the south?"

"Yes," said Larya. "Paddle on wood when water is deep in cold season." A picture of a Lind lying astride a large tree trunk impinged itself in Jim's mind. Jim had wondered how the Lind traversed the channel when tides were high and the smaller islands were submerged and not available to rest on. They used wood to give them buoyancy and paddled over the sea. A certain type of redwood floated exceedingly well over a long immersion time. Jim had tested it out for himself. Just how efficient was that? His estimation of the Lind went up another notch.

"These men know that there are humans in the north, the Larg will have told them," decided Jim.

Zanatei nodded. "Yes," he said simply, "we think so."

"Land is dry there," said Afanasei. "Settlement is good land for humans."

"Good arable land, of course, they would want such land for themselves. The south is mainly desert if I remember correctly. The only arable land is that bordering on the rivers?"

But Afanasei was not finished. He was the first of them to realise that it was not just the land that would draw these man north.

"They wish mates also."

There was the rub, Jim realised with increasing dismay. The convicts would covet the land and the women in the settlement, to start families of their own. They would massacre the men and take the women and younger children for their own, at least the strongest of them would. The humans in the north were outnumbered by at least four to one, not good odds in a fight. These were vicious men, sadists and murderers being well represented. The Larg would support them, of course they would. Help with this summer campaign and allies in the north for the future. If the south won, the Lind and the colonists would have to retreat further and further eastwards into Lind lands as the Larg and convict descendants prospered and multiplied.

It didn't bear thinking about. But he would have to think about it, they all would.

Jim rose to his feet. "Our plans have changed. Time is of the essence. I'll have to warn the settlement at once. Those remaining here when I go west will help teach you about how humans fight and what you must do."

He strode towards the entranceway then turned and issued one last comment. Unconsciously, it emerged from his mouth much like a command. "I'll brief Francis. Listen to him whilst I am away. He knows what he is talking about."

With that he exited the daga at a run, Larya following at his heels.

Zanatei and Afanasei looked at each other.

"A good man I think," said Zanatei, "a good choice as Susyc of our armies. True, he has never been inside a battle with the Larg but Larya will prepare him. You go with Jim to meet with the other humans?"

"Ceja," answered Afanasei. "I go. I respect Jim and believe he will be a good leader. He has a good grasp of tactics too I think. Jim to be Susyc for Lind and human?"

"I will send message back to Gtratha advising his appointment. I think they will be amenable."

Afanasei nodded, well satisfied with his pack-leader's answer.

Emily, Thomas, Laura and Francis were having a most unexpected and interesting afternoon ensconced with those Lind who dealt with healing wounds and diseases amongst the Lind.

They made the acquaintance of an inconspicuous red root with quite amazing medicinal properties. When rubbed on to injuries it not only numbed the wound but cleaned it as well. The Lind had used it for antiseptic and numbing properties in this way as long as any Lind could remember.

When Laura poked at it experimentally with her index finger she was flabbergasted by its effect. Her finger had become numb within a few seconds and stayed that way for quite some time, over two hours by her chrono.

"No side effects so far," she said.

"For Lind Smaha is good. Cleans and stops hurts," said the female Lind who was talking to them. Her name was Talya.

The discussion on various medicinal uses for various plants continued and Laura's finger began, slowly, to return to normal.

It was at this point in time that the unsuspecting Jim was entering Zanatei's daga.

Thomas and Francis soon became more than a little bored with all the medical talk and moved to the edge of the clearing. They began to discuss Thomas's experiments with spear and knife making.

"I can't get the fire hot enough," Thomas was explaining. "Quite a few implements end up so brittle that they are of no use to anyone. That's why I have to get back to the settlement, to find out how to do it properly."

Francis agreed with the boy. Steelwood was hard to mould into shape and needed the most careful handling.

"I think," he began.

Thomas never heard what Francis thought. At that moment a young Lind female hurtled into the clearing and made straight for Zhenya who was the senior healer on duty.

"Ltscta gin," she gasped.

Zhenya, the senior healer at domta Zanatei, stood up at once. Talya, the healer who had been talking to Laura and Francis approached the messenger, a questioning look in her eyes. They began to talk together rapidly in Lindish.

What she learnt from the young female made her drop her head in dismay. An injured youngling had suffered a serious wound and one that the healers for all their knowledge and experience would find nigh impossible to cure.

"Fell. Sharp. Blood," was all that the humans present managed to decipher and it was only Emily and Thomas who understood that it was believed that the situation was hopeless.

As the hurt ltscta arrived, lying precariously over its dam's back, both Laura and Emily moved closer. As the mother lowered herself so that Zhenya could examine her son, they both glimpsed the large gash along his side. It was bleeding profusely. They were surprised to see that the blood was not red like their own but a dull yellow colour.

"Needs closing," stated Laura in matter of fact tones. Later she was surprised to remember how calm and collected she was, and also that she had managed so remember so many Lindish words.

"Closing?" asked Talya. "How do 'closing'?"

With a start Laura realised that the Lind could not possibly know what she was talking about. The art of surgery was unknown to the Lind.

"I need the wound gel," was the only answer Talya got. Laura realised that if the bleeding was not stopped the lindling (as she privately called the ltscta) would die from shock and loss of blood. Turning to Francis who was standing on the sidelines of the drama wondering what he could possibly do to help, she added urgently, "First Aid Kit in my pack. Go get it."

He went on the word, running towards Tara and Kolyei's daga as fast as his legs could carry him.

"Get it numbed," ordered Laura, pointing towards the Smaha roots then trotting off to the nearby stream to wash her hands.

Talya acted without question and picked up with her mouth one of the roots carefully covered with a large leaf to protect the handler. She brought it over to the injured little one who was whimpering piteously, still lying atop its mother.

Emily took the root, still in its protective leaf covering, and gently rubbed it over the wound and its environs. The whimpering ceased within seconds, then Emily, remembering her first aid classes, applied pressure to the area where the bleeding was fastest.

She got an approving nod from Laura.

Francis crashed back into the clearing, carrying the small medical kit. Under Laura's directions he helped them lift the ltscta on to the ground. The mother stayed where she was, hopeful that these humans could do something, anything that would give her son a chance to live. She knew that a bad wound like this should mean death but these humans were acting as if they could save him.

"Someone hold him still," commanded Laura, concentrating hard as she rummaged in the bag for the gel. Emily and Francis bent down to still the patient. The mother looked anxious. What were they going to do?

Laura took a deep breath. Her hand was poised over the edge of the gaping wound. She looked closer. Good, there did not appear to be any damage to the internal organs. If she could stop the bleeding and close the wound the little one should survive. At least this wasn't the hot season; there weren't as many flies and buzzers around which were a prime cause of infection.

Emily bent over the wound. At Laura's nod, she held together the ragged edge of the blood vessel so that the woman would have both hands free to apply the gel. Thomas, standing beside the two Lind healers who were watching, started to look a bit green and soon excused himself. They could hear him being sick in the nearby bushes.

Once she was sure that the blood vessel was no longer spurting out blood, Laura began to close the outer wound. Centimetre by centimetre, she concentrated hard on each one. Sweat began to trickle down her spine and her back began to ache. The blood was still flowing, but was starting to ease off. She drew together the last section of skin at last, applied the gel and sat back. She was exhausted.

As she worked, Laura wondered what the medics would do when their supply of surgical gel was finished. The days of a fully equipped ship's sickbay with the ingredients and technological means to make the gel were over. She hoped that a gel substitute could be found using native ingredients, having no desire to have to use the emergency needles and thread contained in the kit.

The youngster lay there, half unconscious. His dam nudged him with her nose, urging him to move just a little, to prove to her that he was going to be all right. Thanks to the numbing Smaha root, he had felt no pain during Laura's ministrations.

Laura caught the mother's eye.

"It must be kept clean," she told her, "and he has to be kept warm and quiet."

The mother looked to Zhenya for a translation. There was a burst of Lindish.

Zhenya turned towards Laura. "Kseniya asks; will Akimei live?" she asked, partly in Lindish, partly in Standard.

"I hope so," replied the woman. "I'll look at him again tomorrow. Now he needs rest and warmth."

"Kseniya, Akimei, stay here," said Zhenya. "Is warm here."

Talya and Zhenya continued to watch Laura with amazed gratitude. As Laura went to the stream to wash the blood from her hands they bowed their heads with respect. Bad hurts would not now mean certain death for the victim. These humans could join up the edges and insides too and thus stop the loss of blood that caused the heart to stop. They could not wait to tell the others. As Laura returned to the group Zhenya approached her and crunched up her lips in what the Lind called a smile. Her sharp teeth gleamed whitely.

"Thank you," she said simply, but there was a deep and heartfelt gratitude in her voice. "More humans heal?"

"Yes," said Laura, returning smile for smile, "and they are much better than me at it too."

"You Ruza," the Lind replied.

Laura was not aware of what the word meant. Later, when it was explained to her, she was both proud and embarrassed about being considered a hero by the Lind. She had, by saving the little one, earned a permanent place in all Lind hearts; she had more than earned her membership in the pack, paired or not.

The humans left the clearing after some more pleasantries. Kseniya watched them go. Her tail thumped a large thank you.

As they passed through the domta, the word of their recent doings spread. Many came out of their dagas and watched them pass, bowing their heads in Laura's direction. Others watched silently. A warm feeling came over Laura. Francis, greatly daring, put his arm round her shoulder. Laura made no attempt to remove it.

"I must go find Ilyei," announced Emily. She looked shyly at Laura. "That was very brave, what you have just done."

Francis agreed with this sentiment wholeheartedly. When Laura said nothing in reply he answered for her. "Yes it was," he said, smiling down at her from his six and a half feet in height. "And I know for certain that she hasn't done anything like it before either."

"Really?" exclaimed the girl and then sped off in order to be the first to tell this piece of news to the others.

Francis and Laura walked on together. Francis did not speak; he was content just to have this opportunity to be alone with her at last. They did not notice when their two Lind shadows appeared from the undergrowth and padded after them. Their luxuriant tails were swishing fit to burst; Faddei and Asya had reached the culmination of their wait. The moment had come sooner than they had expected. When Laura and Francis returned to their compatriots they would be a couple yes, but they would also be part of an unbreakable foursome that would continue until they died.

After Jim had finished with Zanatei and Afanasei he went looking for Tara. He found her sitting beside what the children called 'the quiet pool', a place where they went when they needed a bit of solitude. She raised her head in welcome as he entered the glade, watching as Larya went to join Kolyei watching the darting pilli fish as they foraged in the reeds.

Jim sat down beside her.

"From what Larya is telling me you seem to be the repository of most of the secrets amongst your bunch."

"People tell me things," Tara answered. "I like to listen."

"Not just listening I hear," said Jim. "Kath says it was you who sorted out young Alan."

Tara shrugged. "I put myself in his shoes, it wasn't difficult. We both lost our families in the storm."

"I remember," said Jim, "I knew your father, did you know that? You're very like him. He always took the time to listen to people."

"I didn't do much listening to Alan," admitted Tara. "I talked to him, that's all. In fact, I shouted and scolded him more than once."

Jim laughed.

"Kath tells me too that it's usually you who puts a stop to any bickering between the others."

"I hate arguments," Tara said matter-of-factly.

"Even amongst the Lind," Jim continued.

"Who told you about that? Kath?"

"No, it was Larya. She says many of the young Lind want to talk to you, that they seek you out."

"They like to listen to my stories," she answered. "The Lind tell stories to each other all the time and Kolyei thinks it's a good idea and it's easy. Young Lind are like little children; they squabble if they're not kept in order. I just treat them like the little ones at the cabin with Mrs Mackie. I tell them to stop misbehaving or I'll not tell them any more stories. Me and Kolyei do quite a bit of ltsctasitting here."

"And Bill and Geoff?"

"They are typical boys, always trying to get one over each other and the others. They've settled down a bit now though."

Jim stared at this so very grown up twelve year old with bemusement.

"And when you are not keeping the peace, telling stories and babysitting, what does Tara do then?"

"Kolyei and I have fun," she answered in surprise. "We've explored for miles around, not that it's new to him, but we've visited the nearby packs around here and run down to the grasslands too. It's so exciting Jim."

"The redoubtable Kolyei," mused Jim with a smile, "and how is his Standard coming along?"

"Really good," Tara said with pride, "he's the best. We're both pretty much bi-whatever it is now."

"Bi-lingual?" suggested Jim.

"That's the one," Tara agreed. "Is it important?"

"It could be more important than you can imagine young lady. Do you think I could talk to Kolyei?"

"Now?"

"Oh, there's no rush," replied Jim easily, "it's just an idea I've got. It may not come to anything."

Tara remembered her manners.

"Would you care to come back to our daga and have something to drink?" she asked. "Yvonne's found a way to make fizzy berry juice. The jug she gave me is absolutely scrumptious."

"That's too good an invitation to miss," he said rising to his feet and giving her a helping hand up. "Where's Peter?"

"Gone fishing with Alan and Bill. If they catch enough it'll be fried fish for tea tonight and I love fried lungtrel."

"I'm rather fond of it myself," agreed Jim, correctly interpreting her name for the succulent multi-coloured river-fish.

Followed by Larya and Kolyei, they set out for the daga.

"Could you try to explain to me just how extensive are the Lind's telepathic abilities? Larya has tried but my command of Lindish isn't too good yet. Tell me how Kolyei does it."

Tara was delighted. There was little she liked better than to talk about how wonderful Kolyei was.

"I'll begin at the beginning shall I?" she looked up at him.

"That's usually best," he agreed.

Candy Rae

CHAPTER 10

SOUTHERN CONTINENT

For the crew and their families in the south these were surreal months, waiting as they were for the expected blow to fall. They worked hard to make the defences as impregnable as they could and practiced their newfound skills with sword, knife and bow. As the days passed, the tension grew. There was no sign of the convicts. A minority tried to hold on to the hope that the convicts would leave them alone, but deep inside their hearts knew that it was a wish, nothing more.

It was almost a relief when the mounted scouts reported that they had located a small advance party of convicts a day's march away.

"They'll be here by morning," Gerry announced to Camilla as he dismounted from his grey mare. She was still his favourite and he almost never rode any of the others.

So it had come at last. Camilla took a calming breath as she digested the news.

"Get the goats up top," she ordered, "then get the horses fed and ready to depart."

The man nodded. They had no time to waste if the party were to leave unobserved.

Gerry and Camilla had concocted the plan between them. Camilla knew they would not be able to hold out against the men. She had not forgotten the idea she had had when talking to Gerry about the other animals. There was no point in waiting until they were about to be overwhelmed before trying to break out. Those leaving would have to go now.

After a long and heated discussion amongst the adults in Fort, she had managed to persuade them that a few should leave before it was too late – those most at risk from the men.

Those most at risk - that was the moot point. The convicts' main incentives were twofold. The first was revenge, revenge for their incarceration and abandonment and the second was booty – they wanted the crew's goods and chattels, and that included the women. There was an obsessive fear amongst the families of what would happen to the women and adolescent girls.

Accordingly, a search was initiated for any young women with any experience of horsemanship. They had found four. Their experience was minimal, but all four had demonstrated an interest in the horses whilst aboard the *Electra* and two had even ridden them gently round the livestock section on occasion. These four began a crash course (crash being the operative word, they had taken many a tumble) of riding at speed then learnt how to do the same with a pillion-passenger behind them. These young women were already getting their mounts ready, together with Gerry (the only male in the party) and Martine, another of his horse handlers, a woman of thirty whose passion for horses rivalled his.

The six passengers that were to accompany them had been selected by lot. All non-crew females between the ages of thirteen and twenty-five had their names entered on the database and the handheld had randomly selected six. One of those selected later decided not to go; she was a young mother and refused to leave her children. Camilla had respected her wishes, made a mental note to find a replacement and had then promptly forgotten all about it. With a start she realised this and turning, made for the north wall where she knew Anne Howard was helping to finish hammering in the spikes that would form that part of the cliff's defence.

One of those on the list to leave was fourteen-year-old Jenny, Jessica Howard's best friend. Jenny's parents had insisted that she take this chance, although it had been a difficult decision for them, weighing the unknown hazards of this new world of theirs against the impending and more immediate to their eyes, hazard of the approaching men. Jenny herself was torn in two directions. One part of her wanted to remain with her parents and little brother Gavin, the other was absolutely terrified about what these men might do to her when they did break in.

Jessica Howard had resigned herself to remaining behind and facing whatever life dealt out, and that without the comfort of her best friend nearby. Anne Howard had not minced words when she explained, in detail, what was likely to happen. She had cut Jessica's hair short in an attempt to disguise her as a boy but they both knew that it would not fool the convicts for long.

Jenny and Jessica were preparing an interminable number of the spicy-flavoured whiteroots for the evening meal when their task was interrupted by seven shrill blasts of the whistle. They looked at each other; the moment they were dreading had arrived. The convicts had been sighted. Fort would be in a siege situation by nightfall.

"I have to go Jess," said Jenny quietly.

"I know," answered her friend, also quietly. "Got everything you need?"

"Packed and waiting." Jenny's eyes strayed over to the corner of the communal cook shop where her backpack lay; ready for when the call came.

"I'll come with you to the gateway."

Jenny nodded as she wiped her knife on a scrap of cloth and attached it to her belt. When Jessica would have thrown hers down regardless in her haste, she picked it up and slipped it into her friend's back pocket.

They stood staring at each other, committing to memory how each looked at this moment.

"I've got to report now," said Jenny at last and hefted her backpack on to her shoulders. "Mum, Dad and Gavin are meeting me at the gate."

Jenny's eyes were filling with tears as she realised that the coming goodbye might well be the last time she would ever see her parents and little brother. Her parents had been positive, saying that when the danger was passed they would all meet again, but Jenny was almost adult now and knew what was what. The two girls walked to the gateway arms round each other's shoulders. Neither was sure who was comforting whom.

At the assembly point, the six horses were saddled and waiting, their girths being tightened. Their handlers were giving them a light feed before departure and were attaching the saddlebags to the saddle cinches. Jenny's parents were waiting, her little brother in his father's arms. Jessica whispered goodbye to Jenny and stepped back.

All was noise and organised chaos. There were shouts of command as the last items were manhandled within the barricades. As soon as the horses left, the gateway aperture would be sealed shut. The goats complained loudly as they were herded into Fort. Sentries took up their duty stations. The barricades were being given a final check-over by the work-parties still outside before they too came in.

Jessica stood watching, a small forlorn figure amongst all the chaos, then she heard someone calling her name and turned. It was her mother approaching, frantically calling her name as she tried to be heard over the tumult. Cherry and Joseph were following close behind. Anne Howard carried a backpack in her arms. As she reached her eldest, she was talking rapidly.

"Camilla spoke to me. Nell Morrison is not going and you are next on the list. You have to leave now."

"I can't," stuttered Jessica, a dazed expression on her face, "I can't leave you. Cherry and Joseph need me. You need me."

Shocked, she stood unresisting as Anne lifted the pack on to her back.

"You must. I've packed some food and a change of clothing."

Jessica looked into her mother's eyes. They were anguished; this moment was purgatory for her.

"Some personal things as well, holograms of the family, to remember us by. Don't worry about Cherry and Joseph, it's unlikely the men will harm the children. It's you that's in the greatest danger. Got your knife?"

Jessica nodded, too dazed to say more than, "I love you."

Taking her daughter in her arms, Anne murmured into her ears, "I love you too darling. You don't know how much. Now be a brave girl and say goodbye to Cherry and Joseph." Jessica's throat swelled with emotion and her eyes filled with yet more tears and she bent down and opened her arms to receive their embraces. They leapt into her arms, crying noisily but there was no time for more. The horses were ready, they moved around restlessly, their hooves sounded loud on the hard turf.

They had to go before the convict advance party spotted them and gave chase.

The four Howards clung to each other for one final moment, then Jessica became aware of hoof steps approaching and the jangle of a bit moving restlessly in the approaching horse's mouth.

"Ready Jessica?" said Gerry encouragingly, "you get to come with me. Ever been in the saddle before?"

Jessica shook her head. This was all happening too fast for her to take in.

The horse-handler looked at her with sympathy but he couldn't give the girl any more time. They had to be off.

"I'll mount then someone'll give you a leg up. Hold on to my waist tight. We'll try and go a little slower to begin with. Keep to a gentle canter until you get used to the motion. But we must go *now*."

He mounted and Jessica was thrown up behind him. She wrapped her arms round his waist as he had ordered.

As parents, siblings and those who could watched, waving hard to give them all a good send off, the six horses turned and walked towards and out of the gateway. Calls of 'I love you and good luck' followed them as they left. When Jessica looked back she saw her mother standing bravely beside Cherry and Joseph. The three were waving and smiling bright smiles.

As the last tail swished out of the opening, work gangs at once began to drag the large wooden gate into place, in preparation to sealing in all those who remained.

Anne Howard and her depleted family walked away from the gate, the children crying inconsolably at losing their big sister. Anne was no whit behind them. She did not think she would see Jessica again. She hoped that she had made the right decision, sending her into the great unknown expanse of the planet like this but what other choice did she have?

There was a resounding crash as the beam fell into place in the aperture at the gateway. There would be just time for the native glue-like substance to harden before the evening. The work gang swarmed over it, fitting the subsidiary defences into place. There was much hammering of nails into wood as they attached the frames. Before many hours passed, there would be little indication that it had once been an entrance, although the tell-tale tracks leading up to it would give it away if the convicts looked carefully enough. Camilla ran here, there and everywhere trying to convince herself that she had done all she could as she wondered what the next day would bring.

Murdoch's advance party observed Gerry leaving with his party in the distance and noted the direction they were headed. The sergeant in charge sent some of his men back to report, then following orders, dug in and waited for the main army to arrive. He did not have any orders to give chase.

The sentries could see no sign of the southern sergeant and his men.

"Waiting for the rest to catch up," said a grim Camilla, "Gerry did say that he spotted only a few. They know we're not going anywhere. They'll no doubt send scouting parties out when it gets dark."

"Do you think they'll want to parley?" asked Shelley Lambert, her closest friend, at her side as usual.

Camilla nodded. "Should think so, not that any terms they might offer will be acceptable."

"Terms?"

"Something like 'hand over the women and we'll let the rest go'," she said with a wry grin at the younger woman.

Shelley's eyes widened. "I'd rather die," she stated vehemently.

Camilla's soft hazel eyes rested on her. "Yes, I know, but you and I have no children to care for. It's different for the mothers. We're crew and are duty-bound to defend them to the last. We can't expect husbands and fathers to tamely hand over their womenfolk either. But it's a no-win situation I'm afraid."

Shelley stared at her.

"There are only losers," Camilla continued, "these men want what we've got, the supplies we salvaged and us."

"What?"

"Yes, they are stuck on this planet for good, just as we are. They look to the future and for that they need – females. Without us, all that will happen is that they will grow old then die. Without women they have no future."

Camilla was quite correct in her analysis of the situation. A half-day's march to the south, Murdoch called a halt so that he could regroup and make his final plans. The regiments that would form the attacking force had been selected. The reconnaissance parties, led by Duchesne, had already departed. On his report when he returned would hinge their plan of attack.

To the regiments not selected, would fall the task of protecting the non-combatants (and themselves) at their present location. As Murdoch intended a protracted stay here, earthworks were being constructed round the perimeter. He did not want any unpleasant surprises on his return from the fight. He could not forget the large wolves.

Those who had taken part in the abortive rebellion were no longer with them. Thinking that it might well keep the gigantic wolves off their backs at least for a while, Murdoch had come up with a most ingenious solution. He ordered that they should be staked out on the ground and left. He was not to know until much later, but the Larg had been very appreciative of this gesture and had enjoyed themselves hugely at the helpless men's expense.

As a reward for his services, Murdoch made a gift of Gunnarsson to Cracov, now promoted to the rank of colonel with a small regiment of his own. The ex-colonel had not enjoyed the experience overmuch and had been heard screaming for a merciful end well before his agonising death.

"Final plans when Duchesne returns," announced Murdoch late that night, in conclave with the colonels of the eight selected fighting regiments (one of Duchesne's lieutenants was attending in his place). "You eight will form the attack force. I do however have some primary and overriding rules. You will make sure that all your men obey them to the letter. I will punish any who disobey most thoroughly *and* their superior officers."

That got their attention. Gunnarsson's final agonised screeches were fresh in their minds.

"First rule, no women are to die. They must be captured alive and I don't care how many of you men are killed or wounded getting them. I expect that some of them will form part of the defence force. That doesn't matter. They must be captured alive."

He gazed round at the colonels.

"Do you understand?"

"Yes," they all repeated dutifully.

"Second rule, no children are to be hurt or killed. Treat them kindly. Remember that some of them will have lost parents during the fight. Do you understand that?"

The men nodded, although some looked surprised.

"Third rule, no women are to be raped or molested. I don't want to be choosing a female from a flock of soiled goods, and neither do you I am sure. Fourth rule, no stealing, nobody is to take any goods or equipment for themselves. That's it, simple. Any questions?"

"Are all the men to be killed at once?" Baker asked.

"Any surviving guards may be considered an exception. Capture them to play with later if you want. I don't care one way or the other."

Cracov smiled. He liked that idea. He would like to get his hands on some of the guards. He made a mental note to remind the colonels about it.

"What if any of our men disobey your orders?"

"Same fate as Gunnarsson," replied Murdoch with a smile.

"That should stop them," said Cocteau, present at the meeting by virtue of his position as head of the non-combatants. "I'll get those with medical training not already assigned to regiments up to you in the morning. They are ready and waiting."

Murdoch nodded. Efficiency was Cocteau's raison d'être. Such efficiency and dedication should be rewarded.

To Cocteau's gratification, Murdoch promptly gave him a field promotion to the rank of colonel.

"You are in charge back here. Keep vigilant at all times, don't let these beasts White keeps rambling on about creep up on you unawares."

Cocteau laughed; there was no way he would allow that to happen and his face was one delighted smile; a colonel at last, just like the others.

"I'll keep you a good woman as a reward," Murdoch announced. Cocteau's grin grew even wider.

"Young and pretty?" he ventured, greatly daring.

"Don't ask much do you?" answered Murdoch with wry humour. "I suppose you want a pretty one?"

Cocteau laughed dutifully at Murdoch's wit but deemed it wise not to push the General any further.

The other colonels laughed too and Sam Baker winked at Cocteau. On the whole Cocteau was a popular choice to take command back here but they did not envy him his task. Keeping around ten thousand or so ex-convicts safe and relatively content in the encampment would stretch Cocteau's abilities to the limit.

"All agreed then?" asked Murdoch. It was a rhetorical question; he neither expected nor required a reply. "Right, all we have to do is wait for Duchesne's return. He'll be back tonight. We move off in the morning."

Duchesne returned some hours later. It was still light. In these warm summer days, the sun did not drop beyond the horizon until very late. The colonel used a long thin stick to mark out a rough map of Fort and its environs in the sand. The other colonels and Murdoch listened intently, their lives, and those of their men, depended on it.

"They're on top of a rocky crag," Duchesne stated, pointing to it with the stick. "All but the southern approach is protected by almost sheer cliffs, although my men are positive that it can be climbed, but with difficulty. We'll lose a few. We caught sight of some defenders at the top. Most of their people will be stationed at the southern approach, behind the barricades they have built. I have to admit that they have done a good job in the time available. Their commander is a good man. The barricades look to be strong and sturdy and will be hard to breach."

"One regiment at each of the cliff faces to keep them occupied and the other five attack the south?" asked Mahler, colonel of one of the selected fighting regiments.

"That would be my advice," answered Duchesne. "I think too that they might have laser-rifles with them as well. How many I have no idea. My senior sergeant has sharp eyes and is sure he saw at least one glinting in the sunlight."

"They could do a lot of damage," observed Smith. "Take out our best men before they can even get close to the barricades."

Murdoch nodded. "We'll use two of the other regiments. They can go in first. Tell them they're now part of our elite force. Even if we lose all of them to the rifles it'll be worth it. Once the rifle batteries are exhausted your regiments will be able to advance without too much trouble."

All agreed perforce. None wanted to sacrifice themselves and their men when there were others that could die in their place.

Murdoch rose to his feet. "Conference over. I for one intend to get some shut-eye. Tomorrow will be a very busy, yet momentous day."

The colonels saluted smartly and dispersed. Murdoch turned to Cracov. "Ask Smith to tell Taylor and Unwin to see me first thing in the morning." He smiled a dark and brooding smile. This was his chance to rid himself of another two thorns in his flesh. Taylor and Unwin had become expendable and all in a good cause. Cracov suspected the two of having been involved in Gunnarsson's plot but was unable to prove anything because they had not made any overt move. This lack of courage represented by their failure to take part in the earlier revolt made Murdoch despise them all the more.

"Tell Smith to tell them that we need their help in the attack. He's not to explain exactly what this involvement is. Perhaps some of the defences are stronger than expected? They'll feel honoured to be asked. Offer them women."

As Cracov turned to do his master's bidding, Murdoch stopped him.

"One more thing. I'll add a refinement. Tell Duchesne to keep Taylor and Unwin's lot separated from the other eight fighting regiments in the morning. Don't want to spoil the surprise by someone babbling out what we have planned for them."

Cracov nodded. He understood. He would pass on the messages, together with a few of his own concerning the guards.

CHAPTER 11

SOUTHERN CONTINENT

Inside Fort, the defenders were as ready as they could be. It was a difficult night. Men cuddled their wives and girlfriends as if they would never let them go and watched their children sleep. Anne Howard sat on her bedroll; Cherry and Joseph snuggled in beside her. She wondered how her husband and eldest daughter were getting on and was making plans as to how to protect her two youngest when, not if, the convicts broke in.

The next day was a beautiful one. The sun rose above the horizon, bringing with it the promise of clear and sunny weather. It hadn't rained for weeks and the rivers and streams were lower than when they had landed. Summer was almost over.

Parents began to lead their children into the large cave designated as their haven. A large sign was tacked above the entrance, with 'Children and pregnant woman inside', in large black letters. On purpose, no guards were stationed outside, thereby emphasising the inmates' non-combatant status.

Anne Howard went with them. With the departure of the two Jays and the other teenage girls, Anne and another three mothers had been relieved of their positions on the barricades and sent into the cave. Camilla had decided it would be better to have more adults there in order to help keep the children calm and quiet. The four women selected were neither large nor strong. They would be of more use away from the fighting.

As Anne took five-year-old Gavin from his mother's arms, she promised her that she would look after him as if he were her own flesh and blood. Lysbet Quirke stumbled away and Anne cuddled the little boy close. He did not understand the full import of what was happening and smiled at her trustingly, before squirming out of her arms to go and play with the other youngsters in the play corner.

Carla, a year mate of Jessica's and daughter of Johannes Pederson, the other ship's officer with Anne's husband in the desert, moved closer. A tall, blonde girl, she was remarkably attractive, a true descendent of her northern European ancestry. Her mother Ulla was part of the team manning the western cliff face, determined to do her bit to protect them all. A crack shot, she was the only woman to be trusted with one of the scarce laser-rifles, the only rifle allocated to her part of the defences. They were needed more on the southern barricade where the main attack was expected.

The inhabitants of Fort realised that the main convict army had arrived during the hour before noon. Murdoch wanted his men in place as soon as possible. A grim-faced Camilla, standing at the southern barricade, sword in her belt, watched their approach. As the dust cloud drew closer the defenders were able to see that the army was split into organised phalanxes. A mile away from Fort, three blocks of men peeled away, marching to their attack positions at the base of the cliffs.

"They look well organised," said Shelley. "Surprising."

"I'm not surprised," said Camilla. "Someone has taken charge and sorted them out. They're certainly not an undisciplined rabble, whatever they might have been when we deserted them back at the ship."

"We had no choice Camilla, you know that. No point feeling sorry for them now. At least we've had more time with those we love."

Camilla did not answer her. Tears were close.

They were distracted from their inner contemplations by a call from one of the sentries.

"Some of them moving towards us."

A bunch of five men were approaching. One carried a stout pole, on to which was attached a large piece of white cloth.

"They want a parley," said Camilla. She strode towards the

sentries. "Let them get a bit nearer," she ordered, "not too near though, just within shouting distance."

The five stopped of their own accord some fifteen metres from the barricade and Camilla took a deep breath as she showed herself above the top level.

"No further," she shouted down.

Duchesne raised his arm in assent and stood waiting.

"Well?" Camilla prompted.

"I wish to speak with your commanding officer."

"I am she," Camilla shouted back.

He looked surprised at that. He had expected to see Captain Howard and he wondered what had happened to him. However, it didn't really matter at the end of the day who was in command. "I bring a message from General Murdoch. I have his terms to offer you for surrender."

"What are these terms?" asked Camilla in a loud voice.

"You will throw down your arms then you will make a breach in this barricade wide enough for two men to pass. All your men and boys over the age of fifteen will walk out towards us in single file, with their hands held high over their heads. I am also enjoined to inform you that your men will be free to go wherever they want as long as they remain at least fifty miles distant from this spot. As a prelude to their freedom, they will be taken downriver where they will be confined for a maximum of three days before being set free. All women and children must remain behind. That is all."

"And quite enough too," said Camilla under her breath. "Just as we expected as well; almost word for word. I don't believe for a minute that they will allow the men to live either."

There were assenting murmurs from those who could hear her.

"How do I know that you will stand by these terms?" Camilla countered.

"You have General Murdoch's word of honour."

There were a number of derisive laughs from the defenders. One of the ex-guards, who had spent many duty watches on Murdoch's block back on the ship, sidled up to Camilla and whispered urgently in her ear.

"I know him. He was Head prisoner in Block A and a killer. You can't trust him."

Turning towards Duchesne, she shouted down. "And the women and children?"

"We will care for them," he answered. "They will come to no harm."

Camilla snorted expressively as the faces of the defenders went flat at the words. Both sexes were well aware of what would happen to them if they were taken prisoner. As one, they opened their mouths. The word "NEVER" resounded throughout the hills. Those in the cave flinched as the echoes of that shout reverberated in their ears. The younger children began to whimper.

Anne Howard held the children clustered round her as tightly as she could manage. Some began to cry, their faces white in the dim light.

"So be it," called back Duchesne as he walked away. The defenders watched as the five moved back down the hill.

"The die is cast," said Camilla. She hefted her sword aloft in defiance. There was a great cheer of support from the defenders clustered around her.

The next hour passed slowly. The attacking force stood silently in the heat. Then those atop the barricades saw two large groups of men, numbering some five hundred each, being moved into position at the foot of the slope and in front of the groups already positioned.

"Make every shot count," commanded Camilla to those with the laser-rifles.

Taylor and Unwin's men began to march slowly and with some semblance of order up the incline. More ominously, from the defenders point of view, behind them marched the ordered massed ranks of another two groups, Mahler and Smith's regiments had she but known it. They marched with parade-ground precision. Camilla's eyes narrowed. These were the ones, the men to be feared.

A clever man, this so-called General Murdoch, she thought. He either knows or suspects that we have some laser-rifles. He's going to use the ones in front as so much cannon fodder, to make us use the rifles until their power is exhausted. Not that we have any choice.

The laser-rifles fired, cutting swathes of death and destruction in the foremost ranks of men. Their advance slowed then came to a stop. The shocked men stood gazing at their dead comrades for about thirty seconds before the two hundred survivors about-turned and fled the battlefield, down the hill towards the regiments marching up. The defenders watched open-mouthed as the front ranks, instead of coming to a halt and letting these men through, drew their swords on a shouted command. They heard another order and the fleeing survivors simply disappeared as they were cut down and trampled over. Mahler and Smith's men continued their resolute climb up the hill. The batteries of the laser-rifles were by now almost completely exhausted.

They did continue to fire spasmodically for another few minutes and did inflict casualties, but the laser-blasts were neither as long nor were they as powerful as at the start. The rifles began to stutter and then to die. The riflemen, not wanting them to fall into the convicts' hands, smashed them to smithereens against the barricades and drew their knives and swords.

These convicts are well armed. Camilla watched as they drew closer. *These are not wooden clubs and spears.* Sunlight glinted on their weapons, testimony to the fact that they were made from metal torn from the *Electra's* hull. The front ranks had makeshift shields as well.

The defenders had made their own weapons in much the same way, by cannibalising the vehicles to make swords, knives and spear-points. Some crewmembers had experimented with the hardwood that grew in abundance around them and a few had made bows and arrows although Camilla had little faith in their abilities to actually hit anybody. The two hundred guards smacked the stunner batons into the palms of their hands. They could be very effective if they got the chance to use them.

The attackers reached the thirty metre markers and arrows flashed by above her head. Surprisingly some even found their mark. Then it was twenty. The only sounds she could hear were the sergeants' chants as they kept their men in line.

Camilla glanced at Shelley, standing white-faced by her side. The young woman looked at her steadfastly yet her expression reeked of hopelessness. Camilla leant towards her and gave her a quick peck on the cheek. There was no time for more.

There was another shouted command and Smith and Mahler's men started their attack run. When they reached the barricades they began to scramble over. The defenders waited patiently, then, as the first heads appeared above the edge of the parapet, brought their weapons down. The heads disappeared but plenty more took their places. Squads of attackers began hacking away at the barricades at the bottom then, unaccountably, the convicts fell back.

The defenders could hear the moans of the dying at the bottom of the walls. They had not escaped unscathed themselves. Sixteen were dead and more were wounded. The youngsters on first aid duty ran to help. None of the more lightly injured could be persuaded to leave the barricades.

One of the youngsters, his face smeared with blood, looked at Camilla hysterically. "Have they gone," he screamed. "Have we beaten them off?"

His face blanched as another roar sounded from outside. The noise began again. As Camilla leant over the top beam to send one attacker into eternity with a large dunt on the back of his head with her sword and watched him fall (unconscious or dead, she didn't care which), her nose twitched.

"What is that smell?" she yelled over the tumult.

"Burning," shouted a disembodied voice from somewhere. "They've set light to the barricades."

If only we'd time to build them of stone. The smell was growing stronger with each breath she took. "Get water," Camilla cried out, "pour it over the fires."

But there was not enough water in the vats for so many fires and they were soon empty. She could tell that the attackers were feeding the fires too. A stench of oil was mixed in with the smell of burning wood. The smoke grew thicker and caught in everyone's throats. The defenders began to cough, so did the convicts. She could hear spluttering and shouting as the attackers regrouped. The two front regiments formed up again in two ranks but this time they waited for the fires to do their work.

The barricade platform was becoming increasingly hot underfoot as the fires took hold. Then, one section erupted in flames ten feet high. Those atop this section scrambled to the comparative safety of the ground. Camilla stamped her foot. The beams shook slightly. This section didn't appear to be as steady as it should be either. She called a warning to all within earshot as she jumped away from the crumbling structure. She was just in time. The foundations had been irrevocably weakened and a further six metres of the barricade disappeared in a cloud of smoke and hot ash.

This was what Mahler and Smith were waiting for. These two regiments had taken the brunt of the attack so far, if one discounted the sacrifice of Taylor and Unwin's men, and were more than eager to make an end to the fight.

Baker's regiment and two others formed up behind them. They would follow them in.

"Steady," called Smith as one or two men started to edge forward ahead of the others, "and remember the orders. No damage to the women and children."

He waved to Mahler who was red-faced with excitement and raring to go. With a yell, the colonel began to run towards the breach, his men following at his heels.

Camilla was dragging herself to her feet as he burst through the smoke and flames. As he bore down on her, she raised her sword in defence against the downswing. The blades met with a clang and Camilla felt the shock of the impact right down her arm. It felt numb. Mahler raised his sword for a second swing and then his eyes widened as he realised that his opponent was a woman. He hesitated for one fatal moment and Camilla took her chance. Death in her eyes, she swung her sword at his neck. The man's head and body parted company. She stared mesmerised as the head bounced heavily to the ground. Then Mahler's men surrounded her. One advanced towards her.

I've had a good life. Camilla tightened her grip on her sword. The man grinned, daring her to use it against him. She sensed other men closing in on her. If she did not try to break out at once they would seize her without too much trouble. She rushed at the approaching man, closing in on him before his comrades had a chance to react. The man raised his own weapon to counter her sword thrust and the blades met with a loud clash. As Camilla tried to force her sword towards him, the man stabbed at her with the wicked bladed knife held in his other hand, but he was hampered by the fact that she was a woman so was intending to wound rather than kill. He misjudged his thrust, or perhaps Camilla moved just that infinitesimal amount. The knife penetrated her side, slid through her rib cage and entered her lung. As her lifeblood pumped on to the sandy soil she dropped to her knees.

Although the man, dropping his sword in his haste, rushed to her side and began a vain attempt to stop the bleeding, she was dead within two minutes. Her killer's comrades began to melt away, intending to disassociate themselves from this forbidden killing of a woman as fast as they could. The man, futilely trying to mop up the blood, stayed where he was. Too many people had seen what he had done for him to try to hide. He had not meant to kill the woman but that would mean nothing to General Murdoch. Mahler's sergeant, knowing well that the man's life was forfeit, decided to get it over with quickly and stepped forward. He grasped his victim's hair atop his head and pulled back, exposing the throat. With his knife, he severed the artery. Better the quick death by a friend's hand than one of General Murdoch's sadistic punishments.

Rigid with fear, half hidden by the smoke, Shelley was watching. When Camilla slumped to the ground, she knew that her friend was either dead or dying. Jumping up, she ran past the circle of men, evading the arms that stretched out to stop her. Running for all she was worth, she headed towards the eastern cliff. With a cry of anguish and loss, she ran as hard as she could and leapt off the edge. Her body gained momentum as it fell, thumping against and dislodging some unsuspecting attackers labouring up the cliff face. Her body was discovered some days later, wedged in a cleft some distance from the bottom of the base.

Topside, all was in chaos. Mayhem and death were the order of the day. The youths they did, if possible, spare, not knowing exactly how Murdoch would react to the death of a teenager, but some of the youngsters fought as desperately as their parents. Mindful of Murdoch's orders, the men were careful to capture the women alive. Most fought valiantly, side by side with their menfolk, but were likewise overwhelmed, but not before they did a fair bit of damage. Angered by the casualties, the regiments did not even attempt to keep any of the men alive. One by one they fell, hacked to death by squads of angry convicts.

There was one attempted rape. Infuriated at the death of his best friend, one attacker decided to wreak his own type of vengeance and to the stars with Murdoch's orders. He lunged at one woman, who was standing, shocked, disarmed, tears pouring down her face, as she stared at what was left of her husband lying in the bloody dirt at her feet. The woman began to scream.

There were loud shouts and a scuffle. She felt the man being lifted off her, kicking and struggling as he fought with his captors. Colonel Baker had seen what was happening and brought a squad of his men to her rescue. She scrambled to her feet.

"You all right?" Baker asked her in a gruff voice.

She nodded mutely and watched as her attacker was tied up then dragged away.

"He will be punished," promised Baker. Turning to his men, he ordered her to be taken towards the other survivors being herded to an area not far from the cave that held the children.

The sounds of fighting stopped and the regiments viewed the field of their victory.

Some of the women were hurt, but only a few had suffered actual wounds that bled. They were mostly bruised, battered and in deep shock at the events of the last hours and with the death of their men. The surviving lads were shoved in beside them; those that could took their weeping mothers in their arms in an attempt to comfort them.

Carefully, Duchesne stood up. He had been wounded in the thigh, although not seriously. Murdoch had not yet arrived to oversee the aftermath of victory. He would be here soon.

Smith ran up to him. "Get some guards round these women and boys," he urged. "I'm off to find the other women and children."

Duchesne nodded and began to shout out commands. The surviving sergeants were doing the same. In a surprisingly short time, the regiments were back in formation and the medics were starting to tend the wounded.

After due consideration, Murdoch declined to deal with the women and children that day. His men were tired and weary now that the fight was over. There were wounds to tend and the bodies to clear away. The two regiments assigned clean up duty began the laborious process of removing the dead for burning and burial.

Duchesne, unaccountably solicitous of the effect this clean up process would have on the women and young lads if they were forced to watch the bodies of their husbands and fathers being dragged away, ordered his men to remove any weapons from them and then to put them into the cave that held the other women and children. After a guard was set, there they could be left until morning. The convicts listened to the sound of wailing and crying as the news of their defeat was recounted in grim and anguished detail.

With Camilla dead, there was no obvious person available to take command. Anne Howard did what she could, but was fighting a losing battle against shock, grief and loss. As she eventually lay down to grab a few hours sleep she couldn't help but worry about what further disasters tomorrow would bring.

The winning officers were discussing that very thing.

"A successful operation," said Smith, "though I've lost about a quarter of my men."

"Same here," said Baker. "Need replacements if I'm to keep the regiment up to full strength."

Murdoch provided the solution in typical fashion. "Reallocate Mahler's survivors," he decreed, "*He* won't be needing them."

They all laughed.

The General turned to Smith. "What have we got then?"

"I estimate that there are about three hundred and twenty women and perhaps the same number of children," Smith replied. "Quite a few youths but less older girls than I might have expected."

"My scouts have seen some tracks," Colonel Brentwood informed them from the edge of the circle of officers, "and the advance scouts reported seeing a small group fleeing east yesterday."

Everyone's face swivelled towards him.

"What sort of tracks?" demanded Sam Baker, "and are you sure of the direction they took?"

"Definitely going east. One of my men said he thought they belonged to horses. Perhaps these girls were spirited away before we got here?"

"We'll find out," promised Murdoch, "but tomorrow we get what we have out of the cave and have a decent look at them all."

Turning to Duchesne, he added, "I want you to take charge of all the boys over the age of twelve. Break them into our way of thinking, re-educate them. You know what I mean?"

Duchesne did and the men dispersed to get some rest. Whether it was well deserved of not depended on one's point of view. Certainly those in the cave would not have thought so.

The women, children and young teenagers inside the cave waited for dawn. They had been surprised that they had not been molested when the men took over but knew that this was a temporary respite. They began to ready themselves for the ordeals to come. Outwardly they were calm, for the sake of the children. There would be no point in trying to hide in the back recesses of the cave; they would only be dragged outside when the men came to check. They decided to exit with their heads held high. The mothers hoped that the men would have cleared away the bodies of their men; it was not a sight for children to see their brothers and fathers lying dead in the dust.

The call came, as expected, not long after dawn.

"Time to come out now ladies. Families stay together. No harm will come to you and I promise that you will not be separated from your children."

This was unexpected; the women had assumed that separation would be the order of the day, their children taken away. They looked at each other. No one wanted to be the first. Anne Howard took a deep breath. As the Captain's lady, it would be she and her children that must set the example. She began to walk towards the exit, holding tight to Cherry and Joseph's hands.

When she emerged into the sunlight, she saw little evidence of yesterday's battle. Three regiments were formed in rank in a large horseshoe round the open space in front of her. To one side and on rough tables, food and drink lay waiting. In the very centre of the space stood a blocky, greying man, hands on hips and smiling. She shivered. There was menace and a certain satisfaction in that smile. Another large man stood at his side, sword at the ready, eyes alight for any trouble. Although the fighting women and lads had been roughly searched the previous evening, Cracov was well aware that they might have some sharp implements secreted away. He was in no mind to be stabbed from behind by a revengeful female.

Anne came to a halt a few paces from Murdoch who stared at her. He recognised her from the holos he had looked at in Captain Howard's cabin back on the ship. He had liked what he had seen then and liked what he saw even more now. Her short curly auburn hair was tousled certainly and the woman was none too clean, there were no bathing facilities within the cave, but the eyes that met his were steadfast and only faintly tinged with fear. His plans to choose a young maiden took an immediate about-turn. He wanted this woman.

She wasn't young; in her mid-thirties he judged, but the curly-headed children at her side were proof that she was fertile. Perhaps she was the better option. She would know how to please a man and the existence of the children would ensure that she continued to do so. Murdoch had made his choice though he decided to wait a while before he made the announcement.

All he did therefore was instruct her to lead the line of women and children towards the registration table and then to eat the meal he had ordered. A squad of men entered the cave at that point to make sure that no one was hiding inside. When they exited after their search, they lined up at the entrance, thus completing the circle of men.

The registration process took time. The captives ate little of the prepared repast. This gentle treatment was unsettling. After this they were led away to bathe, the only indignity being a thorough search of their persons by medical personnel.

Once they were escorted back into the circle however, their fears were realised with a vengeance. They were lined up in ranks of fifteen, although the children remained at their mothers' sides.

The surviving fighting colonels appeared at that point, with Cocteau and Cracov behind them. They stood in front of the lines of anxious women, talking. Murdoch then arrived, carrying a list in his hand and placed himself beside them. He gave the list to Duchesne, who nodded and stepped forward.

"When your name is called, step forward and form up in front of the lines," he ordered. The names he called out were all male and belonged to boys aged eleven years and over. The boys on his list were soon standing in a tight bunch in front of him. Some were crying, others stood bravely.

"You boys will go now with my sergeant." One of his sergeants, a grizzled veteran of the last conflict to occur on Earth, stepped out into the circle. The lads hesitated.

Duchesne encouraged them with a smile. "Go with this man. He will look after you."

With a final look back at their mothers, the boys obeyed. Sobs were heard from the depleted ranks.

Then the colonels (and Cracov) began to walk up and down the lines, choosing the female of their choice. Cocteau made straight for Carla Pederson.

"Your name?" he asked politely. "Age?"

The girl answered in a trembling voice.

"Fifteen?" he mused reflectively. She was a bit young, but Murdoch had said that those girls aged fifteen and over were to be considered available. He put his hand on Carla's shoulder and began to pull her away from her anguished mother, who promptly burst into tears. Carla let herself be led away, too stunned over what was happening to even try to resist. This scene was replayed as the other colonels made their choices.

To everyone's surprise, Cracov chose a buxom ex-crewmember who was almost as large as he. She did not look too happy about the situation. If those chosen had children, they accompanied their mother; this part of Murdoch's bargain was being kept. As they passed the registration desk, the clerks made small annotations on their lists.

Then Murdoch spoke and his words chilled those remaining to the bone.

"The rest of you will place yourselves at the disposal of my men. You will be treated fairly and may keep your children with you as long as you perform your duties satisfactorily. Any trouble and you will never see them again."

Some of the women fell to their knees in shock. The children started to cry.

"There is one exception," shouted Murdoch over the weeping and wailing. He pointed to Anne, who unlike the majority, was standing silently, her arms around her remaining children. "You and your children will come with me. You have just been promoted from Captain's wife to General's woman."

Anne looked at him, stunned. *So he has worked out who I am?* Mindful of his recent threat, she stepped forward, three measured paces, Cherry and Joseph at her heels.

"I have always wanted a son and daughter," Murdoch encouraged. Cherry flinched.

Oh Peter, where are you? Please forgive me but I've got to do this, for our children's sake.

Murdoch stood waiting for her, right foot tapping impatiently, a habit he had when he believed his patience was being tried. With a sigh of resignation Anne lifted her head high and walked the remaining distance to his side. He took her hand in his, smiled and led her away. He was content.

Now would come the period of consolidation as the men settled into their new way of life. Winter would soon be upon them, they would be busy. True, there were difficult issues to resolve such as not enough women. He would send out hunters to catch those who had got away and there was the problem of these huge carnivorous wolves, but he had made a start.

Cocteau, a shocked Carla held wrist-tight in his hand, moved back into the circle. Anne could hear him issuing orders as to the immediate allocation of the women as she, Cherry and Joseph left to begin their new lives.

CHAPTER 12

SOUTHERN CONTINENT

When the horses and their riders trotted down the hill leading away from Fort the day before it was overrun, they turned sharp north, skirting the edge of the animal corral, using the upturned ground to hide their tracks. Gerry pushed them along as fast as he dared, wanting to be well away before nightfall and any possible pursuit.

Only Gerry and Camilla knew their eventual destination. That way, if caught, nobody could be forced to tell what they didn't know. The escapees rode, silently for the most part, each alone with his or her thoughts. All the young women and girls with him, except for Martine, had left families behind; all were here without them for the first time in their lives. It was dark when Gerry called a halt for the night beside a small river tributary that bubbled merrily at them as they led their tired mounts to water. They had food in the saddlebags, enough for both man and beast for four days, after this they would make slower time as they foraged for food. Luckily, the horses appeared to enjoy the native vegetation and greedily nosed around for the most succulent stalks of the long desert grass once they had emptied their nosebags.

Once the adolescents had eaten, Gerry called them over to where he and Martine were sitting. In the clear light of the full moon, he took out the map that Camilla had thrust into his hands as he was leaving.

"No point in me keeping it," she had said. "We aren't going anywhere and I don't want to make a present of it to the convicts." Gerry had reluctantly agreed with this and had slipped it into the folds of his belt-pouch. He knew that he would not see her again, realising that the defenders were too few to keep up effective resistance for long. Some of the girls had realised this as well and it was with long and anxious faces that they settled down to hear him speak.

"Right," he started, "we follow the edge of the foothills round for approximately three days. The land here is well wooded and should give us plenty of cover; it should hide our tracks. Then we break north at a suitable place and head for the coast. So that you know, we are making for a group of islands about eighty miles east of where we should hit the coastline. Our eventual destination is one of the larger islands on the chain of islands that reaches towards the northern continent. The map is detailed enough to tell us that there is water there."

"Fresh water?" interrupted one of the girls.

"Yes. There are abundant hardwood trees and other foliage on the island and we all know that they require fresh water to survive. There will be roots and fruit there as well. We won't starve."

"Protein?"

"Fish in the sea and these ubiquitous rodents," was the reply.

One or two of the girls sighed with relief.

"What about those at Fort?" a tall blond girl asked. "When will we know when it is safe to return?"

Gerry looked at his questioner, not knowing how to answer, well aware that there was little chance of return for any of them.

What can I do for her? What can I say to her? "Someone from Fort will come and tell us," he lied. "They know where we are going."

She nodded, apparently content. Others, the more thoughtful, looked unconvinced, Jessica Howard especially. She had inherited her father's ability to see beyond the trappings and go straight to the root of the matter. She opened her mouth to speak but Gerry raised his hand in a gesture to stop her. The old saying that she can't see the wood for the trees most definitely did not apply to the Captain's eldest daughter.

She subsided, but didn't look happy about it.

Martine, seeing this, decided to get them all off the subject. "Let's get some kip," she suggested with false brightness. "Things will seem better in the morning."

The following morning there were many moans and groans as muscles started to ache in protest at the girls' unaccustomed exercise. Not having taken part in the riding practice sessions, Jessica especially found it extremely difficult even to remain in a standing position for any length of time. The abused muscles in her thighs and calves trembled with every tentative step she took. She had absolutely no idea how she was going to get into the saddle, never mind how to actually stay there.

Gerry was sympathetic. He berated those inclined to laugh at her misfortunes, informing them in no uncertain terms that she had been thrown a-saddleback without as much as a by-your-leave. They at least had had time for their muscles to grow at least partly accustomed to the exercise.

They tidied their campsite and departed, wondering all the time what was happening back at Fort. Perhaps it was as well that they did not know. By common consent nobody discussed the matter, confining themselves to sporadic and short conversations on the subjects of breakfast and their aches and pains. They did not travel so fast the second day. Gerry did not want to push the horses too hard, especially the two pregnant mares, and they still had a long way to go. Every few hours they stopped and took a short rest and Gerry made them walk beside their mounts for at least part of the afternoon.

A small party of Larg was watching. They however, were obeying Aoalvaldr's orders and stayed well out of sight.

It was almost dark when Gerry first became consciously aware of the uneasiness that had been building up inside him. The woods were far too still. Their footsteps sounded very loud in the silence. His grey mare also seemed uneasy, her ears flickered up and down and she tongued her bit nervously. He became aware that her back was stiffening under him and she began to take short jerky steps. His nose caught the whiff of a totally unexpected smell, of roasting meat. No, that couldn't be; or could it? Silently, he motioned for those behind him to stop; not wanting the sounds of jingling tack to warn of their approach. He dismounted and signalled Martine to get the girls under cover. He himself began to walk through the trees, heading towards the smell, fully expecting to see a crowd of marauding convicts sitting round their campfire, as yet unaware of their presence.

As he drew near, the smell of roasting meat made his mouth water, and he heard the sound of low male voices that then unaccountably became silent. He frowned thoughtfully. He recognised none at this distance, he would have to get closer. As he approached the fire glow he realised, much to his surprise, that there were only four men lying round the fire pit. Gerry unslung his laser-rifle from his shoulder. As he set the firing mechanism to ready, he felt it's quiet thrum up his arm. He dropped to his knees and began to creep closer to the fire. The men seemed to be unaware of his approach, laughing and joking quietly as they watched their meal cook. Hunkering down behind a prickly bush, this part of the hills was infested with these annoying plants, he aimed the rifle at the group. One burst would be enough to incapacitate them. He hoped, as he braced the butt against his shoulder, that the men had no friends skulking nearby. A laser-rifle let off an intense blaze of blue light when it fired, especially noticeable in the dark.

His finger was poised over the firing trigger when the men began to speak again. Gerry, being much closer this time, could even discern what they were saying. The name Camilla was clearly identifiable and then they began to talk about a locator. His finger relaxed and he brought the rifle down from his shoulder, set it to standby and laid it on the ground. There was no way the convicts could possibly have known about the locator. These men were not convicts. It must be the away-team who had been missing these many weeks. He thought for a moment, wondering the best way to approach them. If they were startled he might find himself being fired on before he had a chance to identify himself. Caution would be his best policy.

The men started to talk quietly again. Remaining hidden behind the bush, Gerry called out to them.

"Hello there."

The four were instantly on the alert, two dropping to the ground, the other two picking up their own rifles and kneeling in their firing positions, beginning to sweep the area.

"Who is that?" demanded one. "Come out and show yourselves or I'll fire a complete circle. Be sure I'll get you."

"It's Gerry from the ship. I was the livestock-handler. Is that you Captain Howard? Commander Todd sent a group of us away when the convicts appeared at Fort."

The away-team looked at each other uncertainly.

"Fort?" queried Angus. "What is Fort?"

"Commander Todd must have decided to stand and fight," vouchsafed Tom.

Johannes Pederson raised himself slightly from the ground and looked at Peter Howard. "I know that voice. I think he's telling the truth. I'm sure that *is* Gerry Russell."

Gerry relaxed, ever so slightly.

"I'm coming out," he announced, stood up and began to walk towards them, hands held high above his head.

Peter and the others could hardly believe what their eyes were telling them. Gerry was almost the last person they had expected to see out in the wilds like this.

"Great stars, it *is* you," the Captain announced, as Gerry got close enough for him to make out his features. "Are you alone?"

"The rest are with Martine not far away," said Gerry with a small smile.

"How many?" asked Peter, still rather bemused at these night-time shenanigans. "Where are the rest of the crew? Why did Camilla send you off? What has happened? The locator stopped working the day before yesterday."

"Disabled," was Gerry's answer.

Johannes asked the next question, the one uppermost on his mind. "Where are Ulla and Carla?"

"Safe when I last saw them," answered Gerry evasively. Looking at the four, he continued, forestalling further questions. "Explanations can wait. Let's get the rest of my party in and then we can decide what's to be done."

"I'll come with you," said Peter and began to walk towards him. Gerry answered with a nod, saying in tones that only he could hear, "Jessica is with me but not Carla. Both she and Ulla had to remain at Fort. So did your wife. There was no way we could get them all away."

That piece of information took the Captain aback. The situation must have been bad indeed for Anne to decide to send Jessica away like this.

He stepped back. "On second thoughts Gerry, you go and bring them in, I'll wait here. You armed?"

"Rifle is in the bushes over there," answered Gerry pointing in the direction of the prickly bush.

"Get it," Peter ordered Angus.

Gerry left on his errand, intent on bringing Martine and the girls into the relative safety of the campsite as soon as may be. Angus searched the bushes carefully and on finding the rifle brought it back and placed it with the other two beside the fire, within easy reach.

Whilst the men waited, Peter took the opportunity to tell Johannes that his daughter was not with Gerry's group.

"But that means that they are still at that fort place," Johannes groaned, the blood draining from his face. "I must go to them."

"You can't," said Peter, "not before we know what has happened." He half-pushed the older man into a sitting position, reasoning that he'd better sit down before he fell.

A female voice came from the darkness beyond the campsite.

"We're coming in," it announced. There were sounds of approaching feet from the darkness. A young whirlwind sped ahead of the others and into the campsite. It was Jessica, desperate to see her father. With a squeal of delight she fell into his arms.

"Dad," she cried. "It has been so awful. The convicts are going to take over Fort. Mum sent me away."

Johannes sat up. "I must go to Ulla and Carla." He lunged for one of the rifles, picked it up and started to run out of the campsite.

"Stop him," shouted Gerry. "Stop him someone."

It was young Tom who stopped the engineer and wrestled him to the ground. Johannes fought back like a man demented, but eventually he calmed down. He sat on the ground in a heap, sobbing disconsolately.

Peter disentangled himself from his daughter's embrace and she stood, still and shocked, watching Johannes Pederson cry. She had never seen a grown-up cry before. He went over and sat beside him. "Johannes, there's nothing you can do at the moment," he said. "Fort is probably being attacked as we speak. We have a responsibility to those who are here with us now. You'll not be helping your family if you run off and get yourself killed. We can work out what we can do to help them once we find ourselves somewhere safe to hide out and find out what the situation is back there. Until then we must bide our time." It was the complete Captain talking now and Johannes began to pay attention. He stopped struggling. His shoulders sagged and he sat there, the tears running in rivulets down his cheeks.

Jessica tried to comfort him. "They were safe when we left."

"But what is happening to them now?" he sobbed in a voice stricken with broken emotion. "Can you answer me that?"

Jessica could not. She had come to realise just what a perilous situation her mother had tried to save her from. She was not to find out until much later that it was already too late. Their loved ones had already been incarcerated in the cave and their captors were celebrating their victory.

They stayed silent for a while, lost in thought.

"We have to go on," announced Gerry at last. "If they overcome Fort they will send search parties out to look for us once they realise that some have got away." He and Martine drew closer to Peter, Angus and Tom. "I mean, eleven women. Too great a prize to be ignored. I believe that we should carry through Camilla's original plan, make for the coast then the island chain. If we can escape capture that far we have a good chance to reach one of the larger islands. We can hide there, at least for a while."

"How would we get across?" asked Tom.

"It's fairly shallow water. We can swim. Make simple rafts if we have the time. The horses can and will swim beside us."

Peter nodded. It appeared feasible. They could not stay here. It was too close to Fort.

"We all need some rest first," he decided. "I vote we stay here until tomorrow evening. Get some provisions together. I also think we should travel by night and rest by day, safer from prying eyes."

"Agreed," said Martine. "Now I will get the girls settled if you men will get the horses tethered." She turned away with a small smile and headed towards the bunch of girls.

"Yes," said Peter, "and you Gerry can tell us the full story whilst we are doing just that." The four walked towards the horses.

Johannes said nothing. He sat huddled by the fire pit, too wrapped in his own misery to care.

In the end, it was decided not to spend the entire night and following day resting. In the middle of the night the youngsters were woken, protesting feebly, and after a scratch meal they took to the trail again. Now that there were sixteen humans in the party they were too many to ride so they walked. At dawn they rested, the horses grazing contentedly nearby.

All had a spell of guard duty and when not on duty, most slept restlessly, imaginations running riot at what was happening at Fort. When they set out that evening, their packs would be tied to the horses. With no heavy luggage to carry it was hoped that they would make better time. After all, any pursuit would come on foot and without benefit of a pack train.

Peter was pleased to see that there was even some laughter and chatter as they readied themselves for their first full night's march. They filled their water canisters from the nearby stream. Water was not a problem. This part of the continent was comparatively lush when compared with the desert further south. The succulent water roots would be gathered whilst they walked. They had a distinct advantage over the other edibles growing beside the streams as they were as nice to eat cold as hot and could even be consumed raw. There was still a scarcity of larger game around. The small rodents that infested the area were time consuming to catch, living as they did in burrows and they did not have the time to wait for traps to be sprung.

As they walked, Johannes Pederson plodded along at their rear, taking little interest in anything and speaking to no one. Peter Howard was no whit less worried about Anne and the younger children as was Johannes about Ulla and Carla. He himself was holding himself together for everyone's sake but it was taking a great deal of effort on his part. He thought constantly about Anne, Cherry and Joseph.

The party covered a considerable distance each night. They had no idea if they were being followed or not. They reached the coast at the end of their twelfth night and turned east. They hoped to be able to reach the islands without any trouble.

The woods along the continent's coastline were different from those further south. Instead of desert palms the woods were composed primarily of the soft and hardwood trees that existed in the north, although they were not aware of this. The party, instead of negotiating the woodlands, found that they made far better time keeping to the beaches, and the journey was a gentle one, or at least it would have been if their situation had not been so fraught with tension and worry, but as the days passed, they began to relax. There was still no sign of pursuit and Peter was beginning to hope that the convicts were so involved with their new lives back in the hills that they would decide to leave them alone. So apart from their worries about their loved ones, a holiday atmosphere was becoming predominant, days filled with late summer sunshine and cool breezes from the sea.

One cool morning after their night's march they even decided to hold a barbecue on the beach. Enthusiastically, wood for a small fire was gathered and enough sea fish were caught to provide at least two each. Once the fire was lit they attempted to poke a stick through the gutted fish and roast them on the fire. There was great hilarity as one by one the fish fell off the sticks and into the fire. Jenny scorched her hand slightly digging her half-cooked meal out of the embers. They ate every speck of delicious flesh from the bones. Even the baked roots had never tasted so good.

"Tell you what I do miss," said Jessica, biting into one.

"What?" asked Martine.

"Bread," she answered. "Warm, straight from the ship ovens… crunchy crusted bread."

"Me too," answered Martine, also munching her way through a root, "but more than that."

"What?"

"Pickled onions," was her unexpected reply. "I used to be addicted to them."

They all laughed. They were beginning to forget about their fugitive status.

In fact, their pursuers had found their trail. The men had set out two days after Fort had been overrun.

Candy Rae

CHAPTER 13

SOUTHERN CONTINENT

It was Colonel Bryan Brentwood who led the chase. Anxious to make a name for himself and as a means to ingratiate himself with Murdoch, he had volunteered to be the one to run them to earth and bring the female escapees back.

At Fort, it had not taken them long to find out that a small party had escaped and who they were. Careful questioning of the children had been enough.

Murdoch had given the task to Brentwood for one simple reason; Brentwood was the only one eager to go. To the colonel he promised his choice of one of the girls.

Brentwood had thirteen men with him, all armed with the stunner batons salvaged from Fort and whatever other weapons they felt most comfortable with. Most carried swords and knives. All were aware that there might be large predatory wolves in the vicinity so it was a wary group of men that had set out from Fort on their hunt for the fugitives. They made good time and due to the lack of recent rain, the tracks were comparatively easy to find and even easier to follow. Unlike those they were trailing, they travelled by day.

"They're definitely heading for the coast Colonel," his sergeant informed him. "Wonder where exactly they are making for or if they have a destination planned at all."

Brentwood shrugged his shoulders. "Doesn't matter Sergeant," he said. "Probably not. All we have to do is catch them before they get to wherever they're aiming for." He looked around at the cooking area and frowned irritably. "Now, where's that breakfast? I'm starving!"

"Just coming now, sir," answered the man as one of the cooks approached, carrying a steaming beaker in one hand and a bowl in the other.

"More of these never-ending roots I suppose," grumbled Brentwood, all but snatching the bowl out of the cook's hand.

The cook shook his head. He looked pleased with himself.

"No sir!" he announced triumphantly. "Caught two of those bird things in me trap last night. Managed to cook them this morning. Be right tasty if prepared right, and I have prepared them right, I can assure you."

Brentwood was slightly mollified by this and his face brightened. "Taste good?" he asked.

"Yes sir, try a wee taste, beautifully tender they are."

Brentwood was not entirely convinced by this and smelled the steaming bowl gingerly.

"Sure smells good," ventured the sergeant with a smile. "Any left in the pot for me?"

The cook nodded. A small wiry man in his late forties, the cook lived for his craft. The twelve years incarcerated in the *Electra's* convict blocks had frustrated him almost to the point of madness. With the limited ingredients on offer, he had done his best and it was a good best; his fellow inmates had loved him. When they landed on the planet he had soon realised the potential. He could now cook freely. Always an innovator with taste and dishes he was perfectly suited to carve out a niche on this new world. The planet was a chef's idyll.

He had volunteered to accompany Brentwood on this mission for two reasons. First of all, Brentwood liked good food and was prepared to reward those who pleased him. The chef had an idea that if Brentwood grew more appreciative of his talents he might keep him with him on a permanent basis. Secondly, the chef did not like Cocteau (from whose block he came) and certainly did not like living down in the encampment. Brentwood was his ticket up to the more salubrious kitchens of Fort.

Brentwood took a bite and his face lit up with a smile. "This is good," he enthused. "You're as good a cook as you say. Perhaps you should be thinking about what delicacies you might prepare for when we catch up with the girls."

The cook nodded again, a happy smile on his face. He left his two superiors, lost in thought. Perhaps spicy white-root casserole, or baked roots with fruit?

"Good man that," said Brentwood, munching through his meal. "Try and keep him with the regiment if you can."

The sergeant looked at him and decided that his superior wanted a chat. He signalled to the cook to bring his own portion over to him.

"I'll do my best sir, but I do believe his great ambition has always been to open a restaurant of all things. Seems he was a pretty top class chef back on Earth. He worked in the best places."

"Bribe him if you have to, I want to keep him," ordered Brentwood. "Let's eat."

The pair walked over to a convenient tree trunk and sat down.

"I have plans for the future," began Brentwood, munching hungrily.

The sergeant looked over as if to say something but at Brentwood's gesture, continued to eat.

"Yes, plans for the future and once they come to fruition, I will look after my friends." Looking directly at the sergeant, he added, "And those who helped me."

The sergeant took the point at once. "You can count on me, sir," he said. "I'm your man."

Brentwood smiled. "Good. I think we should have a long private talk before we are very much older about what we both want out of all this. I for one don't intend to be a soldier forever. There are other ways in which one can gain power and wealth."

"And women, sir?"

"You are perfectly correct, women too - I wonder."

"Sir?"

"Women may well be the answer to all our prayers. Sergeant, have you ever considered a career in the brothel industry?"

"Never thought much about it, sir. You?"

"Not until now," said Brentwood considering the point, "but there is a distinct shortage of women around. A shortage of certain commodities drives the price up. I think we need to examine the possibilities here. Do you agree?"

"Yes, sir."

Their partnership was born.

It was just an idea at the moment, but as soon as the two arrived back at Fort they would develop this idea and carry it through. Incidentally, Brentwood was quite correct in his evaluation; the business became a very lucrative one.

The cook however, did not end up in Fort's kitchens. Disgusted at the treatment of the captured women when they returned to Fort he would disassociate himself from Bryan Brentwood and strike out on his own.

Some miles away, Jessica was talking to her father. "It's amazing really," she said. "So much has happened to us. It's like something out of a horrible story."

"Perhaps you should write one," suggested Peter with a slight smile. "I would very much like to read it."

"Really?"

He nodded.

"Okay then, I jolly well will. Only thing is Dad, stories should have happy endings and I don't see any happy ending in ours."

"Don't be disheartened. No matter what has happened, your mother will survive and I am sure she is more than capable of ensuring that Cherry and Joseph are okay."

"But what if these men have taken over Fort?" she asked apprehensively. "How will Mum manage then?"

"I am more than confident in her abilities Jessica," he replied seriously. "It's early days as well, remember. I am sure we will be able to find and rescue them in the future. I am absolutely positive that you will see them again."

"Promise?"

"I promise."

They were walking together, close by the water's edge. The travellers were growing accustomed to the mauvy-yellow sea vegetation and the dry spicy odours were becoming familiar. The sea was different although these differences were far subtler. Like the Earth they had left behind, it was blue, but there were flecks of yellow and red to be seen in the water.

Jessica took her father's hand in her own. "We'll be at the islands soon," she announced, "then we can swim across and we will be safe."

Peter nodded; he also wanted to get to the islands without delay. He decided to speak to Gerry and pick up their pace a little. For the last couple of nights he had had the strange feeling that they were being watched and felt what could only be described as a peculiar probing sensation within his mind. He wondered if any of the others were experiencing anything too.

When asked, Gerry agreed they should go faster. The horses appeared nervous of something, although he didn't know what. Although there was some grumbling at this dictat, it was pleasant to march at the water's edge in the moonlight and the sixteen travellers increased their nightly mileage by a full half and reached the beach next to the first island on schedule.

With Johannes Pederson uncommunicative, Peter found in Gerry someone he could talk to. The two men were forming a close friendship. It was during one of their talks that Peter began to speak about their future plans.

"Our priority is to get to the island," he said, "make an area habitable enough so that we can last out the winter."

Gerry agreed with him. "Come spring the mares will foal," he said. "We need somewhere suitable for that."

Peter grinned. Like Camilla before him, he was beginning to realise just what these animals meant to the man.

"Then," Peter added, "I am going back to Fort to rescue Anne, Ulla and the children. Tom and Angus want to go too. If we can get any others we will try for them as well."

"Is that wise?" asked Gerry. "If Camilla was right and the prime motive for the prisoners' attack was to get their hands on the women they are likely to be well guarded."

Peter nodded. "I know, but I am, *was* their Captain. I can't just abandon them."

Gerry thought about what he said. "I'm coming too. After all, I do know my way about Fort. There's even a secret way in."

Peter grasped Gerry's arm in silent thanks.

Once they had reached the beachy outcrop nearest to the first island, they had made their way back into the trees and camped next to a small fresh-water stream. It was still dark and Peter decreed that they should rest for what was left of the night and attempt to cross to the first island in the morning.

The horses did not seem to be nervous and restless in any way but the watch duties were not relaxed. Jessica and Martine took first stint.

"Storm coming," announced Gerry as he passed them on his way to his bedroll. "Keep a close eye on the horses. Don't want them spooked and have to go chasing after them. Call me if you have any trouble."

"It's as calm as anything," protested Jessica.

Gerry looked at her. "Believe me lass; there'll be a storm by morning. When you go to bed put the groundsheet on top of you to keep out the rain."

Jessica laughed. When their watch was over and they woke Tom and Jenny to do their turn, there was still no sign of any impending storm. However, not long before dawn, an ominous roll of thunder woke them as the promised storm struck. Torrential rain lashed down and the sleepers hurried to gather up their bedding before it got completely soaked. Gerry refrained from telling Jenny 'I told you so'. The bitter wind cut through their garments like a knife.

Sheltering below an overhanging rock, they could manage to fend off the worst of the rain if they positioned themselves carefully, but the party could only watch as the storm grew in intensity. There would be no jaunt to the first island that day, nor if they had known it, the day after. If possible, the storm grew worse with each passing hour and showed little sign of abating. It was sixteen wet and disgruntled people who made the best of the situation before seeking the scant comfort of wet bedrolls on their second night at the campsite. The horses were not much better off, tethered forlornly as they were a short distance away. They looked reproachfully at Gerry whenever he came close, the grey mare even going as far as nipping him painfully on the arm when he ventured a consoling pat.

When they woke the next morning, the storm was easing then died away altogether, leaving devastation behind. Trees lay uprooted where they had fallen. The sun shone bravely over all but could do little to heat their wet, cold and tired bodies.

Brentwood's men had pressed on regardless through the worst of the weather and were rapidly approaching the campsite. They had followed the trail up to the coast but lost it temporarily when their feet hit the sandy beach. However, the deeper telltale tracks and droppings left behind by the horses had not been washed away entirely by the tides. Above the tidemark, hoof prints were clearly visible in the muddy sand beside a small tarn by which the horses had been watered. Brentwood, after some investigation had concluded that the fugitives had turned east. When the storm struck, he drove his men on and on. The first clear morning after the storm his scouts were closing in.

At the campsite and after a hurried breakfast, Gerry took the mares with him to a small area some distance away and behind some trees where there was some succulent grass growing to enable them to graze before they set out. Those left behind at the campsite busied themselves getting the float trees ready to aid them during the swim. The trunks littered the ground and it was an easy matter to drag them to the waterline; they were extremely lightweight, so that one person could easily carry a fairly large chunk of wood. By mid morning all was ready. They could leave.

Peter sent Jenny and Jessica to fetch Gerry and the horses. They carried a meal for the three of them and the instruction to stay with the man and help him lead the horses to the beach once they had finished eating.

Jessica smiled at her father as she took Gerry's pack from his hands; her own pack was already on her shoulders.

Peter bent down slightly and gave her a quick kiss on her forehead. He felt in his pocket and drew out a small silo-backed notebook. "Take this," he said, "it's my notebook … don't know why but I want you to take it with you for now."

Jessica looked at him with a stir of unease but all she said was, "I love you Dad."

"And I you mouse," was his tender answer, "now scoot!"

The two girls were helping Gerry ready the mares when he stopped what he was doing as his ears caught some odd noises from where the others were getting ready.

"What was that?" he asked sharply, half to himself.

"What?" asked Jessica, looking at him over one of the mare's back. She was tightening the saddle cinches, it having been decided that the animals could manage the swim with their tack still on.

"Thought I heard something." He checked that his two mares were still securely tethered and looked at the girls. "Wait here. I'm going to check," he ordered. "Keep out of sight. Make sure the horses stay quiet as well."

He began to move quietly towards where they had left the others. Listening hard, his lips thinned and his eyes narrowed as he tried to discern just what exactly the sounds meant.

He then heard loud voices, loud *male* voices, and then high-pitched screams from the girls. *What is that? Is it the sounds of metal clashing on metal?* Gerry groaned. It could only mean one thing and one thing only. They had been followed and their pursuers had found them. He turned and sped back towards the two Jays who were standing quiet and shocked where he had left them.

"I think…" he began.

"The convicts have found us!" gasped Jenny in consternation, understanding in that instant the meaning behind his white face. "What can we do?"

"You two will stay right here," Gerry commanded in a loud whisper. "Remain out of sight. I'm going to see if there is anything I can do."

They heard the whine of a laser-rifle and a scream.

Jessica made a move as if she was going to rush across to the campsite. Jenny, white-faced, grasped her friend's arm to stop her.

"Jessica," said Gerry urgently. "Listen to me. There is nothing you can do at the moment. At least your Dad knows that you are safely away." Turning to Jenny, as being the more level headed at this point he ordered, "Keep her here. If I am not personally back here within an hour, you still got working chronos?"

Jenny nodded mutely.

"If I'm not back by then you wait until it's clear and then take the horses and swim for the first island yourselves."

"I can't," bubbled Jessica. "I can't leave Dad now that I've just found him again."

The sounds from the campsite were getting louder; they could all hear shouting and screaming and the crash of bodies moving around in the undergrowth.

Gerry grabbed her hand. "Jessica," he implored, "you must. Don't let these men catch you. I'll go help your Dad and the others and I *will* find you again."

With that, Gerry left them and keeping a low profile reached the campsite unobserved.

They had given a good account of themselves. Although taken by surprise, the adults had used their laser-rifles to good effect. Four of their attackers were dead or dying, one almost split in two by the force of the blast. Another two were badly wounded and unlikely to make it through the night. Brentwood had been exceedingly clever; he and his sergeant had both managed to grab an unsuspecting girl and, placing a knife at her throat, demanded the surrender of Peter and his men. The men and Martine had dropped their weapons at once.

Gerry lay unseen behind a nearby bush, not three feet away from the body of Johannes Pederson. He could do nothing. His face became more and more anguished as he watched the convicts punch and kick at the remaining away-team. Once they tired of this sport and the three men lay groaning in the sandy soil, Brentwood cold-bloodedly ordered his men to slit their throats.

The girls in the campsite screamed louder than before. Gerry continued to watch, sick at heart. He now had first hand experience of what these men were capable of and of what had, in all probability, been the fate of the male defenders back at Fort. They would be dead by now, the same as the Captain and his team.

Gerry didn't stay around for long. He realised the men might well start counting soon, and then work out that some of the females they had been hunting for were missing. He had to go back to Jenny and Jessica.

Gerry was correct. Brentwood did start to count, but the horse-master had forgotten something important, the existence of the away-team. Brentwood was looking for twelve people, not sixteen. Although he was surprised to find four men amongst the party, he wrongly presumed that they had set out with the woman and the girls, sent out with them for protective purposes. He was surprised to find that the total number within the campsite was thirteen, one too many by his calculations, but Martine was quick on the uptake, telling him that one of their horses had carried three people, it being a sturdy beast and well able to carry the load. Luckily two of the teenage girls standing quivering with the rest were very slight of build and Brentwood accepted her explanation at face value. None of the girls ever revealed his mistake in the months and years ahead.

Brentwood did not even order a search of the vicinity. Asked as to the whereabouts of the horses, Martine told him that they had been spooked by the storm, pulled their tethers and run away, she knew not where. To her surprise, he didn't question that either.

At that point, Gerry turned away and crawled back to the two girls and his beloved mares, intent on getting them away as fast as possible.

Brentwood and his remaining men rested at the campsite until the following morning and then headed back to Fort.

Obeying Murdoch's orders to the letter, none of the youngsters were in any way molested or ill-treated; the men were kind to them in their own way.

Brentwood got his wish. Returning with his prizes to Fort, he was admitted to Murdoch's inner circle, along with Baker, Duchesne, Smith and Cocteau. He also got his choice of one of the young girls, an ethereal fifteen-year-old blonde beauty, whom he had earmarked as his own during the journey back to Fort.

Gerry did manage to return to Jenny and Jessica unobserved. After Jessica had cried piteously in his arms on hearing about the death of her father, they waited until the men left then Gerry returned to the campsite and buried Peter Howard, Johannes, Angus and Tom. The convict dead he did not bury; merely dragging them into the nearby bushes so that Jessica would not have to look at their bodies when she came to say her final goodbyes.

Deciding that they would definitely be safer on the islands, there was no way of knowing if the convicts would eventually put two and two together and come hunting for them again, they swam the horses to the first island the next day, rested, then island-hopped until they reached one of the largest. On the western edge of this island the three of them made their base, tending to the mares. The pregnant duo were rounding out nicely and coming to terms with their losses.

When winter came in earnest, they were still there, snug and warm in a coastal cave, waiting for spring and an uncertain future.

Gerry was making private plans to return south, remembering well his conversation with his late captain concerning the trials and tribulations his wife and children were almost certainly experiencing in the hands of their captors. He felt deeply that he had to try but was torn two ways. He felt he could not leave Jenny and Jessica to fend for themselves on the island and spent many sleepless nights wondering what was the best option.

He was confident in his abilities to get back to Fort, although he could only guess at what he might find when he got there. A general plan was nonetheless forming in his mind. Perhaps he could slip in unnoticed and blend in with the convicts somehow, then bide his time waiting for the chance to spirit Anne, Ulla and the children away.

Of course, he could not do it at once, but in the spring, it might just be possible to leave Jenny and Jessica on the island for a while whilst he made the attempt. He said nothing to the two girls.

As the uneventful days passed, he became more and more resolved to get back to Fort and see if he could at least save the children, although at that point he did not know what one man could do against so many. He could and would however, give it his best shot.

Candy Rae

CHAPTER 14

NORTHERN CONTINENT

When Jim Cranston, Larya and the other six set out on their journey from domta Zanatei back to the settlement, winter was well advanced. With the cold winds had appeared rain and snow, although the latter had not yet reached the lower levels of the hills. Jim had been desperate to leave before this but had been detained by the need to be fully briefed about Lind culture, society and numbers, together with the preparation of a detailed exposé of what the Lind expected to happen come summer, so that he could brief the colonists.

The four humans were mounted; permanent permission for this had been received from the Eldas of the Gtratha, the rulers of Lind. The riders had a small lightweight pack strapped to their backs containing only the necessities required for the journey. Thomas and Jim were openly armed, belted swords at their side. All carried sharp knives within easy reach.

When Tara asked if she might also carry a sword (she thought she might feel safer with it, at least she could scare potential attackers away), it was her Kolyei who said an unequivocal no.

: *You have only twelve summers. You must have fourteen to fight* :

And that was that.

Francis was remaining behind and Jim had placed him in charge of the human contingent. He stood slightly in front of the others who gathered to say goodbye and he called out to Jim as the party left.

"We'll be fine Jim. I know what is to be done, never fear. Asya will send a message if there are any problems. She has good rapport with your Larya."

Jim had been more than a little surprised, but very pleased to learn that Asya was Larya's daughter and that such family ties augmented telepathic abilities. On reflection he realised that the relationship between Larya and Asya made Francis some sort of relative, but Jim only got more and more confused when he tried to work out just how exactly he was related to the ex-rating.

Many Lind could send thoughts and images, and even actual words to each other over long distances. The Larg could not. Their telepathic abilities were limited to a few miles and that for the most able only. Jim intended to make advantageous use of this unexpected bonus. Francis had the important task, among others, of working out just how they could use this skill in a battle situation. He would also begin to work with the Lind to develop cavalry fighting techniques for vadeln-pairs together with explaining to the Lind how humans fought with edged weapons so that the Lind would be prepared if the *Electra* convicts did ally with their enemies the Larg. The Lindars would need to learn how to adjust their tactics for fighting with humans and against them. He was in for a busy time of it although he fully intended to involve James, Kath, Bill, Geoff and the others. Laura would continue to pursue her chosen profession as healer.

As Jim rode Larya out of the clearing he wondered again at the change in the man. From a dangerous troublemaker aboard the *Argyll*, Francis was transformed into his right-hand man and Jim was pleased and not a little surprised to realise that he had not a single qualm about leaving him here to see through a multitude of important tasks. Jim trusted Francis and that was all that mattered.

The journey back to the settlement was an uncomfortable one. The wind cut through their outer garments like hundreds of sharpened knives. The rain fell incessantly, soaking through their clothes during the first day and never stopping long enough for them to dry out. The Lind coat was far better suited to the inclement weather but the constant aroma of wet fur was not at all pleasant. It made for a miserable journey. They stopped to rest each sundown and spent damp nights squashed together underneath the one inadequate tarpaulin, which kept enough of the direct rain off them so as to ensure at least some sleep.

It was with a great deal of relief that they reached the end of the plains at last and entered the woodlands. The trees sheltered them from the ravages of the wind and from the worst effects of the downpours. It was, however, a wet and bedraggled party that reached the edge of the woods and looked down at the settlement.

They paused for a while to decide the best way to approach. From the cover of the tree line, Jim took out his binoculars and surveyed the lie of the land.

His lips pursed together as his mind registered what he was seeing.

"They're strengthening the palisades," he announced. "Wonder what's happened to make them do that? There are more sentries than I expected to be seen on the walls as well."

"Can't we just go down and ask them to let us in?" asked young Peter in a plaintive voice. He was desperate to see his mother and little sister again.

Tara and Thomas agreed with him, adding their pleas to his.

"Might be better to approach first on foot," demurred Jim. "If there has been trouble I certainly don't want to be spitted by an arrow or these crossbow bolts that Arthur Knott was experimenting with when I left before I get the chance to explain myself."

There were murmurs of agreement from their Lind partners. Afanasei too was of the opinion that caution was the safest option.

"We wait here," he decided. "Jim and Thomas must go."

It was agreed. To Peter's immense chagrin, he and Tara waited in the cover of the trees with the Lind and watched Jim and Thomas begin their descent and start their long walk towards the gates.

As the two approached and became aware of bustle and other movement from inside, more guards appeared at the walls.

A voice called out to them. "No nearer. Stop there and identify yourselves."

Jim cupped his hands round his mouth and bellowed, "Jim Cranston and Thomas Wylie here. Let us in. We have news."

After a long moment, a figure waved them forward and the gates swung open. When they stepped through the narrow opening, the first person they saw striding towards them was Stuart MacIntosh, closely followed by Robert Lutterell and other members of the Council.

"Thought you were dead," was Stuart's first comment. "What took you so long, you rascal?" His face broke into a large welcoming smile. "One of the missing with you as well I see. I assume from Thomas's presence that you found them all in the end? Where are the others? Are they far away?"

"Far enough and one question at a time old friend," replied Jim easily, clapping his one-time commanding officer on the shoulder. "We have a lot to tell you and none too much time."

"And we you," interrupted Robert. "Glad to see you. Honestly didn't think we'd see you again, especially with what has been a happening here recently."

"Trouble?" asked Jim.

"You don't know the half of it," was the grim answer.

"I might be able to throw some light on the situation," said Jim, "but we have some friends waiting patiently outside in the woods waiting for my word to come in and meet you all. Two old friends and five new ones as a matter of fact."

Thomas, letting out a loud whoop of joy and recognition, began to run towards a tall middle-aged woman who had joined the interested folk at the gate, distracting Jim. There was quite a crowd gathering. *The woman must be his mother*, Jim decided. They had the same colouring and build and the lad could be heard recounting his adventures to the woman at top speed. Nearby colonists were gathering round to listen and loud were the exclamations of amazement from that general direction.

Jim decided not to wait.

"May I call our friends in?" he asked. "I have to warn you though that five of them are not human. They are Lind and are set to become our helpmates and allies in this new and dangerous world."

"Lind?"

"What are they?"

"How did you meet them?"

"Was it them who kidnapped the youngsters?"

Jim held up an arm to stop what promised to be a liturgy of questions.

"It would be far better if they tell you themselves. They speak perfectly adequate Standard," he said, grinning from ear to ear. He had been looking forward to this moment. "I do need your assurance that they will come to no harm. Young Peter Crawford and Tara

Sullivan are with them."

Stuart turned to Robert. "See to it will you? Warn the sentries, make sure they understand."

"Aye, sir," he answered with a grin and sped off.

Jim thought hard at Larya, indicating that it was now safe to approach. He sensed her letting the others know then led Stuart MacIntosh and the others over to the palisades. As he climbed the ladder up to the parapet (new since his time, and the walls were much higher) he heard the Council members following behind, talking amongst themselves nineteen to the dozen about Thomas and Jim's unexpected arrival.

He looked up at the tree line and was rewarded by the sight of the five Lind and the two children emerging and starting to walk down the hill. He was pleased to see that both Tara and Peter were mounted on Kolyei and Radya, thus proving to the watchers that there was no danger.

There was a hiss of anger from one of the sentries to his right. The man raised his bow and Jim watched in consternation as he retrieved an arrow from the quiver by his side.

"What are you doing?" an angry Jim yelled at him, "these are our friends." The man looked at Jim, shaking his head. He made no move to un-notch his arrow.

"Seen these creatures before," he said. "Took out one of the farms."

"Not these creatures," insisted Jim, "the Lind would not do such a thing." He sent a telepathic warning to Larya and the approaching party stopped in their tracks.

He turned to Stuart and Robert who were nodding in agreement.

"Last month," confirmed the latter. "Bunch of them, killed everyone, man and beast, wolves as big as carthorses."

"The Larg," breathed Jim. Now he understood why the colonists were raising the height of the palisades and why the settlement appeared overcrowded. The inhabitants of the outlying farms must have returned to the settlement for shelter and protection.

"The who?" questioned Stuart.

"The Larg," repeated Jim. "They come from the southern continent, swim over the narrow part of the ocean using the islands to rest. They are the traditional enemies of the north. Vicious brutes, they enjoy killing. We've come to warn you and to decide how both we and the Lind can pool our resources to meet the threat."

"Bit late for a warning," growled Robert. "When we got to the farm it was all over. Managed to run them off though and killed one."

Jim was very interested in this last piece of information. "Still got the carcass?" he asked.

Robert nodded. "Still there. It was a large farm. Buried the families but still to deal with the outlying livestock."

It was Jim's turn to nod. "I might want to look at the body later." He gazed at the rest of the Councillors, warning in his eyes.

"Those that approach are our *friends*," he emphasised. "They have been battling with the Larg for centuries, eons perhaps. They might be our only chance to beat the Larg off and there are other complications, which I will tell you about when we are alone. The Lind *want* an alliance. Together we have a good chance to defeat them before they spread mayhem and carnage throughout the eastern part of the continent. The Lind may have spirited away some youngsters but I assure you that they meant them no harm and that it was the only way they could think of to make contact with us."

He still saw disbelief and uncertainty on some faces and his voice became more forceful. Out of the corner of his eye he watched as the trigger-happy sentry began un-notching his arrow.

"By all the stars in the sky, all sixteen of us have been living in their land, living happily amongst them, learning each other's language and traditions. We have bonded with them!"

"Bonded?" asked one Jean Farquharson, an older, grey-haired lady who had been co-opted on to the Council by virtue of her great common sense and level headedness. "What do you mean bonded? You mean all this? These are not the same creatures that attacked the farm?"

"Definitely not. They are friends and allies and you must greet them accordingly, not shoot at them."

There was a silence then Stuart MacIntosh nodded. "I trust you Jim," he said. "If you say that they are our friends and vouch for them then I'm with you."

Jean nodded then after a moment Jim saw Robert Lutterell do the same. Apart from Stuart MacIntosh, these were the most forceful members of the Council. It had been them he needed to convince. He looked for any other dissenting faces. He saw none. Francis McAllister had had the measure of it. These people trusted Jim; trusted his judgement. Despite his previous misgivings about leaving the domta, he had been the only person who had the force of character and reputation to enable him to persuade them of the friendliness of the Lind. If he had not been here, the human anger about what had occurred at the farm might well have precipitated a very serious incident, one that would have proved extremely detrimental to the future relationship between human and Lind.

"Stand these sentries down," Jim ordered, "and I'll tell our visitors to continue their approach."

"Some inhabitants are angry about what has happened," ventured Winston Randall. "Might it not be better for some of us to greet them outside the walls whilst others inside make sure everybody knows of their benign intent?"

Stuart MacIntosh agreed with this and Robert Lutterell and some others of the Council were sent to arrange it. He himself would accompany Jim to meet their guests, together with Jean and Winston.

At this point Thomas came bounding up towards them, anxious to be reunited with his beloved Stasya, his family in tow and a gaggle of excited colonists in their wake.

"Stasya says she is coming," he shouted. "I want her to meet my family."

That decided almost all who still doubted, and they began to lose their strained expressions. The boy was so happy and excited. Surely there was little to fear?

Agnes Crawford walked up to Jim at that point, her face glowing with happiness.

"Thomas says Peter is out there?"

Jim smiled at her.

"Thomas says Peter has made an especial friend of one of these creatures? That they talk to each other with their minds?"

At that moment Jim was really glad that he'd decided to bring Peter and Radya with them, glad to have brought such joy back into her life.

She gave him a huge hug. "Thank you for bringing him home," she said in heartfelt tones, too full of emotion to say any more.

Raising his voice, Jim shouted, "Let's go," and looking down at the woman added, "Peter will be so pleased to see you. I think you will like his Radya. She loves him very much and she has been looking forward to meeting you."

"Meeting me?" Agnes squeaked.

"She has tended him well," he answered her. "Don't be jealous of the affection they have for each other. They are bonded, we think for life. The Lind call it vadeln."

"What do I say?" she asked worriedly. "How do I greet her?"

"Invite her back to your cabin of course," said Jim with a laugh. "Mind, it might be a tight fit but she'll squeeze herself in somehow. She really wants to meet Peter's human family."

Jim started through the gate. Spilling after him, Stuart, Jean and Winston walked Thomas and Peter's families, then all those who had managed to listen in and who wanted to be part of the excitement. It was quite a number that eventually exited the gate and approached their visitors.

Jim warned Larya. The Lind came to a halt some distance away. They stood motionless as the party approached, all but one Lind and her rider that is, Radya, Peter still on her back, began to move forward. As Peter's mother broke free from the others and started to run towards them, he tumbled from Radya's back and ran towards her. Agnes swept her son into her arms, cuddling him close. Peter squirmed free after a few minutes of this affront to his ten-year-old dignity and those watching could see him as he talked earnestly to her. Mother and son then turned towards Radya and the boy could be heard introducing them to each other in a clear, piping and excited voice.

"Radya, this is my mother, Mummy, this is Radya. Isn't she gorgeous?"

Radya's polite reply was heard by all close enough to hear.

In perfectly accented Standard and to Agnes Crawford's surprise, she said, "Good day Agnes. I am Radya. I am pleased to meet you."

"I am very pleased to meet you as well Radya," she replied. "I hear that you have been looking after my boy? You have done well. He looks very fit and happy."

"Peter miss Agnes," announced Radya. "I bring Peter here. I am sorry that Peter had to go away but it was necessary."

Agnes laughed delightedly. "Oh, you and I are going to get along just fine!"

A similar scene was acted out as Thomas introduced his Stasya. The crowd that had followed the Councillors outside milled around talking excitedly. None appeared to be afraid. Jim wondered whether Afanasei, Kolyei and his Larya were imparting non-threatening vibes to the crowd. He rather expected that they were.

Tara remained seated on Kolyei's back. She had no family to meet her. She sat there sadly, waiting for Jim and the Councillors to approach, a faint smattering of tears showing in her eyes; then felt her unhappiness ease somewhat as Kolyei telepathed her the emotions of love and belonging.

Winston Randall, recognising her as the girl he and Laura had rescued after the asteroid storm on the space ship, did his best in the circumstances and it was a good best.

"Tara Sullivan?" he asked, walking towards her.

She looked down and saw him, a merry smile on his face.

"Welcome back Tara," he said, opening his arms in invitation. "What about a hug from me?"

So it was Tara's turn to be hugged and fussed over. Kolyei looked on indulgently and wagged his tail.

"Janice and I have been so worried about you, Mrs Mackie as well although she doesn't say much these days."

Tara looked at him enquiringly.

"She is not well and is being looked after in the infirmary now. Perhaps you might like to visit her later?"

Jim was introducing Afanasei and Larya to Stuart and Jean.

"I am pleased to meet you," said Afanasei in Standard. He had been practising this phrase for hours. He lowered his head courteously.

Stuart was immensely surprised at this but with great presence of mind copied the gesture. Jean merely stared up at Afanasei, open mouthed with astonishment.

Larya nosed Jim.

"Inside we go," she said decidedly. "Heat and food."

Jean was recovering admirably from the shock of hearing wolves talking Standard but did manage an answer.

"Yes. Certainly. I think the meeting hall, Stuart. Do you agree? We can have food brought to us there."

Stuart did agree and led the way back through the gate. It was quite a procession that followed him and as they entered the settlement it appeared that all its inhabitants had turned out to watch them pass. Robert's information dissemination had worked. There were many smiles and welcoming waves from the crowd and hardly any disapproving looks.

In order that all could see the truth of this, Jim remounted Larya (at her insistence) with Tara, Thomas and Peter following suit. Afanasei padded along at Larya's side.

"What are they?"

"What kind of animal is that?" asked a wizened old lady.

"They're like large dogs but far more beautiful. Look at the blue stripes on their coats."

Peter and Radya were bustled away by Agnes, she intent on finding out just what exactly had been happening to her son over the last months. The Wylie family escorted Thomas and Stasya to one of the open areas near their own cabin. As many as possible crowded into the available area and some not so available; a few were noticed perching precariously on the roofs in order not to miss any of the fun.

Stuart led the remaining three Lind, Tara and Jim towards the meeting hall followed by those who had decided they wanted to hear the news directly from Jim Cranston's mouth. The vet walked beside Kolyei, one hand on Tara's arm. Tara was glad of his comfort; the settlement seemed to consist entirely of eyes, eyes that watched her and Kolyei's every move. She was reminded of her arrival at domta Zanatei and began to wish she was back there. The domta had become her home. After all these months away, it was the settlement that seemed to be alien to her and not the country of the Lind. Winston patted her hand and caught her eye. He winked solemnly and Tara choked back a giggle.

Kolyei was preening himself as he deciphered the comments of the crowd.

"Don't be stupid woman, they look nothing like dogs. Too large, horses maybe."

"Who ever heard of horses like them?"

"They're wolves," breathed the selfsame old woman, "huge, proud beautiful wolves like those that once lived on Earth."

"That child is riding that one."

"Yes," crackled the old woman's sister, "she's one of the 'Children of the Wolves', like the rumours that have been going round since the children disappeared." Unconsciously she was echoing Yvonne's words, spoken that day at domta Zanatei.

"Mighty odd wolves to let people ride them like that."

And so the whispers grew louder and turned into excited shouts.

"The rumours are true! Look at this. Come and see. Look at the Child of the Wolf."

The crowd grew bigger and noisier in its excitement. People tried to jostle forward the better to see this marvel.

"What food do I order?" asked Stuart of Jim. "I can't very well serve them bread and cakes!"

"Meat," replied Jim, "raw and lots of it. We've been on the road a long time and it's been sparse rations for the last few days. We didn't want to waste any time getting here. There is much to do and say and time is running out."

When all were replete (the three Lind ate their fill in a corner of the hall in case watching them eat the raw meat upset any of their new allies' dispositions) they got down to business.

"You start off," ordered Jim, "then we'll fill in the bits you don't know and tell you what is likely to happen in the future."

Nothing loath, Stuart began the tale, recounting all that had happened since Jim had left on his hunt for the children. The colonists had come across the Larg scouts a few times but had not understood what this meant. They had thought them to be another type of ruminant like the jezdic and zarova. The incident at the farm was the only time when the creatures had actually attacked. Afanasei was of the opinion that the Larg had only attacked in order to gain access to the domesticated herds in the farm's paddock.

"Hunger," Afanasei said. "The Larg are your enemy as much as they are the enemy of the Lind. If humans had not defended the zarova, they would have been left alone by Larg, at least in the beginning."

"Scouts," said Kolyei, nodding his head sagely.

"How do we defend ourselves against them?" demanded Robert Lutterell.

"How many are there?" asked Stuart MacIntosh.

"Scouts," reiterated Afanasei. "Lindars come. Guard farms."

"Lindars?" queried Jean.

"A Lind warrior regiment," answered Tara, as Jim for some reason seemed unable to answer. In fact he was collecting his thoughts. If the colonists were jittery and worried now, after a small attack on a farm by some Larg scouts, how would they react to the news that an army of them was planning an invasion this coming summer?

With Kolyei's encouragement, Tara continued to explain. It was no easy task to describe an alien species to a group of twenty serious-faced adults when one was only twelve.

"Each Lind pack has a sort of regiment of fighters," she said. "Afanasei has just offered to send you some Lindars to openly patrol the area, for protection and also to act as a deterrent so that the Larg keep their distance."

Afanasei looked at her approvingly. This youngling had a good grasp of the situation although he was in no doubt that the more experienced Kolyei was prompting her. Still, at least she had the presence of mind to pick up on the explanations needed when she saw that Jim was preoccupied.

There were murmurs of relief. The Council had talked long and hard about how they were going to protect the outlying farms. The settlement was too small to house everybody comfortably.

The Council uttered their thanks and grateful acceptance of this offer.

It was Stuart who brought up the next subject. He had homed in on one word, initially spoken by Kolyei then repeated by Afanasei.

"Scouts?" he asked, "Scouts for what?"

Jim looked at him. It was time to tell all.

Many hours later, Stuart called a halt, declaring himself too tired to think properly. By this time Tara had fallen asleep, an exhausted little bundle by Kolyei's side.

Jim, Larya and Afanasei accepted Stuart's offer of quarters in his cabin.

"Tara and Kolyei will come home with me," announced Winston Randall. "Janice would never forgive me if they didn't."

"You have enough room?"

"We'll make the room," he declared looking down at the girl. "It'll not be the first time I've made do," he added, resolving to pop her into his and Janice's bed. With that, he stooped down and lifted her carefully. "She's as light as a feather! You sure she's been eating properly?"

Kolyei snorted indignantly and Winston chuckled.

"Let's go," was his command to the large male. "Janice and the children will be delighted to meet you. It's not every day we get guests."

The three of them walked slowly, Winston anxious not to waken Tara if he could help it. An inquisitive crowd followed in their wake, speculating amongst themselves. Winston again heard Tara being described as a 'Child of the Wolf'.

"Is she asleep?" asked Janice in a low voice as he carried Tara inside. "Your meeting went on for so long."

"There was much to talk about."

"I've kept supper for you and set up a camp bed in the girls' room. It won't do her any harm for once if she washes in the morning." Janice was a firm believer in frequent baths.

"Is there room for Kolyei?"

"Her Lind? Where is he? I've made up a bed in the corner there with two old ship's mattresses underneath. Will that do?" Janice pointed to the large pile of rugs in the corner of the living space.

"He's waiting outside," said Winston as he made for the girls' bedroom. "On the way over he told me he expected to sleep on the floor."

"I spoke to Thomas," answered Janice briskly, opening the door to let Kolyei in. "It was made perfectly clear that comfortable bedding would be appreciated."

Kolyei whuffled his appreciation when he viewed the sleeping arrangements.

"Thank you," he said to a surprised Janice. "I will be most comfortable here." He wagged his tail.

"Are you hungry?" she said, greatly emboldened by this show of courtesy.

He shook his head.

"Do you want to see Tara? I've put her in with the girls for now."

"Tara sleeps," Kolyei announced. "I see no need to disturb."

As that was exactly what Janice was thinking, her estimation of Kolyei went up another notch.

"You and Tara must stay here," she found herself saying, "for as long as you like. My children will be most excited at the thought of one of the fabulous Lind staying with us. I'm warning you though, they'll be up with the lark."

"The lark? What is lark?"

"A bird that inhabited the planet we come from. An early rising bird with a beautiful song," Winston answered for her.

Kolyei's face cleared. "I understand. We have a saying very similar. We say 'unst si malinon' when talking about those of our kind who rise from their daga before sun is high in sky. The malinon has a pretty song. You see many when you come to Zanatei."

"Come to Zanatay?" Janice turned to her husband. "What's he talking about?"

CHAPTER 15

NORTHERN AND SOUTHERN CONTINENTS

In the southern continent, another meeting was taking place. All Murdoch's colonels were present and the agenda was a serious one.

It had not been an easy time for Murdoch and his men. He had enforced many rules, some of which had not been universally popular. Dissent was rife.

Henri Cocteau talked of his problems down in the encampment beside the river, an undercurrent of warning in his voice as he spoke.

"It is as you predicated General. I've got ten thousand men down there. As expected, they are having to organise themselves in order to survive. They appear to be forming into groups. Just yesterday a bunch of would-be shoemakers approached me for permission to open a shop and quite a number have formed hunting groups. In addition there are over fifty based at the river who have the laudable intention of becoming fishermen. They're even building boats although I have no idea if any of these so-called boats are capable of remaining above the water for any length of time."

"Hope they have life-jackets," interjected a voice from the back. There was a general laugh at this sally.

"Any more signs of these giant wolves?" asked Sam Baker. There had been no sightings, a fact that was making him and the other commanders not a little nervous.

"None," stated Cocteau. "The hunters are keeping a wary eye open but have seen nothing at all, not even any tracks."

"Don't drop your guard."

The others agreed. They were not finding any signs either even after sending out reconnaissance parties in force, partly to watch and partly to keep their men in training and occupied. Now that the immediate fighting was over, some soldiers were finding time weighing heavily on their hands. Their officers were sometimes hard-pressed to find them something to do. Murdoch would not allow any of the seven remaining regiments to be disbanded, not with what was known as the wolf threat on their doorstep. He also felt more secure with three and a half thousand supporters up at Fort with him, trained and ready to rise in his defence if necessary.

Henri Cocteau's men in the encampment were being encouraged to shake off the regimental discipline of the march north in order to organise themselves to provide the goods and services that both they and the army up on the hill at Fort needed. Many were making a concerted effort to do so and varied were the petitions to form this or that trade, to open a shop or to learn another occupation. There were unfortunately, a very fair number who did not want to do any such thing. These men were becoming the troublemakers and riff-raff of the encampment, and even their ex-blockmates were getting annoyed.

"The main problem is the women, or lack of them," stated Cocteau, determined to get his point across.

In the south, women were becoming chattels, to be bought and sold, with no rights outside the house and bedroom and little even there.

It was a serious point Cocteau was making. Discontent was becoming more vocal and there were fears that the angry words would turn into acts of violence. The commanders were worried.

Murdoch and his circle were at a loss to find a solution. No matter how often the matter was discussed, the facts spoke for themselves. There were just not enough women to go round. Those who owned one were targeted for vilification by those who did not and it was just a matter of time before the discontent turned into something more serious.

Well to the south of the convicts, at the edge of the Larg pack-ranges, Andrew Snodgrass was suffering. The Larg had insisted that he learn *their* language; a learning process that was marked with many a menacing clout and snarl when it was felt he was not learning quickly enough.

He had soon found out that he was indeed the only survivor from the convict base camp.

The Larg way of life was hard and brutal. The Larg did not tolerate any weakness or insubordination in any form. Infringements were dealt with savagely. Andrew spent the majority of his time in a state of abject fear as to what was going to happen next. It was a never-ending nightmare of degradation and mute terror. The worst of it all was that his mind was no longer his own.

At last Aoalvaldr decided the time was right. As foreseen by Zanatei and Afanasei, the Larg intended to form alliance with these men in order to better attack the north. Larg spies had reported back on the existence of the human settlement on the northern continent. Most importantly, from the Larg point of view, the settlement had been built not far from their landing beaches. It was time to enlist convict aid to circumvent this hazard.

: *Alliance* : Aoalvaldr forced the word into Andrew's mind : *No fight. Together invade. Defeat Lind. Andrew alliance arrange* :

Andrew began his solitary walk towards the encampment and Fort and with Murdoch and his cronies pondering the two problems of the threat of the wolves and the lack of women, Andrew duly arrived with the answer to them both.

They jumped at Aoalvaldr's proposal.

Murdoch and his men would invade the north alongside the Larg. There was a rush of volunteers for the army that would invade once it was learnt that there were many women in the north from the WCCS *Argyll*.

The alliance was not, however, to result in the same close relationship that was emerging in the north between the colonists and the Lind. The Larg were not being entirely honest with Murdoch when they told him that the Lind were a peace-loving species and would be easy to defeat. Murdoch did not tell the Larg that he liked the sound of the northern lands and would like to settle there instead of in the south. The southern alliance was not built on trust and mutual respect. The Larg did not think much of their human allies and the men distrusted the Larg. They had, after all, tortured and eaten some of their friends and comrades. It would take a long time for the men to forget.

At the moment both their paths and plans ran beside each other. What would happen if these plans started to go awry? Only time would tell.

In the north Jim Cranston and Robert Lutterell were having a conversation.

"There is no comparison," said Jim.

They had both gone to the devastated farmstead so that Jim could see for himself what the Larg looked like. Afanasei had permitted Robert to ride on his back in order to cut down on the journey time. Robert, after due consideration, now decided it was the most uncomfortable mode of transportation imaginable and vowed to never again attempt it except in the most dire emergencies.

"This Larg is no more like the Lind than a carthorse is a thoroughbred racehorse."

This ill-judged announcement meant that he was soon embroiled in another lengthy explanation to Larya and Afanasei as to just what he meant.

"Ugly brutes," agreed Robert. "Your Larya is far more attractive."

Larya cocked an ear at him. She looked pleased.

"Flatterer," said Jim humorously. "Seriously though, we'd better get back to the settlement. The meeting is scheduled to start soon."

Robert Lutterell sighed gustily and his shoulders sagged, just a tad. It was time to mount Afanasei again and to grit his teeth as he bumped along on his back for the journey.

"Okay," he said and added, "but can we go a little slower than on the way out? I'm aching all over."

Afanasei's tongue rolled out and his eyes glinted wickedly. He snuck a glance at Larya who grinned back. The Lind certainly enjoyed having the untrained on their backs. It was so much fun to joggle them around and to pretend to throw them off. Their best ploy was to stop with a jerk, lower their heads and force the unsuspecting rider to slide down their necks. Robert's face when Afanasei had succeeded in dislodging him had been a picture, half outraged, half embarrassed and very annoyed.

Afanasei and Larya agreed wholeheartedly about the decision to return. The Eldas of the Gtratha were expecting a full report by nightfall and they wished to send good news. Not that the news so far was bad. The humans were accepting them as friends and allies, though Afanasei realised that if Jim had not been there with the authority to plead their case the situation might well have been very different.

Tara slept late.

When she emerged from the small bedroom and peeked into the living space she spied Kolyei sitting by the fireside, a crowd of enraptured children at his feet in front of and beside him.

: *Holding court?* :

Kolyei grinned. He did so love an audience.

Janice realised her youngest guest was awake and sprang to her feet.

"Tara," she cried, "a thousand welcomes. Did you sleep well? Would you like some breakfast?"

Kolyei's 'audience' turned to stare at her.

"Yes please," she answered shyly.

"Breakfast first, then a bath," decided Janice aloud as she bustled towards the stove, shooing aside the smallest children who had taken up temporary residence there, "and a change of clothes. Those are in tatters."

Tara looked at her ruefully. "I did my best." She well knew that her own clothes were in a pitiful state and none too clean after the journey.

"You did well," smiled Janice, "and that fur vest, did you make it yourself?"

"With Emily's help," admitted Tara.

"Emily Stanton?" queried Janice. "No doubt her mother will be here shortly. She is anxious for news and I'll not be surprised if other parents appear as well."

"Emily is fine," answered Tara, sitting down at a hastily vacated space at the table and eyeing the plate Janice set in front of her. She was trying hard not to be bothered by the rapt and envious faces gazing at her.

Janice, realising that Tara was uncomfortable with so many staring eyes, made haste to ask the children to leave, promising that they could come back later. They left with many a reluctant complaint.

Soon only the five Randall offspring remained, sitting round the table with Janice and Tara.

"This is Louis," Janice began, "my oldest."

Louis winked at Tara.

"Brian is next, he is thirteen, then Violet, Lucy and Juliet."

"We've been velly quiet," announced the middle daughter.

"Wif Kolyei," added the youngest, a mite of around three years, Tara judged.

"Shush," ordered the oldest damsel and she introduced herself with a shy smile, "I am Violet and I'm nine."

Kolyei watched Tara eat then announced that he must go and find Jim, Larya and Afanasei.

"We'll take you," offered Louis after a glance at Brian.

Janice nodded. "You do that. Tara, the girls and I have important matters to attend to. She looked meaningfully at Violet who giggled and leant confidentially towards Tara.

"Mummy has new clothes for you," she whispered.

"Pwetty clothes," agreed Juliet.

Tara coloured.

Janice saw this; there was little she missed where children were concerned.

"As I said earlier, you've done brilliantly to hold on to them for so long," she comforted with a pat on Tara's head. "What is the fur vest made of? Camel?"

"Kura," answered her small guest.

"Kura?" the sisters clamoured. "What is that?"

What remained of the morning sped by, first with the promised bath, then a wonderful hour spent trying on the clothes Janice had gathered together. Brian had donated his second best pair of trousers and Violet an embroidered tunic she hadn't worn yet.

Luckily, thought Janice, as she gathered together Tara's new possessions and put them in the wooden chest she was to share with Violet, Tara was on the small side so Violet's underthings would do for both. Hand knitted socks and a pair of new boots completed Tara's outfit. Janice then proceeded to trim her hair into a becoming style and sat back, well satisfied with the results.

"You'll do."

Tara regarded her hostess shyly. "Thank you so much," she managed to get out. Her throat felt tight. It had been a long time since she had been fussed over like this.

"We will all now prepare lunch," Janice declared, realising that Tara needed time to compose herself. "The boys and Kolyei will be back soon I expect and hopefully your father too."

"Soon," ventured Tara. Her head was set in the peculiar little tilt that Janice would come to recognise as her having a telepathic conversation with Kolyei. "Kolyei says soon."

Janice was startled, but recovered almost at once. "I forgot you can converse telepathically," was all she said though.

"It's useful, isn't it Mummy?" asked Violet.

"Very useful," Janice agreed. "Now, who is going to volunteer to cut up the roots and who will set the table?"

"I will." Four hands rose into the air.

It is good, thought Tara as she helped Violet ladle the cooked roots into the serving platter, *to be part of a family again, even for a little while*.

Lunch reached Tara's expectations and beyond. She sat between Violet and Brian and munched her way through the succulent stew, cooked the way only Janice knew how. It was delicately seasoned and melted in the mouth. Even Kolyei partook of the stew though he declined the fresh bread, baked by Janice in the small bake-oven she had insisted Winston build. Tara learned later that Janice was considered the best cook in their district.

Kolyei made the acquaintance of what the settlers called lemon root, something that even he had never eaten before. It was poisonous raw and the Lind could not cook. Both he and Tara learned that, if one cut off the lethal spiky stalks and baked the flesh underneath, it was absolutely delicious.

"I've got used to cooking manually," Janice confided to Tara, "and Arthur Knott has a working model of what he calls a cooking-range. I'm looking forward to getting one when he gets the time to make some more."

"I fear you'll wait a long time," said Winston. "His smithies will be producing other items now."

"What do you mean?" she asked, not stopping from spooning another helping of stew into Brian's bowl. "You didn't tell me much last night."

"War is coming," her husband answered. "Jim brought grave news. Arthur Knott will be kept busy making swords and axes now."

Janice threw a quick glance at Tara who had stopped munching. She had said nothing about the coming war.

Winston noticed and made haste to put her at ease.

"You did right to say nothing love," Winston told her. "Best that the news comes from Stuart MacIntosh and the rest of the Council. There are rumours enough already. Peter Crawford is young and was a bit indiscreet last night."

"War? What war? Who is there on this planet that wages war? Who will we have to fight?" asked Louis.

The Randall children were staring at their father, wide eyed.

"Creatures from the southern continent called the Larg," he explained.

"Like those beasts that destroyed…?"

"The Armstrong farmstead? Yes, the very same. There are thousands of them and that's not all."

"It's the convicts from the *Electra* isn't it?" asked Louis. "I heard some people talking this morning," he added by way of explanation.

"The *Electra*?" said Janice sharply. "The prison ship? But it was destroyed. Everybody knows that."

"It appears that she survived as we did, and has to our cost I fear, landed on Rybak too."

Tara however had another matter on her mind.

"What was that you said about the Armstrongs?" she asked.

The War Council was held that evening. The human leaders were still shocked and dismayed at Jim's news. They needed time to become acclimatised to the idea that they would in all likelihood, be fighting for their lives by summer.

Stuart MacIntosh started the ball rolling when the meeting convened. At Jim's behest, as many settlers as possible were present, filling every available space.

"We are here to discuss how we are going to combat the invasion of the Larg and the convicts from the *Electra*. I need not say that our situation is a dire one. Our newfound allies," he acknowledged Afanasei and the other Lind present with a short bow, "have explained very clearly to us what we may expect from the Larg. I am now going to ask Jim to tell us what he and the Lind feel our next steps should be."

Jim nodded to Stuart as he stood up, Larya by his side as usual.

"Hear me out," he announced. "Questions later." He began by giving a summary of what they knew to date, including a sketchy tale of what had happened to the crew and the families of the *Electra*, and then made abundantly clear to all what would likely happen when their enemies arrived on the northern continent. He finished with a plea for all to keep calm and declared the floor open for any questions. They were not long in coming.

"Is it definite that the Larg will attack?" asked a voice.

"Yes," answered Afanasei. His Standard was surprisingly good for one not vadeln-paired, rivalling that of Kolyei's. "Larg will come. Bad men as well. Defend rtathlians we must do or we will die."

"That seems clear enough," shouted Stuart MacIntosh, struggling to be heard over the excited babble that Afanasei's words produced. "Now we have to make plans as to how we deal with it."

Stuart had been well briefed by Jim, Afanasei and Larya. He was going to make sure that the settlers agreed with the general plan as formulated by the four of them in secret conclave earlier that day.

Jim raised his hand for silence and got it. "You know now that certain Lind and humans bond together. Back at the Lind home live those pairs who cannot be with us today. These youngsters are learning how to fight with the Lind, but we need more vadeln-paired with the Lind in order to make our army effective."

Jim's audience looked surprised.

"Yes," said Jim with a smile at his vadeln-pair, *his* Larya. "We are looking for volunteers to travel inland to the Lind pack-woods and bond with a Lind. I promise that it is an incredible experience and one those chosen will never regret. If we are in agreement on this, the party should be ready to leave soon. I am reliably informed that an escort will be provided. Remember also that although we need volunteers that are prepared to fight, support personnel are also needed, metal smiths, woodsmen in the main but also those with any medical knowledge. The Lind can teach us so much."

Fullarton Crawford, young Peter's father, spoke up when it became obvious by the silence after Jim's plea that many were apprehensive at the thought of leaving the comparative security of the settlement to live with an alien species.

"My family and I are going," he announced in a loud voice. "Peter and Radya are to return and as a livestock farmer I am used to dealing with four-footed friends. I do not fear the Lind. I do however greatly fear the Larg. I know as well that there are no guarantees that the Larg will not venture as far as these Lind lands, but I will feel safer that bit away from this coast when the Larg do attack."

That started the ball rolling and soon other settlers could be overheard discussing the matter and some were calling out their names as being prepared to go. It was eventually decided that five hundred settlers would leave for the rtathlians, at least half of them to consist of men and women between the ages of fourteen and thirty who were eager to form a permanent attachment to the Lind and to fight with them. In fact there would, in the end, be no shortage of volunteers. Many had taken every chance to watch the four vadeln-pairs that day and wished for the opportunity to bond with one of these fabulous talking beasts.

Other settlers saw the pairings primarily as a means to get them out of this dark hour with the threat of thousands of Larg and the convicts descending on their homes and loved ones. None were to know at that point, but these paired Lind and humans were to become the nucleus of a cavalry force that would defend the northern continent for generations to come.

By the time the meeting was over, it was dark. Those lucky enough, or pushy enough, to have squeezed into the hall, departed, only to be mobbed by those outside desperate to learn what had been decided.

Stuart turned towards the rest of the Councillors.

"Productive meeting," he said in a laconic voice.

"People are too scared for any dissent," said Jean Farquharson. "I'm terrified at the prospect of being invaded by rampaging beasts and desperate men."

"We'll beat them off," said Jim, the very image of a confident war leader.

"I hope so," she replied quietly.

Afanasei had been very clear about what the Lind spies had reported concerning the fate of the male crew of the *Electra*. Any disbelief people had harboured had ceased abruptly on hearing this news.

Winston Randall and his family also decided to depart with those going with the Lind. Some of the youngsters training with him in animal medicine would go too, the others would remain behind at the settlement to tend to the livestock and pets. His eyes were bright with anticipation of what lay ahead. He did so love a challenge.

The settlement's defences were to be strengthened even more. The number of smithies and forges were to be doubled in order to produce the number of weapons that would be needed. In the morning the backbreaking process of digging out a deep defensive ditch to surround the palisades would begin. Procedures would be set in place for the evacuation of the outlying farms when the Larg were sighted. The large herds of livestock the colonists were building up would be let loose. No point in giving the Larg a present of free meals. The Lind promised to help the settlers round up the herds again after the Larg had gone.

Training for war was to begin in earnest. Conscription was implemented; all those able to do so would be required to fight. The adults within the settlement found themselves with plenty to plan and discuss that night.

It had been a momentous two days. True, they had received disquieting and dangerous news of their enemies in the south, but many had suspected that this new land of theirs hid many unexpected dangers although Robert Lutterell, up until now, had been the only one to voice his opinion that the attack on the farm was only the prelude to darker times ahead. To balance this, Jim had found the missing children and more than that, returned with allies to aid them in their troubles. The existence of the convicts in the south had come as a shock and was the added complication that had altered a dangerous situation into a potentially lethal one.

It was Janice who went to Tara, who was crying in the bedroom she shared with the girls. Kolyei had told her that Tara needed her and that he didn't know what to do. Perhaps Janice could help? Tara's thoughts were so incoherent that he wasn't even sure what it was all about. Janice didn't hesitate, after telling her three daughters not to disturb them; she calmly wiped her hands on her apron and entered the room.

Tara raised her head.

"What's wrong Tara?" Janice asked, taking the sobbing child in her arms.

"I don't know what to say," Tara sobbed.

"About what?" asked Janice reasonably enough.

"Kolyei's had word from Sindya and Malya," she replied, "Bill and Geoff Armstrong are asking about their family. He's passed back messages to all the others and they're asking why there's been nothing from them. What do I do?"

"Best do nothing darling," advised Janice, mentally berating Jim for not thinking of this complication himself. "I'll speak to Jim. Maybe his Larya would pass the news on."

"She could let Matvei or Faddei know," said Tara, "Why didn't I think of that? Laura's kind, she would break the news, or Kath."

"Such news should come from someone grown up," agreed Janice, "and the reason why you didn't think of it is that you are twelve years old and too young to be worrying about such things."

"Do you really think so?" asked Tara, sitting up and drying her eyes.

"Yes I do. Now you freshen up and come out to join us all in front of the hearth. Kolyei is there; he's worried about you."

"Okay," said Tara, "and thanks Aunt Janice."

"Aunt Janice?"

"Violet said I might," said her guest with a shy grin.

CHAPTER 16

NORTHERN CONTINENT

Violet and Tara were finding that a close friendship was growing between them, despite the three years difference in their ages.

The morning's discussions had bored Tara and she had begged to be excused and fled the meeting hall with Kolyei in search of her new 'cousin', for as Violet had pointed out, if her mother was Tara's aunt, then they must be cousins of a sort.

Tara, after so many months away from 'civilisation', was desperate to feel the wind on her face and asked if she could go fungus hunting at the edge of the woods.

"Is it safe with the Larg about?" asked Janice of Winston.

"Safe enough," he replied, having seen the longing in Tara's face when he had looked up from sorting through his veterinary books. He couldn't take them all he had now decided; there wouldn't be room. Perhaps he could claim them later.

"Between here and the trees," he continued, "is well travelled and didn't Kolyei say there were Lind patrols in the woods keeping an eye out? Anyway, if she goes with Kolyei she'll be perfectly safe. Not much passes him I'll warrant."

He twinkled at Tara.

"Off you go."

"Thank you," she breathed, "and can Violet come too? We'll gather more if she comes," she added artfully.

Violet raised large pleading eyes to her father, much resembling a young puppy begging for a bone and held her breath.

"Please Daddy," she begged.

Winston looked at his wife, wanting to say yes but not sure what she felt.

"If I give you two baskets," she said, "do you think you could manage to fill them?"

Violet grinned and skipped away to the big cupboard and brought out two rush baskets.

"Stay in sight of the loggers," Janice warned.

Kolyei was waiting outside. A crowd of interested onlookers had begun to gather and the excited Violet felt very self-conscious as her father lifted her up behind Tara with instructions to hold on tight.

Kolyei turned to him.

"I will not let Violet fall," he said and trotted off, the crowd giving way before him, Violet laughing aloud at this unexpected treat.

It felt good to be outside the walls of the settlement Tara decided, as they loped up the hill. She waved to the loggers as they passed, remembering her promise to Janice. Kolyei agreed. He had found his first experience of living in a human habitation more than a little strange. The natural habitat of the Lind was woodlands; open plains made him edgy and human homes in the middle of the plains edgier still.

: *It is good to be outside* : he agreed : *feel the wind, listen to the trees* :

Behind her Violet chattered incessantly, but Tara knew by now that she could 'mentally' speak with Kolyei and listen at the same time.

"Can we go faster?" cried Violet and screamed with joy as Kolyei stretched out his lope.

"It's like flying," she shouted.

Then Kolyei slowed down.

: *Here* : he sent.

After spending the last months at the Zanatei domta, Tara had learnt what was edible and what was not.

The two dismounted, Tara neatly, whilst Violet slithered down any which way and they began to gather the fruits of the forest.

"Roots first," ordered Tara, "the fungus last otherwise they'll bruise and be spoiled."

Kolyei himself decided that a rest was in order and found a secluded spot, out of the wind, where he could keep an eye on them.

Tara was affected by Violet's exuberance and he was pleased to watch her normally grave little face break into smile after smile every time Violet said something amusing or simply outrageous.

He listened in.

"Are you going to stay with us always?" Violet was asking. "I wish you would. I've always wanted a big sister. It's hard being the oldest girl. Isn't the wind funny. I never felt wind 'til we got here."

"Neither did I," Tara answered. "I was born about eight weeks after we left Earth."

Violet ignored that as she sniffed deeply. "The air smells good. *Are* you going to stay with us?"

"I live with Kolyei in his home," Tara explained. "He, we, wouldn't be happy at the settlement, but that won't matter. I think you're coming west with us and if you do you'll see us almost every day."

"What's his home like?"

"It's a big forest with trees much bigger than these ones. Kolyei and I live in a house made of them."

"A tree house!" exclaimed Violet, her voice filled with wonderment. "Does it have an upstairs? Will I live in a tree house too?"

"Probably."

Violet thought about that.

"I still think you should stay with us," she said tenaciously, loathe to give up on what she desired the most.

"We'll see," said Tara.

"That's what Mummy says when she thinks the answers going to be no. I like Kolyei. I'd like to have a Lind as a friend like you."

"He's more than a friend."

"Is he yours?" she pushed.

"No more than I am his," Tara answered.

They worked in companionable silence for a while as Violet tried to work this out.

"If he's not yours then whose is he? We have a dog called Tanni and he's ours."

"I am his and he is mine," answered Tara but Violet didn't understand. In her world, she and her sisters and brothers belonged to their parents just as Tanni belonged to the family as a whole.

She looked at the baskets.

"We've almost filled them completely with roots. Can we pick the fungus now? Mummy doesn't let us gather them in case we pick the poisonous ones."

"I know which ones are safe to eat and which aren't," agreed Tara. "I'll show you but you must promise not to try and pick them when I'm not here."

"I promise."

Violet cast an adoring look at her. Tara didn't notice. Her eyes were scanning the ground searching for the blue tint of her favourite mushroom.

Kolyei did. He chuckled to himself. Violet was a persistent youngster. He wondered how long it would take her to persuade her parents to offer Tara a more permanent position in the family, providing of course that Winston and Janice weren't already considering the idea. He rather suspected they were. He sniffed suddenly as he heard someone approaching from the interior of the woods.

: *Watch out! Something is coming* :

The two girls had heard it too.

It was too noisy for a Lind, Kolyei knew. He rose to his feet. It did not sound like a Larg but it was better to be safe than sorry.

"Stay beside me," Tara commanded Violet, holding her knife in the workmanlike manner taught to her by Francis McAllister.

The man who emerged from the undergrowth was old, dressed in skins and was weighed down by a huge backpack.

"It's Daniel Trapper," squealed Violet, dropping her basket and dancing over to him.

"Well, well, well," the old man said twinkling down at her, "a young lady that goes by the name of Violet Randall if I'm not mistaken. You've grown child."

He turned frankly interested eyes in Tara's direction.

"And who is this?"

"That's Kolyei's girl," said Violet with pride. "She's staying with us."

"And who in the name of the wee man is Kolyei?"

"Kolyei isn't a wee man, he's a Lind," Violet answered seriously, all important at being the first to tell Daniel of the momentous events transpiring at the settlement. "Haven't you heard *anything*?"

He looked at her.

"Young ladies," he began, "I've been up in these here woods this last two months or more. What is a Lind?"

Kolyei rose to his paws.

"I am a Lind," he announced in stentorian tones.

Daniel nearly dropped on the spot.

Violet invited Daniel to dinner, saying that her father would be pleased to see him again after so long.

Kolyei volunteered to carry the heavy pack and Violet too. The four of them returned to the settlement.

It was as they walked that they learned of another Larg sighting.

"It looked a bit like you, but heavier, thicker legs and body," Daniel told them.

"We must warn the Lindars," said Tara.

"Already done," answered Kolyei, "he'll not get far. The Larg always send scouts west to find out what we're up to if they're planning an attack. He's the fifth this moon time, not counting the ones who killed at the farm."

"This confirms they're coming doesn't it?"

Kolyei gazed at her wisely.

"Who are they and what are coming?" asked Daniel in confusion. "I don't understand."

Winston Randall told him more than he actually wanted to hear when they reached the Randall cabin. Daniel only waited another three days at the settlement before, bags packed, he left to travel west again. Tara and Kolyei never saw him again.

"What can we take with us?" asked Janice some days later, looking round at their possessions. "I've worked so hard to make this a real home."

"We'll take what we can carry," answered Winston, a comforting arm round her shoulders. "Anything else, like that rosewood dower-chest that was your mother's, we are to load on to the wagon and it will follow. We can easily build more cupboards, tables, chairs and the like."

For the four youngest Randall children, their move to Zanatei was a huge adventure, the three girls especially not really aware of the danger threatening from the south. Louis was not so carefree about what was prompting the move west. He was old enough to fully understand the very real danger they had found themselves in.

"Where will we sleep on the journey?" asked Violet.

"On the ground," replied Tara. "These sleepbags are jolly comfortable. When I left with Kolyei I only had what I'd gone out in. Laura Merriman lent me hers for the way back. Clothes for the journey, sleepbags and then cooking and eating utensils are all we'll need."

"Food is being arranged," added Kolyei.

"We won't starve," agreed Tara.

"We can gather nuts and berries as well," Brian declared enthusiastically.

Janice listened to their enthusing with dry amusement.

"And when we arrive?"

"Most welcomed you will be," announced her four-legged guest.

"Kath, Emily and the others are getting ready for you," added Tara. "Ilyei told Kolyei they're building basic furnishings, including beds though they'll be a bit rough and ready."

"I like beds," announced Kolyei. "They are much better than cold, hard ground." He grinned and Tara laughed at her vadeln-pair affectionately.

"Every Lind I have met approves of the human tradition of beds. Thomas and the other boys built ours not long after we arrived at Zanatei. They've become very popular."

"And Francis McAllister," queried Janice, "what is he doing?" She didn't have much time for the ex-rating, 'irresponsible troublemaker' being the most common epithet she used to describe him.

"He learns," said Kolyei. "He finds out how we Lind fight Larg."

Janice shooed the three youngest away at this point, not wishing them to hear yet more talk of war.

"Go along and play. There's no school this morning."

"No school," repeated Lucy with glee and they sped away, intent on finishing their game of rounders.

"Three days," fretted Janice. "How am I going to get ready in three days?"

"Brian and I'll help," said Louis. "We can begin to dismantle the furniture we are taking so that it can be loaded on to the wagon."

"I can help pack the clothes and bedding," added Tara shyly.

"When did Dad say the wagon would be here?"

"Tomorrow morning," answered her eldest. "We're to share the wagon space with the Wylies, the Crawfords and the Amptes."

"What about your possessions Tara?" asked Janice suddenly. "Mrs Mackie told Winston she had kept them in case you returned."

"I had forgotten," Tara admitted.

"Go and ask about them now. Violet will go with you if you ask her. She is dying for another chance to ride Kolyei."

"Can you manage without me?"

"Of course we can. Now, trot off and get them."

Janice then set her mind to the knotty problem of how to fit everything they wanted to take into the limited space of the jezdic wagon.

In the end Winston himself went to central stores for Tara's box. He placed it on the big table in the living area where the Randalls usually ate.

"What's in it?" queried Tara with interest.

"When you ran off Jim went down to the cabin and went through your things looking for clues as to where you'd gone. He insisted that your personal possessions be stored until you came back. Made quite a song and dance about it if I remember. He was convinced he'd find you all and that you'd come back someday."

Carefully, Tara lifted the lid off and peeked inside. It was full to the brim of neatly packed items.

"Why, it is Mama's walnut box," Tara cried with delight as she lifted the precious artefact out. "Mama kept her jewellery in it. It's very old, it belonged to her grandmother."

She laid it reverently to one side and looked inside the carton to see what else was there.

"The holos," she said as with trembling fingers she took them out one by one. "This is Mama and Papa on their wedding day and this is Mama holding me when I was a tiny baby."

Soft tears began to flow and Janice was glad she had arranged that the girls and the two boys should be someplace else this morning. She moved over to Tara and took her in her arms. Tara leant into her as she cried her grief away. After a while her sobs died down and Tara dried her eyes with the kerchief Janice offered.

"What are the other holos?" Janice asked gently.

"This one is Mark, my little brother. It was taken on his fourth birthday."

"He looks a jolly little chap."

"He was, most of the time. When he was good he was very, very good, when he was naughty that was different."

She pulled out the last holo. It was larger than the others and showed a traditional family portrait of the whole family, Tara's mother sitting, Mark on her lap, her father standing proudly behind and Tara herself standing leaning into her mother. All four were smiling happily at the holocamera.

"I mustn't cry," said Tara firmly.

"It's okay to grieve Tara," Janice soothed. "It's natural, nothing to be ashamed of. Let's put these holos aside for the moment and see what else is here."

Tara peeked into the carton again.

"There's something soft, wrapped in a shawl. "This shawl was Mama's favourite," she confided, "I'm glad it's here. There are no other clothes or anything, just some ornaments and books." She was busily unwrapping the shawl. She had felt something wrapped inside it.

"It's Toddles," she cried, "my old teddy bear. Mark had a toy giraffe but I never saw it after the storm."

"He looks well loved," said Janice.

"Oh he *is*," said her young guest, rubbing him against her skin. "I used to talk to him in my mind. I never thought I'd be talking to Kolyei the same way. I used to pretend he was talking back to me … childish I know."

"I did the same thing when I was your age," said Janice, giving Toddles a quick pat and thinking back to her own childhood and her own fluffy bear.

"Did you?"

"Of course, all children do. The three girls have dollies. I listen to their pretend play all the time. They don't realise I'm listening in of course."

Tara was piling up the books and papers she had found at the bottom of the carton on the table.

"These belonged to Papa. He used to read them. He hated reading from the screens all the time. Said it hurt his eyes."

"There are no books on screen any more," said Janice. "The computers are only used for what the Council calls 'necessary projects'. These might well be the only copies that there are. What are they?"

"Story books," replied Tara, "grown up ones. There's an old one of mine as well. He gave it to me when I was eight."

She held up an illustrated book with a front cover that said, 'A Child's Book of Fairy Stories'.

She picked up another.

"This one is *'Fables of Old Ireland'*. I used to read bits of this one myself sometimes and here's his copy of *'Kidnapped'*. *'Catriona'* doesn't seem to be here but here are *'Watership Down'* and *'Pride and Prejudice'*. I didn't like that one much. In fact, I think it was mother's and not father's at all. The rest are his workbooks. He was an analytical botanist."

"There are quite a few," Janice noted. "What do you want to do with them?"

"I'm going to keep the story books."

"You could send the textbooks to the repository," suggested Janice. "Jean Farquharson is collecting books such as these."

"Is she setting up a library?"

"Something like that. Why don't we put all you are keeping back in the box for now? Brian and Louis can help you take the others over later. The girls will be back soon. You can help me prepare the meat for tonight's stew."

"Did someone say stew?" came Kolyei's voice from the doorway. He padded into the room.

"What is that?" he asked, pointing with his paw to the object Tara was holding.

"It is a book."

"What is a book?"

"It's sheets of durapaper stuck together, with writing on them telling the stories."

"What is writing?" he asked.

It took time to explain. Tara didn't manage to help Janice in the kitchen area that day. Kolyei was fascinated and asked Tara to tell him what the marks and squiggles meant.

"Each squiggle as you call it is a letter, letters make words and words sentences. All the sentences together make the story."

"A story?" Kolyei's eyes brightened. "I would like to listen to a story."

Tara laughed.

"Later," she promised.

"Will you teach me how to understand the squiggles?" he asked then.

"Are you sure? It takes a long time."

At the Zanatei domta, the twelve children and their partners had listened to many stories. The pack storytellers held many in their memories and recounted them at every opportunity and to whoever would listen. At night the Lind would gather and the call would go up for one of their favourites.

There were many about brave deeds in battle but on the whole the Lind preferred not to listen to tales of war. Favourites were those that told of bravery and endurance in the hunt. Legends about the past were firm favourites. There were even some love stories.

"I could read you the story about the leprechaun at the bottom of the garden who fell in love with a beautiful young maiden," offered Tara.

Kolyei settled down, ears cocked.

"Sit down beside me," he said persuasively. "I like it when you sit close."

When she was settled, Tara began.

"Once upon a time..."

"What time?"

"Don't interrupt. All fairy stories begin with 'once upon a time'. You'll get used to it."

Tara began again. This time Kolyei listened and didn't interrupt although he had a great many questions.

Her voice was clear and carrying and before long children and some adults began drifting towards them. Engrossed in her reading, Tara didn't notice and it was with surprise when she raised her head after reading out *'and they all lived happily ever after,'* that she realised she had an audience.

She blushed in embarrassment.

Violet broke the spell.

"That was wonderful Tara. Please read us another."

Other voices joined in her plea.

"A short one then," she said, "after someone gets me a drink of water. My throat's gone dry."

There was a rush as the children ran off to ask Janice to get her one.

After they had settled down again (during the interval more children had arrived, summoned by sisters, brothers and friends and Janice was heard to wonder how more could be fitted in), Tara read the tale of *'Cinderella and the Glass Slipper'*, from her own book. They listened enthralled and completely silent.

There were meows of disappointment when it ended and Tara closed the book, declaring she couldn't read another thing that day.

: *Tell them to come back tomorrow :* suggested Kolyei.

Tara did, then Janice appeared and sent them away to their own homes for tea.

Over their own meal Janice declared that all the mothers were in Tara's debt. They hadn't had as peaceful a day for a long time and that Julia Ramsay who ran the settlement nursery had asked if she could bring her young charges round the next afternoon.

"You could tell them some of your own stories," said Kolyei who wanted to hear them again.

"I don't know," protested Tara, the thought of it all rather daunting. Kolyei picked up on this and turned to his hostess.

"Others, will they help Tara read?"

"I'll do one," offered Louis with a friendly grin at Tara.

Tara looked at him gratefully and with a hint of hero worship on her own account. Louis was a big boy and it appeared to Tara wonderful that he should volunteer like this. She was yet to learn that the offer was just like Louis. He loved his three little sisters to bits and would do anything for them (anything sensible and not dangerous that is) and often looked after them when Janice and Winston were busy.

As Janice had plans about the future of her young guest, she was pleased to see Louis treating Tara as one of the family.

Another result of that afternoon was that Tara found herself teaching Kolyei his letters. She found him a quick student and eager to learn. Of course, the fact that he could pick concepts and explanations straight out of Tara's mind was a big help.

By the end of their first lesson he knew all the letters of the alphabet, both upper and lower case, and had read the first line of *'Puss in Boots'*, slowly, very slowly, but with great accuracy.

Tara found her remaining days at the settlement exceedingly busy. In the mornings she taught Kolyei after she had helped Janice with the chores. After lunch she attended the nursery where she regaled Julia Ramsay's charges, and as many others who could manage it, with stories. Kolyei went too and sat in the middle of the group, the tinies swarming over him. He enjoyed himself immensely. Then it was back to the Randall cabin for tea, bath and bed.

The happy interlude didn't last.

Two mornings later the alarm rang out from the sentries on the palisades, not the seven hoots of danger but rather the one that informed those inside the settlement that, as expected, their allies had appeared out of the woods. It was Tarmsei, leading his ryz down to the settlement. He would command the escort to domta Zanatei.

As Jim and Larya sped out to meet them, they were very well aware of what was happening in the Zanatei pack-land and elsewhere in the Lind heartland. Through Larya, Jim was constantly kept up to date. At least six packs had been asked to provide volunteers for the embryo cavalry force, to try and vadeln-pair with one of the young humans who were even now assembling for their departure for the west and Larya had reported, with a great deal of humour, that there was a waiting list of applicants.

The five hundred were ready and waiting. As there were no draft animals apart from a few jedzic, most of the equipment they were taking would have to be carried on their backs, although Larya intimated that as there were plenty of escort guards detailed for this duty, there was a fair chance that the Lind would assist.

Tara and Kolyei were going with them although Jim had considered asking that they remain at the settlement at least for a time to help with translating. The male Lind had refused point blank to be separated from Radya for any longer. Jim had his own private thoughts on the matter but not that private, Larya had laughed as she listened in. She considered this incipient romance very interesting indeed. The two would have to wait quite a long time to cement their relationship if that's what it was because Tara and Peter were too young to be thinking of a permanent attachment at this stage of their lives.

Jim, leaning against Larya, watched the procession leave, this their hope for the future. He watched the Lindar form a shield around their new allies as the party began to walk towards the woodlands. Afanasei and Larya would stay in contact with Tarmsei, Stasya, Radya and Kolyei. The cavalcade should make it to the domta without any trouble.

Jim would have been far happier if more women with children had decided to leave with them. He believed that they would be far safer with the Lind than at the settlement.

Many women, when asked, had refused to leave their men. They felt safe behind the palisade walls, especially now that they were being strengthened and the ditch dug. They felt nervous about taking their children to live with the Lind, to a place with no barriers to keep the Larg out. In vain Jim tried to persuade them, saying that they could be evacuated far quicker on Lind backs from the domta if things went badly for them all but it was to no avail. A scant twenty extra women he persuaded to leave their men, although some that did decide to stay, arranged for friends and families who were leaving to take their children with them until the danger was over.

He had work to do here at the settlement before he, Afanasei and Larya could follow them to the domta, before he could follow them home. He would have to liaise between the two species and prepare the settlers for the Larg onslaught but he was not discouraged. Together they would come through this. Together, Lind and human would build a nation in which both species would live in harmony. His arm round Larya's neck, he waved goodbye one last time then turned and headed back through the gates.

Candy Rae

CHAPTER 17

NORTHERN CONTINENT

Those who set out for the Lindish rtathlians were in high spirits and although the impending threat of war managed to dampen this enjoyment a bit, it did not dampen it so much that anybody would notice.

The overcrowding in the settlement might well have had something to do with it. It had gotten much worse since the Larg had been sighted and killed all living creatures within the Armstrong farmstead. Despite their worries about the more obvious dangers that would exist inland of the settlement, many colonists yearned for the space and adventure that was promised when they had originally set out from Earth for Riga. They had most definitely not enjoyed the experience of being forced to hide behind palisade walls in cramped and often unsanitary conditions.

The wagon train arrived at pack Zanatei's domta one pleasant, though cold, afternoon.

Francis and Asya met them. Winston Randall, walking beside Tara and Kolyei near the front of the straggling column, spied the pair waiting in the distance although Kolyei had known of the man's intention to meet them some time before. He had decided not to mention it, preferring their appearance on the skyline to come as a surprise. Kolyei tended toward the dramatic and certainly Francis and

Asya's appearance was theatrical enough for anyone.

It had been a most fulfilling journey for young Tara. Starved of much human affection since the deaths of her parents and little brother, she hadn't realised just how much she had missed being part of a proper family. Winston's wife Janice took the lonely girl into her heart, giving her the human love she craved and a sense of belonging to a family that, however hard Kolyei and the other children had tried, they had not been able to give.

"Janice and I will be as a father and mother to you," Winston promised one cold night in the middle of the plains. "We wanted to before, but old Marion Mackie insisted that she needed you and I have to admit that you did appear to be happy with her, but she used you as a maid of all work, did she not?"

Tara did not know the term but she knew what he meant. "I wasn't unhappy," she said charitably. "I think she was fond of me in her own way. I didn't know that you had asked about me." After a moment, she added wistfully, "I wish I had though. I thought everyone had forgotten all about me."

Winston gave her a huge hug, but didn't reply. 'Least said soonest mended' was his motto.

Kolyei too was welcomed in the Randall household. He happily let the three little girls swarm all over him, permitted them to pull on his ears and even allowed the youngest to ride him during the journey. When Janice apologised for the children's more rumbustious behaviour he merely answered that it was pleasant to play with younglings that did not bite and chew. Janice had laughed and gone away. Kolyei was in his element with Winston as well, answering his many questions patiently and clearly. Winston could not wait to reach the domta and learn more about the medicines and creatures of this new planet. Janice had her own questions to ask. A trained midwife, she hoped to be able to adapt her knowledge and expertise to aid the Lind as well.

Kolyei was shy about answering these more delicate feminine enquiries and directed the woman towards the female members of the Lindar whenever the topic was broached.

"Ask Radya," he would say. "Radya is female, I am not."

"Who is that waiting for us?" Winston asked of Tara as they sighted the waiting pair. Kolyei answered for her.

"Asya and Francis. They run battle training."

"The cavalry?" asked Winston with interest.

"Vada," corrected Kolyei.

"When will our volunteers meet the Lind who wish to pair?"

Again Kolyei answered. His command of Standard was coming on in leaps and bounds, his syntax and vocabulary expanding day by day. In fact, his Standard was almost indistinguishable from the humans. Gone were the single words that the humans found difficult to interpret. Not many Lind were nearly as proficient although Emily and Ilyei were almost as good.

"Other Lindars come," Kolyei answered, "in part to prepare for Larg. Also they want to find out what humans are like. Many want to vadeln-pair if a willing and suitable human they can find."

"Where are they?" asked Winston.

"Not in Zanatei domta at present. They have doms in the lian."

"Oh, a kind of staging area?"

Kolyei looked puzzled and Tara explained. She only ever needed to explain once. Because she and Kolyei often spoke and thought in Lindish as well as Standard, as did the other vadeln-pairs, they found that it was far better for the other member of the pair to explain any misunderstood terms and concepts than to involve others and become embroiled in lengthy discussion.

Afanasei considered that Tara and Kolyei's pairing was by far the strongest of them all although Jim and Larya, like Emily and Ilyei, ran them a close second. Tara and Kolyei seemed to instinctively know what the other was thinking. Certainly when emotions were involved Kolyei appeared to know exactly what his human partner was experiencing.

Francis and Asya fell into step beside them. Although he had been well warned by Jim, Winston was amazed at the change in the man. Gone were the habitual frown and the faint sense of menace he had previously portrayed as a crewmember on board the WCCS *Argyll*. The Francis that took Winston's hand and vigorously shook it was a happy man. His eyes twinkled and he was grinning fit to burst.

"Good to see you vet," were his cheerful words. "Welcome to domta Zanatei. Zanatei himself and the rest are waiting to greet you all in the teaching clearing, the only area big enough to accommodate us all."

Winston turned to Asya. "We are pleased to have reached our new home at last."

Asya's lips crinkled up at that; she appreciated politeness. It had been one of the attributes that had drawn her to Faddei when she was seeking a mate *: I like this man :* she thought at Francis.

"Hello," she replied, pronouncing it hillo. Turning to Tara and Kolyei she greeted them as well.

"Ctrath," was what she said to them. Tara knew by now what she meant and repeated the word in the usual expected formal manner although Winston looked mystified. He thought for a moment and a small sigh exuded from his lips. He had not entirely realised until this moment that as well as learning Lind medicine and teaching them his, he would also have to learn Lindish. Tara had told him that all those who had chosen to settle with the Lind would be expected to become bi-lingual.

This worried the veterinary surgeon. Languages had never been a strong point of his. He did not expect to pair with a Lind although Kolyei told him that it was easier to learn Lind if one was linked mind to mind. He would have to manage somehow.

As they walked into the domta, Francis filled them in with some details that they might otherwise not be aware of.

"We have been waiting for you. I'm afraid that you are all in for a very busy evening. First there is the welcome feast from the pack and only then can we seek our beds. We'll be up at first light in the morning too. There is much to see to."

"Like what?" asked Tara suspiciously. She had planned to visit her old friends and to settle in again. Their daga would require a good clean for one thing and she would have to check its weatherproofing. Tara had had her fill of sleeping under the stars. She wanted a roof over her head once more.

"Like the visits from the Eldas from at least six other packs. Then the Lind from those packs who wish to pair will visit. The Gtratha has insisted that only members of the Lindars may choose a vadeln-pair and then only with humans of at least fourteen years. We've been requested to have all our hopefuls ready and waiting just after the midday meal tomorrow."

"They will be ready," answered Kolyei.

"Most of them can't wait," added Tara.

"Really?" replied Francis in surprise. "Thought everyone would be a bit nervous about all this. It's happened very fast."

"Not nervous," interrupted Kolyei. "Excited. Many saw us at settlement and then met many Lind on journey. They want to share what we have."

Francis looked at Asya affectionately. "Well," he admitted in an embarrassed tone of voice. "I couldn't imagine life without Asya now." He coughed. He still felt uncomfortable talking about his emotions in public.

"I love Tara too," admitted Kolyei.

"Something else before I forget," Francis said. "It's been decided that any later, non-Lindar pairings are for the over-twelves only, both species. Younger than that and they don't know what they are getting into. These general pairings are permitted after tomorrow and I fully expect that more Lind will choose over the next weeks."

"I'm only twelve now," protested Tara indignantly, "and I know exactly what's what. Peter is only ten."

"There will always be exceptions," comforted Francis, smiling at her. "What do you have there?"

Tara was taking a sealed envelope out from her belt-pouch.

"It is for you from Jim," she said. "I promised I'd give it to you as soon as I saw you."

The column began to walk the last mile, heading towards the teaching clearing. It seemed to Tara that history was repeating itself because again the entire pack turned out to greet them. The only difference this time was that interspersed between the blue-stripe colours of pack Zanatei were the envoys of other packs. Some had purple, green or yellow markings. To Tara's surprise, she spied a small group whose markings were pink! She thought however that she much preferred the blue of Kolyei and his rtathen. The blue matched her eyes for one thing.

Tanni, the Randall dog, sat on Kolyei's back looking around him with wide, scared eyes, his more usual terrier exuberance stilled by the sight of so many and to his eyes, gigantic Lind.

The feast was waiting. Great haunches of zarova were being turned over a fire pit and there was a glorious smell of roasting roots. There was not much variety of fruit available. Winter was too advanced for many varieties to be ripe but here was an abundance of greenfruit that came from a bush that gave up its fruit all year round, although the winter berries were inclined to taste bitter.

Zanatei and the rest of the pack Eldas sat waiting. After some urging from both Kolyei and Tara, Winston approached them. He had been informed in great detail what he would be expected to do and what to say.

Zanatei uttered the traditional welcoming words, used only when one pack was making formal acceptance into its ranks of one from another.

"Dedta domta," he intoned in a booming voice. "Dedta rtath Zanatei."

Then for the benefit of those not fluent in Lindish he kindly translated. "Welcome to our pack-home. Welcome to pack Zanatei."

Winston bowed low in acceptance.

Then like a flood, the ltsctas approached the waiting colonists, it having been decided that the sheer volume of many adult Lind might prove unsettling for the newcomers. The little ones milled round the humans, welcoming the travellers in well-rehearsed and squeaky voices.

"Welcome. Dedta. Eat. Jeza." Their short tails wagged constantly and the colonists laughed at their antics. They looked so earnest, much like young human children given an important task to complete. As one the new arrivals dropped their knapsacks and headed towards the waiting feast.

There were cries of welcome from those paired during the first contact. Emily dropped the spoon with which she was stirring the spicy gravy and flew into her father's arms then turned to greet her mother and brother Steven. All those families whose children had disappeared at the same time as Tara had made the trek. The clearing was filled with the sound of joyful reunions. The only ones who didn't take part in this were Tara and Alan, whose families had died during the cosmic storm and the Armstrong twins. Bill and Geoff stood solemn-faced to one side of the clearing apart from all the jollifications. Mark, however, dragged Alan towards his parents where he was greeted with great goodwill.

Predictably, their initial hunger satisfied, it was the children who made the next move. Spotting the ltsctas playing to one side they began to gravitate towards them. Soon a boisterous game of rough and tumble was in progress, much to the amusement of all adults present, of both species.

"Assimilation will not take long, at least for the young," said Laura Merriman, walking up to stand beside Winston. She looked at the man carefully. "You look well and I see that you have adopted a daughter." She smiled.

"I have indeed. Young Tara has fitted into the family as if she has always been one of us."

"Just remember that she is paired with Kolyei and that bond will always be the most important in her life," she warned. "I know, to my great surprise, Faddei paired with me just before Jim left. We are a four, Asya is mated with my Faddei." She blushed. "Francis and I… well…"

"Jim told me," reassured Winston. "No need for any embarrassment. Janice and I are pleased for you both."

He left her watching the scene and moved over to stand beside Zanatei and Francis. He observed that some adult Lind were beginning to approach individual groups of humans, introducing themselves and inviting them to share their family dagas until they could build dagas of their own.

The humans and their families began to disperse, intent on settling into their temporary abodes before darkness fell.

Emily, and the rest of the human youngsters already vadeln-paired led their families back to their own dagas. Kolyei nudged Tara in the direction of Janice Randall and her children, imparting a very clear picture of her leading her new family to theirs. Tara's face broke into a smile. She nodded and hastened to go over and invite them home. Kolyei would bring Winston along later.

Janice's words were complimentary as she led her brood inside. Someone, Emily probably, or perhaps Kath, had swept it out and tidied it up a bit.

"What a lovely home," said Janice, "an actual growing house and you have made it really nice. I think the sooner we get a place of our own though the better; it will be hard to fit us all in."

"Kolyei and I will help you," said Tara shyly.

"I can help," announced Louis, looking down at his new sister. He was fifteen, nearly sixteen, tall and strong for his years.

"Are you not attending the pairing tomorrow?" teased Tara.

"Don't you want a friend like my Kolyei?"

"Of course I am," said Louis. "I want to attend, but I am terrified about it. What if I don't get chosen? If I am chosen, I will need to learn how to fight and go into battle."

"You would have had to fight anyway when these convicts arrive," said Janice at that point. "At least if you are in the cavalry you will be doing so with an experienced friend at your side. I for one will feel much happier about it all if I know that you are astride a creature that can think for herself and can get you out of trouble if necessary."

"There is that," said her eldest, looking much happier although the nervous look continued to haunt his face.

Back at the clearing Zanatei, Francis and Winston were deep in discussion when Kolyei approached, Asya at his side.

"Come over," invited Francis. "We are discussing how we are going to organise the pairings tomorrow. Want to make a bit of a ceremony out of it. There's a waiting list of Lind wanting the chance to pair. I've been talking quite a bit to them recently about cavalry tactics. They think some of them at least will work against the Larg. That training will start as soon as both parties get used to each other."

Zanatei looked at Kolyei.

"You, Kolyei will not fight. Tara is too young."

Kolyei had expected this. The Lind never sent their young into battle against the Larg. His fellow warriors of the Lindar would understand. There could be no dishonour in remaining with the old, the mothers and the young at the domta.

Francis watched Zanatei. Jim's letter had hinted otherwise. He had sent detailed instructions that *everyone* partnered with a Lind should receive weapons instruction, especially Tara.

"If I have deciphered Jim's intentions correctly, you will, however, be kept more than busy behind the lines, a long way behind the lines," said Francis with the air of one conferring a favour, "a part of the battle to come but not in it."

Kolyei sent him an inquiring look.

"You and Tara have been appointed by Jim to be in charge of communications. It's an important and essential task and one that should keep Tara safe. You understand what military communications is?"

"I do," replied Kolyei, trying without much success to appear modest about his linguistic abilities, and failing miserably. "We are the best," he continued, unable to resist.

"You see what I mean?" asked Francis of Zanatei. "I told you he and Tara were the best choice."

"Tara is very young," Zanatei demurred.

"We'll attach a guard detail to look after them. Believe me, they'll be worth their weight in gold."

Zanatei was not convinced and showed it.

Predictably, the Lind asked for an explanation of his last term. Francis soon regretted using it as he began a long involved explanation of what gold actually was. It proved surprisingly difficult. As the Lind did not wear jewellery, they had distinct difficulties understanding the human need to adorn their bodies and as they lived in an elementary barter economy, they found the understanding of monetary value pretty nigh impossible. It took Francis quite a time to get the message across.

That evening many of the newcomers gravitated back to the clearing where they had been promised a night of entertainment, Lind style.

It would begin with a traditional and well-loved tale, to be recounted by the renowned storyteller Janzei of pack Malkei. Then would come the singing and the humans were warned, they would be expected to 'take a turn' as well. So those who could play an instrument brought it with them. When the Lind had spied the violins and flutes – the larger instruments had been too heavy to carry to the domta – they became excited. The humans learnt afterwards that Afanasei had told them of the musical evenings in the settlement in one of his regular reports to Zanatei. The Lind loved music.

Janzei stood up and signalled his intent to start his tale with one measured howl. The listeners grew silent. Kolyei and Tara joined him in the circle. They were to translate.

"This oldest tradition," Janzei began in Standard, and then reverted to Lindish.

"A long time ago…"

Tara translated, with help from Kolyei.

"When the waters were low and the lands one, the Lai came to us out of the sky. We were as other creatures in these far-off days. We could not talk and we ran in herds just as do the kura and the jezdic of today. The Lai were magical beings and looked favourably on what they saw. The Lai wanted to help us become more than simple creatures. Long were their magics as they strove to give us a great gift; the gift of speech. After a long and hard struggle, they succeeded and we began to speak simple words. Their task complete, the Lai flew away, to where we do not remember, but they left us with the promise that in dire need, they would return. We could not find them though we hunted high and low, but we do not forget."

"An interesting tale," said Janice to her husband when the story drew to a close. "Is it true?"

"Probably not," he answered, "but a good one all the same don't you think?"

Janice was lost in thought. "How did the *Larg* learn to speak?" she asked.

Tara and Kolyei sat down beside her. He had heard her question and decided to answer it, Tara helping with the more difficult words.

"We were once one," he began quietly, "then the ground shook and the waters rose higher than now and the lands north and south were sundered. A long time passed and when the seas fell away the Lind went south to find out what had happened to them. We found that our cousins had changed beyond recognition. They had become hard and cruel, thinking only of killing and war. They had changed physically as well, becoming larger and more muscular, better adapted to the harsh southern lands. We are no longer the same. They want our rtathlians and herds. Summers have been dry in recent seasons and their own herds are not enough to feed them all. That is why they come."

Kolyei sighed. Like his fellow Lind he deplored the need to have to fight the Larg, but knew that if they did not defend their rtathlians the Larg would take full advantage of the peaceful nature of the Lind and would be free to rampage throughout the northern continent.

There was silence for a few moments.

"I agree," said Janice at last, "war is a waste of lives, but I begin to understand why we must fight."

Tara changed the subject.

"You are meeting with the Lind healers tomorrow then? Laura is coming to take you there … yes?"

"We're both going," replied Winston. "Also the kids have been informed that their lessons are to begin at once. I believe that they are fair aggrieved at the prospect."

"Lessons are fun here," said Tara as she remembered her own. She turned to her new sisters and brothers who were looking doubtful. "I promise," she added.

They still looked unconvinced.

It was at this point that the instrumentalists began to play a popular ballad. Conversation ceased as everybody listened and some children began to sing along. The Lind were ecstatic and presently began to hum along with the tune as they committed it to memory.

By morning the entire domta was singing it, the Lind adding their own variations.

Candy Rae

CHAPTER 18

NORTHERN CONTINENT

The Lind made quite a ceremony of the momentous day when more than three hundred men, women and teenagers paired with Lind from seven different Lindars.

Zanatei had not been jesting when he intimated to Winston Randall on his arrival that there were many more Lind wanting to pair than humans eligible to do so.

The human contingent gathered after the midday meal and made their way to the main pack clearing in front of Zanatei's daga where the pairings were to take place. Like Louis, many felt apprehensive about what was to come. Tara, escorting her new big brother, tried to set him at ease. Louis was most definitely nervous and he kept talking about how unfitted he was for the honour, worrying aloud about his fears that the Lind would not like him.

"Louis," said Tara in exasperation. "Will you please *relax*? Kolyei has explained it all to you more than once. He thinks that you will be fine; anyway there is nothing you can do about it. Either a Lind will choose to pair with you or she won't. Even if you're not chosen today it doesn't mean that you are not acceptable. It only means that your Lind vadeln hasn't arrived on the scene yet."

"I know," answered Louis, "but you telling me again and again doesn't make me feel any better." His stomach was in knots and he felt sick with fright.

They reached the clearing, amongst the last to arrive. Tara left Louis with a sisterly and encouraging pat on his shoulder and went to join Kolyei who had found a good spot to watch. He made room for her with difficulty. There were many spectators and the clearing was packed to the gunnels.

Directed by Afanasei who Zanatei had put in charge of the arrangements, those humans presenting themselves for pairing formed a loose circle.

Zanatei, as resident Elda, emitted a high pitched howl, the pre-arranged signal for the pairings to begin and the Lindar volunteers began to nose around the humans, seeking exactly the right one. It was the pink-hued Lindar of pack Ranetei who were the first to make their move. Disappointed, some trotted away, not being able to sense the right thoughts, emotions and feelings from the humans. Others began to nose and sniff at individuals with more force than decorum.

Then it happened, the first vadeln-pairing was made. In a sudden move, a young lad, who was, incidentally, Emily's older brother Steven, took an eager step forward. He stared at the large pink-striped female standing impatiently in front of him. She nudged him in the chest and he took an involuntary step back (the nudge was a hard one). His face broke into a smile.

"I am Alanya," she said, then she thought at him : *You wish? :*

"Steven, and I do wish, very much," he said aloud.

The young man stepped up beside her. She nosed him to her side.

"Ptatch," she ordered.

Steven knew that word, it was Lindish for ride and he had heard it often during the trek to the domta.

Alanya lowered herself so that he could mount. He swung his right leg over her withers and settled himself. She stood up then and with a triumphant smile, walked out of the clearing. Steven had a bemused expression on his face. His parents (and Emily) let out a whoop of joy.

It was a wonderful day. Louis Randall need not have worried. A large violet female approached him early on in the proceedings. She had made a beeline for him as soon as she had sighted him. Louis was ecstatic. Janice was less so because this meant her son would definitely be off to the war in the summer.

Back at the settlement and under Jim, Larya and Afanasei's direction, the defences were being put in place. The colonists began to practise fighting at the palisades. Warned by the Lind as to how the convicts had managed to overcome the southern fort so easily, the palisades themselves were coated with a fire-resistant substance and the ditch around the palisades was growing deeper (and wider) with each passing day as the colonists attacked it vigorously with mattock and shovel. Inside, the palisades were being strengthened and buttressed within an inch of their lives.

A massive programme had begun to arm the northern armies, for armies they were learning to become. Unfortunately the *Argyll* had settled deeply into the marshy ground where she had landed. The settlers, short of metal with which to make weapons and armour, ventured (gingerly) back out into the marsh and removed every scrap of salvageable metal within reach. Now only parts of the higher superstructure remained above the water level. The ship would soon disappear completely with nary a sign of her passing.

Arthur Knott, the smith, made good use of the materials on offer. It was decided that the Vada (the name for the Lind-human cavalry) should be armed with long thin sabre-like swords, similar to those used by the light horse cavalry regiments of early modern Earth.

The sabre was a strong weapon and perfectly suited to what Francis McAllister had in mind for his vadeln-pairs. The metal hilt had a cantle-shaped pommel, with a back strap, knuckle-bow and three curved quillons. The curved blade was double-edged like all cavalry swords. He and his assistants made four hundred of them, as well as some light armour for the riders. Relays of Lind permitted loads of these items to be tied to their backs and sped back to the Zanatei domta with them where Francis received them with many thanks and a great deal of relief. The Vada had made their base at the foot of the hill on which Zanatei domta was situated.

Once the sabres had been despatched, Arthur turned his attention to outfitting the defenders of the settlement, and to his pet project of making as many crossbows as possible. These had a fairly plain, straight stock, a sinew bridle binding the lath to the stock and a cylindrical latch nut with a long iron trigger. They were held in the same manner as a firearm, some defenders rested them on top of their shoulder and manipulated the trigger with their thumb. The bolt's point was used as the front sight when aiming. Crossbow training began as soon as there were enough to go round. They proved to be a rather wicked and accurate weapon although it took a long time to wind up the wires.

The settlement rang to the sound of smithies and metal shops in action; people went to their beds each night with the ringing tones of hammer on anvil sounding in their ears but the piles of swords, knives, helmets, armour and shields grew daily larger as winter progressed.

The morning chosen by Francis and Asya as the one when military training for the embryo Vada was to start was cold although to his relief it was not snowing. Crisp frost covered the ground even close to the trees, and the men, women and teenagers shivered as they waited for the class to begin. Not that it mattered; they would soon be warm enough for anybody's liking, too warm probably.

There were over three hundred vadeln-pairs waiting. For some of the siblings and parents who had elected to watch, this was a poignant moment; many of the boys and girls were disquietingly young. Francis thought so too, but rules were rules amongst the Lind; at fourteen one fought.

Although the majority of those chosen were over eighteen, some forty were much younger. One young lad had vadeln-paired on his fourteenth birthday. He was naturally considered adult in Lind terms and therefore eligible to join a Lindar and fight, but to his mother, standing to one side, he was still her son, far too young to go courting death in war. His Lind was, however, a veteran of her Lindar and if any Lind could keep the woman's son safe, it would be she. Louis Randall was amongst these forty youngsters, aged from fourteen to sixteen, bunched at the rear. There was no way Francis was going to include them in the shock front ranks, however experienced their Lind.

The Lind were saddled and waiting. Francis and the others had spent long and tedious hours designing a saddle that was both comfortable and which also gave the rider the security and stability required to enable him or her to fight without falling off. Francis believed that they had got it right at last.

The zarova leather saddles bore little resemblance to those that countless human generations of horse troopers had used. They were thinner and more flexible for one thing; the backbones and withers of the Lind were not the same as horses. The saddles were designed with that in mind and the Lind could still weave left and right with the suppleness of the wolf. The saddle was secured on to the front of the body with a martingale, a girth fitted round the stomach. Behind the saddle, and after a lot of thought, a heavy flexible strap was fitted horizontally from left to right and attached to the girth to keep the saddle from moving forwards.

To compensate for the fact that the saddles had no pommel or cantle, the riders were actually strapped to the saddle with thick leather straps designed to keep the rider aboard no matter what convoluted cavorting the rider's Lind got up to. It had the added advantage that if the rider was unconscious or badly wounded, they would still remain in the saddle, enabling his or her mount to escape the melee with his or her rider. If a rider needed to separate from his partner for any reason he or she need only unhook the buckles or could even cut the straps away. The rider's feet rested in stirrups, also made of tough zarova leather that provided the rider with a platform on which he or she could brace their feet when fighting.

There were no reins. The rider's free hand held on to the saddle front where a handhold was sewn. The rider sat forward, almost at the withers and gripped tightly with the legs. They had no shields. Francis was in two minds about that but had decided they'd be too difficult to manage for now. Maybe later they could be introduced when the riders had more experience.

The riders wore armour, also designed to be as flexible and light as possible and made of hardened leather. The Vada strength was intended to be in its speed and Francis did not want to weigh the Lind down.

All the humans wore a steelwood helmet, then leather lower and upper arm and leg guards and wrist plates. Many wore breast and back plates made of boiled leather and the others would have them as soon as they were ready. The Lind had realised the advantage of armour at once and many could be seen sporting a wide leather collar designed to protect their vulnerable necks from the sharp-edged Larg teeth.

Francis blew his whistle and the front rank formed up. On the second blow of the whistle they began to move forward. Asya stood beside Francis, mentally imparting the orders to the Lind who seemed to react that much faster than their riders, one or two of whom would have fallen off if they hadn't been strapped on. On her order, they wheeled left, keeping in formation remarkably well for a first attempt. Francis decided to pick up the pace and watched as they circled round the training field, the majority, by now, at one with the faster gait. One of two of the riders began to grin complacently at Francis. That was a mistake. He smiled an inward smile and passed a very private order to Asya. Her eyes twinkled as she passed it on. The Lind stopped dead in their tracks, and one or two of the riders, caught unprepared, banged their heads painfully against their mounts' necks. Francis groaned. They would have to do much better.

They did do better and as the days passed Francis became rather proud of his three hundred.

Even the threat of the coming war could not completely dampen Francis McAllister's joy with his new life. His Vada's expertise grew daily and Francis began to believe that they would play an important part in the campaign. He reported this increase in abilities to Jim (via Larya) who listened to his frequent updates with a great deal of relief. Jim was fighting against time to get the settlement ready. More Lind spies had returned, there was definitely an alliance forming between the Larg and the convicts. They would be facing a combined attack from the south come summer.

So Francis kept his Vada at it morning, afternoon and evening.

The younger vadeln were not exempt.

In vain did Agnes Crawford plead that Peter, at ten, was too young. Francis listened but would not be swayed.

"Jim and Larya have ordered this and I can't make exceptions to the rule. Jim and Larya are my superior officers. I am sorry Agnes but learn he must."

What Francis did not say was that Jim had expressly ordered that Tara must learn and that it would be best if all the pre-teens joined her. He wondered again what Jim's plans were for the girl.

Tara had accepted that she must train with the calm acceptance the adults at the domta were coming to associate with her. Only her eyes betrayed her fear.

Francis did make one concession. The young ones were to be

trained separately from those who made up the main Vada ranks and detailed an ex-crew member from the Argyll, Ross and his vadeln Lililya, to take charge. A thin, wiry man in his early thirties, he showed a distinct aptitude for teaching.

Emily and Ilyei joined Tara, Peter and the others, her medical studies under Talya's tuition being put on hold for the duration.

Under Ross and Lililya's kindly eyes, the youngsters learned how to use a sword. They lacked strength and stamina and Ross, instead of lessons on how to charge and attack, taught them instead how to defend themselves and how to evade a fight. Of the forty or so vadeln-pairs that formed what was called 'the baby class', much to their embarrassment, only Kolyei and Ilyei and a few others amongst the Lind were old enough to have fought in a battle before.

But life was not all work and no play.

The eleven original children and Kath often met together, despite the fact that they were no longer the only humans at the domta. There was an unspoken feeling amongst them that they were a special type of family and should keep together.

Tara and Peter, being the youngest, had formed a close friendship over the past months, much to the gratification of Radya and Kolyei whose attachment to each other had begun to blossom. Emily and Thomas also began to be seen as a couple despite their young age. As Janice Randall had said to Emily's mother, teenagers grew up quickly in these troubled times.

The Lind, naturally enough, saw nothing strange in such a phenomenon. In their eyes, both Emily and Thomas were adult. Stasya and Ilyei were pleased as well, Ilyei saying to anyone or any Lind who would listen, that Stasya had a well-turned paw.

"I hate arms practice," declared Peter one evening. "I wish we didn't have to do it."

"You should see what the grown-ups are doing," said Tara. "Louis came back to the daga yesterday and he was black and blue. I don't think he slept a wink last night he was so sore and bruised." Those teenagers aged sixteen and deemed strong and mature enough had been moved from the 'baby class' to join with the more adult in training.

"Dad says Francis is pushing them because he must," continued Peter. His voice faded as he gazed around him. "Where is Kolyei?"

"He was called to see Zanatei. Is Radya with him?"

"She went hunting," he answered. "Said she would return by bedtime."

"Your mum still insisting you go to bed early?" teased Tara.

Peter squirmed in embarrassment and complained, "She's so clingy – wants me beside her the whole time."

Tara could understand why. Her thirteenth birthday was some weeks away but with her quaint older air about her, which made adults forget her years, they said things in front of her that might have been better left unsaid. Kolyei too was older than Peter's Radya and had a different perspective on some things.

"What do you expect?" she said. "She's your mum and when we all disappeared like we did she must have been frantic with worry. Probably thought you were dead. Bear with it. It will pass."

Peter did not look convinced.

Tara felt much older than him at that point, a feeling she was to retain for many years to come.

"At least Jim and Larya will be home soon," she said. "I've missed them."

"Aren't you happy with the Randalls?"

"Yes I am. It's not the same though. I wish Mama and Papa were still alive, and Mark. They would have loved it here, Papa especially, he did so love adventures."

"Are you calling the war an adventure?"

"Not an adventure exactly, more like a nightmare," she answered.

The two sat together in an awkward silence then Peter stood up with relief as he sensed the approach of his Lind-partner.

"Radya's here," he announced and sped away, intent on spending time alone with her before his mother searched him out for bath, supper and bed.

Left alone, Tara remained where she was, lost in thought and remembering happy times past. She wondered absently where Kolyei was. His meeting with Zanatei must be important to keep him away so long. Had she known what was being discussed, her thoughts would not have been so easy.

At the settlement, the colonists continued with their preparations. The palisades were high and strong. Procedures were in place to evacuate the farmsteads. Beacons were set up along the coastline manned by both human and Lind, who would carry the human on duty with them to safety once they were lit.

It was decided that the majority of the adults able to fight would remain behind the settlement walls. Both Jim and Stuart were positive that the convicts would make straight for them, intent on capturing the women inside. A force of around a thousand would march out the gates when the time came and join with the Lind in fighting the Larg outside on the hill.

The Lind would, as usual, wait for the Larg on this high ground at the edge of the woods. The Larg much preferred the open plains on which to fight. Their superior strength was not such an advantage when they were forced to attack uphill and through the woodlands which were the Lind's natural habitat.

Signs of the impending conflict were manifesting themselves as Jim returned to domta Zanatei. The rtathlian was full, and more than full with all the Lindars arriving from the west to aid their brothers and sisters. When Jim, Larya and Afanasei arrived, Jim was amazed at the numbers and diversity of the different packs surrounding him as he rode in.

They had come back to domta Zanatei to discuss the final deployment plans. Word had come north that the convicts and the Larg were mustering. The so-called General Murdoch was committing an estimated ten thousand men to the fight, some two-thirds of his total manpower. Intelligence was suggesting that he did not consider the campaign as a hit and run raid but was intending a more permanent sojourn in the north.

The Larg numbers were also many. More Larg kohorts than usual would make the crossing to the north, intending to take advantage of Murdoch's aid to extend their summer depredations further west than ever before.

The Lind were responding to this threat in their usual courageous manner. More and more Lindars were arriving. Some of the far western packs appearing had not needed to actively fight for generations, but Afanasei assured Jim that they would fight well, notwithstanding their inexperience. Jim believed him. He had faith in the abilities of the Lind.

Towards the end of winter, the last of the Lind spies in the south began to drift back north, intent on returning before the Larg reached the island chain in any numbers and they were cut off. The sea level between the islands was already dropping.

The Lind Jsei was one of these spies. He began his crossing back early one wintry morning, intending to rest on one of the larger islands for much of the day ahead before setting off again at nightfall. When he reached one large island about seven out from the southern coast he pulled himself out of the water, shook himself and started to trek across to the other side, where he thought he remembered having seen some caves in which he could hide. He took the inland route, one not frequently used by either Lind or Larg. He was much surprised to see strange tracks on the ground beneath his paws. Bending down to take a closer look, he sniffed warily and then he became more confused. These were not the prints of the Larg, in fact, they were the prints of a something that he had never seen before and they were as large as his own.

Jsei decided to investigate.

As he approached the western side of the island he found further evidence of occupation. There were more tracks and then some most peculiar smelling droppings. He also smelt fire but not the more familiar forest variety. Having spent a number of days in the pack Zanatei domta before coming south he recognised it at once. It was the aroma of roasting meat. He stopped and tried to make sense of the information. He knew for a fact that none of the Lind's new human allies had ventured on to the island chain. Logically therefore, the fire must belong to the men of the south who were allied to his enemies.

As he crept towards the smell under the cover of the bushes he began to hear voices, human voices but he could not sense the presence of any Larg. Jsei became even more confused.

Gerry and the two Jays were making lunch. The mares were nearby. They began to move restlessly, having caught Jsei's scent, even though the Lind scout was downwind of the group.

"What's up with them?" Gerry asked, reaching for his knife.

The girls went white. The three had been very careful during their sojourn on the island, keeping their fires low and out of plain sight and not venturing to the east of the island. Gerry had, in their early weeks, found some tracks there that he had not been able to identify and they had concluded that it would be much safer to remain hidden as much as possible. They most definitely did not wish to meet the owners of these tracks.

Gerry stood and looked around, fingering the sharp edge of his knife. The girls had their own knives at the ready.

Jsei was in a quandary. Who were these humans and what on Lind were these other creatures moving restlessly round the paddock? He lay there, watching and listening. Jsei's Standard was not as proficient as Kolyei's but he knew enough to make some sense of what he was hearing.

"It can't be those men," Jessica was saying. "They would have attacked by now, surely?" The three of them had seen nothing and the mares had stopped milling around although they stood still and tense.

"Perhaps it is some others who have escaped Fort?" was Jenny's suggestion.

The three began to relax, just a little bit but although they went back to their fire, they kept looking round for lurking danger as they began to eat; the island teemed with small burrowing creatures closely resembling a rabbit, but with very short ears and no tail.

After a while, Jsei decided that he would have to make the first move. He had realised by now that these could not be southern men but had to be fugitives from them.

Thinking hard of all the Standard words he knew, he called out to them.

"Hello. Humans. Jsei."

The words were a distinct shock to Gerry and the Jays.

"Who was that?" asked Jenny in fright, dropping her plate as she stood up. The contents spilled on top of the fire and hissed.

"Don't know," Gerry answered. "Doesn't sound human."

Jsei tried again.

"Hello. Argyll."

The three looked at each other.

"The *Argyll*?" exclaimed Jessica disbelievingly.

"The *Argyll* was one of the ships in the convoy," offered Jenny. "Do you think they reached the planet as well as us?"

"Possibly," answered Gerry. "If that's the case then I think that whoever or whatever is hiding out there may well be friendly, but there are no guarantees."

"I vote that we invite the voice in," stated Jessica in a manner reminiscent of her father. Gerry remembered how good Peter had been at making decisions and forcing them through, however unpopular. Jessica continued. "Perhaps they have found out about the Electra and it's a rescue mission."

"Of one?" he countered.

Jessica ignored him.

"I agree with Jess," ventured Jenny. "Let's find out. I'm scared and I want to know exactly what is out there. Ask whoever it is to come in so we can see it."

"With its hands up?" questioned Gerry.

"If it has hands, then yes," said Jessica, fingering her knife.

The creature that emerged in answer to their invitation was like nothing the three had expected to see. It was fully as large as any one of the mares. Jsei advanced four steps then stopped, looking at them inquiringly.

"Stop right there," ordered Gerry. "Tell us how you got here, what you know about the *Argyll*. Just tell us everything you can."

It took Jsei a while to work out what the man was saying but eventually he managed to tell all he knew, stretching his abilities in Standard to the absolute limit.

By nightfall, Gerry was quite decided on what their next move must be.

"You two Jays must go with Jsei to the north."

Jessica turned a stricken face towards him. "What about you?"

"I'm going back south to see what I can find out."

"You can't," exclaimed Jessica in distress. "You'll only get yourself killed and then what will we do?"

Gerry looked at the girl. Again he noticed how like her father she was.

"I am not planning on getting myself killed. I fully intend to get to the north someday and see how you and Jenny have got along with the mares. One of them is carrying a colt. I'm sure he will be a fine fellow and will father many more. I'll not tell you which mare was inseminated with the male gene. Let that be a surprise to you both."

He chuckled and then his face took on a more serious expression. "You have to take charge of them in my absence. Make sure they don't come to any harm. Care for them as I would. I know how to get back into Fort. I also know the surrounding area like the back of my hand. I have to find out what has happened to the women and children back there. In fact, I am hoping to rescue your mother Jessica, and Cherry and Joseph too."

He faced Jenny.

"And I think, young woman, that you will be very glad I went back when I return with your mother and young Gavin. Won't you?"

Jenny nodded. After a moment's thought Jessica did the same.

Jsei remained silent. He would have made the same decision as the man if he had been in the same situation. He informed Gerry of all he knew about what was happening in the south and warned him about the Larg and the alliance between them and the convicts. He also told him of the hiding places where Gerry could hole up if necessary and they made plans for future contact.

Gerry escorted the two girls to the northern shore of the island the following morning and helped them tie the horses into two lines. The waters were getting lower and Jsei promised further Lind help once they reached the next island of any size. The girls said a tearful farewell to Gerry then, leading the mares, they followed Jsei into the water. When they looked back their protector had vanished from sight.

The promised help came the next day but it proved difficult to get the horses across the water, the currents were strong and one couldn't quite ask them to sit atop a tree trunk. The Lind laboured long and hard to get the recalcitrant animals north. Some eight days later they splashed ashore. Kath and Matvei met them on the beach.

When they reached the settlement they learnt that they were lucky to be alive. During their time on the island, many Larg scout parties had used the eastern edge of the island, passing from south to north and back again. It was pure chance that they had never been discovered.

The Lind were fascinated by the horses and asked endless questions. There were clear similarities between the horse and the striped jezdic, the half-wild animals that the settlers were trying, with limited success, to break to harness.

After due consideration by the Council, it was decided that they should not stay at the settlement, so shortly after their arrival, Jenny and Jessica found themselves on the move again. With a Lind escort, they travelled with their charges to the safety of the rtathlians, there to tend the mares and to oversee the births of the colt and filly. The two girls passed through the Zanatei pack lands, resting there for only a few days before setting out again, bound for domta Ratvei. Jsei had claimed Jenny and Jessica for his own pack, citing the fact that, as it had been he who had rescued them, thus he had the right. The Elda agreed that it would be good for morale if another pack beside the Zanatei had the honour of having humans residing in their domta. The pack welcomed them with open paws.

The horses were an added bonus. They settled in well in a natural paddock and a rudimentary stable was built at the edge of the domta. The Ratvei Lind grew accustomed to their presence and became quite knowledgeable about horse care.

Jenny, not so deep thinking as her friend, settled in more easily. Before long she vadeln-paired with a young male of the pack, Savei by name. Although pressed, Jessica decided not to accept a similar honour, at least for the time being. She often rode Gerry's favourite grey mare. She missed the man terribly and often wondered over the coming months how he was surviving in the south at Fort.

When the young were born, she named the colt after Gerry, in remembrance, and the filly she named after her little sister Cherry. She did not believe she would see him, or those who remained of her family, ever again.

CHAPTER 19

NORTHERN CONTINENT

Francis sat down in what Jim called Tara's Grove beside the newly appointed Susyc of the northern armies with a grunt.

When Jim and Larya had returned to domta Zanatei, to his great astonishment, Jim had been appointed Commander, or Susyc, of the joint-defence of the north. He and Larya were the two most trusted to command by both species.

Francis had managed to find out where Jim and Larya had hidden themselves only after nagging at Asya for over four hours. Only then had she sighed and mentally contacted Larya. Larya had been loath to pass Jim's whereabouts on, stating as an excuse that her partner needed peace and quiet to think.

Francis had pressed his point across, stating that two heads were better than one and, after some thought she had given him directions towards the rocky outcrop in the very centre of the domta, her only comment being that it was four heads, not two, now that both of them were vadeln-paired and that he mustn't forget this again.

Francis chose to ignore that tart reminder.

Jim acknowledged their arrival but said nothing more and Francis decided that he'd better start the ball rolling.

"How are we going to defeat them?"

"I'm thinking about it."

"Think harder."

"You don't think I'm not trying?" Jim replied with some heat. "This is as new to me as it is to you."

"What's your problem?"

"Problem is that the Lind have a time-honoured way of dealing with the Larg."

"You don't know how they will cope with any changes you come up with?"

"Correct."

"Want some advice?"

"What?"

"Order the changes. They have appointed you leader of the joint-command."

"Susyc," said Jim absently, "not Leader."

"Whatever. The crux of the matter is that you are in charge and everybody else must obey you."

: *Francis speaks truth* : Larya bespoke him. : *Every Susa must obey the Susyc* :

"My thoughts are this," Jim began. "Correct me if I am wrong you three, but traditionally the Susyc has been the first Lindar Susa to reach the battlefield and was usually from one of the four packs who inhabit this area, they being the nearest. The Lindars fight separately. There is no cohesion and the Larg take full advantage of this, exploiting the gaps that appear in the lines."

"Get on with it," interrupted Francis. "You're stating the obvious."

"One line."

"One line? What do you mean?"

"I want a continuous and unbroken line of Lindars standing and fighting on the slope in front of the woods, three ranks deep at least."

: *Ryz* : corrected Larya.

"Behind them back-up ranks and behind them the reserve ranks."

"Will there be enough to cover all the ground?"

"I believe there will. Larya and I got approximate numbers from Zanatei. We can do it. I know we can. I'll plug any gaps in the front lines with the second line and keep the reserves until I need them."

"And how are you and Larya going to know if and where the front ranks are weakening, tell me that?"

"I'm going to allocate a vadeln-pair to each Lindar. They'll tell me through Larya."

"Looks like you're going to be busy," said Francis with a wink in Larya's direction.

"Only the most urgent," she answered in a placid tone. "Even I cannot manage all. Jim has worked it out."

She looked at her vadeln.

"Tell Francis the rest."

"You've expressed many concerns about the fourteen-to-sixteen-year-olds fighting with you in the main Vada ranks. I'm going to use them for communications. They'll be safer with the main lines than with you and, because of our allies' wonderful telepathic abilities, they can remain well behind the rear ryz. They don't need to be right at the battle-line to keep in touch with the Lindar Susas."

"It might just work," Francis admitted but the worry lines did not fade from his face.

"The communications vadeln-pairs will not report to Larya unless the matter is critical, but to the main communications unit, well to the rear, which will filter the information."

"Who is to run the communications unit?"

"Haven't made my final decision yet," was the bland answer. "The Gtrathlin has volunteered a team of ten and I have accepted but I need a pivot, a vadeln-pair if I can manage it, the Lind having enough experience to know what is important and what is not. If they can both understand and think in both Standard and Lindish it would be a help."

Francis realised that there was only one pair capable of this. Asya confirmed it with her next words. *: Kolyei and Tara :*

: Tara is a child : was his rejoinder.

: Kolyei is good at human speaking and Tara speaks our language best of all :

"It took some explaining to the Lind," Jim continued, "but I can't be everywhere, see everything. They saw sense eventually. If we keep together on the ridge and in contact, that is our strength and the superior weight of the Larg is counterbalanced. No matter what, we stick to the ridge like glue."

"The Lindars won't like that."

"I think you'll find they like being torn to pieces even less. That's what happened the last time the Larg arrived in great numbers. The Larg feinted a retreat and the Lindars, wrongly sensing victory, followed, with predictable results. From what Zanatei told me, they didn't even attack together. Each Susa decided when to go on his own."

"Did the Susyc not try to stop them?"

"Oh he tried, believe me."

"And you're sure you'll do better?"

"I have taken precautions. Each Susa and their Ryz Commanders will take an oath of obedience and loyalty to Larya and me personally. I am assured by Mariya, who is the present Gtrathlin, that all will do so."

"If you and Larya fall?"

"The oath encompasses my second-in-command."

"Who is your second-in-command?"

"Why, you are of course," answered Jim with a grin at Francis's stunned face. "I have no intention of getting myself killed though, so don't hold your breath."

"Me?" Francis was aghast at the prospect.

"I can't think of anyone better suited to the job."

"What if we have to make a run for it? What then?"

"The Larg are built for strength," answered Jim, "not speed. In a worst case scenario and I or Larya have to order a retreat, the Lind can make good their escape through the woods and live to fight another day, but I don't intend that to happen. We will hold the ridge. We must hold the ridge."

Summer arrived. The snows melted from the hills and early flowers started to bloom. The fruit bushes were flowering and fruit buds began to form. There was new growth everywhere you looked. If it hadn't been for the invasion threat looming over them the colonists might have felt they were living in a paradise. The kura and zarova herds were increasing daily. Many young were being born and they browsed and played in the pasturelands, the dams watching over them. The Lind took to the human idea of capturing and raising kura herds at their own domtas. The small gentle kura and the not so gentle zarova now lived in paddocks beside the Zanatei domta, for use by both human and Lind. The humans were amazed at the way the Lind managed the wild herds. They had definite rules governing this.

No animal in foal was to be caught for food and none of the young. The old and sick were fair game and also the males. In this way, they succeeded in keeping the herds healthy and plentiful. The Larg, if they were allowed to spread over the continent, had no such rules; they would hunt and kill indiscriminately, for food, but also for fun. They would decimate the herds in a huge area within days of their arrival.

At Zanatei the Vada drilled constantly; to begin with they had provided the spectators with a great deal of amusement, now they were perfecting their skills. Gone were the days when riders toppled out of their saddles (notwithstanding the leather restraining straps – supposed to be designed to prevent such an eventuality) as soon as they raised their swords to practise a blow. After long hours of practice, they now sat as glued to their partner's back, no matter what antics their mounts got up to in an attempt to dislodge them. They were a well-rehearsed team, charging flank to flank at mock targets. Everyone possessed well-fitting armour. The Lind wore neck and chest armour, specially designed, after a lot of false attempts, not to impede movement. The Larg's (and also the Lind's) favourite place to strike was at their opponent's neck and chest. Now when Larg teeth tried to close on this area all they would bite into would be, instead of the jugular, a good inch of treated leather. Long and tedious hours were spent softening the leather and moulding it into just exactly the right shape, trying to get the happy balance of protection and flexibility.

Added to their number were now twenty or so vadeln-pairs who were older than the others. Some men and women, angry at the dictat that restricted the pairings to those up to the age of thirty, had taken matters into their own hands and had approached older members of the various Lindars, offering themselves as riders. Some very experienced older Lind had responded, glad of the chance. It was these older pairs who found themselves commanding the individual troops and as the younger duos of both species respected age and experience, it seemed natural for Francis to promote them.

Jim Cranston and Larya were impressed with their progress and wished there were more of them.

"Many Larg will die," announced Larya with satisfaction.

"You bloodthirsty woman," answered Jim humorously. *: Thought*

you Lind deplored the need to kill :
  : Have fought Larg before. Sometimes killing is only option :

Stuart MacIntosh was to command the defence of the settlement itself with a liaison unit of Kath Andrews, Matvei and another three unpaired Lind. Matvei's Rozya and her vadeln James Rybak remained at the domta because her young were too small to be left. The liaison party would be in direct contact telepathically with the communications Lindar. Emily and Ilyei were also allocated to communications and to provide medical assistance. Thomas and Stasya had been sent to be the communications link to one of the Lindars and the girl worried constantly about them both. Young Peter Crawford and Radya were to remain with James and Rozya at the domta. The boy was considered far too young and vulnerable to face the carnage that was a battlefield. Tara however, as Francis had suspected, was not to be so lucky.

Jim had managed to persuade Zanatei that Tara and Kolyei were to go east with the army as the pivot pair of his communications strategy. He needed a vadeln-pair, both halves of which were fluent in both Standard and Lindish and one where the Lind half could maintain a strong multiple telepathic link. Afanasei could have done this but he was not partnered with a human.

In fact, most Susas, ryz leaders and Eldas could multi-link in this way, to a greater or lesser extent. Kolyei was unusual in being as proficient at multi-linking so young. It was not only Kolyei's telepathic skills that had made Jim choose him and Tara; his linguistic skills were coupled with acumen and experience.

"Good communications is the key to victory," Jim had told Zanatei. "We must meet the Larg as an army, not as individual Lindars and I won't be able to see everything from the ledge I have chosen as our command-post."

"But Tara," exclaimed Zanatei in distress. "She is not adult. Have you lost whatever senses you have? It is our duty to protect her, not to send her into the many paths of danger."

"She'll be behind the lines, well out of danger."

"Nowhere is safe in battle," cautioned Zanatei.

"Do you have any better ideas? They are the only choice, unfortunately."

: I wonder what Janice will say : mused Larya. *: I do not think she will be pleased :*

Larya's prediction proved quite correct and Jim had to talk very fast to get her to agree.

"I will hold you personally responsible for her safely," she warned him, an angry glint in her eye.

Jim was positively sure that, if anything untoward happened to the girl, Janice would personally arrange his painful demise.

A medical section, or Holad, was to be provided to aid both human and Lind. Laura and Winston were in charge of the human contingent with Zhenya, senior healer at Zanatei.

Robert Lutterell commanded the thousand settlers who would march out of the settlement to stand and fight with their allies. Reports from Matvei complimented their preparedness for battle and their determination.

Although Arthur Knott had the knowledge to make duplicates of the old twenty-first century pistols and other firearms, he did not have the time to fabricate the machinery and tools needed. When the colonists set out from Earth, they had never in their wildest dreams expected to find themselves in a war situation. Riga, the planet they had originally been making for, was a peaceful one. High-tech machinery and tools had not been stored in the *Argyll's* holds. Weaving looms were the most technologically advanced machinery they possessed. Mustering a large workforce, they had, however, managed to make many swords, helmets, armour and other weapons and Arthur's crossbows were much in demand.

The infantry swords were short and wide-bladed, resembling, as the more historically minded knew, those used by the Romans on Earth. They were around twenty-two inches in length and the blade just over two inches wide. They were blades designed for short stabbing strokes, for men and women fighting in formation and from behind a shield wall. The infantry's shield was similar to the Roman model as well, being rectangular, curved and comparatively easy to produce in the numbers required and time available. It was made out of wooden upright slats set together with animal glue and then covered with yet more stout leather.

Robert's men practised formation fighting, and copying their Lind allies, the infantry fought in three ranks, the second rank carrying wicked, stabbing spears as well as swords. They also practised forming the traditional fighting square, which had proved itself time and again during the battles of the Napoleonic Wars in the nineteenth century. This time however, it would not be horse cavalry that the square would be facing, it would be the Larg – a completely different proposition.

It did not take the settlers long to realise that for the human element of the army to be really effective, they would need to use some form of rapid-fire weapon. The field army's need for such weapons was the greater because these troops would not have barricades to hide behind, as did those defending the settlement.

The crossbows, although excellent, took far too long to reload after firing. Bows and arrows were an alternative but it took years to train a fast and accurate bowman. The settlers did not have years, they had months. The famous longbowmen of England in the Middle Ages had begun archery training at an extremely young age. Weekly practice at the archery butts had been the law for all able-bodied males.

Stretching his improvisational and technological skills to the limit, Arthur Knott came up with a solution. The army needed to be able to fire volleys of arrows at their foes so he designed, what he himself named, his 'contraption' that was able to fire pre-loaded arrows a fair distance and thirty at a time. The arrows were loaded into a wooded frame he called a magazine that was placed on the main frame of the contraption itself. The firing mechanism was spring-loaded and the magazine was drawn back and then loosed. Distance and trajectory could be altered by the manipulation of wheels and cogs. The settlers worked hard to manufacture the contraptions. They would require any number of arrows as well and children as young as eight were to be seen on the arrow production lines. The term contraption was soon shortened to contrap.

Zanatei thought the infantry would turn out to be an invaluable asset to the Lind defensive plans and told Larya so in no uncertain terms. They would form a solid phalanx of support to the Lindars in the centre of the battle line. The Lindars would be placed to either side of the infantry, the more experienced Lindars to the front. Each Lindar consisted of three ranks, the oldest and most battle-experienced in the front rank, the younger Lind forming the rear rank.

The Vada Jim would use on the flanks as skirmishers and also as a shock force if things got tight.

On the low stool, inside her and Kolyei's daga, Tara sat and stared at the bundle of equipment sitting on the ground in front of her, front and back armour, arm and leg guards, helm on top; to one side the gloves reinforced with steelwood plates, to the other side the neck guard.

As she glanced over to the bed she saw her sword, newly sharpened.

She shivered and wished Janice, Winston and the others still lived in the daga, small and cramped as it had been. She could do with some company.

In six days, unless the call came before, she would ride out to war. In six days what they had been training for these last months would be another step closer. Kath and Matvei were to leave next morning with the other Lind who had been posted to the settlement.

Tara wrapped her shawl tighter and shivered.

Kolyei was out hunting so she was alone, alone with her thoughts.

Kath found her there as the light was fading.

"Care for some company?"

Tara raised her head.

"Company?"

"Us twelve original starters are meeting at Moira and Andei's daga. It was Alan's idea. He didn't think any of us should be alone tonight."

"But we didn't really start it all, did we?" asked Tara scrambling to her feet.

"No, but Alan thought it'd be nice to have a last chin-wag."

What neither of them said aloud was the chance that this would be the last time they might all be together. People were killed in wars. All the history books said so. Kolyei had said so.

Anything was better than sitting alone in misery. "I think I'll come," Tara announced.

Geoff and Bill appeared to be running things. There was a table simply covered with titbits, not made by them Tara was convinced, but she was sure that Yvonne and Brenda would have obliged. These two and Moira were sitting together as usual as were Thomas and

Emily. Mark, Alan and Peter made up the last group.

"At last," cried Alan, "she's got here eventually. Told you she would."

"Come and sit down," said Mark, patting the ground between him and Peter. "It's a bit hard though."

Tara grinned. How often had he said that? She sat down, accepting a mug of root beer from Alan.

Geoff and Bill were to fight with the Vada under Francis and Asya. They were eager to go and avenge the deaths of the rest of their family.

"I'm going to kill as many as I can," stated Bill.

"Me too," agreed Geoff, fingering his knife.

"Don't do anything stupid," warned Kath. "Your parents would want you to live, not throw your lives away."

The twins looked at her as if she was a particularly stupid kura.

Tara shivered. She did not like what she saw in Bill's face.

By now Tara had reached a modicum of acceptance of what had happened to her parents, as had Alan, but she didn't think Bill and Geoff would pay much attention to Kath's warning.

Tomorrow their fellowship would split up.

The next hours passed in a pleasant blur of laughter and reminiscences. Geoff and Bill drank too much as usual. Moira, Yvonne and Brenda giggled too much, also as usual. No one spoke more about the war.

They would have sat there all night but Kath reminded them of her early start and the party broke up with the promise to meet up again once it was all over.

As the eldest of the original twelve, Kath felt it was up to her to speak the last words.

"Me and Matvei leave in the morning," she said. "We twelve started out together." There was a catch in her voice. "You're all like brothers and sisters to me and when all this is over and we come home I want us all to meet here again, so be careful."

Kath and James spent the night in Tara's daga, giving Rozya and Matvei time to be alone. Tara and Kolyei squeezed in with the Randalls.

Tara rose early the next morning to say a private goodbye to Kath.

"You and Kolyei keep an eye on the twins," said Kath as she leant down from Matvei's back to plant a quick kiss on Tara's forehead. "They're so full of hate I'm scared for them."

"I'll try," promised Tara, "and so will Kolyei but it is Francis and Asya you should be asking."

"Don't think I haven't but do it anyway."

Tara nodded and stepped back. She watched as the small group detailed to the defence of the settlement sped away in the pre-dawn light.

When the first beacon was lit, warning that the enemy were mustering at the island chain, they were as ready as they could be.

"Lindars have been warned," announced Afanasei after he had sent out his telepathic announcement to all of the Susas.

"Beacons are lit," added Zanatei in an abnormally loud voice.

"Right," said Jim. "Time to go." : *Where are Francis and his Vada?* :

: *Vada dispersing to eat:* answered Larya after a moment of concentration as she communicated with Asya.

The Vada would leave within the hour. The riders' personal belongings had been ready for days.

"Has the settlement been warned?"

"They will see the beacons. Matvei with tell those who have not."

Jim grunted his approval. He and Stuart had drawn up the evacuation plans for the farmsteads. With Lind help, those still outside the settlement walls would be inside by nightfall. It was estimated that it would take the invaders over nine days to reach the north in any great numbers but it was better to take no chances. In the past Larg advance parties had arrived well before their main army. They would have been waiting on one of the islands for this moment and even ten Larg could do a lot of damage, as the settlers knew to their cost.

Ideally, Jim would have preferred to attack the Larg as they landed, when they were more vulnerable. It was just not possible, though if he had been facing just the ten thousand humans Jim would have tried to hold them to the beach. The Larg however, would quite likely make mincemeat of any force out in the openness that was the flat, low-lying coastal area. Jim therefore agreed with the Lind that such a move would be as folly born of madness. Their only chance was to remain behind the fortified walls of the settlement and wait for the attack.

"Can you hear Matvei?" Jim asked.

"Yes," replied Larya, "he has very strong thoughts. Human domta gets ready now."

Tara was sitting quietly in the Randall family's daga when the word arrived. She looked at Janice.

"It's time," she said in a scared voice. The three little girls and Brian looked at her, their faces as white and strained as hers.

Brian was ashamed of the fact that Tara, who was younger than him by some months, was going to the war whilst he was to stay behind. He put an awkward arm round her shoulders. Janice was too busy comforting Violet, Lucy and Juliet to be of much help.

"Kolyei will keep you safe," he said. "Never fear. And you are not going to the front lines. You won't see much from the communications unit. Dad told me that you are to be in an area near him and the other medics and that's some way to the rear."

Tara nodded but was not much comforted. Kolyei had deemed it wise to warn Tara about what to expect and had recounted tales of his own battle experiences. They had not been pleasant hearing.

Not for the first time Tara wished that there was someone else competent enough to command the communications pivot, anyone else, just so long as it wasn't her and Kolyei.

She opened her mouth to speak to Janice but at that moment Louis and Ustinya popped their heads through the doorway.

"Mum," he called out, "the Vada is on notice to depart. Any chance of something before we go? We've been training all morning and are absolutely starving."

Ustinya nodded in confirmation. A large violet-brown and beautiful female, she towered over everyone in the daga, even Kolyei. A native of pack Vanya she adored her Louis and consequently fitted into the extended Randall family with ease.

Radya was, it has to be admitted, jealous of the fact that Ustinya was now linked with the Randalls, and Kolyei. Tara's Kolyei was attracted to Ustinya and it showed. Radya and Peter had been frequent visitors to the daga as a result. The humans had watched with interest the Lind plays of affection and courting. It was yet to be seen whether Radya would succeed in her mission to oust the Vanyan

Lind in Kolyei's affections. He had been rather nonplussed by Radya's reaction and he and Tara had recently spent a lot of time away from the daga. He was, in fact, off visiting his pack-friends at the moment but Tara had decided to help Janice with lunch.

Louis had altered during the time since he and Ustinya had been vadeln-paired. He had become far more weather-beaten and his muscles had developed in response to the demands of weapons training. The training had also toughened him up. He was a young man now, confident and assured. Janice wondered sometimes what had happened to her boy.

She bustled around preparing the meal; her thoughts in a tangle. She had hoped that this day would never come, that the Larg would have second thoughts about coming north and that she would not have to watch her husband, eldest son and new-found daughter going off to the war.

She did manage to serve the meal and didn't spill more than a little. Her hands shook as she spooned the vegetables on to the plates. Louis and Tara busied themselves preparing the raw meat set aside in the cool room for the family Lind.

When Winston and Kolyei arrived, the family ate their last meal together. They were all quiet, even the three youngest. The daga was normally filled with laughter and good-natured banter.

Winston had spent the morning in meeting with the war leaders. He had a lot to think about.

Intelligence supported Jim Cranston's assumption that Murdoch and the Larg did not possess the same telepathic skills and communication abilities, as did those in the north. None of Murdoch's men had actually bonded with any of the Larg like he and the other vadeln-pairs. There were reported language difficulties. It was an alliance, not a partnership. They were using each other; of that much the returning spies were certain. Murdoch thought of the Larg as allies only to help him overcome the settlement. The Larg were using the convicts to negate the settlers' effect on the power balance in the north, but, as Winston spooned the last of his wife's delicately flavoured stew into his mouth, he could not help but wonder and worry.

Candy Rae

CHAPTER 20

SOUTHERN CONTINENT

Many miles south and over the sea, Gerry had reached the convict encampment beside Fort without too much trouble. He had decided to hide himself in plain sight amongst the riff-raff that roamed the fringes of the ramshackle buildings near the waterfront. He knew that he would find it difficult to find a way to gain access to Fort itself. It was well guarded and there were too many army personnel about; the regular regiments all knew each other well. Gerry knew that, perhaps now that the campaign against the north was about to begin, there might be more of a chance.

He did manage to get in touch with Carla Pederson, Johannes Pederson's daughter, not long after his arrival. Cocteau guarded the girl night and day; Gerry only managed to speak to her the once. The girl appeared reasonably content as Cocteau's woman and largely indifferent to Gerry's offer of help to escape. In a hurried conversation she informed her would-be rescuer that she did not want to leave, but thank you very much.

Henri Cocteau was kind to her in his own way and she much preferred to remain where she was rather than to try and reach the coast through Larg infested territory. She promised to keep Gerry's existence in the encampment a secret but offered nothing more. She did not know where her mother Ulla was and was far too scared to try and find out.

Carla did give Gerry the added piece of information that General Murdoch had claimed Anne Howard and the children and that they lived with the General in his quarters. Armed with this information, Gerry bided his time, knowing that eventually his chance would come. As for Martine, Jenny's mother, and her little brother Gavin he could glean no information at all.

Not long after his arrival Murdoch had stripped the area of men able to fight, conscripting those hale enough and who did not volunteer. Gerry watched Murdoch and his army leave for the coast with much satisfaction. After some more weeks scavenging at the waterfront Gerry found out that the man in charge of the animal corrals was suffering from the resultant chronic staff shortage. He decided to see if he could find some work there. He was sick of scrounging for food and shelter among the ne'er-do-wells.

When he presented himself to the overseer, the man looked Gerry up and down and hired him on the spot. There were not that many able-bodied men under fifty capable of a full day's work left in the south. The man wondered fleetingly how Gerry had managed to escape the draft but decided not to ask. One didn't look a gift horse in the mouth.

Gerry's appearance helped. He was careful to keep himself looking scruffy and dirty. This had been difficult for him as he was a fastidious soul by nature. When the army press gangs had scoured the waterfront looking for recruits, he had dirtied himself even more and affected a slight, but distinct limp. Lined up with the rest of the other unfortunates for Duchesne to make his selection, he had hunched himself over and tried to look much older than he was. Duchesne's eyes had passed over him without a second glance.

"Any experience working with cows and sheep?" the overseer asked.

"A bit sir," Gerry mumbled. "Afore I got caught worked wif horses."

"Well there are no horses here. I did hear that they ran away and the Larg got them."

Gerry kept his face impassive.

"Can I work for ye then, sir?" he asked.

"Yes, yes," said the man. "Start tomorrow first thing and get yourself cleaned up. You smell disgusting. I'll find some decent clothes for you."

Gerry slouched away, content.

As the days passed in the corrals, he wondered how Jessica and Jenny were getting along, tending his beloved mares in the north. The chestnut would have foaled by now; he wondered what the little colt was like. His thoughts drifted to Jessica more than Jenny although Gerry told himself it was because he had been close to her father. To Gerry, Jessica was still a child, but she had a wise head on her shoulders and seemed much older than her years. He was confused about his feelings for Peter Howard's daughter. Perhaps it was as well that he was far away from her presence. At least the two Jays were safe. He himself was well fed and no longer needed to associate with the unfortunates with no occupation or the means to get one down in the encampment.

Only one of the regular regiments had remained in the south. Colonel Brentwood was in charge of Fort and the surrounding area. He was to guard the women and ensure that law and order prevailed. Gerry thought it somewhat ironic that Brentwood, an ex-convict, was responsible for upholding the law but, he reasoned, his task would not be too difficult, as most of the able-bodied from the encampment had been drafted.

Anne Howard had heard of the army's imminent departure with a great deal of relief. It meant that she would have some months respite from Elliot Murdoch's attentions. On the occasions when she was presented to the other colonels and senior tradesmen from the encampment, he was scrupulously polite but the man took great delight in humiliating her in private. She learned how to manage to survive as his woman and Murdoch had no idea of her true feelings. He often bragged to his colonels of how much Anne loved him.

Murdoch was pleased with his choice of Anne. Some weeks previously Anne had felt the familiar tightening of her breasts that indicated that she was pregnant. She had mixed feelings about bearing Murdoch's child. The start of her three previous pregnancies had been filled with pleasurable excitement and she and her husband had celebrated mightily. Anne had enjoyed these pregnancies; she knew she did not feel the same about her fourth. It was not the child's fault that its father bore the ultimate responsibility of murdering his mother's husband. Perhaps she would feel differently as the pregnancy progressed as she felt the new life growing within her.

The only good thing about it was that Murdoch's behaviour towards Anne and the children had changed the instant he had been told he was to become a father. A pleased smile on his face, he became more benign towards her. He even had some kind words for Cherry and Joseph. Life became bearable, if still predominantly unpleasant. She mourned for Peter and would never, for as long as she lived, forget the dreadful night when Colonel Brentwood had returned with his young female prizes and regaled his fellow colonels with his tale of the skirmish at the water's edge when Peter had died.

Gone were the days when women actually joined their men when there were guests. Anne, serving Murdoch's guests with food and drink, had managed to keep her face impassive as Brentwood described what had happened to the men in the clearing, in graphic detail. When he reached the part of his tale describing his order to slit the men's throats she had bitten back a sob and fled from the room. It would have been disastrous for Murdoch to realise that the away-team had met the twelve fugitives from Fort and had not been part of the original escaping party. As far as Anne knew, they were not aware of, nor did they care about, the disappearance of the *Electra's* power-core. To Anne's unbounded relief, Jessica had not been amongst those who had returned. In secret, Brentwood's blonde told her of the three who had not been present when Brentwood had found them. Anne knew that Gerry would have done his very utmost to get Jessica and Jenny to safety. Knowing of the existence of the settlers in the north, she hoped that they had made it that far. Anne had not lost hope.

Gerry managed without too much difficulty to get himself assigned to the unpopular and onerous task of climbing the hill with the fresh meat for Fort's kitchen a few days after starting with the animals.

As he entered Fort carrying his burden, he looked around, curious to see what changes Murdoch had made. These were few. He heard children's voices and turned. The children were in the middle of their daily lessons and to Gerry's eyes appeared well fed and comparatively happy. His eyes opened wide when he recognised the woman who was teaching them. It was Anne Howard herself. He stumbled and almost lost his load of meat. One of the guards, interpreting the stumble for mere clumsiness, took a kick at him and uttered a curse. Anne looked up from the book she was reading from to see what the commotion was about.

She recognised Gerry instantly. He could see that, although she made no visible sign beyond opening startled green eyes. He could do nothing to make immediate contact and merely followed the rest of the meat bearers towards the kitchen. There, they were given something to eat and drink by the kindly head cook before being ordered back down the hill.

Eyes downcast in the manner suitable for a southern woman, Anne Howard watched him leave and resolved to find a way to talk to him. But how? It might be possible. With Murdoch away the restrictions that governed her life had relaxed.

Inspiration came to her as she looked at some of the older children.

"How would you like it if I asked Colonel Brentwood if some of us could visit the animal corrals?" she asked in a bright voice. "I think it would be good for you educationally, don't you?"

The children smiled, much enamoured at the idea of a trip outside the walls of Fort. It did not often happen.

"I will ask him later today," Anne promised.

Anne's smile was much brighter than theirs. Perhaps there was a way out after all.

Candy Rae

CHAPTER 21

NORTHERN CONTINENT

Kolyei, a white-faced Tara at his side, appeared at Jim's daga. Kolyei poked his head through the doorway. Jim turned to look at them.

"Communications ready?" he asked of Kolyei.

"Yes."

Jim looked at Tara, pity in his glance. She would be the youngest member of their army and he so regretted the necessity of having to take her. She looked very small and vulnerable standing beside Kolyei, clad in leather armour, the small sword strapped to her belt. Jim hoped she would not have to wield it. If she did, and the Larg armies did reach the rear lines, they would have lost the battle. Then it would be every creature for himself. Kolyei would, however, do all he could to escape with her to the west. Kolyei was known for his fleetness of paw.

"The medics are assembling as well," volunteered Tara.

"Let's be about it then," decided Jim and led the way out of the daga. He glanced over at Afanasei, Elda of pack Zanatei's Lindar. Afanasei, incongruous as it may seem, winked at Jim. The two had a good rapport. Zanatei Lindar would fight close to Jim and Larya; they were positioned in the battle plan at the very centre of the battle-lines.

It had taken Jim some time to fully understand the Lindar chain of command.

Zanatei was his pack's Chief Elda; that was how the pack came by its name. When Zanatei died or retired, the new Chief Elda would bring his or her own name to the pack but Zanatei was not in command of the Lindar. Afanasei held that position. In the field he outranked Zanatei. Other Lind, subordinate to Afanasei, commanded each of the three lines, or ryz, in the Lindar. Zanatei commanded the middle ryz. Tarmsei, honoured amongst the Lind for having been the first with Kolyei to find their human friends, commanded the front. A part-white Lind whom Jim did not know led the first-timers at the back.

The smaller packs could field around three hundred warriors, others, like pack Zanatei, over six hundred. Over forty packs had sent their Lindars in defence of the rtathlians. Some had already arrived in the woods above the settlement. Jim had the Lindars, the untried Vada cavalry, at his disposal and Robert Lutterell's thousand. Over four thousand would man the settlement walls. Against them it was estimated there would be a comparable number of Larg, if not more, plus Murdoch's ten thousand men.

Larya and Afanasei by his side, and followed by Tara and Kolyei, Jim joined his troops.

The sight that met his eyes was one of organised chaos. The humans were saying their goodbyes and there were calls of good luck and the like. In contrast, the traditional farewells from the Lind family groups were silent. Touching nose to nose they had no need for words, their telepathic abilities more than enough to say all that was needed.

Radya approached Kolyei as Tara was readying his harness prior to mounting. The Lind female looked sad but had lost that look of annoyance she customarily wore when Ustinya was anywhere around.

"Keep safe," she uttered quietly. She then touched her nose to Kolyei's, a long lingering touch. Tara, standing watching all this, was reminded of her own parents gazing at each other. She realised then that, if she and Peter had not appeared in their lives, these two might well have mated by now. Young as she was, she understood the pairing rules. Perhaps, when they were a lot older, she might think of Peter the same way.

"I do hope so," she thought. "Otherwise Radya and Kolyei will never be able to mate." She knew that she was too young to be considering a permanent attachment at thirteen but she would keep it in mind. One never knew what would happen in the future. So much had happened to her during the first thirteen years of her life so far. She still, however, thought of Peter as a little boy and would for some years to come. However, the seed had been planted now and Tara was growing up.

But first they had to deal with the Larg.

Whilst she stood there, lost in thought, Radya slipped silently away.

Zanatei Lindar was ready. Afanasei raised his snout as he prepared to utter the leaving howl.

The families moved away.

"Mount," ordered Francis.

The Zanatei Lindar began to leave the clearing. Francis waited until the last disappeared through the trees, a young female off to fight her first battle against the Larg. Only when her bushy tail had swished out of sight did he order the vadeln of his Vada to follow.

As the Vada moved across the plains they could see signs of the passage of the other Lindars. Occasionally they caught sight of them in the distance. Each Lindar would make their own way to the rendezvous, where they would meet up with Robert's infantry from the settlement before settling down to wait for the Larg.

With the beacons alight around the settlement, Stuart MacIntosh ordered the evacuation of the last outlying farms. Once the majority of the livestock had been freed there was a steady stream of refugees to be seen trudging towards the comparative safety of the settlement walls.

Sadly he watched as the groups arrived. Their Lind protectors escorted them to the gates then departed west towards the woods in order to rejoin their Lindars. He was pleased to note that many of these farmers and their families had grown attached to the Lind who had protected them over the last months. The children hugged their four-pawed friends and said tearful goodbyes, the older ones at least, well aware that their Lind were going into battle and that they might never see them again.

Kath stood by Stuart's side. Being the human half of the main communications pair within the settlement they were rarely far away. Kath wished James was with her. She had to make do with third-hand messages from her lover, passed by Rozya through her daily mind links with Matvei.

"The Lindars are making good time," she announced to Stuart. "The last of them will be here in two days. The Larg are taking longer than usual to make the crossing."

"Mmmm," muttered Stuart, "I expected them sooner rather than later."

"The Lind know what they are doing," comforted Kath, "though I think even they are surprised."

"I have been reliably informed that the convicts have been making rafts to enable them to get their equipment over. That will hold them up. I only wish we knew exactly what the equipment is. The reports have been most unclear, probably because the Lind doesn't fully understand what they are seeing. I don't suppose the Larg are all that happy about the delay though."

Matvei joined in at this point. "This is not usual," he agreed.

The delay was causing some logistical headaches for the northern commanders. Stuart had realised that this problem might occur, and taken steps to counteract it. To enable the Lindars to be fed during the waiting period, he ordered, just in time, the farm holdings nearest to the settlement not to let loose their livestock but to drive them to a small valley some half mile north of the staging area. There, the animals waited slaughter in order to feed the thousands of Lind arriving. An adult Lind took a lot of provisioning.

When Jim and his fellow travellers arrived, he refused point blank to avail himself of Stuart's offer of quarters in the settlement, preferring to remain with his troops. Furthermore, he insisted that Robert bring his infantry up the hill to join them at once. It would enable the men and women to get used to the mass of Lind encamped in the lian. Robert also used the time to good effect by practising battle tactics with the Lindars stationed to his immediate left and right so that when battle was joined both species would be used to the concept of fighting beside each other. The Lindars watched carefully as the infantry drilled, but were totally mystified when Robert ordered them to form a square in preparation for cavalry attack and found it difficult to understand what the manoeuvre was all about.

Jim filched the last reams of durapaper from the settlement and the final battle orders were prepared. All the human commanders had a copy. The Lind could not read, except Kolyei, but were verbally told the orders again and again and they committed them to memory. Each Lindar did have a vadeln-pair assigned to them and they each had a copy. Jim hoped that the youngsters would have the presence of mind to tell their Susa if they realised the plans were going awry.

Jim had done all he could; regular meetings were held but there was not much discussion about the war. They talked of the good things in life. The humans recounted tales of both Earth and life on the spaceship to a rapt audience of Lind. The Lind then told of life in their rtathlians. It was good to relax just a little.

The breathing space also gave Jim and Robert Lutterell a chance to catch up. Two evenings after Robert brought his infantry to join with the Lindars, the two men sat at their campfire mulling over the past year.

"It's just a whimsy of mine," began Jim with a smile, "but think what would have happened to us had our positions been reversed."

"What do you mean?" asked a mystified Robert.

"Imagine if we had landed in the south and the convicts here, amongst the Lind."

"Hadn't thought about it."

"Well," Jim continued, "if we had survived the landing and there's no reason why not, as the *Electra* obviously did..." He stopped, lost in thought.

"If we had landed in the south?" prompted Robert.

"...We would all be dead," was Jim's flat response. "The only reason I can see why the Larg have made friends with the prisoners is because they believe they will be useful to them. We would not have been so fortunate."

"You have a point. And if the convicts stop being useful?"

"The Lind believe the Larg will turn on them. I agree."

"Good," said Robert. "I for one would rejoice."

"And the women and children down there, what of them?"

Robert looked blank.

"And in the future?" pressed Jim, "when their children and

children's children are in danger. What then?"

"That is not our problem," stated Robert. "Our problem is here and now. There might not be a future if we do not win this battle."

Jim took a cautious sip of the beverage the colonists optimistically called tea. It was as far from the real thing as a vuz was from a rabbit. He added three teaspoons of sweetener and then another two, reflecting that he would much rather be drinking the caffeine drink the children served at Zanatei. It was called kala and tasted so much better.

He pushed the mug aside and pulled the map towards them.

"Are these contour lines correct?" he asked pointing at one section. "Maybe Larya and I should go and check."

But Robert was thinking of something else, his face fixed in concentration. An unflappable man, Jim had always thought but with little imagination. He now surprised him.

"It's not that I don't care you know," he said, "about the *Electra* children and I was as worried as you when our kids disappeared."

"You were thinking, are thinking, of the welfare of us all," Jim finished. "You think I didn't realise that? Don't tell me that with all that we are about to go through you are fretting about what I might think? Stop worrying. Now – these contour lines – I must make sure that this point has enough Lindars in place to hold no matter how many Larg attack it."

"Relax man, you've done all you can. No one else could have accomplished what you have done, brought us here, set up the defences and planned it all out. With you in command everyone knows we will win."

Jim remained quietly confident in public. Only Larya knew of his inner worries and wisely, she kept them to herself.

"I've never fought in a battle, never thought I ever would," Jim fretted when they were alone. "Don't get me wrong, I'm not afraid of dying."

"I shall not allow you to find the blue pastures on your own," Larya comforted him. She spoke in Lindish. By now Jim was as fluent as was Tara.

She then remembered what Zanatei and Afanasei had advised her. It was time to show Jim what war against the Larg entailed.

"I will show you if you will open mind," she offered.

He started to breathe quicker as his mind and Larya's became as one. He began to sweat and his body to tremble; so terrible was that which he was experiencing.

The images that Larya imparted to Jim were of horror, blood and carnage on a large scale. Jim also 'felt' what Larya had experienced during the last time the Lindar of rtath Zanatei had fought. He could almost smell the death and pain.

Then, just as he felt he was going to scream aloud, she cut the link and Jim dropped to his knees.

"How many times?" he managed to gasp out.

"Thrice have I fought and thrice have I survived," she answered. She was sorry that she had had to do this to her partner, but if he was to lead the northern army into battle, he had to know, of that she was sure. Better that he got over the shock of what war really was now and not during what was to come, when he would have to have a clear head and not be so full of sick shock to be an effective leader.

"I know that you can do this," she said, "and you see now that we must fight and stop them. We shall be together, whatever happens. Now you must think of what I have said to you and harden yourself against feeling the pain and deaths of those that you love. After the battle comes the pain and the loss, not before."

"I will do my utmost," said Jim, rising from his knees.

"You will lead us to a great victory," said Larya, pride in her voice.

The Larg kohorts arrived on the shore one after another. Rafts and boats appeared with men and equipment and they began to disembark.

Jim stood the Lindars down apart from the sentries. The Lind were surprised when the Larg made no immediate move to attack. With their excellent night vision it would not have been the first time they had fought at night but Jim understood why. The convicts would want to wait until dawn and the Larg perforce would have to wait with them so that the two armies could attack simultaneously.

In the woods, the Lind ate a light meal. There was just enough livestock in the ravine to go round. The final Lindars joining the army arrived. They had come a long way and Jim was again amazed at the diversity of colours and build amongst the different packs, especially those from the far west. Instead of the two-colour markings that he was used to, these Lind had far more variegated colour patterns, some very colourful, some a dull sandy brown, more similar to the Larg.

A small group of Elda came with them. These important Lind were completely white. They were a delegation from the Gtratha, the Council that was made up of a white Lind from every Lind pack that existed, and led by the Gtrathlin. They would not fight in the lines, being far too important personages to be risked. They settled themselves to one side of where the communications unit had taken up their position, their very presence good for Lind morale.

It was a difficult night.

In the morning, Afanasei sent the 'stand-to' command to the Lindars and they took their assigned places, the foremost ryz right at the very edge of the tree line. The infantry were very careful to remain under cover and silent as they took up their own designated position. They all had very specific orders to stay exactly where they were until Jim gave the order. He was in no mind to sacrifice any of the advantage of height and surprise and he wanted to force the Larg to attack uphill.

Tara woke when the sun began to peek over the horizon, she felt a bit groggy; she hadn't slept well. She was scared and more than scared. She took a deep breath and struggled out of her sleep-bag. As she washed she stole a glance at Emily who was busy dressing. The elder girl was nervous; her hands fumbled with the buttons of her tunic.

"Let me," said Tara in a too quiet voice. "I'll do you up then you can do me."

"Do we put our armour on now?"

"Might be best," replied Tara. "Where's Ilyei?"

"Gone for a drink. Kolyei went too." She looked up. "They're coming back now."

"Ok," said Tara struggling with her leg greaves. "That's funny, they fitted well enough yesterday."

"That's because these ones are mine," said Emily with a giggle. "Yours are over there, idiot, where you left them last night."

Tara passed Emily's over and began to fasten her own.

"We'd better hurry up," she ordered. "Mariya and the others will be here soon and Kolyei said we should be ready."

"Armour is so fiddly," complained Emily as she stood for Tara's inspection and gasped when her friend began to pull and tug at it.

"Ouch. You don't need to be so rough."

"Just checking it is on right. Now you check me."

Emily did so and noticed Ilyei and Kolyei sauntering towards them as if they hadn't a care in the world. However, this nonchalance was all bravado. Attuned to Kolyei's mind, Tara knew he was almost as agitated and nervous as she and presumed Ilyei was in a similar state.

"Where's the map board?"

"Over there. You mount up and pass it to me."

Jim watched the scene unfolding from the command vantage point. He could see the settlement on its shallow hill some two miles below the tree line, the land bare except for some dugo bushes around a small group of cabins, now deserted. It was from one of these cabins that Tara had left that momentous morning when she had been the first human to vadeln-pair with one of their four-pawed allies. The hills on which the Lindars and Robert's infantry stood were steep, almost sheer in places. Outcrops of grey rocks were interspersed amongst the ochre grass and showed up starkly in the morning light.

The ground at the base of the hills was wet. The ground had not had the chance to dry out from the winter rains and the boggy land east of the settlement down to the shoreline would make it hard going for at least the human element of the opposing army.

In the distance, on the shore and penetrating some half a mile inland, he could make out the dark mass of what were the Larg kohorts. Their vanguard was beginning to move. They would reach the hill within the hour. Jim knew how fast they could run when the occasion warranted it. The Larg would not dilly-dally; they would want to attack as soon as enough warriors were in position but Jim would not order any of the Lindars to show themselves until the Larg began their climb up towards them.

Murdoch's army was halfway to the settlement. There were no Larg with them.

The Larg vanguard slowed down then stopped. The lines wavered for a moment then surprisingly, the Larg all sat down.

Jim knew then that he would not be facing any men in battle that day. All the convicts were making for the settlement. The infantry would be invaluable now that they would be facing only Larg. Through Larya, he passed this piece of information on. Ustinya and young Louis would pass the message on to Robert Lutterell. The commander of the infantry would adjust his tactics accordingly.

Larya, unmoving, stood beside him. They knew the name of the leader of the Larg army, one Aoalvaldr, a well-known, brave and successful commander and canny tactician. Afanasei had met him in battle before. That time the Lind had managed to drive the Larg off without too many losses. He glanced over and saw Afanasei down to his left, hunkering down at the far edge of the pack Zanatei Lindar's front ryz. He must have felt Jim's eyes resting on him. He lifted his head slightly and looked up at the man. Jim waved. Afanasei lifted a paw in acknowledgement before lowering his head behind the dugo bushes again.

By now Kolyei and Tara had arrived at the clearing behind the lines allocated to communications and found the Gtratha members already waiting for them. Tara thought it looked familiar.

"Is this where…?"

"We met?" queried Kolyei. "Yes, it is."

He looked around.

"It has changed little."

"Except for downstream," Tara pointed towards where the Holad were setting up. "Can I dismount?"

"For the moment," Kolyei agreed, "but not for long."

"I know, when the fighting begins. I don't see why. It's much easier to talk aloud when I'm standing beside you."

"It is safer so."

Kolyei was the pivot in the communications network. He knew what he must do. He sat down and made himself comfortable. He had practised this.

Mariya, as Gtrathlin, came to stand beside Kolyei, the other whites ranged around her in a loose semi-circle and facing the battle lines. No Lind would stand with his or her back to the enemy by choice.

Tara slipped into telepathic contact with Kolyei and merged with Kolyei's initial mind-link with Mariya.

: *Good* : the Gtrathlin Mariya encouraged them. Tara heard her voice in her mind. It sounded as if it was coming from a great distance and was of a lighter timbre than Kolyei's.

That contact established, the three pushed their awareness towards Jim, and Larya and Tara became aware of their presence also.

The focus pivot was complete.

It was now up to the Susas and the others to establish contact.

Gradually the telepathic network was built up.

Finally Emily and Ilyei joined Tara and Kolyei. The two girls sat side by side, the large map-board on their laps.

They waited.

Tara felt that she would do anything to end the tension.

"Try to stay calm," advised Emily.

"I *am* trying," answered Tara, map-pen tightly clasped in one sweaty palm.

On the tree line Jim and his army waited unmoving and silent. Like those in the settlement, those on the ridge were about to fight for their lives and for the freedom of the northern continent.

Candy Rae

CHAPTER 22

NORTHERN CONTINENT

The Vada made sure their armour was secure. They were also careful to keep as quiet as they could. Francis felt a thrill of pride. They had achieved so much and now it was time to fight, to put that training into practice.

The infantry was stationed in the centre of the allied lines and directly in front of the command post. The men and women gathered there had the determined look of those prepared to do their duty, whatever the cost. They all carried the short sword of the infantry and their shields were strapped to their other arm. When in place the shields would form a wall of wood, leather and strength through which, despite their size, the Larg would find difficult to force through.

Behind the shield wall and the infantry ranks sat a long row of Arthur Knott's arrow contraps, ready and waiting for the order to fire. Each crew consisted of six humans and one Lind. Even if the Larg had seen them being manhandled and lindpawed up the hill they would have had no idea of their purpose and what damage they could do. A full Lindar from pack Ranetei guarded the contraps.

Sharp stakes lining the approach were another protection. The Larg would have to negotiate them, further slowing their advance. These stakes were not as effective as they would have been against cavalry. The Larg were far more intelligent than horses; they would weave themselves in and out of the stakes, but they would slow them down.

"Are the Larg aware that we are in the woods?" asked Jim of Larya.

"Yes."

"They'll get a surprise when you don't move down the hill to meet them," said Jim with a malicious smile.

"True."

"Remind each Lindar not to show itself beyond the tree line before the order is given," Jim reminded her. "I want the Larg caught off-balance. Hopefully they will not have realised just how many Lind we have."

Even Zanatei had been amazed at the numbers who had arrived from the west.

When the members of the Gtratha were asked about it their answer had surprised Jim and the others. "Humans give us hope."

"Do you still think that the Larg will attack us and the convicts the settlement?" asked Jim. "If we see any of the Larg kohorts sidling over to the settlement we'll need to warn them."

"The Larg will not wish to attack human domta. They will think it is better that men fight other men."

That fitted in with the rest of the intelligence gathered from the south. Although General Murdoch and Aoalvaldr had an alliance, the two branches of their army would fight their own separate battles.

"Larg use bad men to keep our humans away from Larg," added Larya and Jim came back to the present with a start.

It took Jim a moment or two to work out exactly what she meant.

"Get a surprise when they come up against Robert's infantry," he said with grim humour.

"They will not expect it," agreed Larya. She wagged her tail in satisfaction.

Larya was correct. The Larg kohorts did not expect to face any men in battle. As far as Aoalvaldr was concerned, humans fought humans and Larg fought Lind. He knew of the friendship between the northern settlers and the Lind but not of its full extent. Murdoch's men were there to keep these humans occupied whilst he dealt with his traditional foes.

He had made concessions to his convict allies. The coastal plain on which the *Argyll's* crew had settled Murdoch could do with as he wished. Aoalvaldr's prime concern was the Lind. He needed to defeat their army so that the kohorts could move freely throughout the western part of the northern continent to gather in the large herds of kura and zarova. He did not intend to kill all the herds. The waters between the continents were low this hot season; the kohorts could easily drive the herds south over the island chain. When he arrived home with them he would be a hero, bringing so many animals down to the packs where the local herds had been decimated over the last few seasons due to the lack of rain.

He had made another concession with the full agreement of the Largan, the Chief Larg. The area of hilly and wooded lands beside the southern river where the convicts made their home, from the encampment north to the coastline, he ceded to Murdoch and his descendants in perpetuity. If they could also hold on to the western edge of the northern continent it would be even better as this would ensure that the Larg would have a friendly ally in the north, a stepping stone from which they could raid the northern continent any time they wished.

Aoalvaldr was confident that his army would be able to defeat the Lind. He splashed ashore that dawn with a sigh of satisfaction. He was on his way to becoming the most renowned and important Larg the world had ever seen, of that he was sure. Perhaps he would oust the Largan and take command of all Larg. That was his ultimate aim.

Kath watched the long columns of men approach from her place on the settlement parapets. Matvei leapt up beside Kath. He had no need to use the ladders provided for the humans. As Stuart MacIntosh watched him leap, he was relieved that he had taken Afanasei's advice and dug out the ditch in front of the palisades. If Matvei could jump that high and with such obvious ease it would be an easy matter for any attacking Larg to perform the same feat from without. The ditch was also filled to the brim with boggy water. It was an obstacle to be reckoned with and any attacking force should find it very difficult to negotiate.

In the distance he could see the tawny-brown mass of the Larg army as it swarmed across the level ground from the beach, heading directly for the woods. To his immense relief, none detached themselves from the main force to augment the human contingent marching in measured tramp towards the settlement. It was, he realised, a huge army. Jim was not exaggerating when he had said that he would likely be facing ten thousand.

To his consternation he saw the silhouettes of what he recognised as catapults being manhandled towards them. These were not in the reports. He hoped that the anti-fire substance with which they had painstakingly covered the walls would work. The houses and other structures within the settlement were not so coated. If the convict army used lighted ammunition they could be in a good deal of trouble.

From his vantage point on top of the hill Jim also watched, an inscrutable expression on his face, as the Larg army headed in his direction. For a moment he had the irrational idea that they were heading straight for him … personally. They were, he was thinking, like a swarm of locusts, spreading ever outwards as they advanced and just as deadly. Unfortunately for the infantry and Lindars standing waiting atop the hill, the Larg had the considerable advantage in that the sun was rising behind them but it could not be helped. Not even the Gods of the ancient civilisations had been able to alter Earth's orbit or the sun's rising to give their own side the advantage of the rising sun in battle.

He lifted his binoculars up to his eyes, and after activating the anti-glare mechanism, scanned the plains to the northeast. The convict army was nearing the settlement. They were making good time but he judged that they were unlikely to be in an attack position for a few hours yet.

The honour of 'first blood' would fall on the allied field army.

Jim knew what to expect. Lind and Larg were fairly evenly matched number-wise. He and his allies did have one major advantage and an important one; they held the high ground and he fully intended to hold on to this. If the Larg were allowed a pawhold on the upper slopes the allies would lose their advantage, not an enviable way to fight when one was fighting for one's life.

The Lindars would break with their more usual practice and not follow any enemy feints and retreats downhill. Instead the Larg were to be forced to attack uphill again and again. If the Larg broke through, the Lind reserves would move forward and, plugging the gaps, force the Larg back down the hill. The battle would be fought and won on the narrow slip of high ground in front of the tree line.

On the plains below, the last Larg reserve kohorts came ashore. These were the ones who would round up the northern meat herds after the Larg had won the battle. They would only be committed to the battlefield if Aoalvaldr required more troops in order to defeat his enemies. As yet, there were no sightings of Larg skirmishers probing the Lind flanks.

According to tradition, only once had the Larg succeeded in outflanking the Lind. The Larg favoured the frontal assault, relying on their heavier weight and their brute strength to punch through the Lind lines, splitting the army into segments, and then repeating the manoeuvre again and again until they had surrounded and isolated individual Lindars. The Lindars they then wiped out one by one.

In battles past, the Lind had, unconsciously for the most part, aided this tactic. By their very nature, the Lind defended their own rtathen first, other rtathen second. So as the battle progressed and pack-mates fell, they would tighten up their own ranks, leaving gaps between each Lindar. The Larg always took full advantage of this and would send in more warriors wherever a gap appeared. Not this time, this time the Lind lines were continuous and Jim had ordered they remain so. All Lindars had instructions to keep close to one another, no matter what pack. Contingency plans had been made for the reserve Lindars to fill in any gaps without delay.

Slightly in front of and to one side of the command promon tory stood the solid ranks of Robert Lutterell's infantry battalion. They would stand firm. They could not outrun the Larg if the Lindars were defeated. Beside the infantry sat Lindar Zanatei, ready to aid them when needed. One ryz, Jim rather thought it was Tarmsei's, was congregated at the infantry's vulnerable right wing and another at its left. Arthur Knott's arrow contraps were stationed behind them, in the middle of the reserves. There were not enough of them to cover the whole front and the right and left wings of the army had been allocated less than the centre.

The Larg vanguard reached the bottom of the incline. They looked particularly menacing in the morning light. The uncanniest aspect of their advance was that it was absolutely silent. There were none of the shouted orders that a human army would make as the ranks jostled for position. Jim loosened his sword from its scabbard clips and turned toward Larya.

As he did so he felt rather than heard a subliminal growl from left, right and behind him and felt the hairs at the back of his neck respond. The sound at last grew audible until the human contingent felt that the entire hillside was growling as the Lind reacted to the advance of their ancient enemy. The Larg responded. There were no battle howls yet, only the menacing hum.

: Time? : Jim asked Larya.

: Absolutely : she agreed, leaning her head towards him, inviting a caress.

Leaning against her, Jim obliged, taking comfort from her closeness and the warm bulk of her body. He then busied himself making sure that her armour was fitting just so. His stomach clenched and unclenched.

Larya sensed his disquiet.

: I love you : These words Larya gently inserted into his mind. She turned her head slightly and looked into his eyes. *: I am with you :*

Jim felt comforted. "I love you too," he whispered. "Ready?"

He felt her body trembling with adrenalin. He took a deep breath.

There was a howl from the Larg lines.

"Tell Kolyei that it is time. Warn the infantry." To save confusion, all the general command battle orders were to be disseminated via Kolyei, Tara and the communications unit.

He watched as Louis and Ustinya leant towards Robert Lutterell. This almost instantaneous communication between the battle sections was a godsend to any commanding officer.

"Sir," Louis shouted in ringing tones, "battle warning from the Susyc."

Robert nodded. "Form up on the tree line," he ordered.

The command rang out. The nervous men and women had been standing at ease waiting for this very order. They came to attention with a crump of booted feet.

The Larg began to advance up the slope.

"Battle Order One," Jim commanded.

He sensed Larya relaying his command to Kolyei, then as one, the Lindars rose up from their prone positions behind the trees and advanced to the ground right at the very top of the hill. There was the jingle of equipment and shouted orders as the infantry followed suit.

"Shields," shouted out Robert.

The front rank lifted their shields into position. There was a thump of hardened leather against leather as the shield wall consolidated and then solidified.

The second rank formed up behind and grounded their spears. They would be able to stab at their enemies through the shield wall, unconsciously copying the way the ancient Roman armies had conquered most of their known world. The warrant officers (six per rank, left wing, centre and right wing) began to walk slowly between them and the third rank, making final adjustments to stance and equipment and generally checking that all was in readiness. Jim could hear their low murmurs of encouragement.

The Larg continued to advance.

If they were surprised at the emergence of the human infantry on the skyline, they did not show it, or at least not by very much. There were a few startled yelps but that was all.

The lead kohorts began to trot a little faster. They continued to increase their speed until the vanguard met the stakes. There were some pain-filled yelps of surprise and then the arrow salvoes arched high into the air above them and descended on the brown bodies of the Larg.

Down at the settlement the lookouts watched the battle begin.

"There are thousands of them!" gasped out Jean Farquharson. As a member of the Council, she deemed it her duty to station herself on the southern walls, where they expected the first assault to fall.

Kath stood nearby, one hand placed on Matvei's withers in a gesture of comfort. It was his Lindar up on the hills above. He, Matvei, had led the front ryz for many seasons. If he had not been ordered to this duty at the settlement he would have been leading his ryz into battle. He wondered how Tarmsei was coping. It was the youngster's first taste of absolute command. Tarmsei, although an experienced fighter, was young for his post and it was Matvei himself who had recommended he replace him as commander of the ryz. It took a lot of courage and level-headedness to control a ryz in battle. Afanasei, accepting Matvei's judgement, had promoted Tarmsei over the necks of other, older and more experienced warriors.

"Don't panic Jean," said Kath bracingly. "There are thousands of Lind up there. In fact, I am more worried about our human foes who, if you have noticed, number around ten thousand and are heading straight for us. I don't like the look of these catapult things they are pushing along either."

"What will they fire with them? Rocks? There are very few sizeable hunks of real estate out there."

"Not rocks I think," answered Kath. "Remember the reports we got about when Fort was overrun?"

"Do you think Stuart is right then and that they will use fire against us? We've coated the walls with that evil smelling gluey stuff."

"Yes, but all wood burns eventually and inside the walls all our buildings are made of wood and we haven't coated all of them. There wasn't enough. That's why Stuart has ordered every able-bodied soul who can see light and hear thunder, and who is not manning the walls to fire duty. The fire-control parties have been filling every available bucket they can put their hands on with water for days now. Surely you saw them?"

"Been in the medical centres helping out there," was the laconic reply.

"Mmmm," said Kath. She hoped that she would not be an inmate in one of the centres before the day was out. Some of the medics on duty had received very sketchy training at best. She herself was better. But her duty station was on the walls, with Matvei, providing the vital communications link between the settlement and the field army.

"Our troubles will start soon enough, their front regiments are almost within striking distance."

Murdoch's men were getting alarmingly close. The battle for the settlement was about to begin.

Up on the hill, the Larg advance slowed appreciably as the front kohorts tried to negotiate a way through the initial line of stakes without impaling themselves in the process. Their pace had at once been reduced to a walk as their bodies were forced to weave through them, only to come up against the second row of larger and sharper stakes. The arrows continued to fall and many were hurt.

It was at this point that the Larg command suffered its first major setback of the day. The second string of kohorts had not been ordered to slow down when the first hit the stakes. They increased their pace and pressed ever on, forcing the front troops further up the hill and into the stake lines. They were unable to brace themselves against this and howls of pain and anguish could be heard as the stakes penetrated flesh and bone.

Under the misapprehension that this meant that the front kohorts had already met the enemy, those behind pressed harder, anxious to reach the battle lines without further ado. There were more anguished howls of pain and frustration. Belatedly, the Larg command ordered the second group of kohorts to cease their advance, then to retreat some paces so that those in front could have room to manoeuvre.

Jim watched the scene unfolding below him with a great deal of satisfaction. A great many of the Larg shock troops had been impaled on the stakes. The lead kohorts paused indecisively for a moment and then, first lesson painfully learnt, approached the stakes again. From above, the allies watched as their huge jaws gripped the stakes and began to work them to and fro, loosening them from the ground. Then they eased them out and dropped them. They heard the snarls of satisfaction as the kohorts moved uphill to demolish the second line of stakes. Many died beneath the arrows that continued to fall, but there were others ready, willing and able to take the place of their fallen comrades.

Jim wished he had some individual arrows and crossbows with which to consolidate this advantage whilst the Larg were still downhill. The arrow contraps sent large volumes of arrows down on their enemies but could not take out individuals. He needed snipers, but did not have any.

He had positioned a reserve force at each end of his lines, not wishing to be outflanked. To his immense relief the reports relayed to him by communications said that, true to form, the Larg did not appear to be attempting any such manoeuvre. Traditionally they attacked the Lind from the front, which was why Jim had placed the most experienced and battle-hardened Lindars in his army's centre. Aoalvaldr was not going to break with tradition, at least not for now.

At last the kohorts managed to remove enough stakes. They paused for a moment, and then in response to a silent order, how Jim wished that the Larg did not have telepathic abilities similar to the Lind, they spilled through and bounded up towards the allied lines. Like a swarm of rabid dogs they leapt into the attack and hit them. The top of the hill became in that instant full of snarling writhing bodies as Lind and Larg met in time-honoured fashion.

Jim didn't think he would ever forget what met his eyes and ears as the combatants tried to get at their opponents' vulnerable throats and bellies. There were ear-splitting yowls of pain as tooth, chela and claw found purchase. To his right he saw Tarmsei at grips with a large tawny Larg. *How have they managed to get past Robert's infantry?* There were streaks of ochre blood on the ryz leader's flanks but he was holding his own. He watched as some of the ryz, wounded, tried to disentangle themselves from the melee and drag themselves to the rear. Lind members of the Holad bravely aided their pack-mates. Jim saw bodies lying still and quiet in the churned up soil. Their battle was over. Their mates and ltsctas would wait in vain for their return to domta and daga.

Then two Larg kohorts attacked the infantry stationed directly in front of the command post. The men and women braced themselves. He watched mesmerised as the front rank hurled their huge bodies at the shield wall. The wall held, but only just. The second infantry rank held on grimly and he was pleased to see, was able to jab at the attackers pressing against the front shields with their spears.

Stab and withdraw, stab and withdraw. To the infantry it felt that the horror would never end. The air was filled with shouts of command as the warrant officers encouraged their men and women, ordering replacements forward if they saw the lines weaken. Behind the infantry, Zanatei's ryz waited, ready to bounce into the attack if the Larg broke through again.

The arrow contraps continued to fire waves of arrows over the heads of those directly in combat and down on to the next wave of kohorts advancing up the hill.

The Larg pressed harder. Men and women fell to the ground, dead and wounded. The shield wall wavered, that critical amount that indicated to Jim that it was beginning to disintegrate. He tensed. But just as the infantry felt that they could not hold on any longer there was a deep howl from further down the hill.

The kohorts in front of the infantry growled in frustration. Why were they being ordered to withdraw? Why? They were about to break through the two-legged creatures' ranks. They obeyed with reluctance and ran back down the hill. The infantry emitted a huge sigh of relief.

"Form up," ordered the warrant officers. "Medics, get the wounded to the rear."

Robert Lutterell watched as his depleted force got ready to face the next attack. Water bottles were passed forward and the thirsty men and women drank greedily.

"Why did they stop?" asked one.

"They were almost through," agreed another.

Robert knew why. The Lind lines had held. The Larg had not managed to force them back enough to gain a pawhold on the more level land atop the hill. The kohorts would have to reform and try again. The allies had won the first round.

The Larg were confused. Unlike in previous battles, the Lind had not followed them down the hill to harry at their hind paws thus enabling the Larg to turn on them at the base of the hill. The heavier Larg had the advantage on the flatlands. This time, the Lind stood silent and still on top of the hill, impassive and watched as their foes retreated.

Aoalvaldr, although equally surprised, did not show it. He had hoped that the Lindars would be lured downhill where he could counterattack but no matter, he had other tricks up his forepaw. There were other ways to skin a rudtka. Instead of ordering the kohorts to attack again he decided to try and lure the Lind downhill. He ordered a further retreat to the streambed and there he waited for the attack he was sure would come, positive that the Lind would not be able to resist.

Aoalvaldr waited and waited some more. He grew ever more impatient and growled to himself loudly and often. It took him some time to realise that the Lindars were not going to take him up on his kind offer of a suicidal attack downhill. He was disappointed, the first of many disappointments he would experience that day.

In the communications' clearing Tara and Emily heard the roar as battle commenced.

: *The Larg attack the centre* :

Tara marked the map with the appropriate annotations. Her hands shook.

She 'listened' hard as Kolyei continued to send news of the battle's progress, heart in mouth, until eventually she heard Kolyei broadcast : *Larg retreat. Our Lindars to hold their positions :*

She breathed out in relief.

"Larya says to send Lindars Msnei and Vlrnei to advance and strengthen the lines," Kolyei told Mariya.

She passed the order across to the Susas of packs Msnei and Vlrnei.

Emily marked their movement on the map.

"This is working," announced Mariya in jubilation. "The Larg are confused."

"Now we have to hold," warned Kolyei. "The Larg will be readying for another charge."

CHAPTER 23

NORTHERN CONTINENT

From the parapet walls of the settlement Stuart MacIntosh watched, his binoculars glued to his face.

"They seem to have beaten off the first charge," he announced.

"Hope we can be so lucky," said one of the crossbowmen on the parapet beside him. "The convicts are surrounding the walls and setting up the catapults. They're lighting fires too."

Stuart swung his binoculars round. The man was right. They would be surrounded soon and then it would start.

The Lind stationed on the west, north and east walls reported to Matvei that a thin line of men was forming up just out of the range of arrowshot. They were not outside the range of the crossbows. Stuart surmised that Murdoch had not considered the possibility that the *Argyll* passengers and crew could make such weapons. There was also an arrow contrap embedded into the ground behind the closed gates. When it fired it would do a lot of damage. The reports from Tara and Kolyei from the hill had mentioned to Matvei the effectiveness of the weapon. Arthur Knott had smiled grimly and wished aloud that there had been time to manufacture more.

"Most of the convict army is, as expected, congregating in front of the southern gates," shouted Stuart's new number two (Robert Lutterell had resigned this post to take charge of the field infantry). The rugged, down-to-earth farmer of middling years who had accepted the post had his head well screwed on. He knew what he was about. "The main attack will come from there. Not yet though. They'll want to soften us up a bit first before they send their men in."

"Are the fire parties ready?" asked Stuart. "If they do use fireballs we'll be so busy putting out fires we'll have no-one to man the walls."

"That's what they will be hoping for and they'll be watching out for signs. We know the gate area is the weakest point. The ditch is not so wide or as deep there. They'll try to bridge it then batter down the gates," said the man.

"Don't think we'll bring any reinforcements up to the parapet yet. Leave them at the second line of defence on the other side of the river," ordered Stuart. "If they do break through the gates these river barriers are our only hope."

They heard the blast of a horn, long and clear. The defenders spied a flurry of movement round the enemy catapults, as the rods were winched back to their fullest extent and they watched as smoking bundles were placed in the cradles. The catapult operators let go of the levers. The bundles soared high in the air and towards the settlement. Most fell short but a few descended on the walls. The convicts manning the catapults could be seen making adjustments to the trajectory mechanisms.

The majority of the second wave fell inside the walls. Murdoch did intend to set fire to the wooden buildings inside the settlement.

Those stationed on the parapets would hear the sounds of whistle blasts as the fire parties located the burning areas and proceeded to extinguish the flames before the fires could take hold.

The catapults were winched up again and a third salvo was let loose, then a fourth. Some defenders looked nervously to their rear.

Despite the best efforts of the fire parties, some fires began to grow as they fed greedily on buildings and other combustibles. The smoke emanating from the fires did not dissipate; there was not enough wind to make that much difference. Some of the defenders began to cough as the smoke reached them.

"They're moving." Murdoch had decided that it was time for his main assault on the gates. He ordered the regiments forward and Stuart watched as they began to march towards them.

There was a shaft of blue-white light and the torso of one of the defenders fell off the parapet and on to the ground, his severed arm thumping down beside the twitching body a second later.

"Laser-rifles!" screamed someone and everyone ducked their heads. "Where did they get those?"

"Can't have many," shouted another, "but if they do we'll all be dead soon."

To their immense relief, although the laser fire continued it did so only sporadically.

It was what were becoming known as the regular regiments who were spearheading the assault. Baker, Cracov and Smith's regiments were in the front, closely followed by van Buren, Gardiner and Duchesne's. The men carried bridging planks with which they intended to cross the ditch and also the large hardwood battering rams, hewn from the southern woodlands and towed over to the north by a group of disgruntled Larg who did not understand the need for such accoutrements to go to war. Were not tooth and claw enough?

The regiments marched forward to the beat of a drum. There was the occasional blast of laser fire but Murdoch had only three rifles which Brentwood had taken from Peter Howard's away-team (the ones captured at Fort had proved to be beyond repair) and these were not enough to make a difference. They did inflict casualties, but the majority of their targets were hidden behind the fire-resistant walls that the blasts were unable to penetrate. Their power would not last long.

The crossbowmen were congregated behind the southern parapet, weapons primed and ready to fire. Every bolt would have to count as it took an experienced crossbowman at least three minutes to reload the weapon. Stuart waited for the enemy to come within range of both the crossbows and Arthur's contrap.

"Ready."

Here we go. Stuart raised his right hand into the air.

The men settled the crossbows on their shoulders. Arthur Knott readied his contrap.

Stuart brought his hand down.

The lethal little bolts whirred towards the approaching regiments and the defenders watched as they hit the front ranks. The arrows arched higher than the bolts and rained down on the regiments to the rear of the first three. Men fell to the ground but the advance did not falter. Their comrades stepped over them and continued their measured tramp.

Individual arrows continued to fall but there was a problem with the mechanism of the contrap and Arthur Knott could not decrease the range, neither could he fire. Stuart could see him struggling with it and the man glanced up at Stuart, despair on his face. With inanimate stubbornness the loaded arrows remained in their cradle.

Before the crossbows could be reloaded the attackers would be at the ditch. Kath could see scaling ladders being readied. These men might not need to wait for the planks to be set in place if they could tip enough ladders against the walls to allow enough of them to climb up and over.

Occasionally, the sharp blast of a rifle shot through the air and hit any defender unlucky enough to be in its line of fire. The force of these individual blasts could cut a man in two with ease and some areas of the parapet were covered with sticky warm blood.

Jean Farquharson watched mesmerised as to her left a blast found its target. The woman so hit fell to the ground. Great spurts of arterial blood splashed out from her neck and over the ground as her heart continued to pump. Jean knelt down beside her, applied pressure to the severed artery and called for a medic, any medic, however inexperienced. The young lad who appeared could do nothing. A minute or so later the woman died in Jean's arms.

The crossbows fired another irregular volley as the attackers reached the ditch and began to lay the bridging planks. The defenders drew their swords and closed up against the parapet. It would be cold 'steel' from now on.

The Commanders of the field army watched the battle unfolding at the settlement.

"Looks bad down there," observed Jim, "the fires seem to be taking hold. I can't even see the far away buildings for the smoke. Scaling ladders will be up soon."

"Help we cannot," said Larya. "Larg will again attack." She looked over and down at the mass of Larg milling around at the base of the hill.

"Taking their time."

"They regroup," said Larya. She pricked up her ears. "Robert comes," she added.

Jim walked to and looked over the edge of the promon tory that was his and Larya's command post.

The commander of the infantry was to be seen climbing with difficulty up through the jagged rocks that surrounded the foot of the command post. He wanted to speak to Jim face to face.

"Jim," he called up. "I'll not come any further. These creatures are too strong by half. Lost a good few last time round trying to keep the shield wall intact. Have to tighten the lines up, move the wings closer to the centre. Would be suicide to leave any gaps. It can't be helped if we have to have any chance of withstanding them again."

"You have to hold!"

"We *will* hold. I've never led a more determined bunch of people in my entire life."

"Deepen your ranks. I'll get an experienced Lindar to fill in the space."

Robert nodded once and sped away, calling with urgent voice to his remaining warrant officers.

Larya informed Kolyei and as Jim turned round, he saw a Lindar moving rapidly forward to plug the gap on the infantry's left wing. The infantry now stood in four ranks instead of three. If the Larg fought through the first two ranks, the third and fourth could take them on. It was indeed a defence 'in depth'. Jim grinned at her. He hadn't even needed to ask. Larya grinned back, tongue lolling out.

He watched as the purple and brown Ratvei Lindar settled into their station on the right flank of the infantry. Another, less experienced, Lindar took over the guard of the arrow contraps. They were just in time; the kohorts were advancing.

To the rear, Kolyei and his communications team were busy. He himself dealt with the command unit directives and was finding it tough going but the group of Elda were backing him up assiduously. Experienced in the ways of war with the Larg, they filtered out much of the information that was passing between the Lindars and also kept a weather ear out, two ears if they could manage it, for what was happening at the far edges of the lines, both north and south. No more than Jim did they wish to be outflanked. The next Larg attack would again be at the centre. The Larg intended to punch a hole through in the traditional manner and so split the allied lines. If successful the

Larg would swarm through the gap and wreak havoc from behind. If this were allowed to happen, the allies would lose the battle.

The Vada were put on immediate alert.

Again the infantry waited for the onslaught. One of them was a woman called Geraldine Fitzpatrick. *When I signed up for the colony I know I was looking for excitement and adventure.* She peeked over the shoulder of the man in front of her. *I certainly wasn't expecting anything like this.*

She could hear the warrant officer's voice behind her.

"Remember second rank; get under the shields any chance you get."

This was good advice. During the first assault the men and women with shields tended to raise them up slightly, a reflex action caused by the sheer size and bulk of the Larg to protect themselves from the slavering mouths looming above and over them. Whilst the Larg front rank forced itself against the shields, intent on devouring the infantry soldiers' heads, it left their lower torsos vulnerable. If a soldier in the second rank was quick enough he or she could strike at the Larg from below. Then, as the Larg bent down to combat this attack on their nether regions, the front ranker could hit them from above. The strategy seemed to work.

A tall woman of medium build, Geraldine was the last but one second rank soldier on the right of the infantry lines. She looked over to her right at the Lind warrior waiting quietly beside her and the stocky man who held pole position. It was a good-looking animal, its purple stripe pattern very distinct. The Lind turned its head and looked towards her. To Geraldine's total surprise, it winked and for some reason she became less jittery about the looming assault. She gave it a fleeting smile and turned to face the front once more.

Again the snarling, vicious Larg hurled themselves at the infantry. The man in front of Geraldine staggered backwards as a gigantic tawny monster shoved hard against his shield. She smelled the foul stench of its breath as it used its weight and bulk to force its way through and watched as it took an enormous bite out of the man's side. Geraldine lunged forward as the head loomed within reach of her spear. With all her might she thrust her weapon straight at the creature's face. It penetrated quite a way and she struggled as she tried to pull it free. The Larg body dropped like a stone. The legs twitched once then stilled.

There was no time for self-congratulation, another shield man came forward and took his place and Geraldine pressed herself into his back to help him brace himself and to take advantage of any killing opportunities. She noticed only then the gash on her arm. She hadn't felt the Larg's claw rake down her skin.

She was in a half-crouched position, trying to manoeuvre her spear through the shield wall when she realised that the man was no longer there. She was now the anchorman of the infantry right wing. She picked up his discarded shield and drew her sword.

The Larg were pressing hard. Aoalvaldr was desperate to finish the battle and had ordered his Kohort Commanders to push as hard as they could at both points between the humans and the Lind. It seemed that the entire Larg army were trying to force their bodies through. There seemed to be no end to the numbers that bounded up the hill. Much honour would accrue to the leaders who managed to break the lines and the kohorts were desperate to put an end to whatever it was that was sending the sharp pointed wood slivers overhead and into their midst with devastating effect.

If this attack did not succeed, Aoalvaldr would have to think again. A flanking movement had worked before, he had been a junior member of a kohort during that successful hot season so as a precaution he ordered his reserves to take position so that they could deploy southwards at a heartbeat's notice.

In the midst of the bloody fight, Geraldine became aware of a large warm body pressing into her right side, filling the gap left open when the anchorman had fallen. It was peculiarly reassuring to have a Lind so close. They met the next Larg together. Jsei met his foe in the traditional manner and went straight for the throat. It seemed so easy. The Larg was going for Geraldine. Jsei's attack distracted him and their enemy hesitated for an infinitesimal yet fatal instant. Geraldine took immediate advantage and performed her next move, just like the drills practised over the preceding months. Her warrant officer's voice was ingrained in her memory.

"Shield on left. Hold it up! Sword ready. Swing back right arm. Left foot forward. Push shield toward opponent. Strike as hard as you can, chest, face, body, and legs. Maximum damage is what we are after."

Her sword swung forward in a low arc and with a grunt Geraldine struck at the creature's thick neck. Bright ochre blood fountained up from the wound like a volcano.

"Well done," said a strange voice to her right.

She nearly dropped her sword in surprise. Jsei winked again. Geraldine smiled and Jsei thrust his body up against hers once more and she settled her shield on her left arm.

Together, they looked round for another foe to fight but there were no Larg to be seen.

"Have they gone?" gasped Geraldine of the Lind. It seemed quite natural to ask.

"They have gone back down hill," agreed Jsei. "Rest now."

He sat down and looked at the woman, a quizzical expression on his face. It was obvious to Geraldine that he wanted her to sit down beside him. As she did so she felt his body wince.

"You hurt?" she asked.

"Me Jsei," he replied, deliberately misunderstanding her.

Geraldine laughed then saw the blood oozing from his flank.

"You *are* hurt," she said briskly. "Let me tend it."

She proceeded to do so, his wound being, thankfully, a minor one. Jsei sighed with relief as the numbing root took hold. "Your forepaws are clever. I will not need Holad now."

Geraldine looked at him through lowered eyelashes as she finished tying up the gash on her arm and then put away the contents of her first aid kit. This was the first time she had actually spoken to a Lind. It was, she was finding, an uplifting experience. In her mind a beautiful image emerged of her and this Lind peacefully walking through the forests together. In the picture, it was late summer, perhaps early winter. There was utter contentment portrayed in the image. No Larg were to be seen. Young Lind played beside them as they walked.

: *What your name?* :

: *Geraldine* : she 'sent' back without thinking. The Lind's eyes crinkled.

: *Geraldine?* : There was a wealth of meaning behind the question.

Geraldine looked at Jsei, surprised that she could 'hear' him and he her; there was only one answer she wanted to make, could make.

It needed no words from Geraldine to accept what Jsei was offering.
His gaze when he looked at her was one of quiet pleasure.
"We rest. When battle over talk and think much… yes?"
She agreed with a smile.

Tara turned a face filled with anguish towards Emily.
"Kolyei says Andei is down."
"Down?"
"Dead."
Emily's face whitened as she realised what must have happened.
"He cannot 'hear' him," sobbed Tara. Her hands shook as she gripped the mapping pen and bile rose in her throat.

Moira and Andei's duty post had been with a Lindar close to the centre of the allied lines. Andei had been passing regular reports to Kolyei regarding the repeated attacks and then as Kolyei had told her, suddenly there were no more messages.

"Maybe they're just hurt, or unconscious," stammered Emily.
"Kolyei says no," trembled Tara. "What do we do now?"
"We keep going," answered the fifteen-year-old Emily. "There's nothing we can do to help them." She made another annotation on the map in front of her. "Lindar Hanvsei has moved forward. Try to keep calm Tara. Blubbing about it won't help and you never know, they might still be alive. Don't go to pieces on me. I can't do this on my own."

: *Helvetei and Barindya Lindars to advance* : sent Kolyei at this point and Tara fumbled as she noted down the advance movement.

: *Detach yourself* : he ordered. : *Concentrate on the map* :

Tara took a deep breath. Both Emily and Kolyei were right of course; there was nothing she could do and she mustn't go to pieces. Jim and Larya were depending on her and Emily to keep the map board up to date so that they could direct the battle. She couldn't let them and the others down.

She 'felt' Kolyei take a moment to shunt her thoughts about Moira and Andei to one side of her brain with a start of surprise. She hadn't realised he could do that and she found she was able to concentrate again.

As one by one her friends joined in the battle she managed to keep from becoming emotionally involved by the simple expedient of not thinking of her friends fighting for their lives but imagining them as ever-changing marks on the map. It seemed to work.

She and Emily, as they kept at it, realised that Jim was ordering more and more Lindars forward, their friends with them. The Larg were getting desperate and Aoalvaldr was flinging wave after wave up the hill in an effort to overrun the Lindars. The lines were holding but for how long?

The girls' battle was here, behind the lines, but Tara and Emily were amongst the few who knew what was happening at the settlement. It was their job to pass on updates to Larya. What they passed on did not make good hearing.

"They're fighting in the streets," Tara mentioned during a lull in message passing.

"I know," grimaced Emily. "Jim can't do much to help them either." Both girls had attended Jim's pre-battle conference. They knew that overall victory depended on victory atop the hill.

"Defeat the Larg," Jim had declared, "and the convicts will be unable to sustain their position."

Knowing this, both Kolyei and Ilyei were filtering the information sent by Matvei. There was no point worrying Jim about something he could do nothing about.

Geraldine and Jsei were not the only two who had acted in tandem to fight off the Larg. Robert Lutterell turned to Ustinya and Louis.

"Can you tell others of that Lindar to fight closer to the infantry?"

Ustinya considered the question carefully. She looked at Louis to translate. It was often much easier that way. "Yes," she said at last.

"Ustinya says that those who wish to fight alongside the humans will do so. The Lindar has noted what is happening too. Lind watch out for their rtathen fighting at their side in the ryz. One warrior attacks the Larg head, the other goes underneath."

"You want me order them to help humans?" asked Ustinya of Robert, a wary eye on what was happening in front of her.

"If they can," he answered. The duos can guard the infantry flanks that are susceptible to breakthrough. They can stop any incursions."

Ustinya's eyes became unfocused as she endeavoured to make telepathic contact with the Ratvei Susa. Robert watched as some of the pack detached themselves from their own ryz and placed themselves in position amongst the infantry. The men and women without a Lind beside them formed up in between the twosomes, tightening the shield wall.

They waited, silent and unmoving, for the third assault that day. The infantry took large gulps of water from their canisters. Fighting was dry work. Those standing beside the Lind offered them some as well, an offer gratefully accepted, although the Lind took but little.

Jim watched the second retreat and nodded. There had been no major breaches in the lines and only four reserve Lindars had been thrown into the battle. His tactic of standing firm on top of the hill appeared to be working.

"When do you think the Larg will attack again?" he asked of Larya. "Check with Afanasei, Mariya and the others. I know Aoalvaldr has committed less than half the forces available to him."

The reply came.

"Regroup. This is usual. Do not drop guard."

Jim scanned the battlefield where hundreds of bodies lay. The arrow storms had stopped swathes of attackers further down the hill. He could see many a wounded Larg dragging himself downhill. He felt sick.

Larya was quick to put a stop to this kind of thinking. It was extremely unhealthy from her point of view to feel any sympathy for their foes.

: *Do not feel sorry for Larg. Larg will kill and eat you if given chance* :

He looked at her wryly and took a deep breath as he answered. "You are right as usual." His stomach however, took a while to settle down.

The Larg were reforming at the streambed, a few lengths outside the range of arrow shot. They had learned to fear these wicked and sharp wooden slivers. Arthur Knott's contraps were well on their way to becoming indispensable on the battlefield. Jim ordered the Lindars protecting them to be on their guard. The Larg must not be allowed to take them out. As there was no sign of another Larg charge beginning in the immediate future Jim ordered the quartermasters to send up both food and water. He was sure that the battle still had a long way to go.

Then Kolyei began to send to Larya an increasing number of reports of movement of the as yet uncommitted kohorts. Some Larg who had been fighting in the centre were also moving south, their places being taken by reserves. The import of this was clear to Jim. Aoalvaldr intended to attack his right wing. If he won there, his kohorts would sweep behind the rest of the allied army and attack it from the rear. That he was also deploying fresh troops to the centre probably meant that he would attack there at the same time. Jim had to decide in a hurry which one would be his opponent's main attack and which one the feint. It was a split-second decision. If he opted for the wrong one it could be fatal for them all.

He turned to Larya.

"Right," he said aloud, "tell Kolyei to order three reserve Lindars from the centre to move right. He'll know which ones. They are to sit in the woods with the right wing reserves and emerge to fight the Larg in any way they see fit."

"I agree," she said, "so do Elda and Afanasei."

Their approval made Jim feel much better.

"The left reserve Lindars are to spread themselves out behind our centre and right wings."

Larya passed this on. Jim heard noises in the woods behind him as the reserves threaded their way through the trees to reach their new positions.

Below, Jim could see Louis telling Robert about the new troop deployments. The man looked up at Jim and sent him a short wave of acknowledgement.

The allies watched as the enemy force repositioned.

Jim waited. He took a moment to look towards the haze of smoke that was the settlement. He knew from Matvei and Kath that the colonists were in trouble with a capital T but he could not send any help; he had no troops to spare.

The inhabitants of the settlement were indeed in a great deal of trouble. The fires had taken hold. The flames fed greedily on the dry timber roofs and walls of the cabins and storehouses.

Kath and Matvei felt, rather than heard, the penultimate heavy crash of steelwood upon steelwood that was the battering ram destroying the gate joists. The final bang that actually felled them was almost an anti-climax. The gates tottered then with a resounding crash of dust and splintering wood fell inwards. Baker and his regiment were not long in taking advantage of this and they spilled through the gap and into the courtyard. A ragged hail of arrows hit them but it was not enough to stop their forward momentum.

Kath craned her neck to look in the direction of the gates in dismay. She watched the dust cloud appear as the broken gates hit the ground. She was still on the parapet where she and Matvei were successfully dissuading those men who had climbed up the ladders that it was not a good idea to try and jump on to the parapet right where an angry woman and furious Lind were waiting, teeth bared and upraised sword at the ready.

She spied yet another ladder clumping against the wall and ran to help, Matvei at her side. Sometimes all that was needed was for Matvei to look down over the parapet at those climbing up. Underneath him, the more timid of their enemies would refuse to climb, much to the anger of their officers. Matvei noticed that these selfsame officers showed no inclination to lead by example and take pole position on the ladders. It appeared that in the southern officers' eyes, discretion was the better part of valour.

Murdoch's regiments had tried to scale the walls twice already and had been beaten off but that was before the gates had fallen in. Kath knew that those lined up in the courtyard would not be able to hold the regiments off for long as the convicts surged through the empty gateway.

"This is very bad," announced Matvei. "Ptatch, now!" The two words were a command. Kath obeyed.

She did so and from the vantage point of Matvei's back saw what happened next.

Along the parapet came the shouts of the commanders ordering the men and women to leave the perimeter walls and to retreat behind the secondary barricades on the other side of the river. It was not a wide river, but it cut deeply through the gentle hill on which the settlement was built.

Matvei and Kath fled with the rest, Matvei making a gigantic leap to jump over both river and barricade. Those on foot ran as fast as they could, those already manning the secondary defences giving a helping hand when they could. Once all that could escape the outer area reached them and had climbed over, the rope ladders were pulled in.

CHAPTER 24

NORTHERN CONTINENT

Jim watched the Larg troop movements, a knot of apprehension tying his stomach in knots. There were too many kohorts moving south for that to be the diversion. He had made the right decision in moving his centre and left reserves to the right. Aoalvaldr's next attack would be on the allied right wing. The centre would still be under attack, of that much he was certain, but it would hold firm. The body of Larg in the centre were only waiting for their compatriots to their left to attain their attack position then they would start up the hill again.

Aoalvaldr was hoping for two things. First of all, that the defenders' weakened centre would not be able to resist a third attack and that his forces would be able to break through and split the allied army in half. Secondly, that his attack on the Lind right wing would be successful and that he would be able to envelop the entire allied right in a pincer movement.

Jim could not weaken his left wing more than he had done already. There had been less Lind stationed there from the outset. As it was so much higher and rockier than in the centre it was most unlikely that the Larg would choose to attack there but there were no guarantees. On Afanasei's advice the Lindars on the left wing were also the most inexperienced. There was only one experienced Lindar from a warrior pack similar to pack Zanatei stationed with them.

There could be no help from that area.

Jim knew that the critical point of the battle was upon them.

"Warn," he commanded Larya.

She did so, a troubled expression on her face; she well understood the significance of what was to come.

"They'll attack simultaneously," said Jim. "I think they have committed all their reserves."

Larya nodded.

"All Larg will fight."

"We'll beat them off," was Jim's confident answer, shouted loud enough for everyone within earshot to hear. His troops needed all the encouragement they could get. "They've no more reserves. One more effort and we've won."

"We chase Larg to sea?" asked Larya with a grin. The Lind had copied this human expression and their lips would curl up, showing an array of very large, pointed teeth. Those not used to this often misconstrued the expression as a snarl. Those vadeln-paired knew better, a snarl-grimace was quite a different proposition, coupled as it was with a certain Lind look in the eye that boded ill for all those who had the misfortune to face it. Many Larg had faced it and died that day.

"They must wait for orders to chase," said Jim sharply. "Tell Kolyei to *reinforce* that order." Not for anything would he abandon the advantage of high ground until there was proof positive that the Larg were unable to counterattack and in definite retreat.

"Larg command group moves," Larya said.

Jim looked at her. How on Lind had they managed to find that out?

: *We Lind have sharp eyes* :

Jim made another decision. "Vada to right wing."

Their presence might well make all the difference. Even three hundred or so mounted troops could do a lot of damage.

A few moments later, Jim received confirmation through Kolyei from Larya.

"Francis and Asya say 'wilco'. What is 'wilco'?" Larya asked in a puzzled voice. Larya was incredibly curious to know the meaning of new words in Standard; she was very much like Kolyei in this respect.

Jim laughed and promised to explain later.

"Elda go now," said Larya at that point.

"Go, go where?"

Larya pointed with her forepaw and Jim, turning in the direction she was pointing saw all but two of the Gtratha Eldas leaving the centre and heading south. These experienced whites knew that the battle was fast approaching its critical stage and they were off to aid the right wing. Their very presence would give heart to the defenders, especially those who had never faced the Larg before.

There was a long drawn out howl from the south and the kohorts in front of the centre started up the hill once more.

The melee began again as the front kohorts hit the allied ranks.

Geraldine and Jsei met the charge with grim determination. She was not in the second rank now but stood at the front, shield strapped to her left arm, Jsei to her right. Jsei's presence was like a solid rock of comfort in her mind; for the first time she felt confident that together they would survive all this and that the allied army would prevail.

A large tawny body came thundering towards them. Jsei crouched down, indicating that he was going for its belly. Geraldine raised her sword, ready to strike. Their enemy leapt at her left side with such force that it shattered her shield and she staggered back somehow managing as she did so to bring her sword down on the beast's shoulders. She felt the scrunch as the blade hit bone. The Larg staggered but kept on coming, landing on top of Geraldine. His weight knocked her gasping to the ground but she managed to keep what remained of her shield above her torso. There she lay, dazed and could only watch as the horror that was the Larg's face closed round her throat. His mouth drooled saliva and some fell on to her face and into her mouth. She felt herself retch as the liquid reached her taste buds. Then Jsei was there.

He leapt at the Larg, his mouth grabbing hold of its neck as it tried to get at Geraldine. With a strength he hadn't known he possessed, Jsei forced his enemy away from his chosen human. Geraldine realised that nothing was holding her pinned down any more, and scrambled to her feet. The Larg and Jsei were in a writhing embrace as both tried to bite at the others neck. Their front paws mauled at each other. *You bastard, you're not going to kill my Jsei.* She joined in the fray and her sword came down once, then twice. The Larg tried to get away from this joint attack but Jsei had it by the throat now and escape was impossible. Jsei's mouth closed. There was a gush of bright ochre blood and the Larg was dead.

Jsei moved away from the carcass and in one fluid movement was facing downhill again, ready to face another enemy. Geraldine stepped up beside him as another wave of Larg hit the lines.

Along the infantry lines this scene was repeated again and again. The kohorts found it virtually impossible to win against an infantryman armed with shield and sword fighting with a Lind warrior.

It was not long before this information was being disseminated en masse amongst the Lindars. The reserve Lindars behind the infantry moved forward to join with their human allies. The right wing of Lindar Zanatei merged with the humans like a well fitting glove would slip on to a hand. Robert Lutterell found himself fighting hard with Afanasei at his side. Louis and Ustinya and the other cavalry youngsters attached to these Lindars, fought the cavalry way as taught by Francis darting in and out of the melee when they spied an opportunity. Their two-edged swords were proving extremely effective.

All was confusion as the battle surged to and fro, the Larg hurling themselves at the defenders as they desperately tried to force a way through. Another kohort arrived at the top of the hill and joined in the battle. The smell of spilt blood was overpowering. The combatants no longer fought in rank. They no longer battled in front of the tree line. Individual fights were being fought between the trees as groups of Larg managed to force their way in to be met by the reserves. All was chaos and the sounds of killing and being killed filled the air. Interspersed with the growls and howls, human voices were yelling and shouting. The dead and the dying lay on the bloody ground. The crews of the arrow contraps fought desperately alongside their Lind allies.

The outcome of the battle for the centre hung in the balance.

: *Jim, mount up!* : Larya's 'mind-voice' screamed at him.

With a start Jim looked at her then at the group of Larg swarming round and up the base-rocks of the command post. They were forcing their bodies through the defenders, through the blue striped ryz who were trying desperately to stop them.

: Advance the rest of the reserves now! : he 'shouted' as he swung himself into the saddle. There was no time to fix the restraining straps.

A group of Larg managed to evade the ryz at last and began to climb, intent on destroying the two who stood atop it.

: They know you are Susyc : Larya informed Jim. She mentally prepared herself. *: They think to kill us :*

All thoughts of directing the battle vanished as Jim drew his sword. His legs gripped Larya with all his might. To fall off would be fatal. As the first snout emerged they leapt forward and Larya's chelas reached for her enemy. Jim tightened his free fist in her neck ruff as he brought his sword down.

The Larg collapsed like a pole-axed zarova, but there was no time for congratulations at their first kill. Two more Larg scrabbled on to the ledge. Larya swung round. They were caught up in a swirl of thrashing bodies. Jim killed the first of the two with comparative ease, ignoring the searing pain as a claw scored through the protective leathers on his thigh. Larya downed its partner and managed to get her mouth round its neck. Blood spurted from its severed jugular. More arterial blood spurted out and up until the ground was soaked with it. Larya held on until the body stopped its spasmodic movements.

Jim was drenched in blood, and Larya not much better. It showed up brightly on her coat.

"Gtran's teeth," he exploded. "That was close. Are you all right?"

"Small hurts only," she answered.

"Thank the Lai," iterated Jim, and dismounted, the better to peer over the side of the ledge. There were no longer any Larg there.

"Get Kolyei on line."

: Kolyei says centre is holding. He needs orders :

: Regroup. Tighten the lines. Fill the gaps :

Jim extracted his first aid kit from his pocket and began to smear Smaha salve on Larya's muzzle and chest, which were criss-crossed with bleeding welts.

Up on the hillside, Afanasei and Robert had seen the attack begin on Jim and Larya's command post. With great presence of mind in the midst of the chaos, Afanasei ordered a detachment of the second ryz to go to their aid. Zanatei himself led them back towards the rocky tor where at least the same number of Larg had managed to break though. Three Larg were already half way up the rocks. The remainder of the tawny beasts turned to meet them. It was thanks to this that Jim and Larya had only the three Larg to deal with.

Jim sent a mental thanks to whomsoever had ordered the rescue party and raised his binoculars once again to his eyes as he reappraised the battle. Larya kept a wary eye on what was happening below. He was relieved to see that his soldiers were holding their own. Although small groups of Larg had endeavoured to break through, there were not enough of them to consolidate the advantage. Lind and human refused to give up and fought for every inch of ground. Some individual Larg began to turn and retreat back down the hill and to Jim's eyes not all those so doing appeared to be wounded. Tails between their legs, the more inexperienced kohorts began to leave the high ground. There were sporadic cheers from the beleaguered infantry. These cheers gave the Lindars to either side of the human soldiers the heart to continue. They fought even harder and even the most experienced Larg kohorts began to realise that this attack on the centre was not going to succeed.

Here, they had been well defeated.

On the right wing, it was a different story. The Lind were being pressed hard and were beginning to fall back. Some Lindars had ceased to be a cohesive unit. The Elda were ordering the first reserves into the fray. The hilly inclines were shallower here and the Lind were finding it that much harder to hold their spreading lines. The battle was becoming a fluid one and in such a battle, the smaller and lighter Lind were at a distinct disadvantage. Jim watched the undulating mass of death and carnage. If these lines folded, they would all be in desperate peril.

He turned to Larya.

"How many Lindars not engaged?"

"Eight," she answered after a moment of consultation with Kolyei.

"Tell them to join with the Vada. They are all to swing round and try to encircle the kohorts. They are to attack from the side and rear."

They were his last reserve troops.

CHAPTER 25

NORTHERN CONTINENT

At the settlement, Stuart MacIntosh made it back to the second line of defence, but only just. He thought, as he scrambled over, that this barricade was much less defensible when compared to the main walls they had evacuated and *they* hadn't stopped the self-appointed General Murdoch for more than a few hours.

Scar-faced Baker's regiment, having led the charge through the gates, made short work of the formed echelon of defenders who fought a brief yet bloody delaying action in the courtyard. This leading regiment, closely followed by those of Smith and Cracov, having overcome this resistance, pressed on, leaving the mopping up operation to the regiment to their rear. Duchesne, in command, was not happy about this but orders were orders and he valued his own skin too much to disobey the General. He began to organise the round up of any of the defeated still hale enough to stand and be counted.

Jean Farquharson watched with growing horror as his men began to prowl the courtyard and surrounding buildings. Any men too badly hurt to stand, they at once despatched, ignoring pleas for mercy. Badly injured women they left where they lay. Long afterwards Jean found out that the men had left them because they had not been told what to do with any injured females. Although these women were not killed, neither were they helped in any way. Jean heard their moans as she lay still and as quiet as she could on the dirty ground, pretending to be unconscious. A stray arrow had lightly wounded her arm.

One man approached her and kicked her hard in the ribs.

"Get up," he shouted.

Jean did not move.

He kicked her again.

"Get up," he repeated.

When she still lay there, his narrow sweaty face began to redden with anger.

Jean thought for a second and then began, slowly, to raise herself up into a sitting position and staggered to her feet.

"That's better," the original man said and began to push her towards a small crowd of women, now separated from the male prisoners and being herded towards the gates. "Perhaps I'll be nice to you later," he leered.

Murdoch had made plans about what was to happen when the walls were breached. He had not believed Aoalvaldr when the Larg Commander said he could easily defeat the Lind. The General had watched the first abortive Larg attack and then the next. He knew that he *would* take the settlement but if, in the end, the Larg were to be defeated was aware that his army would likewise have to retreat back to the beach. Without Larg support their position would be untenable.

Accordingly, the colonels had their orders; to grab what women and female youngsters they could and send them at once and under escort to the beachhead. When Duchesne managed to gather up some one hundred and fifty from the occupied area, he lost no time in detailing two squads to take them there.

Jean Farquharson and the others went stumbling on their way. Holding her injured arm tightly, it was still seeping blood, she brought up the rear. Those in the group were all fighters; Stuart had ordered the evacuation of the south area nearest the gates the moment the beacons had been lit. The women walked silently for the most part, only a few were crying, mostly those, Jean surmised, who had lost friends and colleagues during the fight. Like her, none were badly wounded.

The captured males watched them being taken away. They knew that there was no hope of rescue. From the noise coming from behind the second defence line, their would-be rescuers were in the midst of a savage fight of their own. The men waited for what would be.

Duchesne took a deep breath. He knew what was expected of him. Murdoch was in no mind to leave these men alive, as a threat to his rear. His orders were clear but first he beckoned over his senior sergeant.

"I'm not happy with the directive that only boys under sixteen should be spared," he said. He looked round carefully, making sure that no one could overhear his next words. "For my peace of mind and yours, include all those who are aged up to around twenty with the boys. We can at least try to save them."

The non-commissioned officer nodded his agreement and started to walk towards the prisoners. He picked out an older, dependable looking man at the front.

In an almost-whisper, Sergeant Wallace said, "Tell those up to the age of twenty to say they are sixteen. I can save them, but only if you do what I say with no fuss."

"And us?"

The reply was a sombre shake of the head.

The man gulped but a practical man, he got the point at once. His life and that of the others would be forfeit but here was a chance to save some of the younger men at least.

"I'll get them to step forward. Tell your men to stand back. I've got a bit of explaining to do," he said to the sergeant.

"Be quick about it."

The man turned to face his fellow prisoners and began to talk urgently.

"Guards step back two paces," Sergeant Wallace ordered. "Give them some room. This man is sending out the youngsters." His men obeyed. They were the sergeant's own squad, carefully selected and trusted.

He looked around and spied a storage cabin not far away.

Pointing, he added, "Take the boys in there. Leave a guard on the doors but take no further action."

If the sergeant's squad were surprised at the numbers and obvious maturity of those that stepped forward, they said not a thing. These were not sadistic men and understood what Duchesne was trying to do. Duchesne commanded a lot of loyalty and respect. Of all the regular colonels he had a conscience and men were drawn to his command. They would not report their colonel. They agreed with what he was doing.

The 'boys' were led away.

Duchesne nodded towards his chief lieutenant who began shouting orders to move the adult prisoners towards two empty cabins nestled against the outer walls. The prisoners moved slowly. Fathers looked around to see where their sons were being taken; others looked up at the clear blue sky. Most believed that they would eventually be taken outside the walls to a place of execution. That was, in fact, Duchesne's intent.

The lieutenant was an impatient man. Why execute these men one by one – why not do the lot at once? Individual executions, or even of groups, took a lot of time and was not good for morale.

"Get them inside," he ordered, flushing with excitement about what he was going to do.

Once the men were inside the cabins, the doors were slammed shut and the bolts shot home.

At this point Duchesne heard his name being called from the other side of the courtyard and left the lieutenant to it as he went to deal with the problem.

Back at the cabins, a squad appeared, each man carrying some of the unused catapult ammunition. These were set against the cabin walls and doors. Seeped in oil, they would burn well. The lighted fire starters were set against the faggots and they began to burn, slowly at first, then with increasing intensity. The men incarcerated inside began to shout; many tried to get out, battering against the roofs and walls. Some managed it, only to be killed by arrow snipers from amongst the guards.

Duchesne became aware of both the shouting and the smell of burning simultaneously. He realised what the lieutenant had done and felt sickened to the pit of his stomach. He had not ordered this abomination. There was no way he could possibly stop what was happening; the fires had taken hold and were burning fiercely. If Murdoch found out that he had tried to stop it his own life might well be forfeit. Someone might also think to investigate the boys in the cabin too. However, a mercy killing was one thing, burning people alive quite another.

The lieutenant enjoyed the spectacle as he waited for the

anguished screams to cease. A few of the guards laughed with him but most felt much as their colonel did and wished they were anywhere else but beside the execution site. Duchesne made a mental note to arrange the transfer of the lieutenant to another regiment more suited to his sadistic nature as soon as he could. The stench of burning flesh filled the air. The shouts and screams of the dying men grew in intensity for a few minutes then ceased as smoke and flames overpowered and engulfed them. There was no one left alive when the roofs fell in.

It was at that point that General Murdoch, Andrew Snodgrass by his side, entered the settlement and looked at the burning pyres with satisfaction.

Duchesne hastened towards him.

"This area secure?" barked Murdoch.

"Yes General," answered Duchesne, tight-faced. He felt sick. "Boys captured as ordered. They shouldn't give us any trouble and the women are already on their way to the beachhead."

"Saw them when I came in. That all you could find?"

"Most of this area has been evacuated and any other females are too badly wounded to be moved."

Murdoch looked around.

"I see that some of your men are attending to them," he noted, censure in his voice.

"Can't leave them there bleeding to death. Bad for morale," Duchesne temporised.

"You're too soft by half but at least you got rid of the men," Murdoch grunted, but said nothing more on the subject. Thankfully, as far as Duchesne was concerned, he did not ask to see the imprisoned 'boys'. "Baker, Smith and Cracov?"

A relieved Duchesne knew how to answer this. He watched as more troops progressed through the courtyard on their way to the secondary defences. "The colonists have erected another barrier on the far side of the river. Baker requested reinforcements and intends to assault in force in a few minutes, I believe. The support regiments should be in place by now. These passing through are the last. What news of the Larg?"

Murdoch frowned blackly. "They haven't been able to break through the Lind centre but are attacking to the south. I am assured that it is only a matter of time."

Andrew Snodgrass nodded painfully. Aoalvaldr was forcing regular information into his mind. He now had the grandfather of headaches and there was no sign of any respite.

"Ground's more level there," Andrew added. "Aoalvaldr says he should outflank the Lind before the sun sets."

"Good," said Duchesne.

"The Lind are, by all accounts, doing well enough in the centre," warned Murdoch. "Our Larg 'friends' haven't won yet. Until they do, keep to the original plan."

"Yes, General," answered Duchesne.

They could both hear the sounds of the battle beginning for the barricades.

"I'd best get up there," said Murdoch, glancing in that direction. "Encourage the men, give them a bit of support. Once more into the breach and all that rubbish. A good commander should be seen after all. It says so in all the best history books."

With that parting riposte he strode away, Andrew Snodgrass in tow, his bodyguard forming up around them. It was a large bodyguard. Duchesne did not think anyone could possibly get close enough to the General to do him any harm.

More's the pity, the devil within him thought.

With Murdoch gone the courtyard became quiet. The stench from the burning men was overpowering.

"Put that pyre out," he shouted at the lieutenant who was still ostentatiously warming his hands at the dying embers. He stood, hand on hips and waited until he did so. He stopped himself from retching with difficulty.

I'm going to get out of this army, become a farmer or something that doesn't involve any killing of my fellow man.

Sergeant Wallace joined him as they waited to receive the next batch of prisoners.

Duchesne would not leave the lieutenant to his own devices this time.

Michael Wallace looked at Duchesne. "Not a nice man that," he said eventually, with a twitch of his head in the lieutenant's direction.

"Mmmm," said his colonel. He still looked disturbed.

"Watch your back with that one, Colonel," Michael cautioned.

"He's a murderer and he's ambitious, means to go far and doesn't much care how he goes about it. If he were colonel here I wouldn't much like to serve under him."

"What were you in for?" asked Duchesne.

"Murder. Didn't torture anyone though, nor burn them alive. Merely rid the world of the man who killed my daughter. Always thought of it as justice."

Duchesne considered this. "After all this is over, I'm thinking of taking up farming as a career. Care to join me?"

The sergeant's face split into a grin. "I most definitely would. Consider me your man. I'm city bred though. Don't know much about farming and the like."

"Neither do I, Sergeant, neither do I. We will learn together."

The assault at the river barricades was brief and bloody. The defenders were overrun and the battle in the settlement degenerated into a mess of individual fights as the convict army, victory in their sights, swarmed over the makeshift barriers and into the middle quarters. They began to clear the streets of the colonial fighters, street by street, cabin by cabin, step by bloody step.

Kath and Matvei were in the middle of it all. Mounted on her lifemate, she defended herself with all her might.

: *We go* : decided Matvei.

Kath privately agreed with him but couldn't bring herself to abandon the settlers. She and Matvei were part of Stuart MacIntosh's group, presently stationed at the crossroads in the very centre of the settlement.

"Just a little longer," she pleaded.

She and Matvei moved into a small porch area to allow her to tend a small wound on his flank. From there, she watched as another large group of southerners came round the corner, marching straight into Stuart's squad. At Matvei's urgent mental shout, she dropped her first aid kit, mounted up in a hurry and began to refasten the fighting straps with trembling fingers.

The two groups met with a clash. Clipping the hip restraints into place, Kath watched. The two groups were fairly evenly matched number-wise but the southerners were more heavily armed and as the fight continued towards its bloody conclusion she realised that they were far better fighters than the colonists. She did not know it then but this was Murdoch's personal bodyguard. Murdoch only chose the best. In the midst of the furore, Stuart must have, at some point, realised the identity of the man in the middle of the enemy group. This man stood, sword in hand, but was not getting involved in the fight. Every time one of the settlers tried to force through to him, at least two bodyguards leapt to intercept.

"General Murdoch I presume," yelled Stuart, shouldering the guards aside with one giant heave.

Murdoch grinned. He continued to grin as other bodyguards turned on Stuart and began to hack at him with their swords. Stuart, mortally wounded, fell to the ground.

With a howl of rage, Matvei leapt towards them. Kath thanked the stars that she had availed herself of the cavalry harness offered by Francis. She herself dealt with at least two of the bodyguard and Matvei went for the throats and heads of two more as he strove with all his might to reach the hated enemy leader. The settlers took heart at this show of courage and pressed on with their own attack with renewed vigour leaving Matvei free to make his next move. Before Murdoch had time to raise his weapon, the Lind was looming over him, murder in his heart. Matvei's large jaws opened wide. Murdoch stood mesmerised.

The General about-turned and fled the scene, making for the open doorway of a half-finished cabin. Matvei raced after him but was hindered by the battle around him and so lost momentum. Once clear, Matvei, Kath urging him on, tried to grab their enemy before he reached the doorway. They almost made it but Matvei snapping at his heels, Murdoch squeezed inside and tried to close the door behind him. He wasn't strong enough to force it shut against the mass of angry Lind as the large male placed his forepaws on the central bar and pushed at it with all his might. The wood began to splinter.

Murdoch looked round the room with frantic haste, let go the door and sprinted towards the ladder leading to the upper storey. Heart hammering nineteen to the dozen, he climbed the rungs two at a time and let out an explosive breath of relief as he clambered through the hatch. He heard sounds of movement below and peeked his head over the edge only to come face to face with Matvei, who was standing on his hind legs peering upwards into the gloomy loft space.

This cannot be happening to me, thought Murdoch in panic as Matvei's face came closer. He could clearly see saliva forming down Matvei's jaw line.

Matvei's face disappeared from view.

Murdoch breathed a sigh of relief.

Matvei and Kath looked at each other.

: *What do we do now?* :

: *Can't climb that thing* :

: *The ladder?* :

: *Is that what it's called? No matter. I can't get up there* :

: *I'll have to do it alone* : Kath gripped her sword. : *We can't go and get help, we don't know who is in control of the area and if we leave, Murdoch will escape* :

Matvei nodded, looking around the bare room for inspiration. His gaze turned to the chimney. : *I can see light. What is that?* :

: *The chimney? It's constructed to burn a fire in, but this one's never been used* : She walked over to it and squinted up, Matvei padding behind her.

: *I think I could squeeze up. It's only half built. I can see the sky and I think the bricks stop at the attic level. Can you keep him busy at the ladder? I can creep up unnoticed behind him if you make enough noise* :

Matvei was worried.

: *Very dangerous* : he warned. : *I cannot help you if you go up there* :

: *Do you have a better idea?* :

Matvei shook his head and gave her face an affectionate lick. He padded back towards the ladder. Murdoch's white face stared down at him. He had forgotten all about the existence of Kath. His attention was riveted on the blue-striped Lind who began to growl and snarl. Matvei placed his left paw on the first rung.

As quietly as she could, Kath began to climb, thankful that the chimney was made of rough-hewn stone and brick and thus had plenty of hand and footholds. When her head reached the attic floor she risked a glimpse over. Murdoch had his back to her. His attention was focused on Matvei to the exclusion of all else. She threw a mental shout to Matvei and he redoubled his efforts, snarling even louder and rattling the ladder. She pulled herself on to the floor and began to inch her way towards the enemy general.

Unaware of the danger, Murdoch was beginning to relax. He had realised that the Lind could not climb up to him.

Cracov, or Smith or Baker will send some troops to find me. I've only to stay right here and my men will burst in and kill this beast. I don't need to do a thing.

Keeping in constant telepathic touch with Matvei, Kath began to raise herself to her feet, in preparation to bringing her sword down on Murdoch's unprotected back. Something must have warned him. Perhaps the floorboards creaked. The man tensed and turned round.

"Whore," he shouted. "I'm going to kill you and there is nothing that beast downstairs can do about it."

He lunged towards her. Kath screamed as his sword slashed at her legs and dropped her own as she squirmed out of reach. She did manage to retain her knife. She started to kick at him. Caught off balance, Murdoch flinched back as her right foot narrowly missed his groin. Encouraged, she kicked again and again. Murdoch flinched with each one, then started to grin as he realised she had lost her sword. He crouched forward, poised to lunge at her again.

She had nothing to lose.

With all her might, she threw the knife straight at his face.

Murdoch screamed as the knife made contact, imbedding itself in his left eye. He dropped both sword and knife as he clasped the wound with both hands.

Kath could hardly believe her luck. Crying out in anguish, Murdoch scrambled away from her. He dropped to his knees then fell flat on his face at the edge of the ladder hatch.

Kath picked up her sword. It was time to finish it but before she could act, Murdoch's body started to move, very slowly. With supreme effort, Matvei had managed to clamber up the ladder. He stretched his head up and into the loft. Murdoch's head quite literally disappeared from Kath's view as Matvei's jaws clamped shut around it.

The General had time for one conscious thought. *No.*

Matvei shook the man violently, breaking his neck, then pulled the body towards him. It slithered through the hatch, dropped past Matvei and landed on the floor with an audible thump.

Matvei began to spit.

: *Bad taste in mouth* : he explained.

"Must be terrible!" Kath grinned, taking a deep breath. She began to laugh.

"I'll come down the ladder slowly, my legs are shaking."

Out on the street, the fight between the bodyguard and the settlers was over. The handful of southerners who had survived the frenzied attack had fled. The colonists looked at each other, then at Stuart MacIntosh's body.

"What do we do now?" asked one.

"More convicts coming this way," said another. "I can hear shouts."

"Where are the women and children?" asked the first.

"Mostly at the northern wall area. Hidden in houses. That won't save them though. It's only a matter of time before they manage to get us all."

They looked a picture of misery and dejection as Kath and Matvei re-appeared.

"The field army are holding their own," encouraged Kath as she and Matvei got close enough so that they could hear her words. "Hold on a little bit more. I'll let them know what is happening down here. Help will come."

"But will it come soon enough?" asked the first man, wiping his bloody sword on one of the deceased bodyguard's cloak. "Murdoch?"

"Dead."

Despite the death of the convict leader the settlers continued to be forced back, building by smoking building, but as the word spread about their General's untimely end, the southern attack began to falter. Murdoch had appeared to the majority of the convicts as an almost god-like and immortal figure. He had led them from their first small victory in the south to this gigantic one in the north. It seemed impossible to think that he was dead. And if the immortal Murdoch could die, then so could they. Instead of driving forward with abandon, the non-regular troops began to have doubts. Instead of obeying their orders they began looking around for items to loot.

They started to roam the streets, smashing open cabin doors and ransacking all they found within. The men grew angry as they realised there was little of any worth to steal. The situation was getting out of hand. The regular troops continued to fight, but without the irregulars' support, found the going tough.

The northern quarter of the settlement continued to remain in colonial hands.

Baker and Smith were forced to call a temporary halt to the street clearing operation and begin to rein in their more troublesome troops.

The news of their leader's death did not trouble this duo. It opened up windows of opportunity for both. All the regular colonels bar Duchesne began to wonder if they might be the one who might take Elliot Murdoch's place as overall leader. The jockeying for power had begun.

Once the men got tired of looting and were brought under control, they would complete the takeover of the settlement. The colonists were going nowhere after all.

Murdoch, egotistical to the last, had seen no need to appoint a second in command. He had enjoyed watching the manoeuvring for position. Unfortunately, except for Duchesne, none were aware of their deceased leader's doubts about the ability of the Larg to win their part of the battle. The colonels saw no need to rush the men forward and Duchesne kept his knowledge to himself.

The newly appointed Colonel Cracov was nowhere to be seen. He was eventually found in a deserted cabin, bemoaning the death of his mentor, convinced that if he had remained in charge of the bodyguard his General would still have been alive.

The colonels sent a detachment of regular troops to oversee the looting, to make sure it went no further. To their immense chagrin, although they looked long and hard for the majority of women and children, they found only two more strays, both with babes in arms and with sundry young children in their care. After due consideration, the two mothers were left alone. The two women did not realise until much later just how incredibly lucky they had been.

Sporadic fighting continued in the areas where the two sides rubbed against each other. The southern troops were convinced that as soon as the colonels got themselves sorted out the final assault would begin. This time they would fight on until all the colonial men were dead.

Larya turned a stricken face to Jim.

: I cannot 'hear' Kolyei :
: What ? :
: Something has happened. I cannot sense his mind :
: Broadcast the order direct :

Larya composed herself and took a deep breath.

: I am ready :
: NOW! :

Larya's telepathic mind-send thundered out.

: *All Lindars not on the front ridge and not fighting to follow the Vada to the right wing under Susa Francis's and Asya's command* :

It was time to commit everything he had.

Francis, Asya and his Vada had been waiting impatiently for the order. Kolyei and Tara were sending frequent updates of the battle situation and Francis had known the command would come soon.

Once the additional eight Lindars were ready, he gave the order to advance, in extended formation and in two ranks. Thomas and Stasya were with them, momentarily forgotten. The other youngsters attached to the eight sidled over to join him at the edge of the rear rank. By doing so they were disobeying orders, having been told by Francis to go to Kolyei's communications unit behind the lines if the Lindars moved off the hill. They chose to disobey, wanting to take part in what they saw, in their youthful ignorance, as the glorious charge of the day, just like on the story discs.

Neither Tara nor Kolyei realised what the teenagers had done. They were right in the middle of a great deal of trouble of their own.

The vital communications between the allied forces disintegrated in a heartbeat as several Larg descended on them. The Kranj had managed to fight their way through the lines and past the Lindars defending the contraps. Unable to rejoin their fellow Larg when the order came to retreat to the streambed to regroup, they had slunk unnoticed deeper inside the allied lines. The Kranj Commander realised at once what the small group in the clearing was about, why the Lind were not fighting as they used to. This was his chance to gain much honour. Without this centralised communications system their enemy would find itself at a disadvantage.

The Kranj went at once into the attack. Tara, thankfully mounted, Kolyei had insisted on this, saw the first indication of serious trouble when the Larg began to push their way out through the trees. She managed to shout out a warning but then the youngest member of the allied army and her lifelong partner were fighting for their lives. She was conscious of Emily and Ilyei at her side. The Elda and other communications personnel joined in the fray together with the quarter ryz detailed as guard.

With a growl of rage, Kolyei leapt at the foremost attacker, Ilyei beside him. They forced the Larg warrior between them. Tara and Emily hacked at its exposed back whilst their Lind tried to get at its neck. Tara felt the pain as a Larg managed to bite into her arm. Thankfully, Kolyei twisted away and the Larg lost his grip.

The Lind soon realised that the swords, even hefted by two younglings, were perpetrating a massive amount of damage. The Larg, forced tight between them, could not get into an attacking position, neither could he writhe away. With strength Tara did not know she possessed, the girl took another mighty swing at the Larg. It was enough. The Larg stopped and toppled to the ground. A panting Kolyei looked around the clearing but all the Larg were dead. He heard Tara start to sob broken tears and sent a short burst of calming and reassuring thoughts to his girl, but he had an important message to send before he could comfort her properly. He contacted Asya. In a few clear images, he explained to Asya how the four of them had taken the Larg out. He sensed Asya imaging the information throughout the rest of the Vada.

She sent him back a fleeting 'thank you' and Kolyei turned his attention to a distraught Tara. Emily, that bit older, had already dismounted and was tending to the Lind battle hurts, shock taking second place to their needs.

CHAPTER 26

NORTHERN CONTINENT

The Vada burst out of the forested part of the slopes on the right wing, the eight Lindars formed up on either side. The Larg were not aware of their presence right away; so intent were they on attacking the Lindars in front of them. These Lindars were being hard pressed but knowing about the relief force emerging behind them held on with desperate determination.

The Larg kohorts stopped in shock as Francis's cavalry swung round in a large arc and began their charge. The Lindars already facing the onslaught felt the pressure ease as the enemy turned to counteract the unexpected threat.

Stars, thought Francis as he and Asya pounded forward, *there are thousands of them!* Death was in his heart. He gritted his teeth and pressed on.

The two sides clashed together with yells, howls and screams. Soon the entire area was full of the devilish dance of death and horror as the ground seethed with writhing Lind and Larg intent on destroying each other. The reserve Lindars, although inexperienced, acquitted themselves well; not for nothing had they been in training for just this very moment since they were little more than ltsctas. Swallowed up amongst it all fought the Vada, the Larg concentrating their best efforts there, desperately trying to take these angels of death out. The Vada, trained by Francis, fought as a team, aiding and supporting each other with all their might. When they could, they used Kolyei's tactic. Beside Francis fought the twins Bill and Geoff Armstrong, filled with battle lust and thoughts of revenge for the deaths of their family during the previous winter.

The Lindars holding the right wing, and now freed from insurmountable pressure, began to push a little harder. The two Lindars as yet uncommitted by the Elda waited eagerly inside the tree line. They sensed that the battle tide was moving inexorably in their favour. They knew that they would be engaging the enemy soon enough.

As Francis and Asya downed their fourth Larg, he also began to think that the odds were shifting. Yes, they were taking casualties, but so were the Larg. The ground was dotted with bodies, some were moving feebly, others not, but the northern army was more than holding its own, it was advancing.

"We're winning!" he shouted to his troops. "We're winning! Keep going, don't let up!"

Aoalvaldr took this setback to his plans on the snout. He, like Jim, realised that this was the pivotal point of the battle and ordered the kohorts to push forward. They tried but did not manage to advance more than a few yards. The Larg attack began to grind to a halt.

Sensing victory, the northern allies began to push harder. Their foes did not give up easily. They continued to resist. Intensely loyal to their leaders, it was part of Larg nature not to give in. If not ordered to retreat they would fight where they stood and to the death. Unlike the kohorts in the centre they did not have any contingency orders that allowed them to regroup then try again. Their orders were to keep going, to fight until they dropped.

Imperceptibly, paw-by-paw, they were forced back.

Aoalvaldr was in a quandary. The Lind should not have been winning, not in the open like this. He had no appreciable reserves remaining to throw into the fight and if he transferred the kohorts at the centre streambed southwards, those Lind still on the ridge would be able to sweep down on his exposed right flank. He would then be attacked from both sides at once. There was even the possibility that his army would be encircled with no available corridor to escape. His Kohort Commanders were pressing for a decision. Aoalvaldr procrastinated, loath to order full-scale retreat that could only mean the end of all his hopes.

The deadly game of death continued.

Then, the decision was taken out of Aoalvaldr's paws. Reports came in that more Lindars were emerging from the lian. Sensing victory Jim had ordered all those not directly engaged on the defensive lines to regroup on the low hills of his right wing. Even the untried Lindars from the far west of the continent sped forward. They were delighted to be given the chance.

Like the tidal wave of nemesis, these Lindars hit Aoalvaldr's flank and it didn't merely buckle, it crumpled, it collapsed. Aoalvaldr had no way of knowing how inexperienced these Lindars were, he only knew that he was in trouble, deep trouble. His plans had come to naught. He would have to return to the south, tail between his legs. Where had the Lind found such numbers to defend their rtathlians? Their reserves seemed endless. He did not know that the northern army had committed every warrior it possessed.

In response to the unspoken command from their leaders those kohorts nearest the beach began to slink away. Rage in his heart, Aoalvaldr watched impotently as first one and then another began to scarper towards the coast as fast as his four legs could carry him. Aoalvaldr could only do one thing, accept the inevitable and try to extricate as many as he could. This was not an ordered retreat. This was a rout.

The Larg rearguard stood firm. They knew their duty. The Larg at the streambed about-tailed and sped away. Aoalvaldr went with them. As the revengeful Lindars attacked the rearguard, Aoalvaldr watched from the beachhead as the pride of Larg died. The survivors of the other kohorts were milling around beside him, waiting for the order to cross back over the island chain back to the south.

Aoalvaldr gave the order.

None of the rearguard emerged alive to follow Aoalvaldr back over the island chain.

Neither the Lindars nor the Vada followed them. They pulled back, reformed and waited, ready in case the Larg were foolhardy and tried another attack.

At the settlement, Baker and Smith had taken joint command and were in the process of organising their final attack. They were confident that before long the settlement and all those inside would be theirs. Baker was shouting out his orders when he heard his name being called.

"Colonel Baker, COLONEL BAKER, STOP!"

Baker and Smith turned.

Andrew Snodgrass was running towards him, a panic-stricken expression on his face.

"The Larg lines have broken," the man babbled. "They're in full retreat. The rearguard isn't expected to hold out for long. Aoalvaldr says that he can't guarantee your safety unless you leave at once. He's still holding the beachhead and will continue to do so for as long as he can."

"Can Aoalvaldr's kohorts escort us to the beachhead?"

"No."

Baker and Smith looked at each other. Never in their wildest dreams had they imagined this. Without Larg support there was no way that they could consolidate, in fact there was no way they could hold on to what they had.

Through gritted teeth, temper barely held in check, Smith sent runners to all the colonels ordering a withdrawal. Orders to form up in rank began to reverberate in the air, both at the forefront and to the rear of the occupied areas. Few disobeyed. Grabbing whatever loot they could get their hands on, they took their positions.

Their only chance of survival was to keep together. The Lind, it was hoped, would think twice about attacking the ranks if they kept in formation. Two regiments were awarded the dangerous honour of rearguard.

The settlers watched them leave, too tired to even consider following them. *Let them go*, they thought, *and good riddance*. They had no wish to prolong the bloodshed.

Jim Cranston, up at the command post, was jubilant. Through his binoculars he spied the convict army begin to march out of the settlement gates. Two Lindars who had patiently waited atop the rocky crags to the north for the entire battle he ordered to leave the defence lines and move down to the settlement area and offer what assistance they could to the humans inside. They were warned not to provoke a Larg counterattack.

The Lindar assigned to enter the walls of the settlement itself were to take whatever steps they considered reasonable to eradicate any remaining resistance. Jim was a practical man and furthermore, saw no need to practice restraint towards those reluctant or unwilling to surrender. Reports were beginning to come in from Matvei and the others and Jim was shocked to the marrow to learn about those southerners who had cold-bloodily killed every adult male they could get their hands on. The Lindars concerned were more than keen to get started on their duties and many a tail wagged hard as they sped on their way.

Jim would soon learn the full cost of their victory. He was sure the butcher's bill would be a high one. He dreaded finding out.

He stood, wearily leaning against his beloved Larya as the news began to come in. The battle was won. The long lines of convicts were weaving their way back to whence they came. They and their Larg allies would begin to cross over the shallows to the first island before dusk. By morning they would be gone.

A keening howl began to fill the air. Jim looked round. It seemed that every Lind capable of doing so was sitting up on his or her haunches and singing a peculiar litany of tones.

He looked enquiringly at Larya.

"It is the victory song."

"It sounds so mournful."

"Yes, it greets the victory but acknowledges those rtathen not with us now."

> "No more shalt thee run, hunt and play,
> Under the soft warm sun of day.
> He who has died, he has gone away,
> She who has fallen, she cannot stay.
> Midst trees tall,
> We mourn thee all.
> Midst mountains high,
> We for thee sigh,
> Midst rivers fast,
> We sing of seasons past.
> Midst valleys deep,
> We thy memory keep.
> Midst meadows bare,

> *Thy deaths we will share.*
> *He who has died has gone away,*
> *She who has fallen cannot stay.*
> *Be still, mine rtathen."*

Jim looked at the ground, tears swelling in his eyes. The Lind lament was so sad he felt he could not bear it. Eventually it began to die down, then ceased altogether. Then from Robert's infantry ranks, the men and women began to sing in their turn, an eons old hymn, telling of lost shipmates and comrades. The Lind cocked their ears and listened, knowing that this was the human tribute to those who had fallen.

> *"Abide with me; fast falls the eventide;*
> *The darkness deepens; Lord with me abide:*
> *When helpers fail, and comforts flee,*
> *Help of the helpless, O abide with me."*

As the first verse ended, Jim did begin to cry although he managed to control himself in time to hear the last.

> *"Hold you your cross before my closing eyes,*
> *Shine through the gloom, and point me to the skies;*
> *Heaven's morning breaks, and earth's shadows flee:*
> *In life and death, O Lord, abide with me."*

"What is this Lord they sing about?" asked Larya.

"It is an ancient song," answered Jim. "Some humans believe that there is a being all around us," he glanced up at the sky, "who created everything and everyone. I personally don't but that's my decision."

"Is this Lord like the Lai?"

"Something like," agreed Jim, not wishing to get into a theological discussion about their respective beliefs and traditions. It was neither the time nor the place.

The battlefield fell silent except for the sounds of the wounded and dying.

The badly injured Larg lay, knowing that the coup de grace would not be long in coming. They did not wish to survive and have to return to the south with the resultant punishment for failure and for being weak willed enough not to fight to the death rather than be captured.

Not all the convicts made it home either. Some were wounded and lagged behind. The Lindars did not kill those men without good reason. If they surrendered, fine, they were helped. Some however, although hurt, were not prepared to be taken prisoner. These the Lind dealt with in predictable fashion. Colonel Cracov was one of them. He even managed to wound two Lind before he was killed. The prisoners who could stand were escorted back to the settlement. There they were thrust into the empty jezdic corral outside the walls and left to contemplate their sins. It is on record that none attempted to escape. The Lind guard prowling outside the fence was more than enough to dissuade them.

"Is it over?" asked Tara in a small voice.
"I think it is," said Kolyei. "The Larg flee."
"I'll go and help with the wounded," announced Emily. "Will you be okay?"
"Should I come and help too?"
"Stay here," she answered, giving her a quick hug. "Kolyei may still need to pass messages."
"Tara will rest beside me," Kolyei informed them with a weary sigh and watched as Emily and Ilyei left, Emily's med-bags gathered over the girl's shoulders.

The sights that would meet Emily's eyes were to haunt her dreams for many a day. There was no way the older girl would willingly expose young Tara to the horror that was the aftermath of battle, but it was this day that Emily decided that medicine, in some shape or other, was to be her future.

Lindar Jalkei entered the settlement through the gap where the gate had been and advanced into the now deserted courtyard, noses twitching anxiously and hackles raised. The smell of burning flesh filled the air and irritated their noses. One look at the burnt out cabins close to the walls confirmed their suspicions as to the fate of at least some of the captured settlers. They grimaced with distaste and growled to themselves. Any southerners they captured would receive short shrift, Susyc Jim's orders notwithstanding.

The settlers were only now beginning to realise that the danger was over. Admittedly, there were still some enemy soldiers left behind (by accident or design, they were not yet sure) and some were still holding out in some isolated cabins but the very real threat of annihilation was gone.

Kath and Matvei met the relieving Lindar at the edge of the courtyard. Matvei conversed mind-to-mind with the Susa and then stood impassively as Lind began to pass by him and Kath on their way inside.

Kath could hear shouts behind her ordering the settlers to stay where they were, that their allies were here and preparing to clear the streets of any remaining enemy soldiers. Three blasts of the whistles would tell them when it was safe to emerge from their hiding places.

The Lind of Lindar Jalkei were very efficient. As dusk approached most areas were clear. They also wished to know what they were to do with the many prisoners who had been captured trying to escape to the beachhead. In the end it was decided to put them in the corral outside the walls with the others. Presently, small groups of dejected men were to be seen being encouraged to walk faster in that direction. The Lind were not gentle. The men looked exceedingly nervous and fell over themselves in their anxiety to do as they were told.

Then the colonists began to emerge, tentatively at first, to search for their loved ones.

From one smouldering building, a young yellow-striped female Lind appeared, two very young children perched on her back and two slightly older ones stumbling by her side.

After a burst of communication between her and Matvei, he hung his head, his demeanour one of sorrow. Kath, attuned to his thoughts, realised, with dawning horror, what had occurred. The four shaking youngsters had watched their mother being killed by a bunch of vengeful southerners. She leapt down from Matvei's back and went to comfort them.

The four were not the only orphans tended to that night. Not a few children had started that morning with both mother and father. Many had lost one and others both. Over four hundred colonists, mostly male, had died defending their loved ones, although the full death toll would not be properly worked out until the following day when a full roll call could be taken. That first night, the survivors wanted only to sleep, to tend the wounded and to thank their lucky stars for their own escape.

Kath and Matvei managed to snatch a few hours rest after they had seen to the needs of the four orphans Kath had taken into her care.

As the effect of the Smaha root wore off, Tara's right arm throbbed hard where the Larg had bitten it open to the bone. She would have to remove the bandage Emily had put on soon to smear on some more but baulked at the thought. Emily was busy with the more seriously injured and she couldn't bother her with what Tara considered was a small wound. It was bleeding though, the bandage was bright red in places and she felt sick. So she sat on Kolyei's back, willing herself not to cry and berating herself for not doing something about it.

Kolyei stood still, concentrating on passing the necessary reports to and fro, not that it was so urgent now that the Larg were in full retreat. Linked with Kolyei, Tara listened in with growing weariness as she followed the story of the demise of the invasion.

She learnt of the deaths of both Bill and Geoff Armstrong but it was with a curious detachment, a light-headedness. Disjointed images swam in front of her as she followed the Larg's retreat through Kolyei's eyes.

She swayed in the saddle.

How long she sat there she could never remember afterwards but it must have been an hour, if not more.

She felt someone ride up beside her and raised her head a little. She saw a leg, a grimy and dusty leg, a leg sitting astride a Lind, one with the blue-striped pattern of pack Zanatei.

It's from our pack, she thought dully, *I think*. Her vision was foggy.

A voice came out of nowhere, as if from a great distance, a voice filled with concern.

"Are you all right Tara?" asked Alan. "You look half-dead."

With some effort she made sense of his words and raised a dirty and tear-stained face to his.

"I feel all wobbly," she began, "and my arm hurts."

She fainted then, though because she was attached to Kolyei's back by the fighting harness she did not fall off. Kolyei too looked grey with exhaustion and in need of help. This Alan decided as he dismounted from Kiltya's back in a hurry.

The large male was swaying on his paws. His fur was drenched in sweat and he was keeping his head from hitting the ground with much effort and force of will.

The only white senior still there was Mariya. She didn't look to be in much better shape.

Alan took charge; it was his turn to repay the debt he considered he owed Tara.

"Both of you," he commanded Mariya and Kolyei, "lie down before you fall."

Kolyei relaxed and collapsed in a heap of legs and tail. Mariya sat down, careful of her old bones.

She looked surprised at being ordered about by one so young in seasons but was too tired to argue.

: *Kolyei is exhausted* : she managed to telepath to Kiltya. : *You must join with me to keep communications open* :

Kiltya edged over to her and sat down touching paw to paw. She looked pleased and proud to be asked for help by the most senior Lind of all.

Alan unbuckled the harness and pulled Tara off Kolyei's back. She stirred.

"Is Kolyei hurt?"

"Nothing major," replied Alan, "but you are bleeding."

Tara didn't hear him. She had lapsed into unconsciousness.

Alan carried her over to a natural wallow under a large allst tree and laid her down as carefully as he could.

Sorting the wound wasn't easy for Alan. One edge of the bandage was stuck to Tara's skin where the blood had dried. He decided to leave that bit and cut away the wet. He smeared Smaha over the wound and took a clean bandage from his med-pack, then remembering his first aid lessons, bandaged it up as tightly as he could.

Tara didn't appear to be hurt anywhere else he noticed with relief. He made a pillow with his own cloak and rummaged around the nearby packs for hers, which he laid over her. Then he smeared the Smaha on Kolyei's cuts, pushing him all ways to get at every part of him despite his groans of complaint.

He sat down beside Kiltya then in case a translation between Standard and Lindish was required.

Alan never took his eyes off Tara and got up regularly to check her colour and breathing. She didn't wake but it was a natural sleep of the exhausted; towards dawn he fell asleep himself.

On the lower slopes of the hills to the south of the lines, Francis, Asya and the Vada kept at it well into the night. As he surveyed the field of victory whilst there was still light enough to see, Francis was in despair. Over a third of his beloved Vada were dead. It was scant comfort that their sacrifice and those of the Lind who fought with them had meant the difference between victory and defeat. Many of those fallen had been his friends. Asya too had lost many a pack-mate.

The hardest to bear were the deaths of some of the youngsters who had disobeyed his precise orders and taken part in the charge.

He passed the bodies of the twins Bill and Geoff. They, with Malya and Sindya, had died side by side, overcome by the sheer mass of Larg the Vada had hit during their desperate charge.

Francis hadn't been as close to the twins as some of the others but he had liked the two boys and was nearly as upset and filled with anger as when Faddei had told him about the murder of their family. The entire Armstrong family had now been wiped out and all because of the Larg. Closer to home were the deaths of Moira and Andei – Francis dreaded telling her mother; her father had died during the space storm on the *Argyll*.

He thought of young Peter back at the domta busy making welcome-home presents for the other eleven.

Francis himself found the body of young Thomas Wylie lying in the bloody soil, still strapped on to Stasya's back, his sightless eyes staring. The boy had fought; his sword was still gripped tight in his lifeless hand. It was covered with drying blood.

The lad's face was strangely peaceful in the dusk-light, the only evidence that he was dead the whiteness of his face and the thin line of dried blood that had trickled from his mouth. Stasya herself was still alive but very badly wounded. Blood seeped from a large gash in her chest and there were many smaller gashes on her side where Larg fangs had bitten deep.

At Francis's approach she raised her head and looked at him out of haunted and pain-filled eyes.

Francis could barely make out what she was trying to say.

"Thomas has gone to the blue pastures. I follow him."

Asya hung her head.

"No Stasya," babbled Francis, "we'll get healers here, I've got some numbing root it'll stop the pain. You mustn't die." Francis began to apply the salve. But Asya understood what Stasya was saying. The young female did not want to continue life without Thomas.

"We stay with you," she promised her pack-mate.

Francis had an agonised look on his face.

It was at that point that Francis fully understood what the act of vadeln-pairing actually meant. Few Lind who were paired with a human would wish to continue to live if their life-partner died. He also knew, he didn't know how, that this would be the case the other way round, the bond was so strong.

It was up to him to respect Stasya's wishes. He settled down beside her with Asya and gave the dying female as much comfort as he could. Asya's mind linked with her pack-mate and she brought Francis in on the link. The Vada Commander felt Stasya lose consciousness as her lifeblood seeped away. Then there was an emptiness where she had been and he realised that she was gone.

"We will bury them together," said Francis quietly as he eased his cramped muscles. "They were a brave pair."

"Yes," said Asya, also quietly. "The names will be added to the honour chant. They will be sung about for many moons to come."

Francis wondered aloud how Emily would take the news. She had been growing fond of young Thomas and, whatever the two children had been planning, he knew that Stasya and Ilyei had been hoping to make a four before many moons had passed.

"Ilyei knows. He is very sad. He will tell Emily. They have each other. Steven and Alanya died during our charge too."

That did it. For the first time in his adult life, the hard Francis McAllister, one time ship's troublemaker and the bane of every petty officer's life, burst into loud and bitter tears. Victory was not sweet. War was hell.

"Was it worth it?" he asked.

"Yes. If we had lost battle we would all be dead, if not this sun then next. You must be proud."

After these words, Asya fell silent, waiting for Francis to understand. She sent a message to Faddei at the medical station, knowing that Francis needed Laura, but she was too busy to come.

Francis pulled himself together with a grunt of effort, and leaving the young bodies, rose stiffly and went to the aid of those still alive. They were his Vada. He must be there for them. Asya felt very proud of her man, very proud indeed.

It was full night before an exhausted Laura and Faddei picked their way through the battlefield towards them. She had been helping with the operations on the badly injured. Many would survive this time that would otherwise have not. Lind paws could not hold needles and sew but the human medics had hands that could, the stocks of surgical gel having run out some hours previously.

Her fingers bleeding from the pressure from the surgical needles, eyes red-rimmed with exhaustion and from crying for those whom she had not been able to save, Laura fell into Francis's arms. They rocked against each other for some time, both taking and giving comfort.

"If our baby is a boy, I think we shall call him Thomas," she said.

"Baby?" he asked. "What baby?"

"Our baby, silly," she answered. "I've known for over a month now. You had enough to cope with and I was needed here, on the battlefield with the Holad. I was scared that you would refuse to let me come if you knew."

"You are quite right," said Francis, tenderly taking her into his arms.

Asya and Faddei looked at each other, tails wagging. Their humans could look to the future now. Perhaps it was time they too started a family. Despite her hurts, Asya looked at her mate provocatively from under her eyelashes. Faddei returned her look with one of his own.

Jim descended from the command post. He needed to find both Robert Lutterell and Afanasei. He found Robert tending an injured infantrywoman. The commander of the infantry lifted a grimy face towards the Susyc as Jim approached.

"We won then?" he said, fingers busily tying the knot on the bandage. "Settlement?"

"Sent Lindars to their aid a while ago. The last of the attackers are being hounded to the beach. Perhaps 'hounding' isn't the right word, but 'wolfed' sounds most peculiar and wrong."

"You're letting them go?"

"Can't do much else. We are all too exhausted. There are still some Larg inland as well. They'll need to be hunted down."

"Don't think I want to fight any more," said Robert, "and to think I used to read war and adventure stories for pleasure. Never again!"

"Seen Afanasei?" asked Jim, looking around for him.

Robert indicated towards the tree line.

"Last time I saw him he was over there with some of the wounded."

Jim nodded at Robert and headed to where Afanasei was. The white male had streaks of blood on his flanks but did not appear to be badly hurt.

"Pack Zanatei Lindar?" asked Jim.

"We are Rtath Zanatei no longer. We are Rtath Afanasei now. I was asked and have accepted."

Jim's look begged the question.

"Winston and Emily tried save him but his wounds too great. Zanatei name will live on in song."

Jim sighed. Is there to be no end of it? Who else hasn't made it?

"Be not sad," said Afanasei. "He saved you. I was with him when he died. He was very proud of you."

The words were bitter comfort. Jim's whole body sagged.

"I am sorry."

"You win battle," said Afanasei comfortingly. "All rtaths will honour Ruza Jim. All rtaths honour Ruza Zanatei for saving Ruza Jim. Pack Afanasei will honour you above all." A number of nearby Lind whined approval and some lowered their heads in a gesture of respect.

Jim smiled ruefully; it would take some time to get used to this new status but perhaps Zanatei and the Lind had the right of it. It was not the individual who was the most important; it was the rtathlians and those who inhabited them that mattered. Perhaps to die in battle was not an entirely bad thing when one died defending what one loved and cherished. It was still a waste of life, war was always a waste but he should be proud and honoured to have led these soldiers, Lind and human. He would grieve for Zanatei and the others, but first there was work to be done, the living to care for and the future to plan.

"Go now and visit the injured Jim. I will find you later and we will talk more."

Afanasei watched as the man headed towards the Holad, purpose in his step once more.

He met the weary Ustinya and Louis. The young man was dismounted and was stumbling along at his partner's side. Ustinya was limping, but not badly.

Louis, Jim realised, was absolutely covered in dried blood.

"You hurt?" he demanded.

Louis looked down at his stiff clothing.

"The blood's not mine," he answered in a dull tone.

"Larg got through, Jim," said Ustinya contritely. "I am sorry, communications broke down when they broke through to the rear."

Jim shrugged. "In the event it didn't matter too much," he told them. "Larya managed until Kolyei's mind kicked back into the loop. Have you seen Tara? Is she okay?"

"Ustinya says she and Kolyei are sleeping. We'll go and check on her in a little while though I believe Alan and Kiltya intended to go and see. Where is Larya?"

"With the medics. Nothing serious but her flank needed attention. I'm going to her now."

Candy Rae

CHAPTER 27

SOUTHERN CONTINENT

Tidings of the defeat in the north came to those at Fort, including naturally enough, the news that Elliot Murdoch was no more.

Brentwood rubbed his hands together with glee. Now was his chance to consolidate his position, to gain power, now, whilst the leadership was in doubt. His attitude towards Anne Howard changed at once. Gone was the deference. Only her pregnant state was preventing her immediate transfer from Fort to the encampment down the hill. In a snatched meeting with Gerry, she explained her predicament but she was being guarded too closely to even consider an escape. There were Cherry and Joseph to consider as well. Gerry was making plans to get the two youngsters away but it required very careful planning. The penalty for failure did not bear thinking about.

Deliverance for Anne, of a sort, was however, at hand.

As Baker and Smith led their battered army south they had much to complain about. Any hope either had entertained of assuming absolute power was dead, the incipient rivalry between them redundant, ever since Andrew Snodgrass had translated Aoalvaldr's words.

"Larg make pact with Murdoch. Larg keep word. Humans stay in lands ceded before battle."

Baker and Smith had smiled with anticipation. This was good. Both men had eyed each other through narrowed lids, quite sure that it would be he who would assume absolute power at the expense of the other.

"Largan say we need each other in future. Alliance will stay," continued Andrew on behalf of Aoalvaldr.

Baker and Smith had nodded sagely.

The next two sentences contained the bombshell.

"Aoalvaldr says that the land is ceded to Murdoch and his descendents in perpetuity. No one else. This is not negotiable."

So Smith and Baker would not fight each other for the leadership of the south. Elliot Murdoch's unborn child would inherit.

Their plans took an immediate about turn.

After a few guarded words, Aoalvaldr then led his Larg away south, leaving the human army to make their way back to Fort. To Andrew's immense relief, it was permitted that he stay with his own kind.

"I be back," Aoalvaldr warned him. "In disgrace am I. Punishment is to spend many summers in desert guarding borders. Aoalvaldr be important and have power again. I will contact you when time is right."

Andrew did not want to think about that. Perhaps he could move up towards the coast, out of range of Aoalvaldr's mental shout? He resolved to speak to Baker about it. He had no wish to continue his relationship with Aoalvaldr. Let another take a turn.

"We can be Lords though," said Baker as they marched. "Lord Baker sounds good to me and the real power behind the throne will be ours."

"Perhaps it will be a girl child," said Smith. "Much easier to control."

"We'd better make plans," said Baker. "You got the map?"

Over dinner in the colonels' mess three days later Smith spoke to the other surviving colonels.

"We have a map, fairly detailed. We've split the land into eight sectors, each to be led by a Lord, subject to the crown. Baker and I have chosen ours and have allocated the two southerly Lordships to Colonels Cocteau and Brentwood. The other four are up for grabs, except for one."

He looked over at Pierre Duchesne.

"You get first choice."

Duchesne walked over and looked at the map. Naturally, the four Lordships already chosen were those round Fort. To their north were another two, reaching up to the coast, to the southeast, one, smaller than its northern and western neighbours. There was another in the northeast. This one was vaguely triangular in shape, bordering two so far unclaimed Lordships on its western side, its northern border the beachy coast. It's far eastern tip fell short of the beginning of the island chain by a scant three miles. It had the advantage, in Duchesne's eyes, of being as far away from Baker, Smith and all the rest as possible.

He pointed at it.

Smith's eyebrows rose but he said nothing. His look however, spoke volumes.

"The other three," said Baker with a sardonic grin, "the rest of you can argue over. Remember though, your keeping these Lordships depends on your loyalty to Smith, Duchesne, Cocteau, Brentwood, myself and the Crown!"

With that, Baker and Smith left them to it.

"In memory of our dear lamented leader," Baker was saying to Smith as the two walked away, "I think this country of ours shall henceforth be called the Kingdom of Murdoch. It has a nice ring to it don't you think? I must tell them all in the morning."

Smith grinned.

Duchesne followed not long after, deep in thought. He needed to speak to Sergeant Michael Wallace as soon as possible.

The arguments between the remaining colonels continued for some days. Eventually, after much wheeling and dealing, a solution was reached and the two Lordships on the northerly coast claimed. Nobody wanted the small desert south-eastern Lordship with no rivers or coastline. It was therefore left vacant, and would become crown land for the time being.

The scar-faced Baker sought out Duchesne and when he found him, came to the point in his usual abrupt manner.

"Why that Lordship?" he asked. "You're miles away from Fort where the action is."

Duchesne had thought of an answer he hoped would pass muster.

"It's next to the coast," he temporised.

"So are two others."

"But they don't have much woodland area. I intend to make a fair bit from managing the pockets of hardwood growing there. There's any amount of arable land too."

"It's nearest to the island chain man, first line of defence against the north and you're likely to have kohorts of Larg clipping its edges on their way there and what if the colonists decide to attack you?"

"I've got my regiment," Duchesne said in a mild voice. "I'm sure I'll be able to keep the rampaging northerners off your back. I think too that I'll leave the far eastern tip empty. The Larg can pass through any time they like. I'm certainly not going to try and stop them."

Baker wasn't quite sure if Duchesne was being serious or not.

"We're still in your land now. You staying or coming back to Fort with us?"

"I'll leave half of my men," Pierre Duchesne answered. "They can start building the cabins. I'll come back with you to Fort, pick up my goods and chattels and see what's going on. You going to leave me some of the women we've just captured here now? No point in walking them all the way there and then back again. Say twenty-five?"

Baker considered this, then nodded in agreement. He wanted to keep Duchesne sweet, at least for the time being. He wanted him on his side on the Conclave of Lords who would govern the kingdom for the, as yet, unborn prince. If he gave Duchesne these twenty-five, he would be beholden to him for the largesse.

The internal bickering and power struggle had begun, not for the title but for power and more importantly, control.

When the army arrived back at Fort, Henri Cocteau accepted the land allocated to him with commendable aplomb. Bryan Brentwood was not so happy and persuaded Raoul van Buren to swap, the north-westerly lordship being more suitable for his purpose. He had decided on a new business venture that would, long-term, be very profitable. Duchesne watched these two begin their own game of power play and was glad to think that he would soon be well out of it.

He was pleased to see that Briony, the young girl he had chosen the same day Cocteau had picked out Carla Pederson, was well. He was surprised to find that Cocteau had bought Carla's mother Ulla from Brentwood and made haste to do the same for Briony's mother.

A week later they were all ready to be on their way. It was with relief that he led his half-regiment down the hill and away from Fort. Amongst the baggage train walked a pregnant Briony Duchesne (that had been a surprise), her mother and her two young brothers. The girl was in a seventh heaven of delight at what he had done for her family and was quite prepared to fall in love with her protector. Her mother reserved judgement. Too much had happened for her to be entirely at ease with her son-in-law yet.

Before he left, Duchesne did manage to speak to Anne Howard. It was difficult. If anything, her movements were now even more restricted than when Murdoch had been alive. As the mother of the future heir to the throne, she was being treated like glass. She was not permitted to lift a hand to any work and for the first time in her life Anne had servants who were required to look after all her needs. But her life wasn't an easy one. The incipient animosity between Baker and Smith was growing. Both wanted to marry Anne to cement their power at the expense of the other.

She did understand that she had a friend in Duchesne. He had surprised her the morning before he left for his Lordship, walking in on a snatched conversation she was having with Gerry as the man was making a surreptitious detour from his task of delivering some goods to the kitchens.

"Spy in our midst?" Duchesne said half in jest as he approached.

Anne went ashen with fear; Gerry even whiter. How much had Lord Duchesne heard? How much did he suspect?

Duchesne looked at Gerry and Anne took another frightened breath.

Duchesne's next words surprised both of them.

"Don't panic. Even if you are a spy, I am not going to say anything. I only came here to say something to Anne. I am glad she has a friend she can trust here."

Gerry breathed a sigh of relief.

"I am your friend," he said, addressing Anne directly. "I know that you might not believe it but if there is anything I can do to help, I will if I can. Just send this man here to me. I can't do much but you never know what the future holds."

"Thank you," said Anne simply. "I won't forget. You are the colonel who was kind to the boys aren't you?"

"I did my best," replied Duchesne and walked away.

"Do you believe him?" asked Gerry. "Can we trust him?"

"Yes Gerry, I think I do and I think we can and must. There is something about him that is different than the other so-called Lords. I don't know exactly what happened to him in the north during the campaign yet I feel in my bones that my husband would have agreed with me. Remember, we do need all the friends we can get."

CHAPTER 28

NORTHERN CONTINENT

In the north, three weeks passed while the wide patrols confirmed that both the convict army and the Larg kohorts had gone. Jim felt that there were not enough hours in a day to do what had to be done. It had been an unpleasant shock to realise that the aftermath of a war was often more troublesome than the battles themselves, even when one won.

Stars, it was hot. The command tent was like a furnace, even with the sides open to let in what little breeze there was. Jim sighed and bent his head once more to the casualty lists. It seemed as if he had been reading them forever, making annotations here and there against certain names. He had known many of those who hadn't survived to see the victory and some of them he had served with for years on the WCCS *Argyll*. Larya, lying resting on the floor beside him, raised a sleepy eye in his direction then promptly shut it again before Jim noticed the movement and embroiled her in sad conversation. It was, she reflected; as she drifted off to sleep once more, really far too hot even to think.

Jim felt sorry for those colonists labouring to clear the battlefield in this heat, trying to rid the ground of the Larg carcasses before they became more of a health risk than they already were. The raptors were being drawn to the battlefield like the vultures on planet Earth and guards had to be detailed to chase them away from the allied bodies. The area was full of incessantly buzzing insects beavering away and they were an even greater annoyance than the scavengers.

It was decided to burn the Larg dead and the funeral pyres were rapidly becoming an extra burden for those detailed to the grisly task. The stench of burning flesh filled the air and permeated clothing right down to the undergarments. Jim felt that he would never rid his clothes of the smell, no matter how many times they were washed.

The disposition of the allied dead was a task that Jim had taken upon himself, hence the seemingly endless lists. He had the bereaved to visit too.

Those vadeln-pairs who died together were to be buried alongside their life-mates. It seemed a fitting tribute, although the backbreaking labour involved in digging so many graves was extremely difficult in the dry, impacted soil. The prisoners' grunts of effort as they laboured pleased those who came to pay their last respects. The infantry dead, it was agreed, were to be buried in one large battle mound. Robert himself claimed the honour of making sure that they were put to rest. The harsh-looking mound would grow over and soften with time, but would forever be a reminder of those who died during what had been christened 'The Battle of the Alliance'.

It was, naturally enough, the humans who felt a need to give the battle a name. On their own, the Lind would not have bothered. Once the mound was finished Robert Lutterell marched his surviving men and women back to the settlement. Jim would meet him there that evening for a working dinner.

The Lind accepted the human wish that their own dead should not be left where they lay as in the past. The scavenger birds would have picked the bones clean and more, but that was before humans had begun to inhabit the coastal plains. It would not be possible now. The colonists held land there and the ground was fertile, ripe for growing crops.

A large ravine-like hollow was selected as the Lind gravesite and presently the Lind were to be seen dragging their dead pack-mates towards it with the help of harnesses manufactured by the settlers. Once filled in, the prisoners would heap good soil on top. Through time, it would become as one with the landscape even more than the battle mound. Zanatei's body and those of the other Elda who had fallen would lie with them, the Lind having refused a separate gravesite for them. They did not believe in venerating one Lind above another, no matter how important he or she had been in life or how much valour they had shown in battle. Zanatei would have expected and wished to lie with his brethren.

The humans on the other hand were already making plans to erect a commemorative monument nearby. It was as Jim reflected, a matter of perspective and tradition, with both species respecting each other's wishes although they might not understand them.

Jim hoped that the whole melancholy process would be finished soon.

"What did you do before?" asked Tara.

Kolyei looked at her; the two of them were standing on the rocky outcrop that had been Jim and Larya's command post.

"As now," Kolyei sounded surprised, "we mourned."

"No," said Tara, "that's not what I mean. What did you do with the bodies? I've never seen any signs of old bones lying about."

Kolyei understood now and in a voice singularly devoid of emotion he began to explain.

"Many scavengers fly," he said.

Tara raised her head to look at the huge birds.

"These ones? Is it them, these large horrible looking things that we keep having to chase away? What are they?"

"They are the Xrndli, scent blood, feel death."

"Then?"

"Xrndli do not merely eat fur and flesh but the bones too."

Tara now understood the lack of bone traces from previous battles. "Are you upset that Jim has ordered the burials and burnings instead?" she asked.

He shook his head.

"Why should we be upset? Ashes of Larg lie with Lind. That is as it should be. Legends tell us Lind and Larg were once one. It is fitting bones lie together. Humans live here now. It is best bodies not lie as of old."

"It's better this way then?"

"Different."

"I'll make sure they're all remembered," she declared. "I'm going to write about it, what happened to them."

"We have still the History of Lind to write," he reminded her.
"This *is* our history, don't you see?"
"So it is Tara," came a well-known voice from behind them.
Tara turned. It was Jim, a very tired looking and haggard Jim.
He stood beside them surveying the scene below.
"Write your stories," he advised, "they are important, but don't forget your History of Lind either. You've your whole life in front of you, plenty of time. Kolyei will help you. He might not be able to write but he certainly can spin a tale, or should I say tail?"
Kolyei's perplexed look spoke volumes.
"What I am missing?" he enquired.
"It's a little matter of spelling," smiled Tara. "We haven't got to that bit yet, wait, weight, two, too, tail, tale. Different spelling, different words, different meanings."
Kolyei looked confused.
"You talk in riddles," he said crossly.
For the first time since the battle had ended, Jim laughed.
"I think she's won this round Kolyei my lad."
"Round, what round? Why do you talk about circles Jim?"
Jim laughed even louder and even Tara began to giggle.
The Lind were out and about rounding up the herds once more. Many kura and zarova were needed both for restocking and to feed the large numbers of Lind still at the coast. They were accomplishing this with typical speed and efficiency. The corrals round the settlement were repaired and were being filled with restlessly moving beasts once more.

The Lindars were anxious to depart. It would take many of them over a moon to reach their rtathlians. The wounded would follow when they recovered. Jim made a point of visiting them and was embarrassed at their gestures of respect. Afanasei had been quite correct when he had told the Susyc that the Lind considered him a great hero. Larya basked in the reflected glory and seemed most amused by his discomfiture. She reminded him of his honoured status every chance she got.

To allow those who wanted to depart to do so and to relieve the pressures on the depleted food supplies, a conference had been arranged for the leaders of both species to decide what was to happen in the future. Jim had seen many impromptu Lind meetings in progress during this last day and he wondered what they were up to. Larya wouldn't say a thing and when asked merely looked wise. Jim himself had his own ideas about what was to be discussed, hence dinner with Robert Lutterell before the evening gathering to sort out the proposals.

Robert Lutterell, Infantry Commander and reinstated member of the Council, prepared for the meeting in his usual efficient manner. Since that morning when he had led his triumphant army back through the gaping hole in the walls, much of the continuing reorganisation had fallen to him. With the death of Stuart MacIntosh and all but three of the Council there was nobody else capable or willing to take charge. He was later elected unanimously into the vacant Council Leader's position.

The survivors wanted to get back to their farms and professions. They were already gathering their families and possessions together and moving home. True, their original livestock was gone, but that was a small price to pay for their freedom and the Lind were already bringing replacements in. There were fruit and root crops to attend to. Weeds grew with abandon in the summer sun and the farmers did not want to lose their harvest. The settlement was as overcrowded as ever, especially with so many of the cabins burnt down to their foundations and Robert was keen to ease the pressure.

The specialists who were remaining within the walls were eager to rebuild, intending to take advantage of the devastation to organise the settlement properly. The haphazardly erected cabins of the previous year were gone and would be rebuilt better than ever and in line with a new street pattern.

The area next to the wall where the captured men had been burnt to death would not be built on. Plans were afoot for a memorial garden and a plaque was to be erected. The Lind promised to bring in many exotic plants and blooms from the far west when the time was right, although they had continuing difficulties understanding the human need to venerate their dead in such a public manner.

To all intents and appearances, young Tara was recovering from her battle shock. Thirteen was very young to have killed in battle. Winston Randall, taking time off from his care of the wounded to see her, was amazed anew at the courage she had displayed. Only Kolyei was aware of the horrendous nightmares she was experiencing each night. Linked to her mind, he shared them.

"We go back to our domta soon," he said to her. "We will leave this place of death."

Tara smiled a wan smile.

"Back to the rtath forever?" she asked wistfully.

"Maybe," Kolyei mused. "At first yes. I have much to learn. I must continue reading lessons." His tail wagged. He had an insatiable thirst for knowledge.

"Remember Rtath Afanasei is a warrior pack still," he warned.

"I know," Tara answered, "but I also know that I never want to fight in a battle again."

"What does Tara want to do then? You cannot write all of the time."

"I think, I think that above all things, I would like to teach. I know I'm only thirteen and still have to attend lessons but when I am older I would like to be a teacher of the young."

"I like that idea. Tara and Kolyei, we will travel together, we will learn and teach in Lind Rtathlians? Go to many new places? Explore everywhere and you must write all that we find down on paper sheets?"

"Yes," said Tara, her eyes gleaming with anticipation, "yes please. We will write the history of the Lind down in a book so that the humans can know the Lind better. It would be wonderful to be able to do such a thing. I'm sure Peter would like to join us. I don't think he'll ever be a warrior."

"Then that is what we do." Peter's life-mate Radya was never far from Kolyei's thoughts and he was pleased that the two of them were an integral part of Tara's plans for the future.

Others were deciding what they were going to do in the future. The threat from the south had not disappeared. Trained fighters would still be needed, although it was expected that hit-and-run raids by the convicts would become the norm for some time to come. The Larg had been dealt a heavy blow, but they would be back, if not next summer then the one after, or the one after that.

Francis and Asya intended to return to the rtathlians and there rebuild the Vada. He also realised that the threat from the south would be ever present and that the Vada would, in all likelihood, be in the forefront of any future war. Laura and Faddei would remain with them as a matter of course. She would continue with her healing studies with the Holad. The four of them were looking forward to a long and fulfilling life together, bringing up their children, of both species.

Geraldine and Jsei were going with them. The young woman was still nonplussed about what had happened to her. She was keen to try out cavalry tactics within the Vada. Francis had already earmarked her and Jsei for possible promotion as soon as she mastered mounted fighting.

Louis Randall, to his father's disappointment, was showing no inclination to follow the family tradition and take up animal doctoring. To everyone's surprise he appeared to be falling for Geraldine, despite the difference in their ages, although Ustinya and Jsei might well have been encouraging this incipient relationship. The two Lind were attracted to each other in a big way, despite coming from different packs. Francis believed that the autonomy of the packs would undergo a fundamental and radical change in attitude, during the coming months, for those Lind who were vadeln-paired.

A heartbroken Emily was looking forward to her return to the domta as well, although she was dreading facing her parents after the death of her brother Steven. She missed Thomas and Stasya unbearably; the void in her life caused by their deaths would take a long time to heal.

Kath and Matvei were totally engrossed in the four orphans they had found in the settlement ruins. The six would return to the domta together. James, Rozya and the ltsctas were looking forward to this addition to their family and James was adding two extra rooms to the daga in preparation.

As the settlement meeting-hall was relatively undamaged, it was decided to hold the gathering there. The sun was dipping beyond the horizon as the delegates began to make their way there. The agenda was long. Jim and Robert had spent their meal together making minor adjustments to the list with no help from Afanasei or Larya, who surprisingly, as far as Jim was concerned, did not appear to be as interested in the agenda as he had hoped. When asked why, the two Lind again looked wise and refused to comment.

The Gtratha would be present, together with the Elda of every pack that had taken part in the battle. Robert and the surviving Council would represent the humans of the coastal plains, Jim and Larya the vadeln-pairs, Francis and Asya the Vada and Winston Randall those humans who had chosen to domicile with the Lind. Jim was to take the Chair (it had taken quite some time to explain the concept to the Lind) and Tara and Kolyei were to stand behind him, ready with translations if they proved necessary. Jim hoped not. If they had to translate every word, the meeting would likely continue well into the night.

The major item on the agenda was to be the future of the continental land mass. To help with this, a large map had been produced and tacked on to the wall. It was made from individual duraprintouts held together with tape. The Lind had never seen its like before and all afternoon the meeting hall had played host to long lines of interested and excited Lind, all wanting to look at the wonder. Once they understood what two-dimensional maps were all about, they had had great fun placing their own home rtathlians on it. Emily and Tara had spent hours annotating the map with this information in bright blue ink.

Once all were assembled, Jim opened the proceedings.

"Friends," he began, "we are here to decide what is to happen next. The Larg and convicts have been defeated in battle, but not destroyed. We of the north may well have to fight them again. We have two major decisions to make.

First, we have to make sure plans are put in place so that we are never invaded in such force again and if we are, that our enemies can be defeated.

Second, we must decide what is to happen here. The Lind have welcomed us, allied with us. We have fought and died together. We humans thank you from the bottom of our hearts. If you had not done so, most of us would be dead. Unwarned and unarmed we would have been easy to overwhelm. Thank you all."

There was a burst of clapping and cheering from the assembled colonists.

The Lind looked embarrassed.

The oldest member of the Gtratha stood up at that point and cleared her throat.

"Mariya I am," she said in understandable Standard with merely a few words of Lindish here and there. "Some of you might know me. I am Senior Elda of Lind. I am the Gtrathlin. We thank you. If humans not here Larg now be killing all."

There were muted whines of agreement.

"Humans are friend of Lind."

Mariya nodded to Afanasei, who stepped forward. He cocked an ear at Jim. The original agenda was now redundant. He and Larya had laughed long when they had listened to Jim and Robert talking over dinner. Afanasei was looking forward to this.

He began to talk.

"Lind wish to make all right and proper. Humans live here. Here there is no rtathlians of the Lind, so far to the east. We Lind do decree that all land as far as edge of hills where my own rtath, Afanasei, live, is to belong to humans for all time. Up to river there, and up north to cold wastes. Here there are plenty rivers, woods and plains for humans to live, keep herds and to cultivate."

He stumbled a little over the last word, but it didn't matter. There was a burst of cheering from the human delegates and also from the large numbers who had squeezed in uninvited.

"Wait. There is more." Afanasei drew himself up to his full height. The cheering subsided.

"From river to big river be land for human and Lind together. There are four rtath there. All four wish stay. Human and Lind live and learn together, many vadeln there will be. Other Lind and vadeln live there too if wish. There will also be based our Vada."

Francis nodded. The Lind agreed with him that the Vada would continue. He stood and bowed to Mariya.

"I am honoured," he began, but Afanasei was not finished.

"Not all Lind will wish vadeln. Not all human will wish vadeln. They will prefer to live with own kind. Some Lind wish not vadeln but happy are to live in domta beside vadeln. These welcome in joint lands."

There was silence and a few frowns in the audience as they worked out exactly what Afanasei was proposing.

"Lind know Larg always will be a threat. The Larg will be of great danger to humans at coast. It has been agreed each pack shall spend two moons in turn in human lands, here, in lian above battle plain.

They will aid the humans, help guard coast and will patrol. In return humans will give food for that Lindar so they not need take kura and zarova from human herds. Also humans will tend Lind hurts."

"I'll train them!" cried out Winston Randall enthusiastically. "We want to help!"

There were more cheers.

Jim stood bemused. The meeting had been taken completely out of his hands by their four-pawed allies. The Lind were proposing much more than he had dared hope.

"We can help the Lind in other ways too," he said and looked round at the humans present. "I think we can agree to these proposals, don't you?"

There were enthusiastic nods and wide smiles and more cheers.

"One last thing," interrupted Afanasei. "When every hot season come, young Lind and young humans who wish to pair must come to our joint lands. You will arrange this?"

Robert spoke up.

"May I just clarify? Our youngsters who wish to pair will present themselves to be chosen. Each year at a certain time, is this what you mean?"

"Yes. This mean there will be a fair chance for all."

"I think we can do that," said Robert. "Not all will wish to do so though."

"Accepted," said Afanasei.

And that was that.

With a light heart, Jim moved the discussion on to the other topics. There would be plenty of time for celebrations later.

The rest of the items on Jim and Robert's agenda were hammered out between the two species one by one. It was reluctantly decided that nothing could be done about the women and young girls captured during the battle, at least for the time being. Jim kept quiet about their spy in the south. The least known about Gerry's existence the better for the man's safety and effectiveness. Afanasei and Jim were planning the best way to make contact and planned to talk to Jsei on the subject as soon as they could.

The detailed defence plans for the vulnerable coastline were worked out to everyone's satisfaction and the humans agreed that all youngsters from twelve years old would receive weapon and battle training.

In all, it was a very productive meeting and the future was looking bright for the north, despite the continuing southern threat.

Walking back to Robert's cabin afterwards, Jim spoke up.

"I didn't expect that. Thought we'd have to negotiate a bit."

Larya snorted.

"What did you expect? Lind are happy humans here. Larya is very happy Jim here. Now we have time for each other." : *I glad to be going home* : she added.

Jim had a thought.

"What about the orphans, Robert? There are a fair number."

Larya answered for him.

"Come with us to joint lands."

Jim thought absently that the land needed a name. Saying 'joint lands' all the time seemed rather awkward.

Larya was on to his thought in a flash.

: *No* : was Jim's telepathic denial.

: *'Jimsland' sounds good* : She sent a mental chuckle in his direction.

Robert Lutterell was unaware of the interchange. Perhaps it was just as well.

"I would prefer that the young orphans stay here, but I know we have too much to do with the rebuilding for the foster parents to spend the needed time with them. Many of the children are deeply traumatised and need a lot of time, care and love."

"Ask them," said Larya. "Home for them at domta. Much love."

"I think at least the older ones should be given the choice," said Jim with caution. "I know that Kath and Matvei are taking the four they rescued home with them. James and Rozya can't wait. I didn't know that Kath can't have children of her own and the kids themselves only have an uncle left to them and two grown-up cousins. The uncle has agreed to them going as long as contact is maintained."

"I will talk to the Council," Robert promised. "Now we have to plan how we are going to say goodbye to the Lindars that leave tomorrow. Come with me for a nightcap and we can discuss it."

"Good idea," replied Jim. "I'm as thirsty as a parched kura!"

Robert laughed and led the way inside the cabin. By the time night fell both men were feeling rather the worse for wear after some celebratory drinks. Larya looked at them, sighed and settled down to sleep. She did not care for alcohol.

CHAPTER 29

NORTHERN CONTINENT

Tara and Kolyei had one last visit to make before they left for home. She wanted to visit the cabin from where she had started out on her adventures. As the two of them made their way through the battlefield Tara kept her eyes closed as Kolyei picked his way through although this sector had been one of the first to be cleared.

There was not much of the cabin left standing she noticed as they stopped before it.

"They have used the wood for the pyres," Kolyei said.

Tara dismounted and walked into the ruins. The doorframe was still there but the door that she had slammed shut that momentous morning was long gone.

"My bed was over there," she pointed, "and the cook fire there where the soot is. Mrs Mackie wasn't a very good cook."

She wandered over to the bed-space and looked down. "I wasn't very happy here either when I think about it; I cried myself to sleep some nights."

"I know," said Kolyei. "I was there, remember." He sounded complacent.

Tara's eyebrow rose. She decided to correct him. It was good for her self-confident life-partner to be corrected on occasion.

"I suppose in part," she conceded, "though I didn't know that at the time. All I did know was that something was there inside my mind telling me to be patient; that my unhappiness would stop soon."

"Has it?"

She smiled.

"Yes, I am happy, despite all the horrible things that have happened. You should know that."

Tara turned away then and as she did saw something glinting in the sunlight. Watched by an interested Kolyei she bent down and dug it out of the soil.

"What is it?"

"It's a coin," she answered with excitement, "I wonder."

She rubbed it with her sleeve.

"Zowie! It's Papa's silver coin!"

Joy lit up her face.

"I thought it lost forever. It must have dropped out of my pocket that morning. I never said anything but I was disappointed it wasn't in the box they kept for me. Papa and I talked about it the day before he died you see. It's an old coin, been in our family for generations, even older than the last ones made before credits took over from the old money. Look, on one side is Earth, the planet we came from. You can see the continents. On the other side… see."

Kolyei gazed at the coin in Tara's hand.

"Is an animal," he announced.

"Don't you see Kolyei? It's a wolf, an old Earth wolf. Why, it could even be a Lind!"

They returned to the settlement where Kath was trying to get her new family organised to leave. Matvei was anxious to be off. He moved restlessly from paw to paw as she fastened the youngest of the children they had collected securely to his harness.

Emily and Ilyei, who had volunteered to carry the next youngest and who was already tied on securely in front of her, watched. She leant forward to listen to the little girl's chatter, a pensive expression on her face. Emily always looked sad these days.

The two oldest were standing beside Kath as she struggled with the buckles, the eldest giving her 'helpful' advice; not terribly practical advice if Kath's expression was anything to go by.

Tara giggled.

: *That one is going to be trouble* : she intimated to Kolyei as they sauntered towards them.

Kolyei gruff-growled.

The elder girl began to tug at Kath's tunic.

"Auntie Kath," Tara heard, "who's that girl riding that one?"

Kath glanced over her shoulder but before she could answer the elder brother piped up.

"Don't you know that?" he said in the supercilious manner used by boys to their little sisters from time immemorial. There was a hint of jealousy in his voice as he gazed longingly at Kolyei.

"Bet you don't know neither," she taunted.

"I do though," was his lofty reply.

"Prove it."

"That's Kolyei and his girl. They're famous."

"Why?"

"Cos they were the first that's why. Everyone knows that."

"The first what?"

"Tara was the first of the 'Children of the Wolves'; that's what the grown ups call them."

"Hush," said Kath. "Don't tease your sister."

Tara and Kolyei passed by the small group with identical grins on their faces. Kath looked stressed. Obviously motherhood was proving harder than she had anticipated.

Kolyei desisted from making one of his usual wicked comments although he was thinking them aplenty.

Tara giggled again. She didn't think Kath was in the mood for any wisecracks right now.

Over a week later, the surviving vadeln-pairs had travelled home to the joint lands, together with those humans who lived there and some who had decided to move there for the first time. A number of orphans had elected to join them, older ones for the most part, keen to make a fresh start in a place that held no disturbing memories.

They walked; there was no hurry on this return journey, no Larg to fight at the end of it. It was high summer; the plains were teeming with life. As they travelled, their hearts lightened the nearer they got to the hills.

"Seems funny to think that these plains belong to humans now," Jim said to Laura and Francis. "In the years to come it will be dotted around with farmsteads as the population grows."

"It will take generations to fill it," Laura said.

"Meanwhile our home is growing nearer," said Francis with satisfaction. "Only a day away now."

"You're setting up in the southerly area then?" asked Jim.

"Yes, the Vada needs room and after all these years in space I don't feel entirely comfortable in dense woods. You?"

"Larya and I are heading back to our daga. We intend to rest there right through what remains of the summer so don't be having any emergencies for me to solve."

"Laura very busy be with all the young," said Asya. "No emergencies planned."

"By their very nature, emergencies can never be planned for," said Jim. "Just keep the numbers down to a minimum, that's all I ask."

"All the young?" laughed Laura. I seem to remember saying that it was very unlikely that a woman has more than one at a time."

"True," said Faddei, "but Asya will have more than one. Perhaps six."

Francis just looked up at the sky and opened his arms wide.

"Why me?" was all he said.

Jim laughed, Larya howled with glee. Faddei managed to look proud, modest and nonchalant all at the same time. He succeeded very well.

Kolyei got restless the closer they got to the hills. Tara sensed this restlessness and whispered to him.

"We can race on ahead if you want. Radya is waiting and I want to see Peter too. I'm sure nobody will mind."

With a whine he bounded ahead of the others. They reached the domta a full three hours before the rest and Kolyei evaded all who came to welcome them in, intent on reaching the daga as soon as possible.

Janice was waiting outside, tears of joy on her face.

Tara looked around the familiar surroundings and then at Janice Randall.

"It's good to be home." Her chin wobbled and she felt salty tears in her eyes.

Janice simply held out her arms to the girl she had come to love as her own and Tara tumbled off Kolyei's back and into them. They were warm and soft, much like her dead mother's and just as comforting.

Tara lifted her tearful face towards her.

"We won," she said, "but it's been terrible."

"I can imagine honey," Janice said. "Now you must try to forget." She glanced over to Kolyei who looked at her out of sorrowful eyes.

Then Tara saw Brian, standing proudly beside a blue-striped Lind female.

"Hello little sister," he said. "We wanted to surprise you."

Tara's tears stopped and her face broke into a smile.

"You have succeeded!" she exclaimed. "When did this happen?"

"A few days after you all left," he replied. "Sofiya and I decided to keep it a secret. Thought you might need a bit of cheering up when you got back."

"We should celebrate," she agreed. "It's not every day a brother of mine finds his lind-mate."

She grinned at them all, feeling that she was a real family member of the Randalls at last.

Violet, Lucy and Juliet were jumping up and down in excitement.

"I missed you," cried out Lucy.

"Me loves Tara," added Juliet.

It was Kolyei who, as usual, had the last word.

"We are a family," he said. "That is the most important thing," and was rewarded by the smile that lit up Tara's face, filled with love for him, equally matched with the love he felt for her, his vadeln-pair.

Eight sat round the campfire where twelve had sat before the war, each remembering those who had not returned.

Thomas, his mind teeming with ideas for the future; happy-go-lucky Moira who had not wanted to go to the war but had done so nonetheless; and the twins Bill and Geoff, who had wanted to go to the war in order to avenge the murder of their family.

Nobody wanted to be the first to speak. The eight gazed into the flickering flames.

"I've thought of a poem," said Tara at last, not being able to stand the heavy silence any longer.

"What's the title?" asked Kath in a dull voice.

"I've called it *'Children of the Wolves'*. It's not very good, at least not yet. As I thought of it, it seemed to help me to understand what has happened to us all. It's helped."

"*Children of the Wolves?*" exclaimed Kath. "That's what Yvonne called us at the beginning. People called us that at the settlement."

She looked at the flickering face of Tara who had gone back to staring into the flames. "I'd like to hear it."

"If you're sure," answered Tara. "It's not a very happy poem. It's about all that's happened to us since then."

"I'd still like to hear it," insisted Kath.

"And me," said Alan and the others said the same.

Tara, in her singsong voice began to speak the verses she had composed; she did not look into the faces of the other seven;

"Twelve children set out for the west that day,

Confused, bemused, yet happy and gay."

Before she had gone any further there were tears to be seen on the cheeks of Kath and Emily. Brenda was openly weeping.

With a catch in her voice Tara continued. She was crying now but they were healing tears, they all felt it. She came to the last verse.

"But we 'Children of the Wolves' will live on and shout,

With resounding voice, all eight will chant out.

We'll fight to live with thee and thine,

Free in the land which now is mine!

Be still, my rtathen."

There was silence where Tara's voice had been.

This silence continued for a long time.

Not one of those gathered round the campfire wanted to be the one who would break it.

"What do we do now?" asked Alan at last.

"We stay here," answered Emily. "I'm going to begin my medical studies, properly this time. Winston Randall says he'll take me on."

"It's definitely the Vada for me," declared Alan.

"Me too," said Mark. "Francis is going to build it up again better than ever. He's taking us to the plains to the south of the rtathlians and he told me that he's going to begin what he calls a 'full training programme'."

"Who is doing the training?" asked Alan, "Francis himself?" This was the first Alan had heard of a 'full training programme' and he wanted to learn more.

"I think he'd like to but he told me that the Vada needs a professional and that he was going to approach one. I don't know who or what happened though, so don't ask. Francis hasn't said anything, at least to me. One thing's for sure and Francis knows it, this is not the end of the war. I too feel it in my bones that we'll be fighting the Larg for many a long year."

"I agree," said Kath, "but soldiering is not for me and Matvei. We're staying right here. James and I have a family to bring up."

"Yvonne and I are going to the Vada too," announced Brenda.

"You two in the Vada," exclaimed Mark. "Wonders will never cease! I would have thought you'd be wanting to take things easy!"

"That was before," countered Yvonne. "We've changed."

"Or been changed," vouchsafed Kath in a quiet voice, thus effectively putting a stop to Mark's teasing.

"I just want to stay here with my Mum," said Peter in a whisper. He looked embarrassed.

Mark opened his mouth to say something and Tara noticed. "Leave him be," she said. "He's only eleven, plenty of time to make up his mind."

"And you Tara, what are your plans?" asked Kath.

"I'm staying with the Randalls for now," she replied, her eyes distant.

"Then?" pressed Brenda.

"I'm going to be a famous author," her voice rang out in the clearing, "but first and foremost I am and always will be Kolyei's Girl, one of the 'Children of the Wolves'."

"My girl," agreed Kolyei, "but not a Child of the Wolf, you are a Child of the Lind," and so had the last word, as usual.

Candy Rae

CHAPTER 30

SOUTHERN CONTINENT

Aoalvaldr the Larg lay on the rocky beach enjoying the soft warmth of the noontime sun. In the distance he could see the misty haze that was the island chain, gateway to the rtathlians of the Lind, the bare crags of the larger islands reaching skywards through the clouds.

He began to lick clean his injured paw. The wound was almost healed now and it would not be long before he would be able to run and hunt with what remained of his kohort.

His thoughts were dark, dark as night. The name Aoalvaldr was anathema throughout the length and breadth of Largdom. This disgrace he had expected, in fact, he knew he was lucky to escape the wrath of his superiors alive after such a monumental disaster. To Aoalvaldr's surprise the Largan, the pre-eminent Larg, had decreed that Aoalvaldr was too useful to kill, hence this sentence of exile to the coastlands with orders to watch and learn all he could about the humans who had arrived so unexpectedly on their planet and turned their lives up-paw-down.

Aoalvaldr's thoughts were dark and ranged this way and that over the events of the last moon. *How did the Lind and these humans manage to defeat me and my army, the pride of Larg?* He had been winning the battle; he knew he had, his flanking manoeuvre a masterstroke. The kohorts should have swept round and through the

Lind right wing like a floodtide, sweeping away all in their path.

But it hadn't happened that way.

The Lindars had responded with a floodtide of their own, descending from the hills in an unstoppable and if he thought about it, uniform mass, led by these self-same humans riding his mortal enemies. They wielded the sharp, lethal and evil implements the men of Murdoch called swords and had carved a swathe of death as they had methodically destroyed his army's will to fight.

It was their fault the kohorts had broken.

Aoalvaldr's entire awareness became filled with an implacable determination and hatred. He would destroy these riders, their Lind and all they held dear, even if it took him the rest of his life.

His mouth slavered with anticipation. Saliva drooled out of his mouth and landed on the sand.

He vowed revenge.

When the time was right he would return, his ambitions would be fulfilled, he would become the hero of Larg, exalted above all others. He could still become Largan.

Aoalvaldr stood up, his mealy face pointing north, his teeth showing white in a ferocious snarl.

"I will return," he growled. "Enjoy life while you can. I will return to destroy you all."

Then he turned away from the shoreline and limped towards his lonely daga. After a while he slept, his dreams filled with vengeance and the ultimate annihilation of the Vada of Lind.

CHARACTER LIST AND GLOSSARY

CREW AND FAMILIES FROM THE WCCS ARGYLL

Agnes Crawford: Wife of Fullarton Crawford, mother of Peter.
Alan de Groot: Colonial youngster aged 13 on landing.
Arthur Knott: Farrier and inventor.
Bill Armstrong: Colonial youngster aged 16 on landing, twin of Geoff.
Brenda Urquhart: Colonial youngster aged 15 on landing.
Brian Randall: Son of Janice and Winston Randall aged 13 on landing.
Daniel Trapper: Old colonist.
Emily Stanton: Colonial youngster, sister of Steven, aged 13 on landing.
Francis McAllister: Rating on the WCCS Argyll.
Fullarton Crawford: Animal Breeder.
Geoff Armstrong: Colonial youngster aged 16 on landing, twin of Bill.
Geraldine Fitzpatrick: Colonial Farmer.
James Rybak: Navigation Rating on the WCCS Argyll.
Janice Randall: Wife of Winston Randall. Mother of Louis, Brian, Violet, Lucy and Juliet.

Jean Farquharson: Mature colonial lady.
Jim Cranston: Petty Officer on the WCCS Argyll.
Juliet Randall: Daughter of Winston Randall aged 2 on landing.
Kath Andrews: Rating on the WCCS Argyll aged 17 on landing.
Laura Merriman: Leading Rating on the WCCS Argyll.
Louis Randall: Son of Janice and Winston Randall aged 15 on landing.
Lucy Randall: Daughter of Janice and Winston Randall aged 5 on landing.
Marion Mackie: Elderly colonial lady.
Mark Ampte: Colonial youngster aged 13 on landing.
Mark Sullivan: Brother of Tara Sullivan who died on board the WCCS Argyll.
Moira Craig: Colonial youngster aged 15 on landing.
Peter Crawford: Son of Agnes and Fullarton Crawford aged 10 on landing.
Robert Lutterell: Chief Petty Officer on the WCCS Argyll.
Ross Quigley: Rating on the WCCS Argyll.
Steven Stanton: Brother of Emily Stanton.
Stuart MacIntosh: Commander and second in command of the WCCS Argyll.
Tanni: Jack Russell terrier belonging to Janice Randall.
Tara Sullivan: Colonial youngster aged 12 on landing and whose parents and brother Mark died during the cosmic storm.
Thomas Wylie: Colonial youngster aged 14 on landing.
Violet Randall: Daughter of Janice and Winston Randall aged 8 on landing.
Winston Randall: Vet and husband of Janice.
Yvonne Benoit: Colonial youngster aged 15 on landing.

CREW, FAMILIES AND PRISONERS FROM THE WCPS ELECTRA

Andrew Snodgrass: Convict.
Angus: Rating from the WCPS Electra and one of the away team with Captain Howard.
Anne Howard: Wife of Captain Peter Howard.
Brentwood: Convict.

Briony: Young girl aged 16 on landing.
Camilla Todd: Commander and second in command of the WCPS Electra.
Carla Pederson: Daughter of Ulla Johannes Pederson aged 15 on landing.
Cherry Howard: Daughter of Anne and Peter Howard, aged 9 on landing.
Cracov: Convict.
Gardiner: Convict.
Elliot Murdoch: Convict.
Gavin Quirke: Son of Lysbet aged 5 on landing.
Gerry Russell: Animal Handler from the WCPS Electra.
Gunnarsson: Convict.
Henri Cocteau: Convict.
Jenny Quirke: Daughter of Lysbet aged 14 on landing.
Jessica Howard: Daughter of Anne and Peter Howard aged 14 on landing.
Johannes Pederson: Chief Engineer from the WCPS Electra and one of the away team with Captain Howard.
Joseph Howard: Son of Anne and Peter Howard aged 7 on landing.
Lysbet Quirke: Mother of Jenny and Gavin.
Mahler: Convict.
Martine: Assistant Animal Handler on board the WCPS Electra.
Michael Wallace: Convict.
Nell Morrison: Young mother.
Peter Howard: Captain of the WCPS Electra, husband of Anne and father of Jessica, Cherry and Joseph.
Pierre Duchesne: Convict.
Sam Baker: Convict.
Shelley Lambert: Environmental Officer from the WCPS Electra.
Smith: Convict.
Taylor: Convict.
Tom: Rating from the WCPS Electra and one of the away team with Captain Howard.
Ulla Pederson: Wife of Johannes Pederson and mother of Carla.
Unwin: Convict.
Van Buren: Convict.
Weiss: Convict.

White: Convict.

THE LIND

Afanasei: Male Lind from pack Zanatei, Susa of Lindar.
Akimei: Male Lind from pack Zanatei.
Alanya: Female Lind from pack Ranetei.
Andei: Male Lind from pack Zanatei.
Asya: Female Lind from pack Zanatei.
Aya: Female Lind from pack Zanatei.
Faddei: Male Lind from pack Zanatei.
Ilyei: Male Lind from pack Zanatei.
Inei: Male Lind from pack Zanatei.
Jansei: Male Lind from pack Malkei.
Janya: Female Lind from pack Zanatei.
Jsei: Male Lind from pack Ratvei.
Kiltya: Female Lind from pack Zanatei.
Kolyei: Male Lind from pack Zanatei.
Kseniya: Female Lind from pack Zanatei.
Larya: Female Lind from pack Zanatei.
Lililya: Female Lind from pack Malkei.
Malya: Female Lind from pack Zanatei.
Mariya: Female Lind from Gtratha, Gtrathlin.
Matvei: Male Lind from pack Zanatei.
Radya: Female Lind from pack Zanatei.
Rozya: Female Lind from pack Zanatei.
Savei: Male Lind from pack Ratvei.
Sindya: Female Lind from pack Zanatei.
Sofiya: Female Lind from pack Zanatei.
Stasya: Female Lind from pack Zanatei.
Talya: Female Lind from pack Zanatei, Healer.
Tarmsei: Male Lind from pack Zanatei.
Tavei: Male Lind from pack Zanatei.
Ustinya: Female Lind from pack Vanya.
Zanatei: Male Lind from pack Zanatei, Elda.
Zhenya: Female Lind from pack Zanatei, Healer.

LIND WORDS

Allst: Tall, large leafed tree of the north.
Chela: Lind claw, they have five on each paw. They resemble the claws of an earth cat in that they can tract and retract.
Ceja: Yes.
Ctrath: Welcome (informal).
Daga: Lind den.
Dedta: Welcome (formal).
Dom: Temporary pack-home.
Domta: Permanent pack-home.
Dugo: Small prickly, dense and fast-growing bush, prevalent in the north.
Duntanvad: 12.
Elda(s): Leader(s) of packs and Lind nation.
Eln: Mate.
Gin: Hurt.
Gtran: Large vicious cat-like predators that inhabit the snowy mountain ranges of the northern continent.
Gtratha: High Council of Lind, consisting of one representative from each pack.
Gtrathlin: Leader of the Gtratha.
Holad: Medical section of pack.
Jeza: Eat.
Jezdic: Zebra-like intractable animal.
Kala: Caffeine drink made from the nuts of the allst tree.
Kura: Docile, woolly, short-legged goat-like animal.
Lai: Legendary beings of Lind folklore.
Lian: Woods or forests.
Lind: Peace loving wolf-like denizens of northern continent.
Lindar: Warrior section of pack, it is split into three ranks, or ryz, at the front the experienced large males, in the middle the experienced smaller females and at the back the inexperienced and the older fighters.
Lindling: Human word for Lind young, not often used.
Lok: 3.
Ltscta: Young Lind, younger than fourteen summer seasons old.
Lungtrel: Multicoloured river fish.

Malinon: Northern bird that sings a fine tune.
Pilli: Small darting red fish.
Ptatch: Ride.
Rtath: Pack.
Rtatha: Pack range.
Rtathen: Pack-mates
Rtathlian: Pack-woods
Ruza: Hero.
Ryz: Battle line, a Lindar has three.
San: 4.
Saneln: Family unit of four, two humans and two Lind, mated. The Elda of the Gtratha decreed that joinings of two Lind with two humans was fair and proper and would be called saneln. It was noted that a vadeln-pairing seemed to always be female to male or vice versa. It would also be decreed, after much soul searching by the Lind, that when a Lind was vadeln-paired with a human, that Lind could not pair and mate with another vadeln-paired Lind unless the human duo were also a mated partnership. Some humans would not be so amenable to the notion as it meant that short sexual flings were off limits as soon as one accepted the paired bond.
Satalrdn: Many.
Smaha: Red numbing medicinal root.
Susa: Commander of Lindar.
Susyc: Commander of Army.
Tranet: Edible freshwater flatfish.
'Unst si malinon': Lind saying for 'up with the lark'.
Vad: 2.
Vada: Cavalry (Lind/human).
Vadeln: Paired life-mate (Lind/human).
Volat: Needless slaying of any creature.
Vuz: Idiot (if spoken loudly).
Vuz: Small striped river animal (if spoken softly).
Wral: Large bear-like animals that inhabit the riverbanks of the snowy mountains of the northern continent.
Xrndli: Vulture-like raptor bird.
Zarova: Long necked camel-like meat animal.

LIND PACKS

Barindya: Cream striped pack.
Hanvsei: Maroon striped pack.
Helvetei: Turquoise striped pack.
Jalkei: Yellow striped pack from the far northwest.
Malkei: Green striped pack from the rtathlians.
Msnei: Orange striped pack.
Ranetei: Pink striped pack from the rtathlians.
Ratvei: Purple striped pack.
Vanya: Violet striped pack.
Vlrnei: Black striped pack.
Zanatei: Blue striped pack from the rtathlians.

THE CHILDREN OF THE WOLVES

Tara/Kolyei: Kath/Matvei: Bill/Malya: Geoff/Sindya: Peter/Radya: Brenda/Inei: Yvonne/Tavei: Emily/Ilyei: Alan/Kiltya: Moira/Andei: Thomas/Stasya: Mark/Aya.

THE LARG

Aoalvaldr: Male Larg, Commander.
Kohort: Cohort of fighters, usually numbering around 800.
Kranj: Part of kohort, numbering eight.
Larg: Warlike wolf-like denizens of southern continent.
Largan: Leader of all the Larg.
Rudtka: Small southern burrowing animal, like a rabbit with short ears.

OTHER USEFUL TERMS

CPO: Chief Petty Officer.
PO: Petty Officer.
Riga: The original destination of the colonists.
WCCS: World Coalition Colony Ship.
WCCS Argyll: Colony Ship.

WCPS: World Coalition Prison Ship.
WCPS Electra: Prison Ship.

ABOUT THE AUTHOR

Candy Rae lives in Ayrshire, Scotland with her dog and two ten year old cats who think they are kittens. She has been a fan of fantasy fiction (and sci-fi as long as it isn't too technical) since her first year at university when a friend introduced her to talking dragons.

She started to write one Christmas Day when she sat down and planned her first book, which, after many revisions, became the first book in the Planet Wolf Series, Wolves and War.

Candy Rae used to work in accountancy where she scribbled down words in amongst the figures. She carries a notebook everywhere she goes into which she writes down her ideas. She has been known to drive off the motorway, park the car in the first available spot and write for an hour or more.

Thank you for reading 'Wolves and War'. I hope you enjoyed it. The story continues with 'Conflict and Courage'.
It would be greatly appreciated if you could spare a few moments to add a short review on Amazon.
Check out Planet Wolf's Facebook page.

Printed in Great Britain
by Amazon

78549985R00212